Ancient Enemies

LEGENDS OF LAIRHEIM

BOOK 1

ALSO BY TORA MOON

LEGENDS OF LAIRHEIM (SCIENCE-FANTASY)

Ancient Enemies (Book 1)
Ancient Allies (Book 2)
The Scourge Incursion (Book 3)
Exile's Vengeance (Book 4)
Redemption - A Novel

THE SENTINEL WITCHES (URBAN FANTASY)

Crossroads to Destiny (Book 1)
Descent Into Darkness (Book 2)
Well of Sorrows (Book 3)

INDIE AUTHOR GUIDES

Business & Accounting for Authors
Business Plans for Authors (forthcoming)

To get an up-to-date listing of all my books or to purchase visit
ToraMoon.com

LEGENDS OF LAIRHEIM

ANCIENT ENEMIES

BOOK 1

TORA MOON

Lunar Alchemy Publishing

ACKNOWLEDGMENTS

An author may sit alone at the computer, but no book is completed without help. A big shout out to my beta reader team: Angelique, Kelly, and Liesa. I appreciate your comments and feedback which made this a much better story.

Thank you to all the authors I've had the pleasure of reading their stories and making me want to tell my own. Without story, this world would be a much poorer place.

And especially to my daughter, Sasha, you have made me become a better person by being your parent. I couldn't have asked for a more amazing daughter.

Thank you to all my readers. Thank you for spending time with my stories and letting me be a part of your life. I hope you love them as much I loved writing them.

*To my sister, Angelique, who encourages me
to keep going, to keep writing, and put my
stories into the world.
Without you, this book wouldn't have been written.*

EXTRAS

The world of Lairheim isn't a re-imagining of Earth. It has its own culture, language, and landmasses. I've created several extras and resources to help you enjoy this fantasy world more. You can find these on my website: ***ToraMoon.com/Legends-Extras***.

Extras you may like:

Pronunciation audio - While the appendix includes a cast and glossary, fantasy names and words can be difficult to figure out how to say. I've recorded audios for each name and Posair word.

Maps - There is a map at the beginning of the book to help you orient into the world of Lairheim. A black and white pdf map is available to download for free. Or if you love maps, I've created a beautiful color map you can purchase.

Merchandise - I've created some fun merchandise centered around the books and the world of Lairheim. Check them out in my shop!

Map of Lairheim

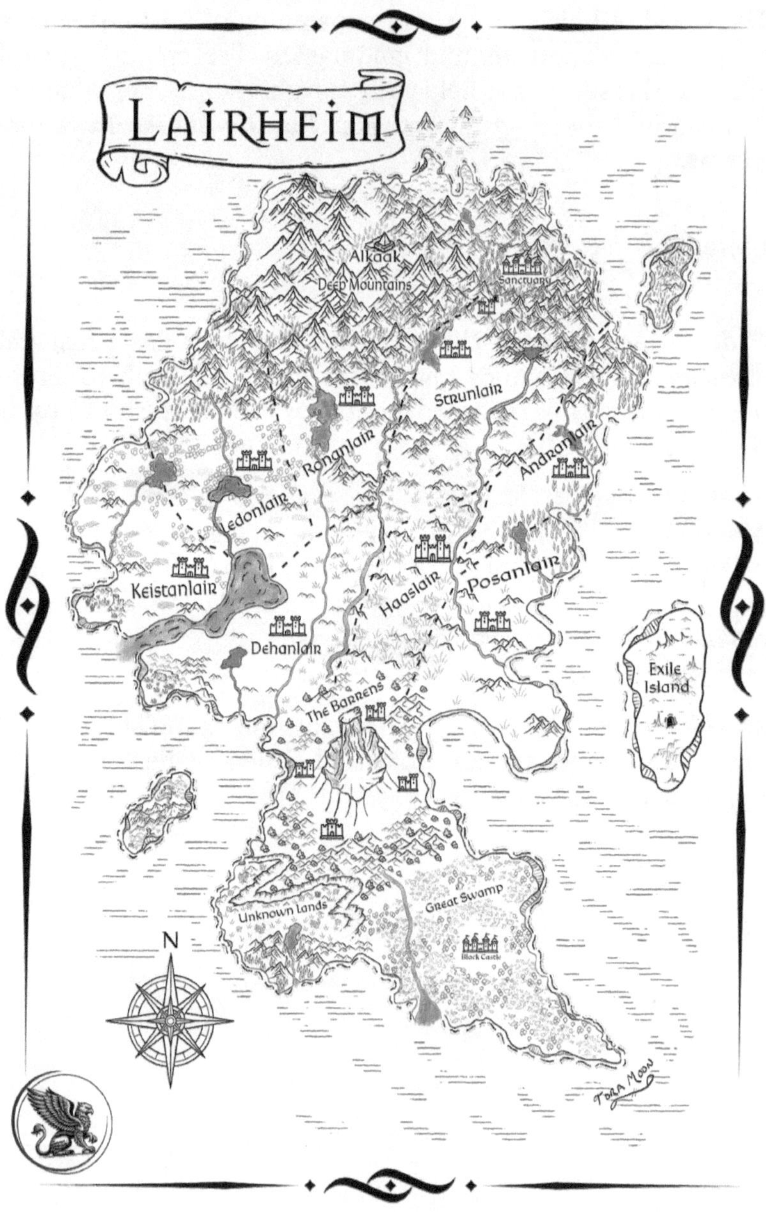

Chapter 1

In the cold predawn light, Rizelya rode in front of a force of fifty fighters. She glanced to her left at her half-sister, Naila. When Rizelya had entered the stable to saddle her horse, it had surprised her to see Naila doing the same. Since becoming the Strunland Keep Alpha, Naila rarely led a fighting-pack anymore. The demands of leading a Territory Keep kept her far too busy.

Like the other ten women in the group, Rizelya and Naila wore red from head to foot: leather shirt, pants, and boots. A hooded cape covered their heads and shoulders. Once they reached the monster's nest, they would toss it aside.

Besides being the color of fire magic, the janacks and brechas, a symbiotic pair of monsters, couldn't see red. The Malvers' monsters had plagued their world since the end of the Great War, over a thousand years ago.

A sigh drew Rizelya's attention to her heart-sister and best-friend, riding on her right side. A few of Kaieli's dark brown, almost black, curls peeked from the hood of her cloak. Like all Posair women, her hair and eye color indicated her Talents, her magical powers. Kaieli was an extremely strong Brown, a worker of earth magic. Her blue-gray eyes showed her secondary Talents were Blue and Gray.

"Kaieli, I wish you wouldn't come to these battles," Rizelya said. "Let the Browns, with less empathic ability, take care of us on the field."

"You know I can't do that," Kaieli replied. "We all have our parts to play in our war with the monsters. Mine is to help the fighters with my healing abilities, and your job, Dear Heart, is to kill janacks and brechas."

Rizelya's lips tightened into a hard line. As much as she didn't like it, Kaieli was right. Many fighters were alive and healthy because of Kaieli being on the field with them.

Rizelya's own dark auburn hair and brown eyes proclaimed her a Red with some Brown. The Red's fire magic was an effective means of fighting and killing the monsters.

Over the past seventy-five years, the formation of the monsters' nests had fallen into a pattern. The Posairs could predict when one would develop fairly accurately. This allowed them to kill the monsters before they escaped into the wilds. The nest they rode toward should mature soon.

After an octar of riding, the group pulled their horses to a stop in a clearing. A large corral sat in the center, shaded by trees, with water barrels on one end. The fighters dismounted, loosened the girth straps on their horses' saddles, and led them into the enclosure. Kaieli and the other two healers riding with the group agreed to wait with the horses until the battle was over. They removed blankets and baskets from the back of their saddles. Two of the thirty warriors stayed behind to guard the horses and the healers.

Rizelya grabbed her weapon, a helbraught, from its place on her saddle. Each woman carried one. Affixed to the staff was a two-foot long, slightly curved blade. It easily penetrated the thick hide of the monsters. Rizelya looked with longing at the other women's helbraughts. All of them were several inches longer than hers. The user's height determined the length of the staff. It meant she had to get closer to the monsters. On her belt, she carried a helstrablade, a dagger also made from helstrim. If needed, she could feed her magic into it, like she did with her helbraught's blade. A blade made from helstrim never needed its razor edge sharpened.

The men had their own weapons: claws, teeth, and venom. Ages past, the men had traded their ability to work all but the most minor magic for the gift of shapeshifting. A wolf and a warrior-wolf were their two other forms. At a signal from their leader, the men shifted into their wolf form and slunk into the forest.

Eiden, the only non-Red female fighter in the group, threw back the hood of her cape and the sunlight glinted on her sunny-yellow hair. She grinned at Rizelya. Flecks of green flashed in her gold eyes. A few years ago, she'd cajoled Rizelya into teaching her how to fight after Rizelya caught Eiden following the pack into a battle. Tradition taught the Yellows' air magic wasn't effective against the monsters. Only Reds could damage the monsters with their fire magic. Being a double Yellow made Eiden's air Talent impressive and strong. She was able to cool or heat air, and she had a gift for solidifying it. Even so, Rizelya felt responsible for Eiden and would keep her safe.

The group of nine women strode silently down the path, their hooded capes flaring as they walked. The shadowy shapes of the wolves flowing in the trees kept pace with them. A hush fell around them. Predators stalked the forest this dawn, and they were hunting.

The wind shifted slightly, and Rizelya drew in a deep breath and snorted from the reek of brechas and janacks.

Rizelya moved her helbraught in front of her. She fed a small amount of fire magic into the blade. Glancing at the forms shadowing the women, she nodded to herself. *Yes, the men have caught the smell too.*

The foul odor became more pervasive as the group drew nearer to the nest site. Although the timing of the nests was in an established pattern, the size never could be predicted. Sometimes, the stench would indicate how many monsters they'd have to fight.

This one smelled big.

Rizelya suppressed a shudder.

Naila didn't pause when the monster stink wafted over them. Instead, she led the group toward the nest, her pace strong and confident. She held her helbraught loosely in her hands. Rizelya admired her much older sister, who carried on the family tradition of becoming a Keep Alpha. Everyone expected Rizelya to become one, too. So far, she had evaded being even a squad-pack alpha.

A few milcrons later, the group reached the demarcation where forest and swamp vied for dominance. The pools of malignant magic caused both swamps and monster nests to develop. Rizelya had heard there were even swamps in the middle of the dry plains.

She, along with the rest, stopped at the edge of the marshy ground.

Soon the battle would begin...

Rizelya adjusted the grip on her helbraught when a large red wolf, his pelt dulled with age, slipped out of the forest and approached Naila. A shimmer, and a man stood where the wolf had been a moment before. Rizelya hissed in agitation and worry. *Damn old man, he shouldn't be here. He's too old. Now I have one more person to protect.*

"The nest is about fifty feet from the trees, Naila," Histrun said.

"How many?" Naila pushed back her hood, revealing a thick braid of bright red hair with bold streaks of gold in it. Her light yellow-gold eyes narrowed.

"Huge." He shuddered. "I haven't ever seen one this big."

Trepidation coursed through Rizelya at the news. At over a hundred years old, Histrun had experienced many battles with the monsters. He didn't join the fighting much anymore, spending his time training the young warriors. Pride made him come today to watch them in their first battle.

"At least ten janacks and twice that of brechas." Histrun turned his head and spat.

Rizelya wasn't the only one who cursed. This nest was three times the normal size. It made her glad Naila had joined them. They could use her vast experience. She had been a cunning leader in her time as a fighting-pack alpha. They might not have enough fighters, even with the extra eight warriors-in-training. If they'd known it would be this large, they would have brought another fighting-pack with them. A team of eight Reds and thirty men easily handled a usual sized group of adult monsters. If the monsters were ready to leave the nest, they were in trouble.

Adults were hunger incarnate. They would consume anything that walked on two legs or four, flew, or crawled. Plants were the only thing they didn't eat, and those they killed with the slime they excreted. The thirty monsters could annihilate all life in this valley within the eight days of a chedan if they weren't dispatched before they left the nest site. Luckily, their lifespan was short, only one to two chedan.

"Stage?" Naila's voice was rough, barely above a whisper. Years ago, a janack mangled her throat, ruining her voice and making it difficult for her to talk. She lifted a hand to rub absently at the scar covering her throat.

"Adult. They'll leave the nest as the day warms up."

Naila gestured and the group of women split into pairs, each with a group of wolves and two of the unproved boys following them, to surround the nest. Each pair took a stance at a cardinal direction point. The wolves spread out to form a large circle around the nest, being careful not to get too close to the swamp. No one entered the swamps alone. There were too many dangerous plants and small beasts hidden in their murky depths.

Naila and Eiden joined Rizelya in the western quadrant. Rizelya would have her hands full, keeping the monsters from escaping their assigned area and ensuring Naila and Eiden's safety. Both of them would scoff at her, but it had been a long time since Naila had led a fighting-pack. She was a good Keep Alpha and loved by her people. If anything happened to the leader, Rizelya might as well become a rogue wolf. While she was at it, she'd better stay safe, or Kaieli would be difficult to live with. Rizelya looked over at the side where Histrun waited with the young boys. She'd protect him, too.

A tingle in the air told Rizelya that Eiden was forming a shield of cold air around the nest. It was a new technique she was trying for the first time. It would give them a few more milcrons to get into position before the janacks detected their body heat.

Rizelya drew in a breath when she saw the size of the nest. Histrun hadn't lied; it was huge. The creatures stirred with the warmth of the day. Spiky shapes intertwined with slick tentacles as the janacks caressed the spikes on the brechas' backs. Rumbled growls from the brechas were answered by clacks from the janacks.

Rizelya poured her fire magic into her helbraught, readying for the fight to come. The glow around the circle showed the other women were also preparing their blades.

Naila waited until the groups on the far side of the nest reached position before giving the order to change in mind-speech.

Soft snarls filled the glade as the men began to transform into their warrior form. The perfect blend of wolf and man made them more powerful, stronger, and faster than even their wolf form. Shifting from man to wolf, or back, was easy. Just a thought and they traded one form for the other. The transformation to their warrior form took more effort and was painful as limbs stretched, muscles bulked, and claws lengthened. Standing, a warrior towered over his brothers by two feet or more and had fifty to a hundred pounds more mass. They became a match for the monsters.

A growl and yelp of pain nearby snared Rizelya's attention. *Leistrun must be caught in the change.* Murmured instructions confirmed her guess as Histrun helped the teenager through his shift. Rizelya felt a moment of pity for the young men. *After this fight, they will truly be warriors—or dead. Mother, grant mercy that we all go home.* She smiled at the snarl of satisfaction as Leistrun completed his change. It shouldn't be much longer for the men to finish.

As if on cue, a howl sounded across the glade, picked up and answered by the other warriors. The nest squirmed as the howls reverberated over and over. The ground vibrated with the challenge. Sensor stalks poked up, tentacles unwound from spiky limbs, rumbled growls and clacks grew more intense. The shapes of individual monsters began to separate from the mass, and those on the outer edge moved toward the sound of the howling warriors.

On an unseen block of air created by Eiden, Naila stood above them all, giving her an advantage in directing the fight. *South!* she shouted in mind-speech.

Light lit up the southern part of the circle as the women fed more fire magic into their helbraughts. The sensor stalks of the outer janacks whipped around. Fire erupted in front of the women, drawing more of the monsters' attention.

A group of two janacks and five brechas broke away, trundling toward the heat. Once they moved away from the nest, a thin stream of fire erupted on the ground behind them, blocking any retreat to the nest. Warrior-wolves raced behind the creatures. The fire grew, forming a curtain behind the warriors, until it surrounded the group of monsters and warriors.

The inner fire separating warriors and monsters dropped, and the warriors swarmed the beasts from behind. Their long, sharp claws sliced through the tough hides. A tentacle from a janack flew off, putrid green ichor splashing the warriors. Their pelts protected them from the acidic ichor. The fire in front of the women flared, burning any ichor before it reached them. The brechas engaged the warriors. Any monsters attempting to cross the ring of fire faced the women's fiery helbraughts.

Rizelya turned her attention away from the fight as Naila called out, *East!* Helbraughts glowed in the east, and another similar group of monsters broke off from the nest. The janacks' clicks drove the brechas forward.

The glade rang with snarls and growls as the warriors attacked the janacks. Once they were destroyed, the brechas would fall into cannibalistic disarray.

The nest rumbled. Naila, with long experience from past battles, cried, *North!* just as three janacks with their accompanying brechas erupted from the nest and headed to the northern section of the circle. Before they were engaged, two more janacks and six brechas scrambled out and swarmed toward Naila and Rizelya.

"What in blazes?" Naila's low voice sounded startled. "That's never happened."

Rizelya threw a shield of fire around Naila and Eiden. Histrun was too far away for her to cover. She looked at the nest. It wasn't empty. "May the Mother be merciful. There's more than we thought!"

"Guard me," Naila told Rizelya as another group of brechas scurried from the nest to attack the southern contingent from behind. "Not typical nest."

Rizelya felt Eiden put a shield of air around Naila just behind her fire. Rizelya nodded in approval. The warriors in her group howled and rushed to meet the monsters coming toward them. Fire now surrounded the entire clearing. Rizelya heard a scream, and the fire flared out of control in the north. A Red had been hurt; but she didn't have time to wonder who it was.

A tentacle reached toward her. She slashed with her glowing helbraught, feeding it a bit more fire magic. A slight resistance, and then the blade slid through the tough hide, severing the tentacle and flinging ichor. Her helbraught blazed, catching the ichor and burning it to ash. A young warrior—it looked like Leistrun—attacked another tentacle that was reaching for her.

Claws dripping with venom, he slashed, cleaving it from the janack. It would take a few moments for the venom to go through the ichor system of the monster and reach the bulbous head-body; until then, the janack was still deadly. Other warriors were attacking the other tentacles, working their way to the head, staying away from the open maw filled with huge, sharp teeth.

A brecha swiped Leistrun, catching him in the hip. He howled. Rizelya used her helbraught as a spear and drove the brecha away. Leistrun nodded thanks and turned back to the beast, ignoring the blood running down his side. The warrior grabbed the brecha by what passed for its throat and ripped it out, jumping from the fountain of green ichor. *If he survives his wound, he'll be a warrior to watch.*

Leistrun paced in front of her, keeping any monsters from attacking them. *No, not in front of me. He's protecting Eiden.* Eiden's helbraught glowed with a pale-yellow light. She was keeping her own against the monsters.

"Rizelya, with me!" Naila called. She added in mind-speech, *Something's different about the janack still in the nest. We need to destroy it now!*

Rizelya quickly scanned the glade. The warriors in her section were taking care of the monsters—but just barely. One janack was down and the other would soon follow. It took a moment for her to realize what was wrong. None of the brechas that the dead janacks had controlled were assailing their nest-mates. They were still attacking the warriors and Reds. Several human bodies littered the area. Monster parts were strewn in utter abandon.

As she ran toward the nest, the remaining janack sent out four more brechas. "Dear Mother!" Rizelya swore. "There shouldn't be any brechas left in the nest. Damn, there shouldn't even be the thirty already on the field."

She fed more fire magic into her helbraught, slicing through the spiky limbs of the brechas blocking her way to the remaining janack. Her eyes widened when a thin shield of air formed around her. Ichor slid off it, not touching her skin or clothes. Soft growls next to her let her know several of the warriors had also broken away from the perimeter fight. She let them have the brechas. Rizelya focused all of her attention on getting through to the nest and the last janack.

Naila and Histrun reached the nest moments before Rizelya. She frowned in consternation. *Stupid old man! He's supposed to stay on the sidelines to help the new warriors.* She grudgingly admitted he was moving well for someone at his age. The janack rising on two of its tentacles gave her other things to worry about.

Heat stalks tracked the small group. It was the largest janack Rizelya had ever seen. Its stomach and head were over ten feet in diameter, and its tentacle were over thirteen feet long. Gulping, she realized her helbraught wasn't long enough to keep her away from its snapping teeth. A ring of fire sprang up behind them, keeping any monsters from attacking them from behind. She added her strength to Naila's fire-ring. None of the beasts should be able to get through the double fire. Nor could any of their people join them.

It was just the three of them and the massive janack.

Rizelya noticed a weird protrusion on the top of the janacks' head as a tentacle whipped toward her. She jumped back, but before she could bring down her fiery blade, the tentacle ricocheted, knocking her to the ground. The tentacle rose to crush her. She jabbed her helbraught into it and rolled, dragging the blade with her. Only her momentum allowed her to shave off a chunk of the tentacle. She continued rolling to escape the falling mass. Ichor sprayed as it reached for her again. She ran forward to cut away more of the tentacle closer to the body. It took a hard thrust to get her helbraught blade into the hide of the janack.

Usually the sharp blade, made sharper with her fire magic, easily cut through the tough hide of either a janack or brecha. She jerked on the blade to slice more of the tentacle away. A piece fell, flopping on the ground. The rest of the tentacle shot toward her. She parried and ran under it until she was as close to the head as possible. She added more fire magic to her blade and shoved it into the tentacle. Pulling her blade across it, she sliced deep into it, but couldn't cut it off. Avoiding the raining ichor, she slid under the tentacle to get to the other side. Another burst of fire magic into the blade and a deep thrust, and she finally finished the cut. She jumped and ran to the edge of the fire-ring to get away from the tentacle falling to the ground.

As she reached the fire-ring, she felt a slamming against her senses as brechas assaulted the fire-ring around them. "What the frag!" she cursed. Brechas didn't willingly run into the magic fire of the Reds. She glanced up, noticing again the peculiar protrusion on the janack's head. Narrowing her focus, she heard a faint, strange humming coming from it.

The janack's clicking sounded angry. Naila and Histrun were both battling tentacles of their own. Rizelya happily noted they were both unharmed and fighting well. So far, she was the only one to sever a tentacle. Histrun darted in toward the body while Naila distracted it by thrusting her fiery helbraught at the mouth. A tentacle grasped for Naila, coming from behind her. She sensed the movement and jumped to the side, swinging her blade and chopping off a small chunk. Histrun missed his strike when the janack jerked its body out of his reach.

She stood watching them for a few milcrons. Realization struck her. This janack acted like it could not only sense them but also track their movements. Testing her theory, Rizelya walked slowly to the right. Several of the heat stalks waved and leaned toward her. They followed her when she moved in the opposite direction. As she brandished her helbraught at the janack, the strange protrusion turned toward her. A tentacle snapped down. Rizelya dodged out of the way. The protrusion shadowed her until she reached the fire-ring and, apparently, out of its range.

In all the years Rizelya had fought these creatures, not once had this happened before. *Something isn't right about this janack, well about this whole nest.* If Naila and Histrun kept the monster's attention on them, she might have a chance of reaching the head. She could then sever it from the thin neck connecting it to its body. Histrun's venom was taking too long to have an effect on it.

Each time she rushed toward the monster, heat stalks turned her way and a tentacle slammed toward her. Again, she danced to the edge of the fire-ring. Unbelievably, it was still being bombarded by brechas, many of them burning. It seemed as if all the brechas had abandoned the fighting on the outer ring and stormed the fire-ring surrounding the nest and the strange janack. This far back, Rizelya could hear the weird humming sound coming from the janack even more clearly. The more cuts it received from Naila and Histrun, the louder the hum and the fiercer the attacks on the fire-ring by the brechas. *Dear Mother, they're trying to rescue and protect it! This is new. I bet it has something to do with that strange protrusion.*

Rizelya sensed her pack-mates behind her, attacking the brecha mob. Her quick respite showed her neither Naila nor Histrun were making any progress in reaching the head-bulb. She fed more fire magic into her blade and rushed in again at the monster. A tentacle reached for her. She sliced through it with ease. At the edge of her mind, she sensed Eiden, and a sudden idea struck her.

Eiden! she mind-called. Only with pack-mates could they communicate by mind-speech. *Can you make a cold-air shield around me?*

I don't know... Eiden's reply was thoughtful. *I haven't tried that before...*

A few moments later, the air around Rizelya was freezing. Small ice crystals danced in front of her.

Whatever you're doing, it's working! Keep it up while I try to get to the head. This won't end until this damned janack is dead. Even as she said it, Rizelya knew it to be true.

This time, when she rushed forward, the heat stalks kept their attention on Naila and Histrun. She jumped, using her helbraught as a lever to vault up on a tentacle. She raced up the tentacle toward the head. Luck was with her; the tentacle she had chosen was on the opposite side of its mouth and gnashing teeth. As large as this janack was, it could eat a horse whole.

The weird protrusion seemed to sense the danger and whipped to face her.

The sound was no longer a hum. It was loud and deep, piercing Rizelya's head, making her feel like it would explode. Her fingers loosened their grip on the helbraught. The tentacle she stood on bucked and thrashed, attempting to throw her off. When that didn't work, the end of it reached to curl around her. She leaped onto the head, the tentacle missing her.

Rizelya gritted her teeth against the pain in her head. As she did, she realized the sound was almost mind-speech, convincing her to let go of the helbraught and stand still. It was all she needed. *No one is ever going to mind control me!* She tightened her grip and swung the blade with all her might at the protrusion. The blade met resistance, then slid through.

Immediately, the humming ceased, and the brechas stopped throwing themselves at the fire-ring. But the danger wasn't over until this monster was dead. Rizelya fed more fire magic into her helbraught blade, more than she had ever attempted before. The blade glowed dark red and orange. Tiny flames licked across its surface. She drove her helbraught deep into the janack's head.

Exploding a janack was dangerous—the falling debris could injure the fighters—and was a last resort measure. They had already tried all the normal methods. Cutting off the tentacles was proving to be more difficult than usual. The blades seemed to need more fire magic to do the job, and Histrun's venom wasn't working fast enough. There was something different about it, other than just its size and the peculiar protrusion. There was no other choice; she released her fire magic into the janack's head.

She heard a sizzling noise, jumped off the janack, and raced to the edge of the fire-ring. As she did so, she simultaneously yelled and mind-spoke, "Run! It's going to explode!"

Rizelya threw a shield over herself just as the janack exploded. Gray ichor, green slime, and parts of tentacles plummeted to the ground. The fire-ring flared as Naila cast a fire shield under the ring to contain the fallout of the explosion.

Rizelya huddled under her shield while the burning remains of the strange janack rained on her. She could vaguely hear the commotion of the other warriors and Reds battling the rest of the janacks and brechas.

Are you and Histrun okay? she mind-spoke to Naila.

I am. Histrun flew out of the fire-ring. Did you see the strange protrusion?

Up close. It was tracking the fighting, and I heard a hum. It seemed as if the janack was directing the others. This is so weird.

I didn't notice. I was too busy trying to stay alive. Ah... the 'rain' has stopped.

Rizelya looked around. No more monster parts fell.

Go ahead and release your shield, Naila said. *I'll keep mine up so we can examine this thing.*

Rizelya let her shield go and slowly stood up. Naila's fire shield and ring still surrounded the remains of the strange janack. Rizelya glanced at the fighting behind the fire-ring. There was only one janack left. A warrior drew its attention while a Red slashed at it with her glowing helbraught. The severed head flew to the ground. The janack shuddered. Its tentacles thrashed in its death throes. One caught a young warrior unaware, tossing him several feet. He lay still.

A number of forms were spread out on the battlefield. Most were changing from warrior to human, but two were motionless, staying in their warrior form. They were lucky more weren't dead the way this fight had gone. Only one of the Reds was down, although the rest of them had wounds seeping blood. The women were checking each other for splotches of ichor and using their helbraughts to burn it off. Later, the healers would treat their injuries and purge them of any remaining toxin.

First, the area had to be cleansed. Eiden was holding up Leistrun as he limped toward the path leading to the horses. Once the Reds burned the ichor off each other, they crisscrossed the field, burning all the monster bits and parts they could find.

It was the only way to keep the monsters' malignant magic and poison from spreading.

A galloping horse drew Rizelya's attention. Kaieli flung herself from her mount, bag in her hand, and raced to the nearest motionless form. The other Browns weren't far behind. Kaieli directed them to the various wounded while she worked on the woman. Her injury was serious, if Kaieli was working on her, but she hadn't passed into the Mother's arms yet.

There would be time later to find out how the pack had fared in the battle. Rizelya's job wasn't finished.

Her head throbbed and her right arm burned. Surprised, she looked at her biceps. Blood flowed from where ichor had eaten through her shirt. Raising her helbraught, she placed the glowing blade on the wound. It hissed as it neutralized most of the acid. Later she would have Kaieli remove the rest. If left untreated long enough, the acidic ichor turned poisonous. She didn't have time to go to the healers now. She'd be fine for another octar or so.

"You okay?" Naila asked, looking Rizelya over as she joined her.

"Yeah, just a scratch." Rizelya noted Naila's own wounds, most of which were also cauterized. "Here, you missed a spot." She fed fire into her blade and then touched it to Naila's forehead, where a drop of ichor had fallen. It surprised Rizelya that neither of them weren't more seriously wounded.

Naila looked at the smoking monster debris. She frowned at Rizelya while shaking her head and rolling her eyes.

"Sorry, I didn't see any other way of killing the janack. Nothing else was working."

"I know. Glad you did. Need to find that thing."

They walked around the remains of the strange janack, searching within the burning bits for the strange protrusion. Monster parts were flung all over within Naila's fire shield. They split up when it was apparent they weren't going to find it quickly. They started in the central area with the largest monster pieces and worked outward toward the fire barrier. One would prod something or turn over a bit with an air of excitement, only to be disappointed.

In the quiet, Rizelya heard an odd, high-pitched screech. It was so high she felt it more than heard it. She noticed it became louder when she was in the far south quadrant of their enclosure. She took a few steps toward the barrier. The sound grew louder.

"Do you hear that?"

Naila looked up, eyebrows knitted in confusion. "Hear what?"

"A high-pitched screech?"

Naila stood in an attitude of listening. "Nothing."

"Come over here where it's louder."

Naila left off her search to join Rizelya, zigzagging around pieces of janack, some of which continued to twitch.

"Still nothing." She shook her head when she stood next to Rizelya.

"Damn. You didn't hear the humming either, did you?"

"Nope."

"I think I'm hearing the protrusion. I don't know why I can hear it and you can't."

Naila shrugged.

Rizelya took a step toward the barrier, and the sound grew louder. Her head throbbed. A few steps to the left, and the sound and pain lessened. "It isn't in that direction." She returned to where Naila was standing and went right, and again, the sound lessened. When she stepped forward, the sound and pain intensified. "It's in this direction, I'm sure."

Using her pain as a beacon, she made her way to the fire-ring barrier, the sound and pain growing greater with each step she took. Spots swam in front of her eyes. She found it a hand span from the barrier. Any closer and the thing would have burned.

"Here it is," Rizelya called out. Without thinking, she poked it with the tip of her helbraught. The resulting screech almost deafened her. She dug her helbraught into the ground, white knuckles gripping the staff. A wave of darkness hit her. In it she thought she saw a strange pale gray, gaunt face with dark gray hair and black eyes. The vision faded too fast for her to make much sense of it.

"Riz!" Naila cried in alarm.

Rizelya forced the bile in her throat back down. She squeezed her eyes shut until the fear receded. When she opened her eyes, her sister was looking down at her. She'd blacked out. Rizelya clapped her hands over her ears at the horrendous screeching. Abruptly, it stopped. Grateful for the reprieve, she turned onto her side to find herself staring at the protrusion. "Dark Mother!" she spat, scrambling away.

Naila's air magic encased it, making it blurry, and blocked the sound it was emitting.

"Thanks! That helps."

"Should see it closer," Naila said.

"I'm not going anywhere near that thing." Rizelya dragged her helbraught to her. She tried to feed magic into the blade in case the thing jumped at her, but couldn't. *Huh? Where's my magic?* She scooted as far away from the protrusion as possible while still able to see what Naila was doing, then sat back on her heels.

The protrusion was as long as her arm and translucent, with bumps running along the length. Naila squatted in front of the thing. Carefully, she inserted the tip of her knife into the bubble of air surrounding it, then prodded the protrusion. "It's squishy."

"It was easy to cut off." The sensation of someone watching her made Rizelya look around. It was there and gone in a moment.

You coming over to see?

"Nope, I'm staying right here."

Naila rolled her eyes. She continued with her inspection, flinging comments to Rizelya. "Doesn't want to turn over. Multiple circles." Naila sliced one open.

Rizelya slammed her hands over her ears. "Don't do that! Even with your shield, I can still hear the stupid thing."

"Okay. Won't." Naila turned back to her specimen. *A jelly like substance oozed out.* She lifted the mass near the cut end with her knife. *There's some type of filament dangling from the bottom.*

The hair on Rizelya's neck stood up. Someone was watching her. She glanced around. No one. Everyone else was busy taking care of the wounded and destroying monster bits. Then her gaze fell on the protrusion. Naila tipped it away from Rizelya, and the watching sensation eased. The protrusion rolled until the circles faced Rizelya; and as it did, the sense of being watched returned.

"Burn it!" she yelled. "That damn thing is watching us."

"You sure?"

"Yes!"

It was a testament of Naila's trust in her when Naila fed magic into her helstrablade. The fire touched the mass, and even with the air shield, the screeching hit Rizelya like a hammer. Pain blazed in her head. Again, she saw a flash of the gray woman before she knew nothing.

Rizelya woke up moaning, with Naila standing over her. "Ah crap, I blacked out again, didn't I?"

Naila nodded, then held up two fingers. *That's twice in less than an octar.*

She struggled to sit up. Naila had to help her. "This is embarrassing. I don't know what's wrong with me."

"Don't know either. Kaieli might."

"Is it gone?"

Naila nodded again and pointed.

Rizelya turned her head. A mass of smoldering slime was all that was left of the protrusion. She listened hard and couldn't hear any lingering sound, but her head still pounded like a herd of billocks stampeding.

"The sound is gone, and so is the watcher."

"Watcher?" Naila narrowed her eyes.

"Yeah. Both times immediately before I blacked out, I thought I saw someone with charcoal gray hair and black eyes. Something was wrong with them; they were so skinny."

That isn't good. You need to tell the White Priestess.

"I will." Now the danger was over, Rizelya couldn't ignore the flaming pain from the acid burn on her biceps. Naila was holding her arm carefully. The areas around both of their wounds were inflamed, tinged an awful gray, and beginning to stink. Time was up; a healer needed to purge the janack's toxins from their injuries. Rizelya glanced around and found her helbraught by her side. She used it to lever herself to a standing position. Her head reeled, but this time she didn't pass out. "Let's get out of here. There's nothing more we can do."

"Yes. Need to burn the rest." Naila released her fire-ring around the janack remains.

As soon as the fire shield was down, Kaieli bolted toward Rizelya and Naila, adroitly avoiding the haphazardly strewn monster debris as she ran. Three of the Reds crossed the boundary and began walking around the area, setting all the monster pieces on fire.

"Riz! Dear Heart, what in the Crone's fires happened?" Kaieli stood in front of Rizelya and gently cupped her face. "I felt you pass out twice. I couldn't cross the fire-ring to get to you. You look awful."

"Gee, thanks. I feel awful. Drained."

"Let me take care of your and Naila's wounds, then we'll see what else is wrong with you."

Kaieli went to Naila, which she should have done first, as Naila was the Keep Alpha. Rizelya knew Naila would allow the transgression to slide since Kaieli was Rizelya's heart sister. The only bond stronger within the pack was a bond-mate.

No one noticed when Rizelya's legs gave out and she dropped like a stone to the ground.

Kaieli ran her hands in the air over the monster ichor on Naila. Beautiful bronze light poured from Kaieli's hands and covered Naila's wounds. The light grew darker, deepening to a dark, mud brown as it drew the poison from the monster's ichor from Naila's body. It took a bit longer than usual since they had waited for over an octar to get it removed. Kaieli made a motion and gathered the noxious light into a tight ball. One of the Reds came over and sent a tendril of fire to the ball. It flared, and fine ash trickled to the ground. Naila's wounds were raw and red, but now they didn't have a ghastly gray tinge to them.

"How's Histrun?" Naila asked as Kaieli smeared some ointment on her wounds and bound them with strips of clean cloth.

"He's hurt, but alive. Damn fool." Kaieli shook her head. "He shouldn't be fighting monsters at his age." She turned to Rizelya, her face scrunched with worry when she saw Rizelya sitting on the ground. "What are you doing down there?"

"Seemed like you were taking forever. You getting sloppy?"

"Yeah, and you're getting weak." Kaieli sat next to Rizelya. Bronze light spread out over Rizelya's biceps. Kaieli looked deep into her eyes and asked quietly, "What happened? You don't pass out."

"Not sure. There was a new janack in the nest. I heard it humming during the fight and after I blew it up, I could hear it screaming. I felt fine until then. Then it felt as if my magic and energy were draining away from me."

Kaieli finished bandaging Rizelya's arm. "Light a fire for me," she commanded.

Rizelya lifted her hand to make fire dance on her palm. It was her favorite trick. "What in the Crone's fires!" For the first time since she was a little girl, no fire danced. She reached deeper toward her magic and tried again. No fire. None. Not even a spark.

"That isn't good," Kaieli commented. She pulled a package out of her rucksack and unwrapped it. "Here, eat this." She handed Rizelya a trail bar. It was dense, rich with nuts and fruit, and full of calories. A flask of hot, spiced taevo followed. "It will help revitalize you until we get back to the Keep."

Rizelya nibbled on the trail bar, trying not to eat any fruit. She didn't like fruit, especially dried. As the first bits hit her stomach, she realized she was ravenous. She stuffed the rest, fruit and all, in her mouth, barely chewing. She gulped down the taevo. Finished, she felt slightly better and looked around.

The Reds were done. Nothing but piles of ash were left of the janack. The fire-ring she and Naila had created to corral the strange janack had burned hotter than normal. A hand-width band of charred ground provided a clear demarcation of the area where they had fought. Eiden moved through the clearing. A breeze blew in front of her, gathering the ash into a cyclone. The dirty wind funnel lifted above the trees and toward the swamp, where it dissipated, dropping the ash.

Eiden crossed the boundary, concentrating on collecting all the monster ashes. The little group around Rizelya needed to move so Eiden could finish her task. They couldn't leave with Rizelya lounging on the ground. She lifted a hand to Naila. "Here, help me up."

Naila grasped Rizelya's hand in her strong grip and tugged her to her feet. Rizelya was glad she held her helbraught to help steady her as she swayed. Her head cleared a couple of breaths later, so she started to walk away, only she found herself sitting on the ground instead. She grimaced. *Well, at least I didn't pass out this time.*

"She can't walk back to the horses in this shape," Kaieli said.

"True," Naila answered. She looked around the battlefield. "Aistrun!" she called. He was one of the males still in warrior form. He turned their way, and seeing them, loped toward them.

Rizelya groaned. Of all the warriors, it would have to be him. He'd tease her unmercifully for her weakness. It's what best friends did.

"Carry her," Naila told Aistrun when he reached them.

"I can walk," Rizelya insisted as she struggled to get her feet under her.

"Hey, Little Red. Troubles?" Without waiting for her to answer, Aistrun swept her into his arms. He was careful to keep his claws from her tender skin.

"Wolf!" Rizelya cried. Woe to anyone else, even Kaieli, who tried to call them those names. It had started when they were children, when she was the littlest one training in their group and he was the tallest. At six-four, he was still one of the tallest in the pack and at five-two, she was still the shortest. She struggled in his arms, but it was futile with his greater strength.

"No worry, big bad wolf not eat you... this time." He let his tongue loll out and panted a little. He looked more like a friendly dog than a frightening wolf. Most men didn't talk much in warrior form, and when they did, it was a word or two at most. It was difficult to form the words around the different mouth shape and teeth. Aistrun, however, was a jabber-mouth in either form.

"Let me down. I can walk."

"No can do. Alpha said carry you, so I carry. Can't disobey Alpha, can I?"

He had a point there. Not even as Naila's sister could she disobey an alpha's order. Rizelya gave up and settled against his chest. Aistrun fell into an easy lope as he ran toward the horses. The movement lulled her to sleep. She didn't rouse when he transferred her to someone else's arms.

Chapter 2

Rizelya crossed her arms over her chest and whined, "Kaieli, can I please get out of bed now? It's been two days, and I feel fine."

Kaieli glared at her. "Riz, your magic was drained!"

"So? I'm going crazy with nothing to do."

Kaieli's intense gaze made Rizelya squirm. "It was serious, Riz. Nearly all of your magical reserves were gone. Dear Heart, I almost lost you."

Rizelya reached up and touched Kaieli's face. "You didn't lose me. I'm here and all right." She wiggled, sitting up straighter. "But I won't be if I have to stay here any longer!"

Kaieli laughed. "If you're able to complain this much, you must be back to normal. Fine. You're released from bedrest."

Rizelya gave Kaieli a quick hug, then jumped out of bed. She spun in a circle, arms up in the air. "Thank you, Maiden! I can move again." She picked through her clothes on her side of the floor, finally finding something clean.

"Your sponge bath didn't get all the monster goo off. I'm going to the bathing room. Want to join me?"

"Oh, that sounds wonderful," Kaieli sighed, brushing a wayward curl from her face. "It's been a long three days."

"It wasn't me keeping you busy. I just slept."

"You were the easy one. We've had more fighters injured than usual." Kaieli pulled an outfit from the wardrobe in their shared sleeping room in the pack house. Kaieli's side was immaculate. Besides the clothing tossed on the floor, Rizelya's portion had piles of books and papers on the desk in organized chaos.

Dark circles underlined Kaieli's blue-gray eyes. She walked slowly, keeping one hand on the wall for support as they traversed the corridor of the sleeping rooms. Her usual bouncy curls hung in limp strands.

They went downstairs to the main floor of the pack house, then wound down another flight of stairs to the large underground space. Storage and supply rooms covered half the area. The other portion held the communal bathing room.

Rizelya stopped inside the threshold, glancing around. It surprised her there wasn't anyone soaking in the huge tubs. "Where's everyone?"

"Out fighting."

"Again?"

Kaieli sighed as she stripped off her clothes and filled a bucket with water. "The nests and monsters aren't acting normal, forming out of schedule, and larger. Fighters have gone to battle every day you've been ill. Sometimes more than one nest matures at the same time."

Rizelya gulped.

The two women washed, rinsed, and climbed into the large soaking tubs. As Rizelya sank into the steaming water, the memory of the gray woman she'd glimpsed as she'd passed out floated through her mind. She shook her head, unsure if she'd actually seen it or if it was a figment of her imagination.

Sitting next to each other, Rizelya wrapped her arm around Kaieli, who rested her head on Rizelya's shoulder.

"It's been awful," Kaieli said quietly. "A dozen fighters have returned to the Mother's Womb."

Tears filled Rizelya's eyes as Kaieli listed the dead pack members.

"One of those strange janacks you exploded has appeared in every nest," Kaieli continued. "They're damned hard to stop. It's why so many people have been killed."

"Has anyone else heard the janack?"

Kaieli shrugged. "Naila would know."

"I'll talk to her later."

They silently relaxed in the hot water for another half octar. Finally, Kaieli stretched, stood up, and grabbed a towel. "I have work to get back to, and you need to see Naila."

"Spoil sport." Rizelya stuck out her tongue, making Kaieli laugh.

Rizelya sighed and climbed out of the tub. After they were both dry and dressed, Rizelya sat on a bench. Kaieli combed out Rizelya's long auburn hair, braided it tight on either side of Rizelya's head, and then wove it into a thick braid down her back.

"There, you're presentable," Kaieli said, patting Rizelya's shoulder.

Rizelya turned and wrapped her arms around Kaieli. She buried her head in Kaieli's stomach for a moment, then looked up. "I know you worry about me, but I can't stop being a Red and fighting."

"I know, Dear Heart." Kaieli leaned down and kissed the top of Rizelya's head. "We can't change who we are."

Rizelya wondered anew why this amazing woman loved her enough to become her heart sister. Kaieli's soft and gentle nature made her an extraordinary healer. Her deep brown, almost black hair spoke of how Talented she was not only as a Brown, but in most of the Talents except Red and White. Kaieli's blue-gray eyes were more blue than gray today. They changed colors depending on the type of magic she accessed.

The women climbed the stairs back into the world, hand in hand. Their differing duties would soon separate them.

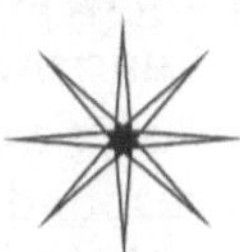

Rizelya huffed when she saw Aistrun lounging against the wall when she and Kaieli reached the main level.

"Hey, Little Red," he said, pushing off the wall. "You're looking better. Hey, Kaieli, the fighting-pack just came in with some seriously wounded."

Kaieli squeezed Rizelya's hand and rushed off.

"Were you waiting for us or guarding us, Wolf?" Rizelya asked.

"Both," he said. "I thought you two needed some time alone. She was really worried about you, Rizelya."

"What's up?"

"Naila and Kelstrun want to see us. I'm not sure if we're in trouble. Again. I can't think of anything we've done lately."

Rizelya and Aistrun strode toward the Keep Alphas' office, located near the front of the house.

The two tended to find themselves in front of the Keep Alphas quite often. It was a good thing they were the best fighters of the pack, or the Alphas might relegate them to doing menial labor. She'd end up in the stables and Aistrun in the nursery, although Aistrun would love the job. He spent his free time telling stories to the children.

Rizelya shrugged. "I've been sick. I haven't had a chance to break any rules. What have you done?"

"Nothing."

When Naila bade them enter, they slunk into the room, eyes downcast.

"Don't look so forlorn. You're not in trouble. This time." Kelstrun wore his red hair clipped short. His short beard circled his mouth.

"Come. Sit," Naila said in her rough voice. The high neck of her turquoise blue tunic partially covering the scar on her throat. Rose embroidered geometric shapes trailed along the sleeve edges and hem. Her light yellow-gold eyes crinkled as she smiled at them.

Rizelya and Aistrun perked up as they crossed the room to sit in the chairs in front of the large desk.

Kelstrun's green eyes narrowed. "You're aware of the changes in the Malvers' monster's behavior?"

"Yes, sir," both of them responded.

"We need to know if this is happening in the other territories." Kelstrun turned to Naila. "You sure they're the best ones for this?"

"Yes." Naila looked at Rizelya, then at Aistrun.

Kelstrun snorted. "They're more likely to find trouble than solve our problem."

Rizelya resisted the urge to roll her eyes. Kelstrun never let an opportunity to express his dislike of them pass. He thought they were slackers. But he did respect their fighting ability.

"They may be trouble finders," Naila agreed. "But good fighters. We decided. They are best. Tell them."

Kelstrun pinched the bridge of his nose and huffed out a breath. He gave Rizelya and Aistrun a stern look. "We're assigning you the task of going to Strunlair Keep and inform our Clan Alphas of the new situation with the Malvers' monsters. You'll stop at the territory keeps along the way to determine if the strange janack has shown up anywhere else. If it has, ask them if they've found a method to kill the damn thing without exploding it. We haven't, and it makes a terrible mess. There have been more injuries—and deaths—from falling debris than from fighting."

"We were lucky." Naila pointed at Rizelya and then back at herself. "You, me, strong Reds."

"Your fight is the only one without serious explosion injuries," Kelstrun continued. "We haven't managed to get it surrounded alone since then. It seems as if the new ones are learning from the mistakes of the others." He slammed a fist on the desk, anger darkening his voice. "Damn! I've read every alpha log we have in this keep, and nothing like this has ever happened before. We've had one janack and two of its brechas escape a nest because we were so focused on the strange janack."

"Oh, Sweet Mother, no!" Rizelya swore.

"What! Where?" Aistrun asked at the same time.

"Near the pasture. They went after the goat herd. We caught them before they reached it, thank the Mother. We haven't had any escapees in more than twenty years."

"When do you want us to leave, sir?" Aistrun asked, his usual buoyant nature subdued.

"In the morning," Naila answered.

"Will it be just us, or will we have company?" Rizelya asked. "I doubt it will be safe for just the two of us." It would take over a chedan to reach Strunlair Keep, and she didn't relish the idea of spending it alone with Aistrun. He was her best friend, and she loved him as a pack-mate or even a brother, but not the way he wanted as a bond-mate. They'd been lovers once, and she'd hoped it would put an end to his desire to be bond-mates. But it hadn't. Her relationship with Kaieli satisfied her. She didn't want to get involved with anyone else.

"Yes, small squad." Naila's eyes twinkled with suppressed laughter. After all these years, she had, at last, discovered how to force Rizelya and Aistrun to assume alpha duties.

"Go see Histrun," Kelstrun ordered. "He has the details and will give you the assignments."

Aistrun groaned. "But I don't want to be an alpha. I'm too young. Can't someone else be the alpha?"

Naila and Kelstrun shook their heads in unison.

"Time you be alpha," Naila grated. "Old now."

"You're what, twenty-four?" Kelstrun speared Aistrun with his eyes. "You should have had a squad four years ago. No complaints." He turned to Rizelya. "You either. Both of you are quite capable, if not for your trouble making, to be squad-pack alphas."

Aistrun hung his head in submission. "Yes Alpha."

"Come on, Alpha Aistrun," Rizelya teased. "We need to find out who is in our squad-pack."

Although Histrun was no longer an active alpha, he was a revered elder with great wisdom. He had been the Strunlair Clan Alpha for sixteen years, the longest term of any clan alpha in any of the eight clans. He and his bond-mate, Zehala, had developed the current method of using fire-rings to separate and divide the monsters in the nest.

Aistrun knocked on Histrun's door. Courtesy, and Histrun's status, forbade them from just entering, even if his door was open.

"Oh, it's you two," Histrun grumbled. "Well, come in."

Rizelya gaped. She hadn't seen him since she exploded the new janack. He sported a black eye and bruises down the side of his face. A patch of his hair had been shaved above his right eye, and a sling held his right arm.

"What happened to you, sir?" Concern for her father filled Rizelya. She didn't have much of a relationship with him outside of his stern instruction. The pack raised the children, especially those born to legendary Alphas like Histrun and Zehala. She tried not to be bitter about it. None of the other children of fighting-pack alphas, famous or not, had much contact with their parents. Even so, she still loved him. Sometimes the close relationship Aistrun had with his parents, who weren't part of a fighting pack, made her jealous.

"You did!" Histrun snapped.

"Well, if you hadn't insisted on going to a battle at your age, you'd be just fine."

"I was *just fine* until you exploded that damn janack. One of its tentacles tossed me clear out of the fire-ring. Busted my arm when I landed."

"Sorry, sir." Rizelya ducked her head. "I heard you'd been hurt. But it was the only way I could see to destroy it. Your venom wasn't working or was taking its sweet time killing the stupid creature."

"I know, I know," he waved away her apology. "Seems like no one can kill them except by exploding the vile creatures. But—" he glared at her "—because of you, they won't let me go out and fight anymore."

"Hey, sir," Aistrun piped in, "that's probably a good thing for a man a hundred and five years old."

Rizelya put her hand to her forehead as she shook her head, groaning. Sometimes Aistrun didn't know when to keep his mouth shut. Her posture also hid her relief. Her father was too old to be fighting the monsters.

"What was that, boy?" Histrun roared as he surged to his feet. The effect was lost when he abruptly crashed back down in his chair, his face pale with pain.

Both Aistrun and Rizelya rushed around the desk.

"Histrun, are you all right?" Rizelya asked.

"Yeah." He nodded after a few moments. "Busted my leg and a couple of ribs, too. I guess I might be getting old. I can't roll like I used to."

"Sorry, sir." Aistrun's voice was full of contrition. "I didn't realize you were so hurt, or I wouldn't have teased you."

"You're a damned cur," Histrun swore, "and a lazy whelp."

Aistrun grinned.

Rizelya sighed in relief. Histrun was okay if he was swearing at Aistrun.

"Now, get back over there where you belong." Histrun shooed them to the other side of his desk. "So, they've finally convinced you into leading a squad-pack, huh, cur?"

"Hey, they didn't do any talking. Just told us we had one," Aistrun snarled. "They know I don't want to be an alpha. She doesn't either." He pointed his thumb at Rizelya.

"Nope, I don't."

"You're both leaders, whether you admit to it or not. Something tells me we haven't seen the last of the changes in the Malvers' monsters. We'll need every alpha possible. Now, for your squad-pack. It's small so you can move fast but safely." Histrun pushed a map in front of them and pointed at it as he spoke. "Here is the route we want you to take. You'll go east, first to Strunell, then Strunville. Then head north to Strundale, Strunheim, and Strunven. From there go to Strunlair. Stop at each of the territory Keeps and talk to the Keep Alphas. You're to arrive at Strunlair Keep by the last day of Sandar."

Rizelya whistled. It was the middle of Neydar now. The schedule gave them twelve chedan to cover nearly a thousand measures. She leaned over the map and traced the route, which circled the entire Strunlair Province, with her finger.

"It will push us and our mounts to their limits, sir."

"It will. We don't have time for lallygagging. We chose you two because you won't feel guilty about pushing each other and your squad-pack hard."

Rizelya and Aistrun looked at each other and nodded.

Histrun picked up a piece of paper and handed it to Rizelya. "Here are the people of your new squad-pack."

Aistrun leaned over to look at it with her. There were four names on the list. Rizelya knew three of them. They were age-mates and had worked with them at various times in different squad-packs. Aistrun and Rizelya were too dominant to stay in a squad-pack for long without the squad-pack alpha feeling challenged. As a result, they'd been assigned to numerous squad-packs over the years.

"These are good people. We can work with them." She pointed to a name. "Except this one. He's new here, and I don't like him."

Aistrun nodded in agreement. As the female alpha, she held the ultimate authority within their little pack. Just as Kelstrun bowed to Naila, Aistrun would bow to her. She trusted him to argue and disagree with her if he felt she was making any wrong choices. But in the end, all the decisions were hers—and so were the mistakes.

"I don't care if you don't like him. You will take him as ordered."

Rizelya glared at Histrun until he snarled. She bowed her head in submission.

Histrun put the map with the indicated route in a packet and handed it to Rizelya. "There are letters of introduction for each of the Keep Alphas which will allow you to requisition supplies. You won't be carrying much with you. Go, they are waiting for you in the meeting room." He turned in his chair to gaze out the window, clearly dismissing them.

Aistrun pushed the meeting room's door open and waited for Rizelya to proceed him. At the table sat the four people who would be their first squad-pack. Rizelya stood at the threshold, assessing her new pack. Over the next lunadar and a half, their lives would depend on each other.

Leistral was beautiful with her dark green eyes and copper-red hair. She exercised her Green Talent by spending most of her spare time in the kitchens. During the journey and staying at safe houses along the way, it would be nice to have a good cook with them. No one wanted to eat Rizelya's cooking. Leistral seemed more resigned than pleased to be in the group.

The other Red assigned to them was Dehali. Her fingers drummed a nervous staccato on the table. She stopped when she saw them at the door. She didn't appear to be a strong fire Talent with her strawberry-blond hair until you looked at her eyes. They were an unusual red ringed with gold. Having the intelligent fighter on her team pleased Rizelya.

Eidstrun was three years younger than the rest of them. Rizelya had worked with him several times. His twin sister, Eiden, was her friend. The siblings were both impetuous. His pale blond hair shone in the afternoon sunlight. A ray caught his golden brown eyes. He stood a tad over six-foot, with broad shoulders and well-defined muscles. His warrior form was one of the strongest Rizelya had seen.

The last of the group leaned against the wall behind the table, glowering at the door with his arms crossed. He was the only one Rizelya didn't know or want. She bet Keandran didn't appreciate being given this task. He recently moved to Strunland Keep from the Andranlair Province. He seemed to be an arrogant know-it-all and followed Histrun around like a puppy. Maybe getting him out of Histrun's hair was why he'd saddled her with Keandran. Most would call the tall, blond handsome. But Rizelya saw the hard coldness in his pale watery blue eyes that ruined his looks.

They must have been scraping the bottom when they chose him, Rizelya mind-spoke to Aistrun. *There's something about him that makes me uneasy.*

Hey, it's only for a lunadar and a half and then they'll dissolve this little squad-pack, Aistrun replied.

Rizelya didn't think they would. Once they became alphas of this tiny squad-pack, there was no going back to being just a fighter. She let Aistrun keep his fantasy.

Well, shall we? Stepping into the room, Rizelya addressed the waiting group. "Hello, welcome to our new squad-pack. Did Histrun tell you what they've assigned us to do?"

"Something about a fast trip to Strunlair Keep taking a message to the Clan Alphas." Dehali moved her hand off the table but continued to drum her fingers on her leg.

"Hey, that and more," Aistrun said. "You all noticed the changes in the Malvers' monsters and the new janack, right?"

The group nodded.

"Damn crazy stuff," Eidstrun interjected. "What's happening?"

"No one knows," Rizelya said, leaning against the wall. "It's the real reason we're traveling to the Clan Keep. We're to discover if this is an isolated occurrence in our territory, or if it's happening in the other Strunlair territories."

"How are we going to do that?" Leistral's eyebrows furrowed in confusion. "Strunlair Keep is only a few days' ride from here."

Rizelya took out the map Histrun had given her and put it on the table. As she explained, she pointed out the route. "Like this. We'll ride east to Strunell and circle around the province to go north to Strunheim and Strunven. From there, we'll proceed to Strunlair Keep. The only one we aren't visiting is Strunhelos."

"Damn!" Keandran swore. "That's a lot of measures to cover. How long do they expect it to take us?"

"Hey, they said fast," Aistrun smiled. "It normally takes nearly three lunadar or more to make the journey. We're doing it one and a half. We have to be in Strunland Keep by the last day of Sandar."

"You trying to kill us, Rizelya?" Dehali glared at her.

"Not me! Blame it on Naila and Kelstrun." She narrowed her eyes and lowered her voice. "This is bloody serious. We have to know what we're up against."

"But why now?" Leistral complained. "Why not wait until the clan alphas send for information?"

"Hey, you know whose plan this is," Aistrun laughed. "Can you honestly think Histrun would wait for the clan alphas Nestrun or Beladi to consider the need to gather this intelligence?"

They all shook their heads, mumbling, "No."

Rizelya glanced at each in turn. "Go get ready. We leave in the morning. Pack light as we're moving fast. Meet at the stables an octar before dawn."

There was some muttering and grumbling. "What was that?" Rizelya asked in a hard voice. She might as well start being the alpha. If they wanted a show of dominance, she'd give it to them.

All of them immediately lowered their heads in submission, except Keandran. He looked her directly in the eyes before dropping his head. "Yes, Alpha!" they shouted. She shooed them off.

"If you don't get into a fight with Keandran before we're two days out, I'll be surprised," Rizelya said. It fell to the male alpha to discipline the warriors.

"I may not want to be an alpha, but I am. I'll wipe the insolence from him."

"Just don't kill him. We may need him."

Rizelya put the map back in the pouch. The new alphas sat down at the table and went over the written orders Histrun had included.

Rizelya pondered the orders. The Keep Alphas were asking a great deal out of her little squad-pack. If the increase in Malvers' monster's nests was occurring in the entire Strunlair Province, it would be a miracle if they didn't run into a nest alone on the way. They weren't a full platoon, and fighting a nest with so few people would get them killed. She prayed another fighting-pack would be there to help them when they ran into a nest. Until then, there was nothing she could do, except collect the supplies they needed and do everything in her power to keep them alive.

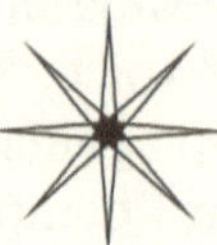

Rizelya tossed and turned, unable to fall asleep. Her mind wouldn't stop whirling. At the evening meal, she and Aistrun had gone over their preparations with Histrun. He'd told them a bit about each of the Keep Alpha pairs they'd meet. Even though he was no longer an active alpha, he kept informed about all the alphas in Strunlair Province. He'd finally shooed them off to bed well into the night.

Kaieli climbed into bed with her and snuggled close. She didn't say anything, just held Rizelya in a loving embrace.

In the dark with Kaieli, Rizelya could look inside and admit she was afraid. "What if I fail? What if I'm not a good leader?" Her fears tumbled from her lips. "What if I get them all killed? There won't be a Gray around to guide them to Summerland."

"Shh, shh, Dear Heart," Kaieli crooned. "All will be well. If they die—which they won't—they'll find their way to a Gray."

"But I don't want them to be ghosts!" Rizelya wailed.

"If it happens, it happens. Nothing you can do about it."

"Just because I'm dominant and am able to be an alpha doesn't mean I will be."

Kaieli snorted. "Now you're being morose. I know you." Kaieli leaned over Rizelya, nose-to-nose.

This close, Rizelya could see the intensity in Kaieli's face. And the love.

"You. Are. A. Good. Leader." Kaieli paused between each word. "Believe in yourself. Trust the training you've received. They've been grooming you since you were born to become a keep alpha, if not the clan alpha. You can't hide from your gifts forever. The only reason you're not a platoon-pack Alpha is because until now you've refused to even lead a squad-pack."

"You're right," Rizelya huffed.

When she was fourteen, she'd followed Naila's fighting-pack every time they headed to the monster battles. Finally, the Keep Alphas gave up and let her join the fighters. As a result, the leaders had offered her a squad-pack at the unheard age of sixteen. She had refused then because she believed they were only giving it to her because of her parents and sister's legacy. And she kept refusing on the same grounds.

"They finally found the only way I wouldn't refuse."

"A dangerous mission and a challenge," Kaieli finished for her, chuckling. "You'll do well, Dear Heart." She snuggled back down beside Rizelya, her head tucked on Rizelya's chest, arm flung over her. She crooned an old lullaby.

Rizelya suspected Kaieli was weaving a light sleep spell as she felt her mind and body relax. Kaieli hadn't even finished a full verse when Rizelya's eyes closed.

Chapter 3

Rizelya arrived at the stable well before the rest of her squad-pack, including Aistrun. Her mare, Kymaya, whinnied when she entered the stall. She rubbed the horse's nose affectionately. Histrun's letters authorized them to replace their horses at the other keeps. She'd only leave Kymaya behind in a dire circumstance. They had been partners since she was thirteen.

Scars covered both of them from past battles with the Malvers' monsters. Sometimes they didn't get to a nest site in time to install the horses in the corrals. Kymaya, as a Haaslair battle-trained horse, bravely fought the creatures. Rizelya ran the curry comb through Kymaya's dark-blue roan coat, admiring the fine blue-gray stripes marking her body. Her mane, tail, and ears were a deep charcoal gray, almost black.

Aistrun came in and nodded to her in greeting. He led his gelding from his stall. Aistrun had fallen in love with Jezhan and his deep red-gold sorrel coat at first sight. The horse was stunning with his pale gold mane, darker gold tail, and white socks on his hind legs. After months of cajoling, Aistrun convinced Jezhan's original rider to part with him. Rizelya often teased Aistrun that the only reason he liked Jezhan was because the two of them made a striking pair. The sorrel and gold horse set off Aistrun's red-gold hair and gold eyes.

The others trickled into the stables. As each person came in, a young apprentice of the stable-pack ran to get their mounts for them. Keandran and Eidstrun also had a remount. They didn't ride a plains-bred horse with their superior stamina. Soon, the riders had saddled their horses and secured their packs and bedrolls to their saddles. As they led the horses into the courtyard, pale pink brightened the sky.

Rizelya mounted Kymaya and walked her toward the keep gate, the other horses clopping behind them. Ready to start their adventure, she waited impatiently for the gatekeepers to open the heavy doors. As soon as a space wide enough for Kymaya appeared, Rizelya nudged her horse through. When her group was out, she kicked Kymaya into a ground-eating trot.

They passed fields surrounded by stone fences to guard them from being invaded by Malvers' monsters. A broad lane of crushed white sheadash stone separated each field and pasture. The rock's magical properties kept the monsters from crossing it, providing additional protection in the event the fighters couldn't stop the beasts before they reached the keep.

Rizelya shuddered. It used to happen often, causing heavy casualties of not only livestock, but people. That is, until thirty years ago, when her parents invented the innovative technique the fighting-packs now employed. She only had to remember the lost lives to know why her parents were so celebrated.

"Hey, what are you thinking about?" Aistrun's cheery voice broke into her thoughts as he caught up to her.

With the fields behind them, they rode through the empty pastures surrounding the keep. The shepherds would herd the animals out to graze in another octar.

"My parents," she said. When he kept looking at her expectantly, she sighed and continued. "I was thinking how lucky we've been since they developed the fire-ring technique that allows us to kill the monsters at the nest site."

"Yeah, my parents' pack talks about how bad it used to be."

Aistrun came from the shepherd-pack, which had lost many members as they had fought monsters off from their livestock.

"Even after all these years," he continued, "they still mourn the loss of my older sister, Aistral. I think it's because she's their only girl."

He never talked about how Aistral had died. Rizelya knew very little about it. Except he hadn't been born yet.

"What happened?"

When he answered, sorrow filled his voice. "The fighting-packs weren't as efficient back then. Aistral had found a ewe with a new lamb and wouldn't leave them. The ewe was comfortable next to the pasture wall." He spat, and his eyes tightened with anger. "Stupid sheep never learn that's a dangerous place. A brecha smelled them out, and its janack reached a tentacle over the stone path and fence to snatch up the animal. Aistral tried to fight it off with only her helstrablade and her Brown Talent. A tentacle crushed her. The squad-pack battling the janack on the other side couldn't save her."

Aistrun pointed at the seven-foot-tall pasture fence they rode by. "Afterward, they built the fences higher, but thankfully, we haven't needed them." He paused, thoughtful. "Maybe they will protect someone if this outbreak is the new norm."

"I hope it isn't," Rizelya said with feeling. "It's too bad killing them at the nest didn't do what everyone hoped, and starve them into nonexistence. After all these years, we don't know where they came from, or why they continue attacking us."

Rizelya halted Kymaya as a memory rose to the surface.

"Watch out!" Keandran snapped as he fought to keep his horse from running into hers.

"Go ride point," Rizelya snarled. When Aistrun started to follow, she said softly, "Wait."

Dehali and Leistral rode by, but Dehali drew up her horse and turned around. "Are you all right, Rizelya? You don't look so good."

Leistral, who had also stopped, nodded in agreement. "You're awfully pale." Her eyes darted to either side of the road. "Did you see a ghost?"

"No, no ghosts," Rizelya said with a laugh. "I'm not a Gray. I'm fine." When it appeared they would argue, she added, "It's nothing to concern you. Go on. Keep the boys out of trouble." She noticed Eidstrun kept a careful distance from Keandran.

"Will do." Dehali leaned over her saddle horn and lowered her voice. "I'm keeping my eye on that Keandran. I don't like him."

"Me either." Leistral shuddered. "There's been problems in whatever fighting-pack he's assigned to. Watch him, Alphas. He likes authority even less than you two do."

"Hey, thanks for the warning," Aistrun said. "We're watching."

The women broke into a trot to catch up to Eidstrun, then guided their horses so they rode on either side of him.

"So what's wrong? You really do look like you've seen a ghost."

"Something much worse, I think." She nudged Kymaya into a slow walk. "I just remembered what I saw when I touched the strange protrusion on the new janack."

"What was it?"

"The face of a woman unlike anyone I've ever seen before. She was pale and gaunt, with gray skin and gray eyes. Malice and hate burned in her eyes. Crap! I forgot to tell the White Priestess about it."

"Does Naila know?" At her nod, he continued, "Then she'll talk to the White Priestess about it. Hey, perhaps she already has, and it's why we're going."

"That's possible. I think I'll ask the Keep Alphas we meet if anyone else has heard the humming or seen someone."

"You heard a noise too?"

Rizelya grimaced at the memory. "During the fight. Did you hear it?"

He shook his head. "No, but then I was in the south area, and part of the first group fighting. I didn't see the weird janack until after you surrounded it with your fire-ring. No one else has mentioned experiencing anything out of the ordinary."

Rizelya's heart plummeted. Why was she the only one affected by the new janack?

They'd ridden past the pastures. The road through the forest beckoned. A fast ride would clear her head. "Time's a-wasting! We have a long journey." Rizelya kicked Kymaya into a canter, racing up the path and passing the others, including Keandran.

Rizelya and Aistrun pressed their squad-pack and horses hard. Using the cycle of trot, canter, trot, walk, the measures flew under their horse's feet. At the quick pace, they'd pass through their home territory within a day or two. The path they followed avoided known nest sites, giving them a couple of relatively safe travel days.

The first time they stopped to give the horses a breather and water them, Keandran complained bitterly about the short rest. Rizelya ignored him, figuring he wasn't used to the fast pace. Although her Strunland pack-mates weren't having any difficulty. When he tried mounting his horse, it shied away from him. Swearing, he finally settled on the saddle, only to have the horse buck, nearly throwing him off. Rizelya frowned at the horse's unusual behavior. Then shrugged it off. She hadn't ridden any horse other than Kymaya since they became partners when she turned thirteen.

During the ride, Keandran's horse fought against the bit. When they slowed to a walk, it sidled every few steps, and kicked up its heels. At the next stop, Keandran changed horses. His remount was even worse. The gelding snapped his teeth at Keandran as he tightened the girth strap, nearly taking a chunk from Keandran's arm. It whirled away from Keandran each time he tried to step into the stirrup. Finally, Keandran leaped to the saddle with a growl. The horse whinnied and bucked, then crow hopped in an effort to unseat his rider. Eidstrun grabbed the horse's halter, bringing it under control.

Shaking her head, Rizelya gave the order to move out. "I've never seen such ill-mannered horses," she commented to Aistrun. "I'm considering asking the horse-master at Strunell Keep to give us different ones for Keandran."

"It might be a good idea." He studied Keandran's horse. It crow-hopped several times, stopping when Keandran jerked savagely on its reins, swearing up a storm. "Is it the horses or Keandran? Eidstrun's pair are Strunlair-bred, and he isn't having any troubles."

Rizelya shrugged. "Perhaps it's both. Remind me to talk to the Strunell horse-master."

Late in the afternoon, they stopped to rest the horses one last time before reaching the safe house.

"I've had enough of those evil horses," Keandran said, plopping on the ground. "You can't make me leave."

"This spot isn't safe." Rizelya turned, removing her foot from the stirrup. "We can't stay here. Get up, get on your horse, and let's get moving. I want to get to the safe house before dark."

"What are you scared of?" Keandran jeered. "The monsters aren't active after sundown."

"Tell me you're not that stupid." Rizelya put a fist on her hip. "The monsters aren't the only danger. Have you forgotten about narhili beasts? I haven't. They'd tear us apart in our sleep if we stayed here." The beasts lived in the swamps during the day and hunted the surrounding area at night.

"Hey." Aistrun bopped the back of Keandran's head. "Haven't you been paying attention? The monsters aren't acting normal. Get up. We're moving." Aistrun turned his back and walked toward his horse, ignoring Keandran's growls.

Keandran surged to his feet. "How dare you hit me!"

Aistrun spun around. His narrowed eyes glowing a dark amber gold. "I am the alpha. It is my place to punish insolent curs."

His calm voice surprised Rizelya.

Aistrun glanced at Keandran's fisted hands. "Are you challenging your alpha?"

In answer, Keandran leaped at Aistrun, shifting in mid-air to his wolf form. Aistrun stayed human, calmly waiting as the wolf sailed toward him. His right hand swung out and slammed into Keandran's jaw, knocking him to the side. The wolf stood, shaking his head to clear it, then lifted his lips in a snarl.

"Really, that's all you got?" Aistrun sneered.

He still didn't shift. Rizelya wondered what he was waiting for until she realized it would be more humiliating for him to trounce Keandran while remaining human. He had guts. Keandran wouldn't know what hit him. Aistrun was a formidable fighter, no matter what form he fought in.

She felt a new power rising within her, that of the female alpha. She cast the Alpha magic over the clearing, preventing Keandran, or any other male, from shifting into warrior form. From her training, she knew the power kept the men from tearing each other to bits during their dominance fights. Aistrun, not taking his eyes off Keandran, nodded. He'd sensed her magic.

Keandran snarled again and charged. Aistrun ducked under Keandran and threw him across the clearing. He landed with a thump and slid, hitting a tree so hard that leaves tumbled to the ground. Keandran staggered to his feet. He tried shifting into his warrior form and growled at Rizelya when he couldn't. He changed direction and launched himself at her.

Aistrun intercepted the wolf's path and punched his muzzle. Blood dripped from Keandran's fangs. He howled, then rushed at Aistrun. The wolf again flew into a tree, swiping at Aistrun as he sailed by. Aistrun shook his hand, spraying droplets of blood. This time when Keandran charged, Aistrun caught him and lifted him high. The wolf whined in terror.

"Aistrun, remember not to kill him," Rizelya called out. She could see the anger burning in his eyes.

Aistrun struggled for a moment. He slammed the wolf down, quickly straddling its body. Aistrun's hand closed over Keandran's throat. The wolf glared at him.

"I won't if this cur yields." Aistrun said, not looking away from his opponent. "If not, he is dead."

"So be it."

The muscles in Aistrun's arms tensed as he applied more pressure. Keandran finally lowered his eyes and whined. When Aistrun stood up, the wolf dropped his head to the ground, tail tucked between his legs, fully subservient.

Aistrun walked to the small creek and washed the blood off his hands.

"Come on," Rizelya said to the rest of her pack. "Let's go."

The fight had only taken a few milcrons. Aistrun was stronger than she realized, to have cowed Keandran's wolf so quickly. The wolf was nearer to the surface of the men in the fighting-packs, and dominance fights were common. It took incredible strength to combat a wolf while human.

Eidstrun's crouch caught her attention. He looked ready to run, and his breath came in quick pants. His wild eyes followed the source of his fear—Aistrun.

She hurried over to Eidstrun, knelt in front of him, and used her alpha magic to spin calm around him. "Eidstrun, be easy," she crooned. "Don't be afraid. It's just Aistrun. You know he won't hurt you." He closed his eyes and took a shuddering breath.

"I'm okay now, Rizelya," he said, his eyes not meeting hers. "He really is scary. He seems so friendly, and then... that." Another shudder went through him. He turned away, gathering his horse's reins, and mounted. Dehali and Leistral were both already in the saddle.

Keandran hadn't moved, still whining. She stalked over to him and snapped, "What's wrong with you? Shift back and get on your horse. Move it, now!" Her anger overflowing at his challenge, which had forced Aistrun to fight him.

He tucked his tail in further and whined more.

"Ah, Rizelya," Eidstrun called, "he can't change. You have to release your hold."

"Oh!" She hadn't realized the Alpha magic also kept the men from shifting into or out of their wolf forms. She'd assumed it only affected their warrior forms. She didn't apologize to Keandran as she let it go.

Panting, Keandran shifted back to human. He lay still, taking shallow breaths. A bruise began to bloom on his throat where Aistrun had held him down. He struggled to his feet, holding his ribs tight. Keeping his eyes down, he said, "Alpha, I think he broke my ribs."

Rizelya could hear a faint snarl in his voice. Even though Aistrun had beaten and humiliated Keandran, he hadn't learned Aistrun truly was his alpha and the better man. If he tried to fight Aistrun again, Aistrun would kill him.

"You'll live. Leistral, wrap his ribs for him. We don't have time for his bellyaching."

Leistral climbed off her horse and rummaged in her pack. Pulling out the first aid kit, she ran over to Keandran. "Lift up your shirt," she ordered.

He growled, and Rizelya smacked him on the head. "Behave. She's helping you."

Keandran took off his shirt. A livid bruise covered his entire torso from hitting a tree a few times.

Dehali whistled. "That's going to hurt like the Crone's fires."

Leistral began wrapping Keandran's ribs. "Oh, quit whimpering. You asked for it. You're lucky to be alive. Damn, he has control."

Aistrun stomped through the clearing to Jezhan, leaping into the saddle, and rode off. Rizelya stopped Dehali from following him. "He'll be fine. Let him be. We'll catch up to him soon enough." She glared at the slowly moving Keandran and put a bit of command in her voice. "That is, if this one gets a move on it."

She wasn't in the mood to be sympathetic. One reason Aistrun hadn't wanted to become an alpha was that he was stronger than most and didn't enjoy fighting to prove dominance. He tried hard to be a likable, nice guy. Smelling Eidstrun's fear would have hurt Aistrun even more than the fight.

Eidstrun helped Keandran onto his horse, for once not bucking as he settled into the saddle. They left the clearing and rode on.

When they arrived at the safe house, smoke rose from the chimney. When Rizelya entered the stable, she found Jezhan's muzzle buried in a bucket of grain. She and the others took care of their horses. Then they ambled into the main building to find their own comfort.

The large house could shelter more than a full platoon of sixty fighters. Their little pack of six didn't put a dent in the accommodations.

Rizelya looked around. Aistrun's duffel bag sat open on one of the beds, and a pot of stew simmered on the wood stove. *He must have galloped the entire way to arrive far enough ahead of us to start dinner, but where is he?* After listening for a moment, she could hear him behind the house, chopping wood. He used the activity often to burn off steam. She put her bags next to Aistrun's and then stretched.

Keandran groaned as he fell into a bed across the room from her. The rest of the group let him have the wide berth and chose beds near their alphas. Rizelya knew it wasn't healthy to have such a division in their small pack, but she couldn't bring herself to coerce Keandran to join them.

Leistral rummaged in her saddlebag and pulled out a parcel. "Ah ha," she said. Without further explanation, she went to the stew pot and stirred it, wafting the steam toward her and breathing deeply. She took some herbs from the packet and added them to the pot. Then she opened the supply cabinet. All safe houses stored basic food like flour, beans, salt, rice, and the ever-present taevo. Leistral mixed together a batch of pan bread and put it on the stove next to the stew. She then brewed a pot of roasted taevo berries, which gave the drink a darker, richer flavor than the lighter beverage made from the taevo leaves. Rizelya sniffed appreciatively, glad Leistral had joined this little pack. They would eat well tonight.

While Leistral finished cooking dinner and the others relaxed, Rizelya slipped out the back to find Aistrun. She threaded her way over the remnants of old foundation stones jutting from the grass. This safe house, like many others, was built on the ruins of buildings and villages from the Before Time. Before the menace of the Malvers' monsters forced the Posairs to consolidate the population into the Keeps. Ruins, like this, were scattered all across Lairheim.

Rizelya loved to explore them and imagine how the ancient ones lived. Once in a while she would discover a cache of old things that had survived: a piece of jewelry, a knife, a statue. Thirty measures south of Strunland Keep were the ruins of a town, even larger than the Keep, with individual houses instead of the communal homes they resided in now. The tall walls of a Keep hadn't surrounded it. She couldn't fathom the number of people living in the Before days to populate so many cities and towns.

The chopping sounds continued. She followed the edge of the stones around to the rear of the house. Based on the layout of the ruins, Rizelya surmised this had been an inn for travelers at one time. Now it served the fighting-packs. Rizelya stopped to survey the large pile of wood Aistrun had chopped. He had taken off his shirt and sweat poured off his face and back.

"How are you doing?" she asked.

Without stopping, he answered, "Fine. I didn't want to prove my dominance over him. I hate it. It's worse than I imagined. Is he okay?"

"A few broken ribs and bruises. You had excellent control."

He put down the ax with great precision and turned to her. "I almost killed him. If you hadn't been there, I would have."

"No, you wouldn't have. He was simply being a complaining jerk. If he had endangered any of us by his stupidity, then maybe he'd be dead right now."

"You're correct. Hey, can I kill him the next time he's being a stupid jerk?"

Rizelya considered for a moment. "If he's still being an ass and a baby—" she kept her tone light "—and we decide we're better off without him, then you can."

Teasing aside, their duty was to protect the rest of their pack if Keandran put them in danger. "Come on, dinner's ready. Leistral doctored up your stew, so now it'll taste great."

He laughed, wiping off his sweat with his shirt, and then hugged Rizelya to him as they walked back into the house. "Hey, you were wrong," he said, reaching for the door.

"How?"

"It only took one day for that cur to get into a fight with me."

They were laughing together when they entered the common room. The tension in the room immediately eased. When dinner was ready, Keandran carried his bowl to a table on the other side of the room, his back to them, and ate alone. After eating, the rest of the group laughed and told stories. By the time they crawled into bed, Rizelya felt they were becoming a solid squad-pack. Except for Keandran.

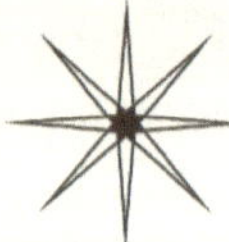

The next day, they rode at the same demanding speed. Keandran continued to complain about his horses and added in complaints about his broken ribs and bruises. Rizelya ignored him. He'd heal in a few days.

The early evening cast dark shadows when they passed the cairn markers signaling the territory border. Several measures into Strunell Territory, they stopped at the safe house for the night.

When they entered the stable the next morning, Rizelya instructed her pack to put on their horse's barding. The rose and turquoise patterns on the decorative reins, saddle blankets, breast collars, and breeching proclaimed them as belonging to Strunland Keep.

"Why are we putting on all this stuff now?" Keandran complained, his voice hoarse and raspy. "It takes so long to take it off and then put it on when we switch horses. We don't need it."

Rizelya sighed. She finished buckling the barding straps across Kymaya's hindquarters to the saddle before turning around. The beating Aistrun had given Keandran wasn't keeping him from being a whiny brat. Maybe it was his normal temperament.

She looked at the pained face of the others. No one questioned their alpha's orders. A fighting-pack needed to follow their alphas at a moment's notice to survive the Malvers' monsters. If Keandran didn't stop soon, he'd get another beating, and this time not from Aistrun. Rizelya watched, bemused, as Dehali stalked up to Keandran.

"Because you were told to do it by your alpha," Dehali ground out.

"She's not my alpha." Keandran folded his arms in front of him in a challenge that screamed, 'Make me'.

"Shut your frigging mouth." Dehali's eyes glowed bright yellow in anger.

Rizelya felt the breath in her lungs pulled from her as the air gathered around Dehali. Rizelya inhaled deeply, then waited to see what Dehali had planned.

"We were given a choice to come on this mission with them as our squad-pack alphas," Leistral said sternly. She stepped to the side of Dehali and glared at Keandran. "No one forced you to be here."

"I didn't think... Histrun's daughter... would be... so stupid." He gasped and grabbed at his neck like he was trying to loosen something strangling him. His eyes bulged as he dropped to his knees.

Rizelya waited until he started turning blue. "Dehali, enough."

Dehali made a flicking motion, releasing Keandran, who heaved air into his lungs.

"I suggest you keep your thoughts to yourself," Rizelya said mildly. "You might not survive. I don't know how they do it in the Andranlair Clan, but here, we obey our alphas and treat our pack mates with respect."

Keandran had the sense to lower his head.

"Get your horse saddled like you were told." Aistrun's cold, hard voice left little doubt he would haul Keandran onto his feet if he didn't stand up on his own power.

Her squad let out a collective sigh of relief when Keandran stood up, head still lowered, shuffled to his horse, and threw on the barding saddle blanket. Everyone turned back to putting tack on their horses.

"We're in Strunell Territory," Rizelya said to Keandran in an exasperated voice. "The barding will let the scouts know we are on official business."

The group soon had their horses tacked and ready. "Let's go!" Rizelya stepped into the saddle and looked up at the sky. Even with Keandran's episode, they were on the road again shortly after dawn.

They rode for several octars without seeing or meeting any Strunell scouts. Rizelya worried the Strunell packs had monster problems. Anxious they'd run into a nest, she slowed their pace to a fast trot.

Late afternoon, Aistrun signaled for them to stop as they reached the bottom of a hill. Rizelya waited, knowing his senses were better than hers. She glanced back and saw Eidstrun intently scanning the area. Something was wrong. As the clatter of hoofs quieted, the faint noise of a monster battle being fought rose in the distance.

"Should we go help them or keep going?" Aistrun asked.

"Go help," Rizelya said. "It will give us the opportunity to see if one of those strange janacks is here, too."

Aistrun dismounted. "Hey, Eidstrun, lead the way. You have the best nose."

Eidstrun nodded, tossed his horse's reins to Dehali, and slid off his horse. He squatted, examined the ground, and then headed north. A shimmer, and he was in his wolf form. Dark brown mottled his pale gold pelt. He looked like a shadow flowing along the forest floor.

Aistrun and Keandran shifted into their wolves and followed Eidstrun. Rizelya didn't expect them to wait for the women. As soon as they smelled the monsters, the men's fighting instinct would take over.

The three women kept low to their saddles, avoiding tree branches as they crashed through the forest. The sounds of battle increased. A familiar howling roar announced Aistrun had joined the fight. Another deeper howl sounded like Eidstrun. She listened but didn't hear Keandran howl his fury at the monsters.

The women stopped at a hill top. As Rizelya picketed Kymaya and Jezhan, a loud humming, like angry jacklewasps, assaulted her. She gritted her teeth. At least the janack wasn't screaming at her. Hopefully, she wouldn't pass out. She grabbed her helbraught off her saddle and stepped to the edge of the hill. From her vantage point, she spotted a humongous janack, sporting the same type of strange protrusion on its head.

"Damn, they have one, too," Dehali said, coming to stand next to Rizelya. "They haven't surrounded it with a fire-ring yet."

"What are they waiting for?" Leistral commented, standing on the other side of Rizelya.

"I don't know."

They watched, getting a feel for the battle flow. The warriors could join a scrimmage, slashing with their fangs and claws and not hurt anything but the monsters. However, if the women didn't insert their fire magic carefully with the other Red's, they could seriously injure someone.

"Look!" Rizelya pointed. "The Reds can't get close enough to form a fire-ring. A group of brechas are attacking them."

As she watched, three Reds ran toward the new janack, their helbraughts glowing. Before they drew close, another janack's tentacle crashed down in front of them.

A woman jumped back, jamming her helbraught into the tentacle, keeping it from crushing her. She pulled hard, but the helbraught was stuck fast. A warrior, with a red and green striped pelt, rolled under the tentacle, his long claws cleaving strips of flesh from it. The Red's blade glowed as she fed more fire magic into it, bursting the tentacle into pieces and freeing her helbraught. The janack shuddered before collapsing. Immediately behind it, six brechas streamed forward.

Two warriors ran side-by-side toward the strange janack. The brechas blocked their way. As they fought, another group of Reds and warriors tried to slip past them. Rizelya gaped. Six brechas broke away from the nest when there shouldn't have been any left in it. The janacks and brechas harried the warriors to keep them from closing in on the new janack.

Aistrun stepped back from the fighting, pacing. Eidstrun's huge form stood preternaturally still. Rizelya couldn't see Keandran.

She concentrated on the central janack. Its protrusion followed the battle, and wherever it pointed, the monsters attacked the Posair fighters. It gave her an idea.

"Dehali, did Eiden tell you what I had her do?"

"What?" Dehali paused, thinking. "Oh, the cold air thing?"

"Yes. Can you do it? Can you form a cold-air shield around me?"

"Let me try. I was working on it before we left the Keep. Stand still."

Rizelya felt a tingle, and then cold air surrounded her. "You did it! How far away do you have to be to maintain this? Can you do one for Aistrun at the same time?"

Dehali thought for a moment as she played with the air streams. "I can't be too far, about ten feet. I think I can split this to cover Aistrun, too."

"What are you thinking, Alpha?" Leistral asked.

"We can reach that janack if it can't sense us. The cold-air shield should do that. Leistral, you guard us. When we're close, enclose Dehali in a fire-ring and make sure she can concentrate. Eidstrun will help you."

At least, Rizelya hoped he would. She wasn't certain they had been together as a pack long enough for mind-speech to work. She and Aistrun had spoken with each other via mind-speech for years.

"Aistrun will go in with me."

The women fed fire magic into their helbraughts and dashed to the battlefield toward Aistrun. As she ran, Rizelya mind-shouted, *Aistrun, Eidstrun, get over here!*

It gratified her when both their heads snapped her direction. They raced to meet her and the other women. She sent a visual of her idea to Aistrun. Sometimes images were easier to send than words. This was one of those times.

It should work, he agreed.

They ran toward the battle. Luck was with them. None of the monsters sensed them. The Strunell Keep fighters were keeping them otherwise occupied.

Now, she mind-sent to Dehali when they were fifteen feet from the nest site. Rizelya mentally cheered when cold air enveloped her. The pack connection was working. Aistrun nodded and mimed shivering.

Rizelya touched her helbraught's tip on the ground, sending fire magic down through the blade and into the earth. A thin trickle of fire encircled the nest and the strange janack.

Remember, we have to destroy the protrusion as fast as we can, Rizelya mind-spoke to Aistrun. *Dehali can't keep our cold-air shield up long.*

I'll distract. You demolish.

They stepped over her boundary. As soon as they did, Rizelya added more fire magic to it, making it blaze twenty feet high and cutting off the strange janack from the other monsters. Aistrun and Rizelya raced to the janack. Aistrun cut to the front of the head, slid under it and shredded a swath across the entire width of its body with his claws. The janack waved its tentacles in frustration. Its protrusion flipped from side-to-side. *The cold-air shield is working! It can't sense us.*

The humming, which had been a background noise for Rizelya, suddenly grew louder, almost deafening. Prepared, she ignored it. She used her helbraught to pole-vault onto the top of a tentacle and rushed up it toward the head. The air warmed around her as Dehali's spell weakened. Rizelya wouldn't have the advantage of not being sensed much longer.

She fed more magic into her helbraught until the blade glowed with small orange flames. Rizelya jumped onto the janack's head and swung her weapon, severing the protrusion along with most of the sensor stalks. An angry scream filled Rizelya's mind. Blocking the sound, she drove the flaming blade into the monster's head, feeding additional fire magic into her blade.

She remembered what Histrun had said about burning debris. The fire shield Naila had taught her would contain the fallout. With a thought, a dome of magic formed above the fire-ring.

Run! It's going to blow!

Aistrun sprinted to the edge of the ring. Pulling her helbraught from the janack, Rizelya leaped in his direction, landed, and ran. She reached him just as the janack exploded. She flung a shield around them both, and they huddled together until monster bits stopped falling on them.

The mysterious screaming penetrated her block and grew louder. Darkness crept on the edge of her vision. She grabbed

Aistrun by the ruff of his fur. "Did you see where the protrusion landed?" She yelled.

"Yesss," he hissed through his fangs as he turned to go retrieve it.

"No! Don't touch it." Using her helbraught, she stood up. She was shaky, but not as much as the last time. "Help me get to it."

She should have expected it. Aistrun picked her up.

"Put me down!"

He grinned at her. "Not my alpha." He jogged to where the protrusion lay. Using the claws of his foot, he moved some smoldering monster bits covering it.

As soon as it was uncovered, the earsplitting screaming knocked Rizelya unconscious. She woke up, still in Aistrun's arms.

He patted her face and growled, "Wake. Wake."

"I'm awake. Put me down," she growled back. When he set her on her feet, she crumbled to the ground. When he tried to pick her up again, she batted away his paws. "No, Wolf! I'm fine. Where's my helbraught?"

"Not fine." Aistrun grumbled unhappily, but he handed it to her, anyway.

As soon as she gripped it, flames burst along the blade's edge. She remained sitting so she wouldn't have so far to fall when she passed out. She touched the blade to the protrusion, remaining conscious long enough to burn it to ash.

This time when she came to, she heard Leistral's muffled voice calling to her. Rizelya frowned, unable to make out the words. Then she realized Leistral was trying to mind-speak to her, and the block she had used to push the janack out of her mind remained in place. With effort, she released it.

...the shield. Rizelya, drop the fire shield.

"Oh!" It surprised her that she'd been unconscious twice and still managed to keep the fire shield in place. It should have been beyond her abilities.

She dismissed the shield and immediately Leistral rushed to where she lay, followed by several strangers. Only then did she realize Aistrun cradled her head in his lap. His furry lap. She sat up quickly, groaning as a thundering headache slammed into her.

"Who are you?" The older woman, obviously the platoon alpha, stood with her hands on her hips. "How did you do that?"

Rizelya held up her hand. "Quieter, please. My head feels like it's going to explode." She looked at Leistral. "Where's Dehali? Is she all right?" Dehali had used an incredible amount of magic to keep the cold-air shields up for as long as she had.

"Safe. She's tired," Leistral responded. "Damn, Eidstrun's strong. He killed a janack by himself! He's fine too, helping with the mop-up."

The Strunell alpha huffed with impatience. She could wait until Rizelya found out about her pack. That meant all of them. Rizelya sighed and asked, "And Keandran?"

"Haven't seen him. Do you think a monster got him?"

"Leistral!" Rizelya chided.

She turned to look at the alpha. The woman was old. Her copper hair had faded, and wrinkles lined her dark brown eyes and face.

"I'm Rizelya de Strunland. This is my squad-pack." She pointed to Aistrun, who hovered over her protectively. "He's my co-Alpha, Aistrun."

"I'm Keshanal, Strunell Keep Alpha," the woman replied. "How did you know how to destroy that thing? This was the first time we've seen a janack like it."

"We fought one a few days ago. Histrun's venom wasn't even touching it. I had to explode it to kill it. Our fighting-packs encountered four others, and they all had to be exploded."

"Four others? That would be four nests in less than a chedan." Keshanal sat down, stunned.

"I thought we had another day before we reached Strunell. Why are you at a monster battle, Keep Alpha?" Rizelya asked, confused.

"We've had larger than normal nests this past chedan. I wanted to see for myself what we were facing." She shook her head. "I didn't expect anything like this." She looked sharply at Rizelya. "Four in Strunland Territory, huh?"

Rizelya nodded.

"That's bad. Are our territories the only ones?" Keshanal wondered, more to herself than to Rizelya.

"It's what my squad-pack and I are trying to find out. Not to be rude, Alpha Keshanal, but do you have anything to eat? I'm starving after the magic I just used."

"Good gracious, my poor manners. Yes, yes, I'll have one of the girls bring you a travel bar." Keshanal stood up, looked around, and shook her head. "A fine mess you made, Rizelya. A fine mess." She strode off, giving orders for the remains to be burned.

Leistral helped Rizelya to her feet. She turned to Aistrun. "You ought to change. We're safe. You need to find our absent pack mate. No one has seen Keandran since he took off into the forest with you."

"We find him." He grunted, then jogged toward Eidstrun. Together, the two warriors loped off the battlefield.

A Brown approached Rizelya.

"Squad Alpha," she said, bowing her head, "Keshanal sent me to see to you. Are you hurt?"

"No, just starving. Did you bring me something to eat?" The woman handed Rizelya a trail bar, full of dried fruit. "Ugh, do you have anything without fruit?" She knew she was whining, but after what she'd just gone through, she didn't want to deal with dried fruit.

The woman took the bar back and rummaged in her bag. "Here, try this. We have a few here who share your dislike."

If the cake had any fruit in it, it was well hidden. Rizelya scarfed it down, barely chewing. "Do you have another one?" she asked between gulps, "and something for a headache?"

"You've a headache?"

"Bad. The damned protrusion screams loud."

Leistral and the healer looked at her with the same disbelief on their faces.

"It screams, okay? I don't know why I'm the only one who hears the freaking thing."

"How's your magic?" Leistral piped up. "Kaieli said last time you encountered the janack, it drained your magic."

Rizelya glared at Leistral, who only shrugged. "Fine," she spat.

"Show me." The Brown sounded almost like Kaieli.

Rizelya held out her hand. A small flicker of flame danced on her palm. "See, I'm fine."

"When we're at the safe house for the night, I want to examine you more closely," the healer said. "For now, there are more serious patients who need my care." She handed Rizelya another trail cake, a flask of taevo, and a packet of herbs before she left.

After eating and drinking, Rizelya felt much better. She stood up with Leistral's help. It took a few moments for the shakiness to leave her legs. She looked around. "We need to move so they can finish cleaning up my mess."

"Yeah, you did make a fine mess," Leistral imitated Keshanal's voice. "I think Dehali is where I left her."

"Lead the way."

When they arrived, the three men waited with Dehali. Rizelya didn't want to make a scene in front of the Strunell pack, so she refrained from commenting on Keandran's absence during the fight. Dehali's face appeared paler than normal. Rizelya gave her uneaten trail cake and the remaining taevo to Dehali.

"Eidstrun and Leistral, go retrieve our horses, will you? We have an escort to Strunell Keep by the Keep Alpha herself."

Eidstrun and Leistral sprinted up the hill where they'd left the horses.

"You," she said, pointing at Keandran, "with me." She stalked off, only half expecting him to follow. It surprised her when he did. Aistrun joined them. Rizelya stepped far enough away from Dehali to keep her from overhearing, then turned on Keandran, allowing her anger to spill out. "Where in the Crone's fires were you? No one saw you during the battle, and you weren't there helping Eidstrun and Leistral protect Dehali. This behavior doesn't suit someone in a fighting-pack."

Keandran kept his head down. "I don't know what happened, Alpha."

His voice was full of a contriteness she hadn't heard from him before. Then he raised his head. His face was white with terror.

"Hey, what happened, Keandran?" Concern filled Aistrun's voice.

"I was following you and Eidstrun to the battlefield, and the next thing I knew, the battle was over. I was clear over there." He pointed at the far end of the valley. His eyes were wide. "I was... I was walking into the swamp."

Rizelya remembered how the first janack had tried to control her mind. "Do you remember hearing or seeing anything?"

He shook his head.

The clatter of hoofs broke into the resulting silence. Rizelya glanced over to see Eidstrun and Leistral returning, leading the horses. "I don't know what's going on. Maybe a Gray at Strunell Keep can tell us."

"The Keep Alpha is ready to leave." Aistrun gestured to where Keshanal waited with her Reds. He looked at Keandran. "We'll get this sorted out."

When Keandran docilely nodded and went to his horse, Rizelya's jaw dropped. The event had shaken him more than he'd admitted. Her little pack joined the rear of the much larger Strunell platoon as they rode to the safe house.

Chapter 4

The next midday, Rizelya and her pack entered Strunell Keep with Alpha Keshanal's group. The Keep was the same size and laid out the same way as Strunland. Thick, fifteen foot tall sheadash stone walls guarded the community. Sturdy doors braced with strips of helstrim blocked the only entrance. If a nest of monsters attacked, a Red could feed fire power into the metal to repel the creatures while keeping the gates intact. A large plaza dominated the inside area.

The Clan House sat directly across from the main gate. As the central hub of the keep, it was three times the size of the other buildings. In the evenings, the population would gather there for dinner and socialization. The community lived and worked in the smaller structures scattered throughout the enclosed area.

To the left of the Clan House was the Temple built from white sheadash stone that sparkled in the afternoon sun. A dome made from clear quartz crowned the sanctuary portion, filling it with prisms of light. Five steps led up to the walkway, where four pillars rose to the ceiling. An eight-pointed star—the emblem of the four-fold Goddess—was carved on the doors. A white-haired priestess exited the building, and Rizelya glimpsed a large fire-pit in the center of the sanctum. Those women who had White or Gray Talents became priestesses of the Goddess and lived in the Temple. They were the spiritual leaders and soul workers. There had never been a man born with White Talent.

Rizelya smiled as a mob of children tumbled in front of them. Several of the boys were in their wolf form. As they played, they shifted back to boys while others transformed into wolves. At adolescence, they were taught the warrior form. But not all men became warriors. She looked over at Aistrun. He was the only male in his herdsman family-pack who had chosen to become a warrior.

The group turned down a side street between two of the fighting-pack houses and stopped at the stables.

Rizelya lost herself in Kymaya's loving presence as she groomed her horse. As she brushed Kymaya's mane, her mare whickered a greeting. Rizelya glanced around the empty stable. The others had taken her and Aistrun's belongings with them.

A large man walked in and headed toward Rizelya. He smelled like horses, and he wore his dark brown hair in a braid hanging down his back. He rubbed Kymaya's nose. Holding it in both hands, he breathed into her nostrils. "Ah, Kymaya, lass, it's been a long time." He looked up at Rizelya's stunned face. "I helped this one's mother foal her and brought her to saddle."

Rizelya ducked under her mare's neck. "You must be Lehaas!"

He grinned. "The one. And now I serve as horse-master here." He walked around Kymaya, observing her closely, running his hands down her legs, picking up her feet, or stroking her hide as he murmured quiet words to her. Finally, he completed his circuit and stopped in front of Rizelya. "She's blossomed under your care."

Rizelya blushed at the high praise from someone from the horse clan. The Haaslair Clan were phenomenal horse trainers. They lived on the plains where both wild and domestic herds ran. Many of the Haaslair men shifted into a secondary form of a horse. A few chose to become half-horse, half-man.

The horse in the next stall neighed and stuck its head over the wall. "Ah, Jezhan! Lad, you are here too?" Lehaas went to the horse, who was craning his neck, and stroked Jezhan's muzzle. "Then Aistrun must be here."

"Hey, right you are." Aistrun stepped up to Kymaya's stall door. "How do you know me? I wasn't Jezhan's first rider."

"I know the riders of all my horses." He leaned in and told them in a conspiratorial whisper, "They share with me those who treat them well and with love." He looked over his shoulder toward the stalls Keandran's horses were in. "And those who don't care for our children, don't ride them. They won't allow it."

Rizelya could believe it. The horses from the Haaslair plains she'd been around were highly intelligent. Sometimes, Kymaya communicated with Rizelya using images and emotions. They had a striping pattern on their coats. On some, like her Kymaya, it was prominent, while on others, like Jezhan, their stripes were subtle. Both of Keandran's horses were keep-bred.

"I saw your boy wearing a bruise necklace. Your doing, Aistrun?"

Aistrun nodded, frowning. "He forced me to show him who was in charge our first day out. He doesn't think he has to follow orders."

Lehaas shrugged. "He'll learn, or you'll kill him. I'm surprised he's made it this long in a fighting-pack. Unlike non-fighting-packs, we don't tolerate insubordinate crap." Lehaas examined Keandran's horses. He lifted their lips and swore. "He's a mean cur! These horses' mouths are bleeding." He crossed the stall to Keandran's tack. A stream of curses seared the air. He brought the bit to Rizelya. "Here, burn this vile thing."

The bit was rough and had short spikes coated with dried blood. "No wonder Keandran's horses behaved so badly and were ill tempered. They were being hurt." She'd never tried doing anything with metal before. Her anger at the mistreatment of the horses flared hot, and the bit quickly became a useless lump.

"If we didn't need to cover so much ground, I'd make the caitiff walk," Aistrun fumed.

"Why don't you leave him here?" Lehaas suggested. Then he added in a voice roughened with menace, "I could teach him a lesson or two."

Rizelya put a restraining hand on him. "No, we can't do that—yet. He is a part of our squad-pack. We'll deal with him. Besides, Alpha Keshanal seems too nice of a person to drop a creep like him on her."

"You be right, lass," Lehaas agreed. "She be a good alpha and takes care of us here. She doesn't deserve such cruelness laid at her feet unknowing."

"Hey, speaking of which, we need to head inside," Aistrun said.

Lehaas returned to Keandran's horses. "Go, I will take tend to these poor beasts." He glared at Keandran's tack. "I will also search his things and see if there be more he be doing to these children."

"Let us know if you find anything," Rizelya said.

Lehaas nodded and turned his attention to the misused horses.

"Damn! I can't believe I missed that," Rizelya told Aistrun as they walked out of the stable.

"Hey, you're not the only one. I don't know how our horse-master failed to notice this type of treatment of the horses. You can bet he won't allow Keandran to ride another horse—ever."

"Maybe he only does this when no one is watching. But now we're aware, we'll see to it those animals don't suffer any further."

"Damn straight," Aistrun agreed.

Rizelya and Aistrun knocked on the Keep Alpha's office door. Bestrun, the co-alpha, let them in. He was a few years younger than Keshanal. Keshanal glanced up at their entrance and put down the papers she was reading. She appeared tired and worried.

The smell of spiced taevo, steaming in a large pot on a side table, made Rizelya's mouth water. At Keshanal's nod, Rizelya filled a cup of the drink for herself and Aistrun.

"Sit," Keshanal told them, gesturing at the two empty chairs in front of the massive desk. "So why are you visiting our territory, Rizelya?"

She handed the Keep Alpha Histrun's letter of introduction. "Our alphas tasked us with taking a circuitous route to Strunlair Keep and stopping at all the territory keeps on our way. We're to find out if the new janack and the unusual nest activity has spread across all of Strunlair Province."

"We know it's in both our territories," Bestrun observed. "It might be safe to assume it's in all of them."

"Histrun sent us," Aistrun said. He leaned back in his chair, affecting unconcern. "He doubted it's an isolated problem in our territory. But he wants to be sure before sending word to the Clan Alphas."

"That sounds like him," Keshanal chuckled. "He was clan alpha for a long time and still doesn't quite trust the young ones."

"What is this new janack?" Bestrun asked. "What does it do? Besides being bigger, how is it different from the others?"

"I think it controls the other monsters," Rizelya answered, looking into her mug. "I don't know why it's suddenly appeared."

"Hey, maybe because we've become so efficient in killing them," Aistrun interjected, sitting up from his sprawl.

"You might be right," Keshanal agreed. "Let's call it a control-janack so we can differentiate it from the others. How did you reach it? Two of my warriors died trying to kill it."

Rizelya leaned forward. "They track with their heat sensors. Well, if there's a shield of cold air around you, they can't sense you. Simple, really."

Keshanal gaped. "Simple? How did you get the air cold? You don't look like you have much Yellow."

Rizelya shrugged. "Not a drop. I asked my talented friend Eiden, and she figured it out. Lucky for us, before we left, she taught Dehali, who is a fairly strong Yellow as well as a Red. I don't know why we haven't done it before this."

"Isn't your friend—Eiden?—a Red?"

Aistrun laughed. "No, just a feisty Yellow."

"You take a Yellow with you to monster battles?" Shock filled Keshanal's voice.

"Yep." Rizelya nodded. "She followed us to a battle, and we sent her back, but once everyone became involved in the fighting, she showed back up. After the third time it happened, we gave up. Now she's an essential part of our fighting-pack. Good thing she was there. Histrun, Naila, and I were fighting the first control-janack we've seen. Nothing was affecting it, not even Histrun's venom. The only way to kill those damn things is to explode them. Exploding is easier."

"Makes a damn mess," Keshanal grumbled.

"Oh, that's the other thing. Besides surrounding them with a fire-ring, you must create a fire shield around the control-janack to contain the explosion. Because they are bigger, their fallout zone is larger than normal. The debris has injured quite a few of our fighters." She remembered Kelstrun mentioning that their fighting-packs were having trouble getting near the control-janack. "I need to send a message back home. They aren't using the cold-air or fire-shields."

"We'll send it. Can your person teach my people how to create the cold-air shield?"

"I'm sure she can. However, the women must have strong Yellow Talent in order to work the spell."

"I'll make the arrangements. In two octars, we'll meet in the practice arena."

Rizelya appreciated the reprieve. It allowed her team to eat and relax. At the appointed time, they walked together to the practice arena. Except Keandran. He'd wandered off.

The large building, where they trained young ones in how to use their Talents, stood alone and well away from other structures. Sometimes, especially Reds working their fire magic, the students could lose control.

Keshanal waited for them with several women. Most had deep yellow hair proclaiming them strong Yellows. But three were Reds with red-gold hair and yellow eyes.

Dehali led the women to the center of the arena to teach them the spell to form cold-air shields. They caught on quickly, and after a few tries, were creating the shields.

"That Eiden of yours is a genius," Keshanal remarked to Rizelya.

"Yep, she is, and she just turned twenty."

"A Yellow in your fighting-pack? Remarkable." Keshanal continued to watch the training. "I never even thought to bring Talents other than Red into the fight. With the cold-air shield, the Yellows will be quite useful. Hmm, I wonder what else we could use. Certainly not Blues, they are too emotional. Come, let's talk." She turned away from the practicing women and motioned for Rizelya and Aistrun to follow her. Keshanal took them to a small office overlooking the arena.

"I've thought about this since our conversation," Keshanal said when they were all seated. "I even went to the White Priestess, and she confirms this is important. We can't wait the lunadar, or two, it will take you to visit all the Strunlair territory keeps on your way to the Clan Keep." She held up her hand, halting Rizelya's and Aistrun's protest. "But it is equally imperative to inform the Clan Alphas of the extent of the problem. So, here's what we'll do." She pulled out a map and unfolded it on the table. "I'll send a team east to Strunville and Strundale. You head north along this route to Strunheim, then back west to Strunven.. But instead of you just finding out what is happening, you'll also teach them the cold-air and fire-shields."

"What about the smaller keeps?" Rizelya asked.

"Don't worry about the minor holdings in the districts, the Territory Keeps will train them."

After seeing how bad the problem was, Rizelya had worried how they would help the smaller keeps. Keshanal had just taken that responsibility from her shoulders. There weren't any individual houses. Everyone lived within the protection of a keep made of sheadash stone and granite and in the company of others to fight the monsters. Each keep, no matter its size, housed a fighting-pack.

"Oh, good," Rizelya let out a relieved breath. "They need help, too. With your schedule, we'll only have time to stop at the Territory Keeps. But what about gathering information for the Clan Alphas? I thought you said it was also important."

"The Keep Alphas will inform the Clan Alphas themselves. I'm adding a note to your introduction telling the Keep Alphas we're having an emergency clan meeting about this problem. I expect the Strunven Keep Alphas will travel with you to Strunlair Keep. We'll send a courier to Strunland Keep and Strunhelos to notify them."

"Hey, isn't it the Clan Alphas who call clan meetings?" Aistrun asked.

"Normally, but the Keep Alphas are authorized to call emergency meetings. And this certainly qualifies as an emergency!" Keshanal looked at them, then back at the map, considering. "This should work. We'll meet in four chedan, on the first day of Sandar, at Strunlair Keep. You'll be pushing yourselves, but you're young and tough. Most of your squad-pack is riding plains horses. They can handle the fast pace."

Rizelya considered Keshanal's proposal for several moments. "I can't see any reason not to follow your plan. We'll still be accomplishing Histrun's goal."

"Hey, it cuts our travel in half, and I'm all for that," Aistrun said. "I'd rather travel only four chedan instead of the full ten or twelve chedan it was going to take."

"Keshanal, we'll need winter supplies, including tents," Rizelya said. "Our original plans had us getting to the northern keeps at the beginning of the summer lunadar rather than late spring. There may be snow in some of the higher mountains."

"You'll have what you need when you leave in the morning." Keshanal thought for a moment, then added, "The northern keeps may not be having the problems with the Malvers' monsters that we're having. The cold keeps the nests from forming. Strunven and Strunhelos Keeps are far enough north that even in the heat of summer and autumn they don't have as many nests as we do here. I hear the southern territories of Posanlair and Dehanronlair are hit worse all year than the rest of the territories. We at least get a break during the winter."

"I don't know how the southern territories do it," Rizelya commiserated. "The control-janack may not be plaguing the two northern keeps."

"Even if they're not," Aistrun broke in, "we still must go to discover what's happening there."

"And tell them how to destroy the control-janacks. There's no reason to think they won't show up in their nest sites eventually," Rizelya finished.

"You're good kids. I wasn't planning on not sending you," Keshanal interrupted them. "If there's a new janack controlling the others, there may be new monsters that can stand the cold better." Keshanal stood up. "I'll make the arrangements for your supplies."

"Do you want our letter of guarantee to recompense you for your aid to us?"

"Posh," Keshanal waved her hand in front of her. "No need, girl. We're the same clan. Anything you require, we freely give.

Besides, sharing the new cold-air shield and the information on how to kill those control-janack, you've more than paid for any supplies we give you."

Keshanal pushed her chair back from the table and stood up. "You've a long journey ahead of you. I don't envy you. Join me tonight for the evening meal. We have some excellent cooks."

Rizelya looked out the office window as Keshanal made her way down the stairs. Dehali now had the Yellows working with Reds. The three Reds with Yellow Talent worked well with their partners. However, the full Yellows were having trouble. They could create the cold-air shield while their partners stood still. But when the fighter approached with their glowing helbraughts, the cold air heated. Rizelya could see the frustration on all of their faces. Dehali seemed especially frustrated because nothing she did helped them maintain their shield when threatened.

As she watched, Rizelya realized the Yellows weren't afraid of the fire. The fighting terrified them. One girl dropped her air shield and cowered on the ground as soon as her partner fed fire into her helbraught. Three kept flinching when their partners started thrusting their helbraughts in mock combat. Two looked promising if they could learn to work with the Reds as they fought. Their movements were similar, and their shields were the strongest of the bunch.

Everyone was taught how to fight, no matter what magic they wielded. Rizelya knew from working with Eiden that most non-fighting Posair women treated the training as exercise or a required necessity. But those with Red Talent found joy in combat as part of their fiery nature. The Reds below had all fought the Malvers' monsters and brought the intensity of a real fight with them into their practice.

Rizelya left the office, jogged down the stairs, and stopped at the small wall bordering the arena.

"Dehali, come over here," Rizelya called.

"I can't figure out what their problem is," Dehali complained when she reached Rizelya.

"I think I know. The Yellows haven't ever trained with a fighting Red before, nor have they fought for real. They're unsure and don't know what to do after they form the cold-air shield."

"Oh, I hadn't thought of that," Dehali said with a sigh of relief. "We're about ready to give up. We think I can't teach them because of my Red Talent."

"No, that isn't it," Rizelya told her. "Eiden is a Yellow without a drop of Red Talent. What she had, that these women lack, is the conviction that fighting the monsters is the best use of her magic. She and I developed a few tricks when I taught her that should help your students. Call them over."

Dehali motioned for her students to join them. "This is my squad-pack alpha, Rizelya," Dehali introduced her to the women. "She's the one who thought up this trick."

"There's a new janack that is difficult to attack and kill using our normal methods," Rizelya said while pacing. She stopped in front of the Yellows, who stood a little apart from the Reds, and directed her remarks to them. "Like all janacks, this one uses its heat sensor stalks to find us. If you block our body heat with the cold-air shields Dehali taught you, then we—" she pointed to the Reds "—can get to the control-janack and kill it. So from now on you'll be part of the fighting-pack. You're important to all of our survival."

The cowering girl fainted. The three who had flinched away from the Reds protested they weren't fighters. Meanwhile, grins covered the faces of the two women Rizelya had picked out earlier. As they stood together, Rizelya could tell they were twins. They had bright yellow hair and green eyes flecked with red. They wore different scarves around their necks, but otherwise they were identical.

The one with the longer hair and a pale lime green scarf looked at her companion. "Told you. They're finally going to let us fight." She turned to Rizelya. "Kami and I have been begging Keshanal to let us join a fighting-pack. We knew our Talents could be helpful."

Kami, who wore a rose scarf, spoke up. "She told us we wouldn't be any good against the monsters. We had too much

Yellow and not have enough Red Talent. Both of us can solidify air. This cold-air shield is brilliant. Although I can't figure out how to keep it steady when my partner fires her helbraught."

"You just need the right practice tools." Rizelya smiled at the twins. She turned to the three who were protesting. "Take your friend and leave. You aren't doing any good here." When they left, she smiled at Dehali. "It's time for the janack illusion spell."

"The what?" the twins asked in unison.

Dehali grinned. "Another invention of Eiden's. She wanted to practice fighting, but pretending there was a monster in front of her wasn't working, so she created an illusion."

"Yep, add a bit of Brown earth magic to it, and it becomes quite solid," Rizelya added. "I have the Brown power."

She turned to the two Reds, who waited to train with the twins. One was tall and had red-gold hair and brown eyes. The other woman was medium height with cherry-red hair with pale green highlights and honey-gold eyes. "You'll get good practice as well. What are your names? I can't call you Red one and Red two."

"I'm Shaydan," the tall one said, "and this is Bren."

"The warrior's venom isn't affecting the new control-janack. Well, if it is, it takes an awful long time to be of any help. The only way we've been successful is by exploding it."

As Rizelya led the group into the middle of the arena, she remembered her first encounter with the control-janack. She'd made a fire shield to contain the janack's explosion.

"Have you created a fire shield within your fire-ring before?" she asked Shaydan and Bren.

They shook their heads and looked at her as if she was crazy.

Shaydan quirked up an eyebrow. "That's impossible."

"No, it isn't. It's how I controlled the debris field yesterday," Rizelya replied. "Looks like you and the twins have become Strunell's control-janack demolition team." She paused, replaying the scenes where she'd destroyed the two new janacks. Both times, a warrior had distracted the monster. "Do you have any warriors you work well with?"

"Yes, Alpha," Bren answered.

"Send for them," Rizelya told them.

Shaydan ran to the observation area where a few Reds sat watching and spoke to a woman, who then hurried off. Rizelya decided the rest of her pack could also use the practice and called them out of the stands.

"Twins," she said, "go work with Dehali to strengthen your cold-air shields."

Rizelya turned to Shaydan and Bren. "While we're waiting for your warriors, I'll teach you how to form the fire shield. Watch carefully."

She formed a fire circle around the two women. Working slowly, she wove the filaments of Red magic together, creating a bubble within the fire-ring that surrounded them. After a few heartbeats, she released her magic.

"Wow! That was amazing." Shaydan's eyes were wide. "How did you figure out how to do that?"

"My sister, Naila, taught me when I was little. I think my mother, Zehala, taught it to her before she died."

"You're that Rizelya!" Bren exclaimed. "Histrun is your father, right?"

"Yeah," Rizelya sighed. She should have expected to be known at any of the Strunlair Keeps. "Shh... I try to keep it quiet. I'd rather be recognized for who I am, not for what they did."

"Gotcha." Bren put her hand to her lips, sealing them shut. "We won't tell anyone." She looked at Shaydan, who nodded.

"Did you catch how to do it?"

Bren shook her head. "Can you do it one more time?" Bren asked. "I was too busy admiring how beautiful it was."

"Me too," Shaydan agreed.

"What did you do?" Dehali asked. Rizelya hadn't noticed Dehali and the twins had joined them and were avidly watching her.

"Yeah, what was it? I just caught the last bits," Leistral commented, walking across the arena.

Flabbergasted, Rizelya realized even her own pack-mates hadn't learned the fire shield spell. She didn't understand why Naila hadn't taught anyone else how to do the shield. It had saved their lives.

"Here, stand with them, and I'll show you. It's a fire shield, and it's how I keep the bits of exploding monster from spreading too far."

"Hey, I'd wondered about that," Aistrun said. "I heard you mention it to Keshanal, but I haven't had time to ask you about it. I was too busy fighting to pay attention to what you did."

"Wolf, you don't have enough Red Talent to do it," Rizelya huffed.

"But I have enough to see it."

"Okay, fine," she grumbled. "But watch carefully." Rizelya didn't mind teaching, but this was beginning to feel like a show. She formed the fire-ring around everyone in the arena, then slowly built the fire shield. She hadn't taken the time to examine it before. Now that she did, she understood Shaydan and Bren's reaction. The weaving of different shades of red was beautiful. The strands of the shield glowed when she pushed her fire magic into it and activated it.

"That is one fine piece of magic," Keshanal observed when Rizelya dropped the shield.

Rizelya whirled around. Her surprise must have been evident, because Keshanal broke into a laugh.

"I came back with the others to see what all the fuss was about," Keshanal told her. "When you mentioned a fire shield, I thought it was just a bigger or brighter fire-ring. This is something different. You'll teach me too." Her mouth formed a tight line of disapproval. "And I'll have words with Naila when I see her at the clan meeting for not showing the rest of us the spell."

Rizelya broke down the steps of the spell and taught the group of Reds, which had mushroomed into quite a few more than Shaydan, Bren, and her own squad-pack. It looked like all the Strunell Keep fighting-pack alphas had joined her in the arena.

When her main students could form the shield well, she called a halt to the practice.

"That's only part of the process to kill the control-janack," Rizelya said. "I only have time to teach Shaydan and Bren, who will partner with the twins, Kami and Tami. They'll teach the Strunell fighters. Leistral, stay here and work with Dehali. The rest of you, please move off the arena floor."

The crowd headed to the edge of the arena rather than to the stands. Rizelya looked up and gaped with surprise. Spectators packed the stands. Quite a few women with strong Yellow Talent sat with the Reds, as well as some men. The attention made Rizelya uncomfortable. She turned her back to the watchers, waiting until only the two Strunell teams and her squad-pack remained on the practice floor.

She glanced at Aistrun and motioned for him to shift. None of the men could tell her where their clothes disappeared to when they shifted into their wolf or warrior forms. They didn't have to strip them off, nor were they torn in the change process. One milcron they were men, fully clothed, and the next, they were wolves. After a bit more effort, they were warriors. Their clothes disappeared as they changed. When they returned to human form, they wore the same clothes they had on previously. Within a few moments, Aistrun towered over her in his warrior form.

"Now, for the fun part," she told the teams. She gripped her helbraught. "Dehali will create the janack illusion. This time, Dehali, add the protrusion and make it larger so it looks like the new control-janacks. When I add my Brown magic, it will look and feel real. Dehali, are you strong enough to hold the illusion and create a cold-air shield for me?"

Dehali nodded. "You can't take too long to destroy it, or I'll lose one or the other."

"Okay, I'll be fast. Aistrun, your job is to distract the illusion, like you did the control-janack yesterday." She directed the other teams to stand out of the way. "Now Dehali, please."

Dehali started the spell, and Rizelya sensed the swirl of magic. She gathered her own power and sent Brown magic to join with Dehali's Yellow. When the funnel of air stopping spinning, a large control-janack stood in the center of the arena. The illusion not only looked like the monster, but behaved like it as well. The fight was on.

Rizelya formed a fire-ring around it and added the fire shield. The illusion turned its maw toward her and Aistrun. She felt the air grow cold as Dehali produced a cold-air shield around them.

The janack swayed back and forth, searching for them. Aistrun raced toward it, hassling it with his claws. Rizelya fed fire magic into her helbraught until it glowed, then ran to the janack. Using her helbraught, she pole-vaulted onto the janack and raced up the tentacles to the head. Since this was an illusion, she didn't have to feed much fire into it to make it explode. This fight was also easier because there wasn't the annoying hum which almost formed words.

She banished the burning bits of the illusion. "That's how to kill one of these things."

Rizelya pointed to Shaydan's team. "Now, it's your turn. Kami, your job is to keep Shaydan and her warrior, Drustrun, safe. They can't get to the janack if your shield collapses. This illusion is real enough that they'll be in danger if you don't maintain the shield around them until Shaydan at least gets on the janack."

"Gee, thanks for the pep talk," Kami said.

Rizelya shrugged. "It's what will happen out in the field. Keep them safe." There wasn't any danger, but Kami and her sister needed to believe there was, so they would treat this seriously. Rizelya, Aistrun, and Dehali moved off to the side. "Are you ready?" she asked Dehali.

Dehali nodded and created another illusion.

Kami kept her cold-air shield on Shaydan until Shaydan shoved her helbraught blade into the janack. Her performance impressed Rizelya. But when the debris threatened to hit Kami and Drustrun, Rizelya quickly banished the illusion. She thought about it and realized the problem.

"Next time, Shaydan, form the fire shield two feet inside the fire-ring. All of you get your butts to the fire-ring as fast as possible when the janack blows."

The illusion formed again, and when the janack exploded, the team remained untouched. The other teams took turns until finally Rizelya held up her hand.

"Enough for today. Dehali and I are too exhausted to form the illusion anymore."

Keshanal had stayed the entire time. "Good tactics, Rizelya." She patted Rizelya on the back. "Your pack should be proud of you. After the evening meal, I want you and Dehali to teach me how to do that illusion spell. Good training tool. Make sure you include a session like this at the other keeps you travel to, and I'll do the same."

After they'd eaten, Rizelya and Dehali met with Keshanal and several of her platoon alphas in the practice arena. They taught them the training illusion. It didn't take long for them to become proficient in casting the spells. Rizelya and Keshanal walked toward the fighting-pack house.

"You're a fine teacher, Rizelya girl," Keshanal said as she put an arm around Rizelya's shoulders and drew her into a quick hug. "This makes me wonder what other things we don't share with each other, even in our own clan, or our own keep."

"I'm sure it wasn't intentional," Rizelya reassured her. "Eiden and I developed the illusion spell recently. We haven't had our Clan Gathering yet. Besides, she and I are so low in the rankings, no one would ask us to show them anything."

Keshanal growled. "There has to be a better way to exchange information and techniques than what we've been doing. It takes too long. It's true we don't have a system in place to share if it's something developed by a lower-ranking clan member."

"Of course, Eiden could have presented it. She's a Yellow, and they're expected to be inventive. But a Red like me—" she snorted "—not likely."

The two women walked the rest of the way in silence. When they reached the pack-house, Keshanal turned to Rizelya. "We'll have your supplies and a multa ready for you an octar after sunrise. May the four-fold Goddess watch your journey, child." She strode off without allowing Rizelya to reply.

Chapter 5

At daybreak, Rizelya and Aistrun arrived at the stables before the rest of their group.

"Hey, Lehaas, bright morning to you," Aistrun said.

"Bright morning, laddie, lass." Lehaas smiled in greeting. "Come to see what else that caitiff did to his fine horses?"

Rizelya nodded. "I was afraid there would be more."

"Anybody who could harm one of the Mother's children for pleasure has to have something wrong." Lehaas led them into his office.

On his desk were a number of bramble berries, long thin cylinders with sharp thorns all along the surface. "I found these under the saddle blankets." Lehaas indicated several of the crushed berries. He lifted a length of leather, studded with sharp spikes, dulled with blood. "This fit under the girth strap. Damn torture device. That caitiff won't be riding those horses again. They be too injured and spooked."

Aistrun reached out and took the leather strap, fingering the spikes. His face was white with anger. "I'm keeping this. He may just find out how it feels."

"Aistrun, you can't do that!" Rizelya knew how he felt, but they weren't cruel.

"Oh, yes, I can. That beast needs to be taught a lesson." Malice filled his grin. "Besides, I'd like to find out what Clan Alpha Nestrun has to say about this. Too bad you turned that bit to slag, Riz. We could have shown it to him."

"Not to worry, laddie." Lehaas's voice deepened in anger. "There be another one in his saddlebag." He tossed the torture bit onto the pile.

"You searched his bags?" Rizelya asked, incredulous.

"Course I did and with Keep Alpha Bestrun at my side," Lehaas said. "The cur be loafing in his room while the lot of you worked in the practice arena. Nice work, by the way. Bestrun sent him on an errand, and while he be gone, we inspected his belongings." He tilted his head toward the leather strap. "The girth strap be in his packs, too. I could see the injuries on his horses, but there wasn't anything left in the stables to make such wounds. The dastard be hiding his devices."

"Thanks. We'll take care of it," Rizelya promised. "I'm sorry. I thought his horses were just bad-tempered and ill-mannered."

"Nah, not them. Sweet things." Lehaas smiled. "They be staying here until they heal. He must've ridden the poor gelding the most, because his belly be torn to shreds. It will be a long time before he can be ridden again."

"So what is the imbecile going to ride now?" Aistrun set down the bit. "We have to take him with us."

Lehaas grinned. "I'll show you." He led them to a horse tied outside his stall, ready to be saddled.

It was one of the largest horses Rizelya had ever seen. At nineteen hands, his withers brushed the top of Aistrun's head at six-plus feet. He had the look of a draft horse, except the wide black striping on a white hide marked him as a plains' horse. His short-clipped mane stood straight up, the deep gray color matching his tail. The horse had pure black socks up to his knees.

"This laddie be Tejen, one of my own stock," Lehaas said proudly. "He won't take any guff from that vile cur." He motioned Rizelya over to stand in front of the horse.

When she did, intelligent blue eyes looked into hers. She reached up and caressed his muzzle. "Why, he's soft," she blurted. "His pelt feels more like a feline rather than a horse." It was also longer than it appeared. Images of welcome filled her mind. "Oh! He's very communicative."

"That he be," Lehaas agreed, "especially to those he likes. He recognizes you as an alpha." Lehaas gave a sly grin and waggled his eyebrows. "And he knows you're Kymaya's rider.

Better keep an eye on those two if you don't want a pregnant mare."

"Hey, he's a stallion?" Aistrun asked, awe and wonder filling his voice. "It'll take a strong horseman to control him with all the mares we have. Kymaya isn't the only one."

"She's the only one he's deemed worthy of his attention," Lehaas laughed. He patted the horse's neck. "Tejen here be sweet-tempered and has a beautiful, smooth gait." He paused. "When he likes you and is being treated like the king he thinks he is. If not, well then—" Lehaas's mouth tightened and his eyes narrowed "— the cur will have a rough ride and one mean stallion to deal with."

"That work's for me." Aistrun grinned. "Either Keandran will learn to behave and treat his horse right, or he will be sore and more grumpy than normal."

"What about a remount?" Rizelya asked.

"Don't need one," Lehaas said. "Tejen be strong and has stamina to spare. Besides, I'm not letting that cur get hold of any other horse. Tejen can give back, but most horses wouldn't be able to."

"Thank you, Lehaas, for the great gift," Rizelya said.

"I don't want to let him go, but I know how important your mission is. Just take care of him for me—" he caressed the horse "—and return him after the clan meeting." He grinned. "And maybe a foal will come back with him."

"Perhaps when this is over, we can discover what kind of babies those two make."

"They would be stunning," Lehaas sighed. He looked up at a commotion at the stable entrance. "I've also chosen plains horses for your other riders. Bestrun said you'd be traveling hard and fast." He rubbed his hands together. "Ah, time for that cur's penance to begin."

Lehaas moved in front of Tejen, blocking him from view. Lehaas's bulk didn't quite cover Tejen's girth. Rizelya and Aistrun sidled next to Lehaas to help hide him.

Rizelya's squad-pack entered the stable and walked toward them. Anger darkened Keandran's face.

"So, do you think he'll say something?"

Aistrun shook his head. "No, not with Lehaas here." He looked at Keandran. "But then again, he might be stupid enough to say something, then he'd have to travel the entire way in his wolf form."

"Don't think I wasn't tempted," Lehaas growled under his breath. "If we didn't have so many troubles, he would be."

"Greetings of the day," Rizelya said to her pack. She smiled warmly at them. Except for Keandran, whom she scowled at.

"Morning, Alpha," Leistral greeted her. "It's a beautiful day for riding."

Dehali snorted and looked away. Rizelya suspected it was to hide her tears. At some point yesterday, Dehali and the twins had become heart sisters. Last night after the training with the alphas, Dehali had happily gone with them to their room. Looking at how sad Dehali was now, Rizelya thought it might not have been the best idea to let her go. But she was Dehali's alpha, not her pack-mother.

The twins entered the stable, looking just as unhappy, and strode toward Dehali. They hugged Dehali and then tugged her between them into the stall with Dehali's horse, Julay. The three women proceeded to tack her horse. Rizelya returned her attention to the others in her pack.

Leistral and Eidstrun flanked Keandran and stood a pace behind him. They knew something was up.

"Keandran," Rizelya said, "the horse-master informs me your horses are unfit to ride any farther."

"They were flea-bitten nags, anyway." Keandran waved in a dismissive gesture.

Rizelya placed a restraining hand on Lehaas, who was growling.

"So, what sorry excuse for a horse is he giving me?"

"Oh, I think you'll like him," Rizelya drawled.

"Hey, this one you won't be able to bully," Aistrun said.

They stepped aside to reveal his ride. Tejen reared and screamed a stallion's challenge, then lunged toward Keandran. Keandran's eyes widened with fright, and he jumped back. Tejen pranced to Keandran, staring him down and making him back up until he ran into Eidstrun. Keandran ducked his head, and Rizelya silently applauded. Tejen had proved his dominance.

"No, this one you'll not bully or hurt," Lehaas growled. His hand on Tejen's halter. "He'll not tolerate such behavior. And, laddie, he be much bigger and stronger than you are."

"You searched through my bags and took my things," Keandran accused.

"I did, with Keep Alpha Bestrun. You'll not abuse another horse." Lehaas leaned toward Keandran until he was nose to nose. "If you do, you'll never ride a horse again."

"Is that a threat?" Keandran sneered.

"A promise. One I can keep." They stared at each other for a long time. Keandran finally looked away and dropped his head in submission.

"Where is his tack?" Keandran's posture drooped in resignation. "What I had won't fit this beast."

"It be there." Lehaas pointed at an over sized saddle. He hovered over Keandran while he put on Tejen's tack, criticizing his every movement and making adjustments.

"Leistral, Eidstrun," Rizelya said, turning away from Keandran. "Lehaas has been good enough to give you each a plains horse, so we won't need to waste time with remounts."

"Oh my! What an amazing gift!" Leistral bounced on the balls of her feet in anticipation.

Lehaas motioned to his stable hands. One boy brought out a beautiful black mare with silver stripes and a white mane and tail, and handed her to Leistral. The other boy led out a large chestnut brown horse with pale red stripes. His unusual mane started out as light gray near his body and melded into a pale red at the ends. The boy handed him to Eidstrun.

"Finally, a horse that fits me." Eidstrun grinned as he took the lead rope.

Rizelya and Aistrun brought out their horses and began tacking them with the rest. Rizelya was tightening Kymaya's girth strap when she heard Tejen's startled whinny. Keandran's yelp quickly followed. She stepped away from Kymaya in time to see Keandran's head whip to the side from Lehaas's blow.

"What do you think you be doing? You idiotic imbecile!" Lehaas roared.

Blood dripped down Keandran's arm. "He bit me!" Keandran yelled, indignant.

"That he did. You tightened his girth strap too tight and with too much force." Lehaas's voice was quiet with anger. "What did you expect him to do? Stand there and take it like the others did?"

Keandran glared at Lehaas.

Lehaas shook a finger at him. "I told you, you couldn't bully this horse. He won't take it."

Rizelya chuckled to herself and turned back to finish gearing up Kymaya. "I like Tejen," she murmured to her horse. "He has spirit."

Kymaya whinnied in agreement and sent Rizelya an image of Kymaya and Tejen rubbing necks.

"Na-uh, no getting cozy with him." She gently tapped Kymaya's nose. "We have a long journey." She finished buckling on her saddlebags. Picking up the reins, she led Kymaya out of the stable and into the courtyard.

Leistral and Eidstrun waited, already mounted. Dehali stood by her horse, tightly embracing Kami and Tami. They were the only ones who knew how to form the cold-air shields and work with the strike force. Otherwise, she'd have talked to Keshanal about letting the twins come with them, at least to the borders of Strunell Territory. She frowned. Quite a few people and horses also milled around the stable yard. *A platoon must be heading out on patrol.*

Rizelya crossed the yard to take a better look at the multa tied to the paddock's railing. The sturdy pack beasts could carry a load larger than their own weight. Under the large bundle of supplies, Rizelya glimpsed the multa's long winter pelt. Pale cream and warm gray mixed with small patches of short, curly pale green and ivory.

"We brought her down from the higher pastures so she'd still have some of her winter coat," Keshanal said, walking across the courtyard to join Rizelya. "Her name is Kressy."

The multa smelled Rizelya's outstretched hand and then turned her attention to Kymaya. The two animals nosed each other, then the multa emitted a happy chirrup. "Looks like she's found her herd," Rizelya chuckled.

Keshanal smiled. "You have winter supplies to get you through the mountains to Strunheim. I gave you a tent in case you can't reach a safe house or it storms. This is a more difficult route to the two northern Keeps than coming from the east would have been. The passes should be open by the time you reach them."

Rizelya bent her head in gratitude. On impulse, she hugged the old woman. "Thank you for everything."

Keshanal patted her back. "There is much good in you, girl." She pushed away from Rizelya to look her in the eye. "You have given me tools to keep more of my people alive. I can't thank you enough." She looked over Rizelya's shoulder and grinned. "Oh ho, Lehaas is getting his revenge on that caitiff."

Rizelya turned around. Keandran sat perched on Tejen's back, who walked stiff legged and came to an abrupt stop. There was no sitting comfortably in the saddle with such a gait. Lehaas stood next to Tejen's halter, whispering to the horse. Aistrun rode up and stopped beside him, and Jezhan appeared almost delicate next to the large stallion. When Tejen saw Kymaya, he whickered at her.

Kymaya looked at Rizelya, then coyly neighed back.

"Brazen," Rizelya fondly chided her horse.

"Tejen will teach him a lesson on proper horse care," Keshanal commented. "I heard what he did to those poor horses." She turned back to Rizelya. "You could have left him here with me."

Rizelya shook her head. "You don't need his trouble. He's my responsibility. Aistrun has the torture devices, and we'll give them to Nestrun when we get to Strunlair Keep. He can decide what to do with the coward." She dropped her voice and said confidentially, "Unless we kill him first."

Keshanal chuckled evilly. "You could, and no one who has met him would blame you." She glanced up at the sky. "Time for you to go. An escort will go with you through our territory." She indicated the fighters mounting up.

Rizelya recognized Shaydan and her alpha partner, Drustrun. Kami's horse waited next to Dehali's. Rizelya opened her mouth to protest.

Keshanal lifted a hand to forestall her refusal of an escort. "They will also scout the area for unusual nest activity. We need to give our new strike force experience. I'd much prefer it if you were there to guide them."

"But what about your plan for them to teach your major keeps?"

"There is time. They'll be with you for less than a chedan and meet me at Strunville Keep. I suspect you'll fight a nest or two before you part ways."

Aistrun had ridden up to them while they talked. "Hey, thanks for the company! We'll keep them safe." He looked down at Rizelya. "That is, if Little Red will get her butt up into the saddle so we can leave."

Rizelya glowered at him as she mounted Kymaya, while Keshanal laughed.

"Go with the blessings of the Goddess," Keshanal told them.

"And you as well," Rizelya said. Then she kicked Kymaya into a prancing walk.

The clatter of fifty horses followed her out of Strunell Keep. The sound made her realize she was the alpha of a platoon. She grimaced. *If Naila and Histrun could see me now, I'd never be a simple fighter ever again.* With the thought dogging her heels, she urged her horse into a trot. She glanced at Aistrun, who was keeping pace with her. He had a grim look on his face. He must have had the same thought. At least she would have company in her misery.

The group traveled on the well-groomed roads leading east from Strunell Keep. The road passed quickly under their horses' hoofs. They rode through hills which nestled the keep's fields and pastures. It turned out Shaydan and Drustrun were the alphas of the platoon. When the pace allowed talking, the four alphas soon became friends. Rizelya enjoyed their conversations, which made the journey more pleasurable. She glanced back to see the rest of her squad-pack chatting with Shaydan's fighters.

Except Keandran. He bounced in his saddle from Tejen's rough gait, riding in a little island of isolation. No one talked to him, and it was obvious from his glower he didn't want to talk to anyone else. When she looked again a few octars later, she couldn't see him.

Midday, they left the well-tended plots and entered the wilds of Strunell Territory. They rode through long valleys dotted with spring flowers. In one valley, she saw ancient orchards behind crumbling old fences without any sheadash stone in them. They had been built in the Before Time.

The next afternoon, the platoon slowed to a walk, giving the horses a rest. The alphas rode to the top of a hill and stopped. Rizelya gasped at the beauty. Below her lay a wide valley with sprigs of bright green grass dotted with thousands of small flowers. A herd of billocks grazed on the lush spring growth. The animals had huge curving horns, shaggy fur, and a hump over their shoulders. They foraged in areas with tall grass and on the edge of swamps. Their large platter-like feet kept them from sinking on the marshy ground. One of their favorite foods was cattails. Billocks were good eating but resisted domestication. They stayed alive in the wilds with the roaming monsters because the immense beasts stampeded easily and were fast.

An enormous bull lifted his head, snuffing the air. The breeze had shifted, carrying their scent down the hill. The bull bellowed, and the herd thundered away.

Rizelya put up a hand to shield her eyes from the lowering sun and scanned the valley. On the eastern edge, tall cypress trees draped with moss smudged the sky. A wide expanse of marshy grasslands and waterways fronted the trees. Exactly the type of area favored by the Malvers' monsters.

"So, what do you think?" Rizelya asked the other two alphas, who were more familiar with the region.

Shaydan pointed to the last of the receding billocks. "Those tell us there aren't any monsters in the marshlands."

"It doesn't mean there isn't a nest forming," Drustrun continued. "This is one of the nest sites, after all."

"Hey, with the way the nests have been developing out of whack," Aistrun added, "we can't move on without making sure."

Rizelya looked around the valley. The air was cooling as the sun slid closer to the horizon. "If there is a nest and the larvae are close to maturity, we should stay and let them mature."

"What?" the other three alphas exclaimed. It went against everything they believed. Covering a nest of larvae with fire was much easier than fighting the mature monsters.

"We need a control-janack for you to practice killing. This is a good spot." She gestured at the valley for emphasis. "This valley is small enough we can contain the monsters."

"Do we have time to go to the nest site and reach the safe house before dark?" Aistrun asked.

Shaydan nodded.

As they rode to the edge of the marshland, Rizelya noted how healthy the plants looked. None showed signs of the toxic slime the monsters excreted as they moved. Ahead, she spotted an area without any plant life. It was about fifty feet wide, with a depression in the center.

The nest site.

Shaydan signaled the party to stop. Rizelya and the other alphas stepped off their horses. Behind them were the sounds of men changing into their warrior forms. A few moments later, a scout-pack of two Reds and four warriors saluted them, then jogged off.

While the rest waited, the breeze shifted, carrying with it the stench of Malvers' monsters. Rizelya wasn't the only Red reaching for her helbraught. A nest was forming.

As the scouts approached the site, they slowed, and the women fed fire into their helbraughts. The blue-white color of the blades meant they were using cold-fire. It burned like acid to eat into the monster's hides. And more importantly, it didn't produce any heat for the janacks to detect their presence. The scouts crept to the edge of the grass and looked down into the depression. They turned and raced back to the waiting platoon.

The older scout tipped her helbraught at Shaydan. "It's another big one, Alpha."

"Juvie," croaked a warrior.

"Almost adult," corrected the woman. "They'll leave the nest within the next two days."

"Thank you." Shaydan nodded, then glanced over at Rizelya. "This is exactly what you wanted."

"It is. If we're lucky, this nest will have a control-janack."

"Hey, they all do now," Aistrun added. "Or at least it seems like it."

Drustrun addressed the scout-pack. "Good work. Go back to your positions. We'll be going on to the safe house."

"What?" the woman exclaimed. "We aren't firing the nest?" Her face paled.

"I don't like allowing the nest to mature either, but it's necessary this time," Rizelya told the scouts. They looked at her as if she had just sprouted tentacles. "For Crone's sake, we're not leaving them to the area."

"We'll kill them," Shaydan added, "but when they are adults. We need to practice the new techniques if this nest has one of those weird, hard-to-kill janacks."

The scouts still weren't happy with the plan. Rizelya knew they would spread the news among their fellow fighters. Gossip passed quicker than a wildfire in the fighting-pack ranks. As they resumed crossing the valley, several men had shifted into their wolf forms.

Rizelya and Aistrun fell back from the lead to ride with their squad-pack. She hadn't talked to them much all day. Dehali looked happy with Kami riding next to her. They held hands as they rode. Leistral and Eidstrun were busy chatting with some of the Strunell fighting-pack.

"Where's Keandran?" she asked, looking around.

"Last I saw, he was in the rear—" Eidstrun paused, then sputtered "—walking." He and the group burst into laughter.

"Hey, why was he walking?" Aistrun asked.

"His horse is giving him fits," Leistral said, wiping her eyes. "Something happened at the last rest stop, and Tejen wouldn't let Keandran get in his saddle. Damn, that horse has some mean moves."

"Tossed him several times," Eidstrun continued the story. "Once, Tejen allowed Keandran to settle into the saddle before he started bucking. He threw Keandran forward over his neck, then reared his head. Cracked Keandran's skull good. He was a bit wobbly."

"And he was limping," Leistral added. "Tejen stomped on his foot. He tried shifting into his wolf form, and Tejen kicked him in the chest. I don't think he broke any more ribs, but Keandran wouldn't let me look at him. Afterward, he was too hurt to shift."

"Should we go find out if he's okay?" Rizelya asked Aistrun, alarmed.

"Naw," Eidstrun told them. "We've been keeping an eye on him. We don't like him, but he's still pack. He's a bit footsore now, but otherwise all right."

"What did Keandran do to deserve an ill-tempered horse like Tejen?" Dehali asked. "I know the others were bad mannered, but this one is downright mean."

"Hey, the others weren't bad mannered," Aistrun said. "Keandran is the mean one. He abused them. Lehaas gave him a horse who wouldn't be bullied." Aistrun told them about the bit and girth strap that had tortured the other horses. When he mentioned the bramble berries, Eidstrun's eyes widened.

"I might have seen Keandran slip something under Tejen's blanket, just before he acted up," he said.

Everyone in the group, including the Strunell fighters, wore harsh expressions at the news. No one was cruel to their horses. They were too necessary for survival. The men could shift into wolf and travel that way, but the women couldn't. It took both Reds and warriors to kill the Malvers' monsters.

"Serves him right, then." Dehali's mouth pulled taut. The rest nodded in agreement. "We'll make sure he doesn't do it again."

They soon reached the safe house. Rizelya stayed in the stable after she unsaddled and curried Kymaya. Aistrun waited with her.

It was well after dark when Keandran finally stumbled inside. Both of his eyes were black, and he held his ribs and limped. Tejen walked behind him, pushing him forward when he tried to stop.

Rizelya rushed to Tejen. "There you go, boy. I'll get you settled in," she crooned. She grabbed Tejen's bridle and led him to an empty stall.

"What about me?" Keandran whined. "That devil horse wouldn't let me ride or shift to wolf."

"You did something to him." Aistrun glared at Keandran. "You were told he wouldn't tolerate any mistreatment." Keandran turned to leave. "No, you stay right here."

A wave of alpha magic washed over Rizelya at the command in Aistrun's voice. She glanced up to see Keandran standing stock-still. She took off Tejen's saddle and blanket. Stuck to

Tejen's hide were two bramble berries, their spikes buried deep in his flesh. She pulled them off and soothed him.

"Poor thing, you'll be okay. Next time, someone will know to check." She glared at Keandran and stalked to him, shoving the bramble berries under his nose. "These were under Tejen's saddle blanket. You put them there, just like you did to those other horses. What is wrong with you?"

Keandran glowered back at her.

"If you keep this up, you'll walk all the way to Strunlair Keep," she told him. "You will not be given another horse. You will not mistreat Tejen." She looked him up and down. "I can promise you'll suffer more than he does."

He started to say something, but she cut him off. "We won't leave you behind. The Clan Alphas will deal with you."

"That is, if you survive," Aistrun quietly added. "You hurt any of my pack, including my horses, again and I. Will. Kill. You."

The color slipped from Keandran's face.

Aistrun waited a few milcrons, then said more gently, "Come on. Let's have a healer look at you."

"We may not like him, but he is our pack," Rizelya echoed Eidstrun's words, sighing as she watched them go.

Other than the minor injuries from the bramble berries, Tejen was fine. She couldn't understand Keandran's behavior. She had never seen someone deliberately hurt an animal before. He was her responsibility until they reached Strunlair Keep. But she had no idea what to do about him. Or for him. With a heavy heart, she entered the safe house for the night.

Before dawn, a scout-pack went to the nest site to keep watch. They wouldn't have to wait long if the monsters were in the juvenile stage. If they didn't mature during the day, they would tomorrow.

Just in case they had to battle monsters, the platoon saddled their horses. Breakfast was being prepared when a messenger thundered to the safe house. He pulled his horse up in front of Rizelya and Shaydan, who had barreled out.

"They're mature, at least three janacks," he said in a rush.

"What about the new one?" Shaydan asked.

The messenger shook his head. "I don't know. I didn't see it."

"The one I fought was hidden," Rizelya said. "We didn't know it was there until the rest cleared out."

"Let's go!" Drustrun bellowed. "We've monsters to kill!"

The fifty members of the platoon rushed to their horses and stepped into their saddles. Rizelya and the other alphas rode out in the lead, with Rizelya's squad-pack and Kami close behind. They stopped closer to the nest site than Rizelya was used to, but then she saw a copse of thick jedash bushes. The slick blue stems and leaves shed the monster's toxins, and the yellow flower's scent repelled them. The tall bushes would hide the horses.

As they approached, a man jumped off his horse. He swung open a gate made from the bushes to reveal a large corral. Inside, Rizelya noticed the temperature dropped, masking the body heat of anything hiding there. She'd forgotten about this protective aspect of the jedash bushes, as there weren't many in her home territory. The fighters tied their reins to the saddle in case the horses needed to bolt from the corral without their riders.

As she left the enclosure, Rizelya looked back to see the few stallions, along with the geldings, herd the mares to the center of the circle. They then stood in front as protectors. Tejen was having difficulty herding Kymaya into the center. She was a battle horse as much as he was and wasn't amenable to being guarded. Rizelya chuckled. Kymaya could be just as stubborn as she suspected Tejen to be.

Two young men closed the gate of the corral and stood guard at either side of it. Rizelya nodded to herself in approval. Someone would watch over the horses during the battle and let them out if necessary. She wiped the thought from her mind. They would all return to reclaim their horses in a couple of octars.

The squad-pack alphas listened attentively as Shaydan and Drustrun gave quick orders. The platoon leaders wouldn't be leading the attack this time. Their job was to destroy the control-janack using Rizelya's new methods. Rizelya's team would stay out of the fight until the control-janack, if there was one, emerged.

Rizelya looked over at Kami, who stood next to Shaydan. Kami bounced up and down on the balls of her feet in anticipation while her tense face told a different story. Rizelya thought she'd do well.

Rizelya stepped over the rise and gazed down at the site. Although she didn't hear the telltale hum, she was certain the nest contained a control-janack. *It's as big as the first one,* she mind-spoke to Aistrun.

He nodded, clicking his massive claws open and closed.

The monsters writhed with increased activity as a sensor stalk shot up from the mass and then another. They knew the Posair fighters were there. The first brechas boiled out, and the battle began.

"This is so weird," Rizelya said to her team, gripping her helbraught, "standing here and not fighting."

"Yesss," Aistrun and Drustrun hissed. They both trembled with the need to fight.

Shaydan grimaced. "Those are my people down there. It's hard to just watch them."

Rizelya rubbed her ears at the faint hum.

"Let's go! There's a control-janack in there." Rizelya winced. The volume of the hum grew louder as more monsters left the nest. She ran down the incline, feeding fire into her helbraught.

"How do you know?" Shaydan asked, catching up to her.

"I can hear a hum. Can't you?"

"No," came a chorus from the others.

"Look!" Rizelya pointed to the south, where a group of monsters broke off from the fighting. "They're heading back to the nest!"

The last of the janacks had left the nest with its attendant brechas to reveal a control-janack. The humming grew into a screech. Rizelya felt the brush of cold surround her as they raced down the incline. She looked over her shoulder. Dehali sprinted next to Kami, shouting instructions. The control-janack didn't turn its attention to them, so she assumed Kami had formed a cold-air shield around her team as well.

Rizelya's eyebrows shot up when Shaydan began forming a fire-ring around the control-janack while she ran. When the six of them crossed the boundary, it flared into a fire shield. Rizelya glanced. Leistral and Eidstrun skidded to a halt at the edge of the fire-ring and then turned. Keandran was missing, again.

The control-janack wasn't alone. Two brechas roamed the nest's perimeter. For all appearances, they guarded the janack. Rizelya hadn't seen anything like it before. The brechas lifted their heads, snuffing the air with their large nostrils. They made a wuffing noise as they dropped their heads. Rizelya realized the cold-air shields blocked their scent as well as heat. The brechas couldn't smell them, and the control-janack couldn't sense their body heat.

"That changes things," Shaydan commented.

"It does," Rizelya agreed. "You two stay as far back as you can," Rizelya told Kami and Dehali. She turned to Dehali. "If we split up and you can't shield both of us, break off and help Kami protect Shaydan. Destroying the control-janack is your top priority."

Rizelya ignored the janack's almost deafening screeches. "My team will tackle the brechas, yours the control-janack," she shouted.

Shaydan and Drustrun looked at her strangely, then nodded.

Rizelya pointed to the brecha closest to them. "I'll take that one, you can have the other," she told Aistrun. He grinned, lifting his lips to show his fangs, and took off for his target.

Rizelya fed fire magic into her helbraught as she ran and swung at the brecha. It moved at the last moment, and her blade sliced into its side rather than its short neck. It whirled, slashing at her with its claws. She jumped back.

The screech of the control-janack beat at her, insisting she drop her weapon. Rizelya shook her head. She swung her weapon in time to block another strike from the brecha. Either her cold-air shield wasn't working or the control-janack was tracking her via her mind. Indistinct words formed, but she couldn't understand them. She'd worry about it later. Right now, she had a brecha to kill.

The brecha reared onto its hind legs, swiping at her with its eight-inch front claws. She knocked them aside with the staff of her helbraught, then quickly brought the blade around and jabbed it into the creature's belly. The glowing blade slid easily into the tough hide. She dragged it down, opening it up. The entrails and the edges of the wound smoked. The monster dropped to all fours. Rizelya swung again, severing its head. She touched it with her blade, feeding more fire magic into it. It burst into flames, burning quickly to ash. The body followed.

Rizelya turned back to the nest. Shaydan raced toward the head of the bucking and thrashing control-janack. Aistrun had killed his brecha and worked in concert with Drustrun to attack the control-janack. An odd sparking sound made her spin around. Brechas smashed into the fire shield.

Leistral and Eidstrun fought a janack with a brecha held in its tentacles. It tossed the beast at the fire shield. Instinctively, Rizelya ducked. The shield hissed and crackled while the brecha burst into flames. She looked up. Several piles of ash darkened the dome. This wasn't the first brecha they'd flung onto the shield.

Rizelya scrutinized the fire shield. Minute cracks spread over it. It wouldn't hold much longer. She rushed to it and added her magic to strengthen it.

An insistent, "Come to me," whispered to her. Rizelya shook her head and realized it wasn't directed at her. She surveyed the area, finally seeing Keandran. He stumbled, like a sleep walker, toward the swamp.

"What in the Crone's fires is he doing?" Rizelya swore. If she left the fire shield, it would shatter. She glanced over her shoulder at the fight with the control-janack. In a few steps, Shaydan would make it to the head and explode the monster.

Rizelya looked back to Keandran, who was almost to the trees. Frantic, she didn't know what to do. She didn't like Keandran, but for him to enter the swamp alone, he would die. But she couldn't allow the shield to falter. Just then the janack Leistral and Eidstrun fought collapsed from Eidstrun's venom.

Go stop Keandran! she mind-shouted at them. *He's going into the swamp.*

They twisted around as Keandran stepped into the trees.

We'll get him. Eidstrun replied as the two raced across the mucky ground.

"Run! It's blowing!" Shaydan yelled as she leaped off the control-janack.

Rizelya turned her attention back to the fight. The janack still had the strange protrusion attached to it. Shaydan had forgotten, or hadn't had the chance, to cut it off before burying her helbraught into its head.

The shrieking was so loud now, Rizelya wondered why no one else heard it. She threw a shield around herself while she kept her eyes firmly on the protrusion. The control-janack burst, flying pieces hitting her fire shield. As soon as the debris stopped falling, Rizelya raced to the spot where she had last seen the protrusion. It lay on the ground, unharmed, and with a scrap of hide hanging on at the base. Gritting her teeth against the pain in her head from the screaming, she placed a small fire shield around it. Then saw darkness.

Rizelya opened her eyes to see Aistrun, Shaydan, and Drustrun looking down on her. "I passed out again, didn't I?" she groaned.

"Yep," Aistrun said. "Why?"

"Damn thing screams a fit when its janack is destroyed."

"What thing?" Shaydan looked worried.

Rizelya waved toward her mini fire shield. "The protrusion." She looked closely at them and scrunched her face. "You can't hear it, can you?"

They all shook their heads. Rizelya struggled into a sitting position. Her head pounded, and black dots swirled in front of her eyes. Standing, let alone walking, would be impossible, so she settled for crawling to the appendage. She released her fire shield. "What about now?"

"Still nothing," Shaydan said. "Dehali, Kami, come over here," she yelled.

Rizelya winced. "Listen. Do you hear anything?" she asked the two when they arrived.

They both cocked their heads in a listening stance for several long moments and then shook them. Rizelya took a deep breath and prodded the protrusion. This time, it sounded angry. "What about now?" she ground out through the pain.

"Nothing," Shaydan said, "but it's obvious you do." She looked at Dehali "Burn it!"

Rizelya screamed as Dehali set it on fire. When she revived, blood trickled from her nose, and Aistrun cradled her head in his lap.

"Hey, Little Red, don't scare me like that," Aistrun said as he stroked her hair.

It took her a few moments to realize Aistrun had shifted into his human form.

"You went into convulsions while that thing burned," he told her. "They really don't like you."

"The feeling is mutual," she croaked.

"How are you doing?" Shaydan asked.

"Head hurts, tired," she groaned, rubbing her raw throat. She tried to sit up, but the effort was beyond her. She didn't dare try using her magic.

Aistrun scooped her up and started walking. "This is getting to be a habit, Little Red," he chuckled. "One I like."

"Well, I don't." She weakly slapped his chest. "Don't get too used to it. You and I are only friends."

"Hey, that's what you keep telling me, and then you end up in my arms. Be careful, Little Red, this big bad wolf may eat you." Aistrun made chomping noises with his teeth, then nuzzled her hair and neck.

Laughter bubbled up and out before Rizelya could stop it. "Ow! Don't make me laugh. It makes my head hurt worse."

"Poor Little Red," he crooned, as he pulled her tighter against him.

Rizelya drifted to sleep. She woke when she felt herself transferred to someone else. She opened her eyes to see Drustrun held her, then noticed they were in the corral. Aistrun was getting on his horse. "Where's the rest of our pack?" she asked.

Drustrun turned a bit. "There," he said.

Eidstrun sat in Tejen's saddle, with Keandran draped in front of him. Keandran sported new bruises on his face and a laceration over his eye. Anger tightened Eidstrun's mouth. He blotted blood from his cut lip.

"Leistral and Eidstrun dragged him back unconscious. I don't know what happened," Drustrun told her as he lifted her up to Aistrun.

"I sent them after him. He was heading into the swamp." Rizelya settled more comfortably on the saddle in front of Aistrun. As much as she didn't want to admit it, she was in no shape to ride alone.

Drustrun's eyebrows rose. "Why was he going there?"

Rizelya shrugged. "I don't know."

"We'll find out at the safe house," Drustrun said. "There's something wrong with that boy."

A young man brought Drustrun's horse to him, and he mounted. "Let's get you where you can rest."

"Good idea," Rizelya mumbled.

Chapter 6

Rizelya opened her eyes, relieved her massive headache was gone. She wandered over to the stove and dished up a bowl of stew. Her mouth watered in anticipation as she inhaled the rich aroma. Either Leistral or someone else with Green Talent had fixed it. A covered basket held fresh, warm biscuits. She hadn't napped long, then.

Rizelya looked out the window and swore. She'd slept all day. This was the evening meal, not midday. She surveyed the large room, noting the other alphas and her pack at a table in the back. A sea of empty tables surrounded it. Rizelya walked over to them, carrying her dinner.

"He's still out. I had to hit him pretty hard," Eidstrun said.

"Who's still out?" Rizelya asked. Aistrun looked up and scooted over on the bench to make room for her. She sat down and started eating.

"Keandran," Eidstrun elaborated. "The fool was running into the swamp. We—" he indicated Leistral and himself "—had a helluva time getting him out."

"He fought us," Leistral grimaced. She held up her left arm, which was bandaged from her wrist to her elbow. "He sliced me open with his claws."

"I finally had to knock him out in order to stop him from dragging us all into the depths of the swamp. Strange things waited for us in there." Eidstrun shuddered. "That's twice I've had to lug that moron out of a swamp." He slumped back with his arms folded over his chest and glared at Rizelya and Aistrun. "He may be part of our pack, but I'll be damned if I'm going to keep hauling him out of every swamp we come across."

"Keandran kept yelling 'I'm coming.'" Leistral shrugged. "There wasn't anyone around."

Rizelya's stomach dropped with dread. "What did he say?"

"'I'm coming.' It was really weird." Leistral rubbed her face. "He didn't seem to recognize either of us. He was in his warrior form and had a wild look in his eyes, almost like he was feral."

"Oh, Crone's fires!" Rizelya swore. She looked at Aistrun, and then around the table, debating whether she should tell them. But they needed to know the added danger they were all in. When she spoke, she lowered her voice. "Sweet Mother, protect us. There is something—someone—controlling those janacks. When I pass out, I see a strange woman, who looks nothing like us. When I sent Leistral and Eidstrun after Keandran, I thought I heard someone calling. It was... imploring... almost seductive."

"Why Keandran?" Drustrun asked.

Shaydan looked at her sharply. "And why do you hear them?"

Rizelya shrugged. "I have no idea."

Shaydan gazed into her mug of taevo, rolling it between her hands. "I think both of you need to see a Gray or a White when you reach Strunheim Keep. It appears there is some connection between whoever is controlling the janacks and you." She looked at Aistrun. "Make sure she sees one."

"Hey, I will, even if I have to carry her."

Rizelya cringed at his grin, full of mischievous glee.

He nodded knowingly at her. "She likes me carrying her."

She reached out and popped him on the nose. "No, Wolfie, I do not."

"Yep," his voice was smug, "you do."

Rizelya made a face at him.

"The battle today gave us a good chance to practice our new skills." Shaydan turned to Kami, pride written all over her face. "You're a powerful Yellow and did well. Your cold-air shield worked, and you didn't flinch when the fighting started."

Kami blushed. "I kept begging Alpha Keshanal to let me fight, but she wouldn't." She squeezed Dehali's hand and gazed at Rizelya. "Thank you both for giving me some way to help my people and battle the monsters."

"We learned something important, too," Rizelya added. When the others looked at her in confusion, she continued, "The protrusion must be destroyed as well as the control-janack. I swear there is a sentient watcher behind the control-janack, who means us ill."

"We'll make sure to pass this information along to the other Keeps," Drustrun promised.

"Hey, we learned something else," Aistrun commented. "Rizelya loves me to carry her off the field." He grinned at her. "It's why she faints when she destroys the protrusion."

Rizelya sputtered in indignation, then glared at Leistral and Dehali as they tried to smother their laughter. They didn't succeed. The rest of the group joined in. Rizelya glared at them all, which made them laugh even more. Finally, she gave in and laughed along with them.

"In all seriousness, Rizelya," Dehali broke in, wiping tears from her eyes, "you can't be the one to destroy the protrusion. Next time, let me or Leistral do it. We don't hear the damn thing. You, it almost kills."

A young man with pale brown hair approached their table and bowed. "Alphas, Keandran is awake."

"Bring him here," Drustrun ordered.

"Sorry, Alpha, he is in no condition to come here. He is still disoriented." He glared at Eidstrun. "The blow to his head gave him a concussion."

Rizelya stood up. "Let's go find out what he has to say for himself. No, the rest of you stay here," she said when Leistral moved to stand up. She and the other alphas followed the young man.

A massive bruise covered Keandran's face and chest, and multiple scrapes wound around his arms. She guessed his legs were in the same condition. He had a small cut over his left eye and one on his chin.

"Keandran," Rizelya said, hands on her hips, "you continue with this and you won't make it to Strunheim, let alone Strunlair Keep."

"Hey, what got into you?"

"Huh?" Keandran looked genuinely confused.

"Why were you headed into the swamp?" Aistrun asked.

"The swamp?" Keandran's eyes widened, and horror filled his voice. "I was going into the swamp? Why would I go there?"

"You tell us," Rizelya said.

"I don't know!" Keandran all but wailed.

Rizelya leaned over him. "What do you remember?"

"I shifted with Eidstrun and ran to the nest... and I... fought?" Keandran paused, and when he looked up, fear darkened his pale blue eyes. "I don't remember anything after I shifted. What happened to me?"

"You headed into the swamp," Aistrun told him. "Eidstrun and Leistral had to pull you out."

"Did you hear anything?" Rizelya asked.

Keandran started to shake his head, then stopped. "I thought I heard someone singing. But that doesn't sound right. Who would sing while battling the monsters?"

"Was it singing or humming?"

"Singing... maybe it was humming. I'm not sure."

"That's okay." Rizelya patted his leg. "You get some rest."

Rizelya drew the other alphas into a corner. "It baffles me why, but both Keandran and I are hearing the control janack and what's behind it. For the life of me, I can't think of anything we have in common. We don't even have the same Talent. He's a Yellow with some Blue while I'm a Red and Brown."

"Perhaps it's his Blue Talent," Drustrun mused. "Both Dehali and Kami are Yellows, and they don't seem affected. Are you positive you don't have any Blue?"

"I'm sure. There aren't any Reds with Blue Talent. Fire hates water."

"You're right," Shaydan agreed. "Until we know what it is, we'll have to keep an eye on all our fighters. We'll ask around to find out if anyone else hears any singing or humming."

"Hey, isn't it unusual for a Blue to be in a fighting-pack?" Aistrun pointed out. "Aren't they too emotional?"

"Normally, yes," Drustrun said. "We don't have any fighters in our packs who have any Blue Talent. His must be very weak."

"How could a Blue be so cruel like Keandran has been to his horses?" Rizelya made a face. "There's something wrong with that boy." No one disagreed with her.

After leaving the valley safe house, the platoon followed the billocks herd as they traveled north. They would top a hill in time to see the animals thundering over the next one. Numerous ruins of ancient villages dotted the low-lying areas, always with a nest site and swamp nearby. Unlike past years, every nest they came across swarmed with monsters in various stages of development. When the nests held larvae or juveniles, they covered it with fire, killing the creatures before they became a problem. A battle raged whenever adults were in the nests, which was more often than not.

Late in the afternoon, they stopped at the bottom of a hill to rest and water the horses. The next safe house was another couple of octars away. A group of men approached Shaydan and Drustrun. "Alphas, the scouts say the billocks herd is just over the hill. May we hunt?" the leader asked.

Drustrun leaned on his saddle's pommel while he considered the request. Then gave a quick jerk of his head. "We could use fresh meat."

The leader motioned to the others, and within moments, they were in their wolf form and slinking away. Soon, a wolf howl signaled a successful hunt.

When the platoon reached the safe house, several men quickly and efficiently butchered the billocks and spitted the carcass over a large fire. The rich smell of the roasting meat made Rizelya's mouth water. There were enough people with Green Talent to scrape together a feast from the supplies. A few people brought out instruments from their packs, and Drustrun broached a small cask of ale. The contingent had been fighting hard and deserved the break.

Many of the men, and a few women, took turns twirling Rizelya across the floor. She laughed with joy, then sobered as a pang of longing ripped into her. Kaieli loved to dance, and would have enjoyed the impromptu party.

As the night wore on, Rizelya sat on a bench and watched Dehali and Kami slip off. Then Shaydan and Drustrun disappeared together. Several other couples, and a few groups, wandered off into the dark corners to celebrate privately. Leistral, Eidstrun, and one of the Reds stopped by and asked her to join them. Rizelya declined, not in the mood for casual sex. She missed Kaieli and the closeness they'd once shared.

She'd experienced the difference a deep connection made and wanted it again.

Rizelya sensed someone watching her, and she looked around. Keandran stood across the room, leaning against the wall, and his arms folded over his chest. During the recent battles, she'd assigned him horse duty, and he hadn't complained. But now as he glared at her, hatred and barely contained anger filled his eyes. He made an obscene and threatening gesture at her and walked off.

"Hey, what was that about?" Aistrun asked, coming up behind her and throwing his arms over her shoulders.

"I don't know." Rizelya leaned into Aistrun's comforting presence. "We'll have to watch him closely when Shaydan's platoon leaves us."

"That we will."

Rizelya turned around and searched Aistrun's face. "Why aren't you with someone?"

"No one I want to be with." He looked away, sighed, and then dropped his forehead on hers. "Except you."

She pulled away from him. "We tried once, remember? It didn't work out. I like you better as my friend than as my lover."

"Come on, Little Red, let me in," he implored with a low, sexy growl.

"No." She crossed her arms.

"At least allow me to sleep with you," Aistrun pleaded. "I don't want to be alone tonight."

"Oh, all right. But—" she pointed at him as his lips twitched in a grin "—keep your hands and other parts to yourself."

As they cuddled on the narrow bed, she put her hand over his and whispered, "I don't want to be alone either."

Aistrun nuzzled her hair and kissed the top of her head. "Sleep, Little Red. The big bad wolf will watch over you."

A smile tugged her lips. Aistrun was a good man and a good friend. Too bad she didn't feel any attraction to him. Sighing with longing, she drifted to sleep.

The platoon left later than usual the next morning. Rizelya observed the fighters as they readied their horses and mounted up. They appeared rested and eager to move on. It had been a good decision to allow the billocks hunt and the celebration. As Leistral and Eidstrun packed up, she could hear the easy banter flowing between them. Dehali and Kami glowed with happiness. It would be hard for them to part in a few days. She smiled at Aistrun as she threw a leg over Kymaya's back. He'd kept his word last night and hadn't tried to make love to her. Wrapped in his arms, she had slept well, without any dreams disturbing her.

As they traveled farther north, the hills grew taller and the mountain range separating Strunell and Strunheim drew closer.

"Today is our last day with you," Shaydan said, as they approached the foothills. "At the next safe house, we'll part ways. My platoon will turn east, while your path continues northeast to the pass."

Rizelya turned in her saddle and gazed over her shoulder at the riders behind them. Other than the subtle differences in barding colors, there was no longer any differentiation between their groups.

"It's been great traveling with your people. The six battles you've fought with the monsters over the past two days have given you plenty of experience with the new methods. Almost more than us. Even better, Aistrun hasn't carried me off the field."

"How is that better?" Aistrun raised his eyebrows at her and winked. "You know you like it, Little Red."

Rizelya rolled her eyes at his antics. "Seriously, it's nice not being screamed at by the damned control-janack's protrusion. Hopefully, when we're on our own, I won't have to destroy it."

"Assigning Keandran to horse detail," Drustrun observed, "seems to be working. He hasn't tried to run into the swamps. You'll have to watch him carefully until a White Priestess, or even better a Gray, looks at him to find out what's wrong with his mind. You should have left him with Alpha Keshanal."

"She offered," Rizelya said with a grimace. "But I couldn't leave him with her. He's our responsibility."

"Speaking of, would you look at that," Aistrun interjected, pointing at Keandran.

Tejen slid into a smooth gait, then, after a few steps, shuddered into a stiff walk. The past few days, Keandran had stopped trying to torment his horse.

Rizelya chuckled. "It looks like Tejen isn't sure if he should relax or continue punishing his rider."

The chatter eased off as the road climbed into the foothills, and the warm days became a memory. Rizelya glared at the sky. A spring storm billowed over the mountains. If they were lucky, they would reach the safe house before it broke. She shivered as a bitter breeze slipped in under her cloak. The cold made it unlikely they'd have to fight monsters at the next nest site.

As she hunkered down in her cloak, she considered the nest's intense activity. She couldn't recall—either in her own experience or from history—when this many nests were active at the same time. That morning, Shaydan had sent a scout-pack on the fastest horses in the platoon to report back to Keshanal. If it continued like this, the fighting-packs would be hard-pressed to contain the monsters. They may again face monster attacks on the Keeps and outlying pastures. Rizelya shuddered. They hadn't experienced that horror since her parents developed the Zehis method the fighters used to trap the creatures at the nest sites.

They climbed higher and into meadows dotted with new sprigs of spring grass. Rizelya and Shaydan rode in a small pocket of isolation.

"This is our summer pasturage for our livestock," Shaydan said. "What do we do if we can't bring them here this year?"

"We do what they did thirty years ago. Our people stick close to the Keeps, and the fighting-packs stay out in the field."

"But do we have enough fighters? We've become so efficient fewer people are in our fighting-packs."

Rizelya shrugged. "I don't know. I guess we'll recruit more fighters." She looked back at Dehali and Kami, deep in conversation, holding hands as they rode. "We know now Yellows are an important part of our packs. Who knows what else we need? The nests are bigger, and the fighting fiercer, so I'm sure more Browns and even Greens will be required to support and heal the fighters. We'll survive. We have so far."

"You're right. All our people are trained to fight, so we can include more in the packs." Shaydan gazed off in the distance, then sighed. "Do you think we'll ever do more than survive? It's all we do—survive and fight the Malvers' monsters."

"Someday we might figure out a way to stop the nests from forming." Rizelya didn't hold on to the hope. The Posairs had been fighting the creatures for over a thousand years without any success in stopping the attacks. "Do you know why they are called 'Malvers' monsters? I've always wondered."

Shaydan shook her head. "No, I don't. The name implies they belong to or came from someone, but who? I've never heard of any people called Malvers."

"Me either. The creatures appeared after the Great War. But not even the White Priestesses know who we fought in that war. I've asked."

"Maybe they just don't want to say. We fought someone, and their magic was bad enough to cause Shandir's Crater. Have you been there?"

"No, thank the Mother." Rizelya made a prayer gesture. "I was out fighting when the alphas chose the guard-pack for our spring rotation."

"I haven't either. We have the summer rotation. I guess I lucked out and get to stay home to fight the monsters here this time." Shaydan grimaced. "Lucky me. In a couple of chedan, our guard-pack should be heading south to relieve your people."

Rizelya shifted in her saddle, drawing her cloak tighter to her. "Do you think the control-janacks are down there too?"

"Probably." Shaydan blew on her hands. "It's always worse there than it is here, especially this far north. It must be horrible there. I don't envy any of our guard-packs. Damn, it's getting cold!"

Rizelya nodded in agreement. The earlier chill breeze was now an icy wind, howling down the pass ahead of the storm and making it difficult to talk. Slivers of ice stung her nose and face. Her teeth rattled together, and she'd wrapped her cloak around her hands in a failed attempt to keep them from going numb. When they stopped a short time later in the lee of a massive tower of ruins, Leistral and Eidstrun wrestled one of the packs off their multa, Kressy. Rizelya slid off her horse and used her privilege as alpha to stand between Kymaya and Jezhan, using their bodies to block the wind. The horses radiated enough heat that she almost stopped shivering.

Tejen wandered over to her and thrust his head under her hand, demanding attention. He pulled back his ears and nipped at Jezhan.

"Oh, stop," she told him. "He's a gelding." She rubbed Tejen's nose. His bulk blocked even more of the wind. "Do you need some love and attention?" she crooned to him as she stroked his neck. He snorted, shaking his head, and looked over at Keandran.

Keandran stood next to Eidstrun, who crouched over the packs. Keandran held his hands under his armpits, and he stamped his feet. The familiar, complaining whine marred his voice. Eidstrun growled and surged to his feet. Keandran backed away. Eidstrun stepped forward, towering over the smaller man, and snarled loud enough for Rizelya to hear him clearly. "We're all cold. I'll get it undone faster if you leave me alone."

"Here, I found them," Leistral called out, jerking a bundle out of the pack. She stood up, shook it out. The bundle turned out to be a thick, fur-lined wool cloak, dyed crimson red with matching gloves and scarf. She carried the clothing to Rizelya. "Here," she said, handing them to her, "these must be for you. The cloak's short."

Rizelya took them gratefully and thrust her shaky, cold hands into the gloves. Leistral hurried back to find her own winter wear. Rizelya wrapped the scarf around her neck and nose and tossed the cloak over her lightweight one. She snuggled into the sudden warmth, grateful for Keshanal's thoughtfulness.

Pushing Tejen out of the way, Rizelya joined her pack, who surrounded Leistral as she handed out more cloaks and gloves. Each set was dyed in the primary colors of each of Rizelya's team's Talents, making it obvious which belonged to whom. Dehali flung on a beautiful coral orange cloak, while Leistral snuggled into her red one that had swirls of green woven into it. Eidstrun's golden brown outer wear matched his hair. Leistral gave Aistrun a deep red cloak with thin gold stripes. Keandran's pale yellow cloak made his skin appear sallow. Rizelya chucked at the colorful group they made. They didn't stand out, though. Shaydan's platoon also wore vivid cloaks.

"There are boots, too," Leistral commented, "but I'll get those out at the safe house."

Shaydan strode over to Rizelya in a crimson and green cloak. "We'll stay here out of the wind while a squad-pack checks the nest site. It's on the other side of these ruins."

A short time later, the squad-pack returned. The leader shook her head at Shaydan, who breathed a sigh of relief. "Thank the Mother! No nest. We can ride on to the safe house."

Everyone remounted and trotted out from behind the ancient walls. Rizelya gasped at the cold, pulling her hood low over her face. Sleet drenched the world. In an effort to escape the storm's fury, they kicked their horses into a canter.

The sky darkened. The wind dashed snow and sleet into their faces. Rizelya could only see the rump of Jezhan in front of her. If the snow became any thicker, they'd have to tie themselves to each other in order not to lose someone in the blizzard.

Rizelya's fingers were numb with cold, even in the gloves. She mentally swore at Keshanal for sending them into the mountain pass this time of the year. If they'd stuck to their original plan, they wouldn't be here and would be warm. She was still muttering under her breath when Kymaya stopped. Aistrun reached up and dragged her down.

"Hey, we're here," he said.

"Thank the Mother and Crone! I hate spring blizzards."

"Come on," Aistrun said and took her arm. "Let's get the horses unsaddled and go inside where it's warm."

She let him lead her into the stables. She had never been so glad for the connecting walkway between the safe house and stables. By the time she entered the house, someone had the fire roaring. Several people, including Leistral, stood at the stove and tables prepping food.

Rizelya wearily slid onto a bench. Dehali put a mug of hot taevo in her hands.

"You look as tired as I feel," Dehali said, as she slumped onto the bench beside Rizelya.

"I am. Thanks." She lifted the mug and took a sip. The dark and spicy flavors warmed her. "Mmm, this is good."

"It's one of Leistral's special mixes. She said it was to warm the body and raise the spirits."

"Does it have spirits?"

Dehali shook her head. "Don't think so."

They sat in companionable silence as they sipped their taevo. By the time she emptied her cup, Rizelya was finally warm enough to shrug off her thick cloak.

"I'll be sad when Kami leaves tomorrow," Dehali sighed. "I never thought love could be so good, nor so cruel."

"You know I can't let you go with her. We need you with us too much."

Dehali dipped her head. "I understand. And Shaydan needs Kami. But when things settle down, I want to transfer to Strunell Keep."

"When we get back, I'll tell Naila." Rizelya patted Dehali's hand. "I'm sure she'll approve it, after you teach more people in our fighting-packs to do the cold-air shield."

"Did you see how good Kami is getting?"

Rizelya nodded.

"She doesn't have a helbraught, instead she surrounded her helstrablade with a cold-air shield. She killed a brecha with it. Once she'd stabbed the beast, she superheated the shield's air around the blade. It was almost as if a Red had used fire on it." Pride filled Dehali's voice.

"She did? That was powerful magic. Hmm... I wonder if the other Talents could do something similar with the helstrablades or even helbraughts. Although I don't know what the Blues could do with their water magic."

Dehali shrugged. "Maybe the same thing Kami is doing with her air magic—turn it to ice and then heat it to boiling? The Browns with metal magic forge the helstrablades. You'd think they could do something in battle with them."

"Remind me to talk to the Clan Alphas when we get to Strunlair Keep. This might be what we need to fight this resurgence of monster activity." Rizelya stretched and yawned. "Right now, I'm going to take a nap. Wake me for dinner, will you?"

Dehali nodded and Rizelya found a cot in a warm and out of the way corner. Rizelya drifted into an odd lucid dream.

Pale, emaciated people with black eyes milled in a dark cavern. Her vision honed in and focused on one in particular. The woman seemed familiar, but Rizelya couldn't figure out where she'd seen her before. The woman appeared to be deep in concentration and wore a strange device on her head. Thin wires connected it to a contraption of various tubes on a table next to her.

Movement swirled inside the tubes. Dark, pus-colored smoke snaked out of a tube. The woman's eyes flew open in jubilation. Droplets coalesced as the smoke spun around a large glass funnel. Thick, viscous beads dripped out of the funnel and into a matte black bowl. The smoke continued to flow, and pearls dribbled until they filled the bowl.

Rizelya watched the scene unfold in fascinated horror.

The woman removed the device and stalked to the bowl, a hungry look in her eyes. She stuck a needle-like claw into it, scooped out several of the beads, and popped them in her mouth. She sighed in ecstasy.

The words were mangled and strange, but Rizelya thought she heard the woman say, "We did it! Our pets have succeeded. Soon we will have our revenge on our ancient enemy. Come, my friends, and eat." More hands dipped into the bowl.

Rizelya awoke with a start, the echoes of maniacal laughter ringing in her ears.

The spring storm kept them cooped up in the safe house. Howling wind shook the shutters and snaked under the doors and windows. The group used the downtime to rest and to repair equipment. But the laughter and good cheer between them held an edge of sadness. As soon as the storm passed, they would part ways and wouldn't see each other for several chedan, if not a lunadar. Everyone in Rizelya's squad-pack had made deep friendships with Shaydan's platoon. That is, except Keandran. Even in the close confines of the safe house, he kept to himself, rarely interacting with anyone else.

On the second day of the raging storm, Rizelya and Aistrun sat in the stables with items from the multa's packs spread around them. She'd insisted they take the opportunity to go over their supplies.

"Keshanal was generous," Rizelya commented. "We have enough supplies to last us until we reach Strunheim Keep, even if we run into trouble."

"Hey, look at this," Aistrun said, and held up a bundle. "A tent. We'll be fine traveling through the pass if we get caught in another storm on the way."

"May the Mother and Crone bless us so we don't have to use it!" Rizelya prayed fervently. She looked around and lowered her voice. "I don't want to be caught out in the open with Keandran. Have you noticed how he doesn't talk to anyone?"

"Yeah, I have," Aistrun whispered back. "There's something not right with that boy. Are you sure I can't kill him?"

"As much as I'd like to, we can't unless he endangers us," Rizelya admonished. "We can't kill him because we don't like him or he's acting strange."

"If he sneaks off into a swamp again, can we just let him go?" Aistrun pleaded.

When she answered, she wasn't able to keep her own longing to get rid of their troublesome pack member out of her voice. "No. If we can, we'll send Eidstrun after him again. If he leaves when it's the six of us fighting a nest, then there's nothing we can do. Killing the monsters is more important than saving him from his own folly."

So have you had any more strange dreams? Aistrun asked in mind-speech.

Rizelya shook her head. When she'd told him about her dream, or whatever it was, he had been as unnerved by it as she had.

They worked throughout the afternoon inventorying and repacking the supplies, then placed the packs near Kressy's stall to be ready to depart when the storm stopped. Back inside the safe house, the fighters had moved the tables and benches to the side of the room to make space for a game of jelehan. Several people were already out of the game and calling encouragement to the remaining players.

Nine game sticks flew around the circle. Someone added a tenth one—a short one—to the mix. Kami snatched it and tossed it across the circle to Leistral, who handily caught it and sent it spinning toward Dehali. Kami and Dehali had sticks in their hands and flung them both to Leistral, Drustrun's stick fast behind them. Leistral grabbed the first one, then the next, quickly tossing them to another player and, to everyone's surprise, caught the third. But she missed seeing a short stick coming at her from the side. Laughing, Leistral bent down and picked up the dropped stick. She tossed it back into play, and bowing, stepped out of the ring.

Soon the circle was winnowed to three players: Shaydan, Eidstrun, and Drustrun. Fifteen sticks flew between them in a blur. Bets against Eidstrun winning swirled around Rizelya. She grinned as Aistrun made the opposing bet. He knew Eidstrun was not only big and strong, but also quick. In a blinding fast move, first Shaydan, then Drustrun failed to catch a stick, while Eidstrun easily juggled the rest. With a grin, he caught the sticks and bowed as the group whistled and cheered. Rizelya chuckled as Aistrun collected his winnings.

A scurry of activity put the tables and benches back in order. The cooks returned to the stove to finish preparing dinner. Feeling restless, Rizelya wandered to the door and opened it. The wind and snow had stopped during the game. She stepped outside, breathing in the cold air, and looked up to a clear sky.

The stars twinkled brightly. Kelar, the largest of the three moons, was full and peeking over the northeastern ridge. With the lunadar half over, both Zelar, the middle moon, and Chelar, the smallest, were waning into their dark phase and wouldn't be seen for the next couple of nights. In another two nights after that, Chelar would appear first, with a new sliver showing on Ahme, the first day of the chedan.

Rizelya watched Kelar rising as she contemplated the strange things happening to her and her world. She offered a prayer to the Mother and Crone to guard and protect them from this latest evil. The chill finally sent her back inside.

She headed to the fire, letting its warmth thaw her out from her sojourn outside. Shaydan wandered over to stand next to Rizelya, shoulders touching.

"The storm has stopped. The night is clear," Rizelya said.

"This is one time when I wish we had a Blue who was a weather worker." Shaydan sighed. "We'd be alerted if another storm is brewing."

"You know, it would be a good idea to include a weather Blue in the fighting-packs. We need more than simply the Reds, and now Yellows, if we are to defeat the monsters. And for more than just shielding, Kami is becoming quite the fighter."

Shaydan frowned at her. "I seem to have missed something."

"Oh, I'm sorry. I didn't realize Kami hadn't told you yet. She killed a brecha in the last fight using her Yellow ability on a helstrablade."

Shaydan's eyebrows rose in surprise. "That is news, good news. Why hasn't she mentioned it to me?"

Rizelya shrugged. "Dehali told me. She was so proud of Kami. I think this is something we need to pursue. We need all of us to stop these attacks."

"I'll mention it to Keshanal when I see her." Shaydan surveyed the room. Her gaze stopping on Kami. "And I want to know what Kami has been doing. She should have informed me. If it is clear in the morning, we'll be heading on our way."

"And we, ours. Make sure to ask if anyone else is hearing the humming from the control-janack. I really hope I'm not the only one." Rizelya couldn't keep the wistfulness from her voice.

The next morning dawned bright and sunny. The sun held the promise of a warm day. While the rest of the fighters readied the horses and multas for departure, the pack leaders sat at an empty table. Shaydan and Drustrun showed the routes into Strunheim Territory on the map to Rizelya and Aistrun one last time.

A scout, who had been there as a courier several times, joined them. "These are all big enough for your group," he said, pointing out several caves along the route. "If another storm catches you, and you can't make it to a safe house, you can shelter in them."

Finally, all was ready, and the two groups separated after ten days together. Rizelya took Kymaya's reins from Leistral. "It has been a pleasure to work with you," she told Shaydan and Drustrun.

"Same here."

Rizelya clasped hands with Drustrun. Shaydan refused her outstretched hand and pulled her into a hug.

"If you ever need a new pack to join, you're always welcome in ours," Shaydan whispered.

Rizelya nodded, then stepped away. She signaled to her squad-pack, who mounted up. Rizelya was the last to climb into her horse's saddle. She looked at Shaydan, and when she spoke her voice was rough. "If all goes well, we'll see you at Strunlair Keep on the first day of Sandar. May the Mother and Crone watch over you."

"And over you." Shaydan lifted her hand in farewell.

Rizelya kicked her heels into Kymaya's side. Without a backward glance, she led her group out of the courtyard of the safe house and turned onto the path that headed deeper into the mountains.

Chapter 7

The day may have been bright and clear, but the sun wasn't having much luck melting the foot of fresh snow. Rizelya snuggled into her cloak's warmth as they climbed higher into the mountains. They stopped at an ancient tower and the first marker pointing the way to the mountain pass to Strunheim Territory. Leistral and Eidstrun built a small fire to heat soup and prepare flat bread for the midday meal.

Rizelya tapped Aistrun on the arm. "Come on, Aistrun, let's climb the tower and look around. I want to make sure we can find and follow the path."

"Good idea. The pass could still be buried under snow, especially after that spring blizzard. If it's closed, we can change our route."

The worn stone steps winding around the tower's interior and the dark walls spoke of a forgotten age. Even so, the tower was in surprisingly good shape. Climbing the stairs, Rizelya fingered the cracks in the stone from some long-ago battle. At the top, they crawled through a small opening and onto the tower balcony, with a low wall surrounding it.

One side of the tower gave her a sweeping vista of the countryside for measures. As she moved around the platform, her view changed to the pass threading up the mountainside through the trees. Safe houses marked the path, tattered flags on their roofs flapping in the breeze. Near the top of the mountain, the tips of the roofs peeked through the snow.

Neydar, the second month of the year and spring, was half over and spring was warming to summer in the valleys of Strunland Territory. It would take longer for the deep snows in the mountains to melt. Rizelya had heard stories of places in the Deep Mountains where the snow never melted. She shivered. She didn't mind the snow for the two lunadar of winter, Eyedar and Hondar. But by the end of Hondar, she was ready for the warmer weather Ahdar brought. She couldn't imagine living in a place where winter never left.

"Hey, looks like we'll find our way, and it's open," Aistrun said, echoing Rizelya's thoughts. "Come on, let's go eat." Aistrun took off ahead of her down the stairs.

The group made good progress up the pass until the next afternoon. Their pace slowed to a crawl as the horses struggled through the deep snow crusted over with ice.

"Eh!" Rizelya cried as Kymaya floundered, dropping several feet. The horse whickered in panic, trying to keep her nose out of the snow.

"Help!" Dehali echoed. Her mare, Julay, striding at the side of Kymaya, plunged into the same hole.

The men raced over, peering over the edge.

"Stand on your saddle," Eidstrun suggested. He dropped onto his stomach, holding out his hand. "We'll pull you out, then dig out the horses."

An octar later, the two mares scrambled from the snow encasing them. Leistral doled out hot mash to warm them up.

"Keandran, you take point," Aistrun ordered. "Tejen's the biggest and heaviest of the horses. Eidstrun, you follow on Luchen. He's nearly as big as Tejen. You two can break a path for the rest of us."

Keandran grumbled but moved to the lead. Rizelya suspected his grumbling was more out of habit. As they climbed into the mountains, he hadn't been as grumpy. She had even caught him feeding Tejen a carrot that morning, and Tejen certainly seemed happier with his rider.

It took them four days to climb the pass and begin the downward journey. On the afternoon of the fourth day, they stopped to take a break. Rizelya wearily slid off her heavy winter cloak and stood in the center of the clearing, where the sun seeped through the trees. During the trek through the cold, the strange dreams had abated. But last night, they'd returned with a vengeance, with a particularly nasty one that left her exhausted. She tilted her head back and basked in the weak warmth.

Eidstrun came up to stand beside her. "This warmer weather means we'll encounter monsters."

She nodded, not saying anything.

"So, do you want me to watch the cur and keep him from going into any swamps? Or can I just let him go?"

"Stop him if you can."

Tejen screamed in warning, turning to face the trees. Rizelya whipped around, anxiously seeking the danger, and swore. She'd left her helbraught on Kymaya's saddle across the clearing where she couldn't reach it.

Eidstrun sniffed, then yelled, "Monsters!"

The stench hit Rizelya. The ground trembled. Birds flew in panic. One wasn't fast enough, and a long tentacle snatched it out of the air. A herd of multas broke through the trees, their eyes wild in terror. They saw the horses and dashed to huddle around them.

Rizelya cocked her head, listening for the telltale humming. "There isn't a control-janack with this bunch. We should be able to take them."

Leistral raced toward her, Rizelya's helbraught in her hands. "Here!" Leistral yelled as she tossed it.

Rizelya caught it and swung it in front of her. She glanced behind her to see the three men were in their warrior forms. Dehali stood guard over the horses. As the herd of multas joined them, Rizelya sensed a shield of cold air go up around the animals protecting them from the janack's heat sensors. Kressy's eyes were wide in fright, and she stuck close to Kymaya. Rizelya nodded to Leistral, and they sent flickers of flame low along the ground, stopping short of the trees.

Rizelya turned her attention back to oncoming danger. "Here they come!"

Two brechas burst through the trees, a janack right behind them. Rizelya and Leistral waited. When no more monsters careened into the clearing, they closed the fire-ring. Flames shot high into the sky, imprisoning the creatures. The janack clacked in anger and turned its attention on the women. Two huge, furry bodies flung themselves at the brechas. Aistrun's red-gold warrior form sprang into the air, covering the several yards' distance, to land on the janack.

Time devolved into a tight focus of cut, slash, flare for Rizelya as she battled the janack with Aistrun and Leistral. This janack lacked a protrusion. No strange noises. No strange faces intruded into Rizelya's mind. Soon it trembled and crumpled into a heap, dead. Rizelya glanced up and saw both Eidstrun and Keandran breathing heavily over the dead brechas.

Rizelya snuffed the fire-ring. Dehali banished her cold-air shield. The three women started to burn the monster bodies and pieces. Rizelya was busy burning the janack when she heard Aistrun snarl. She looked up to see several strange warriors standing at the edge of the clearing.

A woman pushed her horse through the men. She had short copper hair, brown eyes, and appeared to be in her mid-thirties. She surveyed the smoking piles of ash and smiled. "Did you get them all?"

"If there were only a janack and two brechas, we did," Rizelya replied. She dug the staff end of her helbraught into the ground and leaned on it for support as exhaustion rolled over her. The fight, along with the sleepless night, was catching up to her.

"Good. That was all that escaped us," the woman said tersely.

"There was a strange janack with an unusual protrusion in the nest, wasn't there? And you didn't notice the missing ones until after you killed it, did you?"

"How did you know?" She glared at Rizelya in accusation.

Rizelya sighed. "I know because we've been fighting these things for almost three chedan. We've seen them in Strunland and Strunell Territories and now here in Strunheim." Rizelya noticed out of the corner of her eye the rest of her squad-pack closing ranks around her. The men were still in warrior form.

The woman relaxed and extended her right arm in greeting. "Sorry about that. We haven't had any escapees from a nest for a long time, and we're a bit touchy. I'm Laynar."

"Nice to meet you. I'm Rizelya de Strunland." Rizelya gripped Laynar's arm, then indicated the others behind her.

"This is my squad-pack, Leistral and Dehali, Aistrun and Eidstrun, and Keandran ke Strunlair."

After the introductions, Aistrun jerked his head to Eidstrun and Keandran and led them away to shift back. Dehali and Leistral walked back to the horses and gathered their reins. One of Laynar's men broke off and herded the multas together.

"Good thing you were here," Laynar said as she and Rizelya crisscrossed the glade, burning the monster parts. "We were having difficulty catching up to those monsters. They were trickier and faster than usual."

"You've been having trouble killing the control-janack, the one with the protrusion, too, haven't you?"

"Yeah, they're awfully hard to kill. It takes an inordinate amount of time for the warrior's venom to have any effect."

"We can teach you how to kill them. We've found a method which works."

"That's good news!" Laynar's eyes lit up. "Can you show us?" She indicated the men waiting at the edge of the copse.

Rizelya shook her head. "We need to speak to your Keep Alphas first. How far is it to Strunheim Keep?" They had covered the glade and fired a few missing pieces, and now stood next to the horses.

"A couple of days."

Rizelya groaned. "I thought we were closer to the keep."

"The safe house where we'll stay the night is close." Laynar looked at the sky. "We need to hurry to get there before nightfall."

In a matter of moments, the group left the clearing and cantered along the trail. The fast pace didn't give them a chance to talk. The last glimmer of light was fading when they reached the safe house. Exhaustion pulled at Rizelya, and she felt herself tip sideways out of the saddle. Aistrun caught her before she fell. Over the next half octar, Aistrun continued to steady her. Without him, she would have fallen off several times. She sat resting for a long moment, trying to find the energy to dismount Kymaya.

"Here, let me help you." Aistrun reached up and lifted her out of the saddle.

"I shouldn't be this tired. We didn't fight a control-janack." Rizelya's exhaustion kept her from protesting about Aistrun carrying her.

"Hey, I know the dreams are troubling you, so you haven't slept much. Just rest. Let me take care of things tonight." He settled her on a cot, tucking the blanket around her shoulders.

"'Kay," she mumbled. The warmth of the safe house enveloped her, and she sighed and closed her eyes.

The next morning, Laynar waved Rizelya over to her join her for breakfast.

"What's so special about your technique?" Laynar asked.

Rizelya swallowed the food in her mouth. "We've added Yellows to our fighting-pack—" she pointed to Dehali at the next table "— and for good reason. They are integral to the new method."

Laynar raised her eyebrows, and her mouth dropped open. Her spoon hovered in the air, dripping porridge. "You're joking. She's a Red."

"She's also a strong Yellow. You'll see when we demonstrate it for your alphas."

"Why not now?" Laynar demanded, clunking her spoon back into her bowl.

"We're exhausted from going over the pass, and I'd rather do it just once. If we come across a nest on the way to Strunheim Keep, let us take the control-janack. You'll then find out first hand how necessary she is."

Laynar agreed. As they returned to the road, two men split off with the herd of multas in a different direction. Laynar pushed the group into a hard, ground-eating pace, stopping only once to rest the horses. In the late afternoon, she rode past a safe house to push on to the next, arriving at twilight.

"Why the fast pace?" Rizelya asked Laynar as they ate a dinner of beans and rice with pan bread.

"Those rogue monsters didn't escape the day you caught them," Laynar admitted. "They escaped the day before. In the rampage, they killed the multa herder, along with several of the multas. I want to keep it from happening again."

Rizelya nodded in understanding.

Laynar pushed her plate away and stood up. "We'll leave at first light and should be at Strunheim Keep by midmorning." She strode off to talk to her people.

Rizelya let her squad-pack know they'd be leaving early and found her own bed. As she lay there, she realized the very disturbing dream she had the night before killing the rogue monsters coincided with the death of the multa herder. *Why am I having these dreams, or are they visions?*

True to her word, Laynar led the group into Strunheim Keep by midmorning. Without waiting for anyone, Laynar jumped off her horse and rushed into the clan house. Rizelya and Aistrun were dismounting when an old woman, leaning heavily on a cane, exited. Her hair had faded to a dull pink, but her emerald-green eyes still sparkled with intelligence. Rizelya guessed the woman's age to be close to Histrun's; both had passed the century mark some years ago. A man a few decades younger stepped to the matriarch's side, and Laynar flanked her other side.

Rizelya and Aistrun hurried to the stairs leading to the clan house.

Without waiting for introductions, the old woman said, "My granddaughter says you have a method to kill the strange janack."

"Yes, Alpha." Rizelya inclined her head. "To kill them, we must change the way we fight and include more than just Reds in the fighting-pack."

A startled look crossed the woman's face, and the man sneered in disbelief.

She motioned for Dehali to join them. "This is Dehali. She also has Yellow Talent, which the strike force must now include. We could show you in the practice arena." Groups of platoon and squad-alphas gathered near the stairs.

"Then let us be off." The old woman gestured across the courtyard.

Rizelya held back a sigh of irritation. She'd hoped they could rest awhile before giving the demonstration.

Laynar sputtered, her hands on her hips. "But Grandmother, courtesies."

"Yes, yes." The old woman waved away Laynar's protests. "We shall have introductions while we wait for my multa to be brought to me."

Laynar quickly introduced Rizelya's squad-pack to the Strunheim Keep Alphas, Layhalya and Selestrun. "They killed the monsters that escaped from us," Laynar told the alphas.

"Just the six of you?" Selestrun asked, eyebrows raised.

Aistrun shrugged. "There were only two brechas and a janack."

"No control-janack with them made it easier," Rizelya admitted. At their confused looks, she added, "That's what we're calling the janack with the strange protrusion. It seems to control the others."

While they talked to the alphas, a group of youngsters led Kymaya and the other horses to the stable. Alpha Layhalya's multa arrived, and Laynar and Selestrun helped her onto it.

"Well, let's see what you have to show us." Layhalya urged her multa forward.

Laynar snatched at the multa's headstall, taking quick steps to catch up. Selestrun strode on the other side. They carefully watched the older woman. Rizelya and her squad-pack followed with the Strunheim alphas behind them.

When they entered the practice arena, the spectator stands held numerous people, not all of them from the fighting-packs. Rizelya noted several Yellows, Greens, and Browns. The few Blues surprised her. Blues notoriously avoided violence and fighting. As she looked closer, she noted the Blues also had Yellow Talent.

"So, girl, show us how to kill these damn control-janacks," Layhalya snapped when everyone entered the building. She settled on her multa to watch the proceedings.

Rizelya sent Dehali, Leistral, and Eidstrun into the arena. After some inner debate, if she could trust Keandran, she finally indicated for him to join them. He had been behaving for the last few days. She hoped his apparent awe of the aged alpha would keep him from doing anything stupid.

"A control-janack can't send its minions at us if it can't sense us," Rizelya explained, pitching her voice so it reached the entire arena. "To stop them, we need a Yellow—" she pointed to Dehali, who bowed slightly "—and a Red, as well as the normal warriors." Leistral tipped her helbraught at the Alphas, while Eidstrun and Keandran shifted into their warrior form.

"Dehali is now going to cast an illusion spell." Rizelya nodded to Dehali, and in the center of the arena a control-janack emerged, bobbing its head and clacking at them. Gasps erupted from the stands, and several people jumped back, including Alpha Selestrun. The illusion janack looked and acted like a real one would, although it lacked the horrible smell.

Leistral began forming the usual fire-ring around the janack, low to the ground. "We need a strong Yellow to form a cold-air shield," Rizelya told the audience as Dehali formed the shield around the fighters. The janack swung its bulbous head, searching for its prey, which it had sensed a moment before. "The second thing that is different, is what the Red is doing. Leistral isn't just creating a fire-ring, but she's building a fire shield within it."

"That's mighty fine magic work there," Layhalya said, studying the filaments of Red magic woven into a bubble. "You'll teach us, won't you?"

Rizelya nodded. "Of course. We'll teach any Yellows who volunteer to be part of the fighting-packs how to do the cold-air shield as well."

Aistrun took up the explanation. "Now the warrior's job is to distract the control-janack." As he talked, Eidstrun and Keandran began to attack the illusion. "So the Red can get to the head—" he paused and looked at the audience significantly "—and blow it up."

Loud protests broke out. Current practices taught exploding a janack was a last resort.

"Hey, it's the best way to kill them." Aistrun raised his voice over the objections. "Our venom doesn't affect them like it does the other monsters."

"The fire shield contains the monster bits." Rizelya looked at the progress of the training fight. Leistral rode the bucking head, her helbraught poised to strike. "Now, the most important thing, and I can't stress it enough, is to destroy the control-janack's protrusion. If you don't, it will keep controlling the other monsters until it's destroyed."

Dehali released the illusion and cold-air shield while Leistral dismissed her fire shield. Rizelya and Aistrun waited for the alpha's reaction.

Layhalya leaned forward, holding her chin in one hand, while she stroked the multa's neck with the other. After several long moments, she nodded sharply. "You've all done some powerful work." She turned to Laynar. "You learn. Decide who else will make up the new teams." She twisted around on the multa to survey the audience. "Anyone who wants to fight the monsters, and has sufficient Talent to learn this new method, you may do so. Come see Laynar."

Several Yellows and a few Browns and Greens let out an audible breath. These pushed their way through the crowd to reach Laynar before any of the Reds did. Tami and Kami from the Strunell Keep weren't alone in their wish to fight the monsters. Feeling a slight tug on her sleeve, she returned her attention to Layhalya.

"Can your people begin teaching while you tell me what's going on and why you're here?" Layhalya demanded.

"Yes, they can. Eidstrun and Keandran, you stay and help them and the warriors. You've had enough experience in the last two chedan." The men nodded in understanding. Rizelya and Aistrun turned away and left the arena with Layhalya and Selestrun.

It took the rest of the morning to tell the Keep Alphas of their journey.

"Keshanal of Strunell Keep sent a group to Strunville and Strundale Keeps." Rizelya crossed her ankles, resettling into her chair. "We're assigned to stop here and then go on to Strunven. As you can see in the packet I gave you, Keshanal has called a clan alpha meeting for Ahme de Sandar."

"You will remain here until we have learned these new shields of yours," Selestrun grunted, his arms crossed tight against his chest.

"I'm sorry, Alpha. We can only stay for a few days. We have to reach Strunven, teach them, and make it to the Clan-Keep for the meeting," Rizelya responded.

"It worked well for a fighting-pack to escort us across Strunell Territory," Aistrun interjected. "We ran into many active nests, all of which had control-janacks, so they had plenty of practice by the time we separated." He caught Selestrun's gaze. "It could be a good plan here, too."

"It is," Layhalya said, smiling. "We'll assign a fighting-pack to escort you through our territory. In the meantime, you will teach us." She looked them over closely. "And rest. You have traveled hard." Layhalya clapped her hands, and a teenage Red opened the office door. "Laynal will show you to your rooms. We'll meet again before you go." She waved a hand, dismissing them.

Leaving the message packet with the alphas, Rizelya and Aistrun followed the young woman. As they walked to their rooms, they learned she was Laynar's sister. After they cleaned up and grabbed lunch, Laynal escorted them back to the practice arena. Laynal reminded Rizelya of Eiden as she wistfully watched the training.

"Have you gone out with the fighting-packs yet?" Rizelya asked.

"No. I'm sixteen and old enough," Laynal pouted, "but Grandmother won't let me go."

"Go on, join the training, and perhaps your grandmother will allow you to fight with us." Rizelya sent her to Dehali's group.

"Hey, why Dehali's group?" Aistrun asked as he watched Laynal jog over to Dehali.

"She is both a Red and a Yellow, like Dehali, and needs both of her Talents trained."

Rizelya and Aistrun wandered around the various groups, making small corrections and encouraging comments. By the time they released the trainees to clean up for the evening meal, they'd made good progress. The Yellows could form a cold-air shield, the Browns could cast the illusion spell, while the fire shield came easily to the Reds. The next step was to test the Yellow's reactions when faced with the illusion janack.

Laynar and Laynal walked to the fighters' hall with them. Laynal could create a cold-air shield and was close to forming a fire shield, neither one was small magics. Laynal skipped with delight.

"So do you think Grandmother will let me go?" she asked Laynar. "I can do this, and I'm ready. You'll ask her, won't you?"

Laynar sighed. "Yes, I'll ask her and tell her how well you're doing."

"Yippee!" Laynal did a little jig and ran off ahead of them to the hall.

"I don't remember being as excited to go fight," Laynar said, frowning.

"Hey, I was," Aistrun said. "I snuck off and followed Little Red here. We were both younger than Laynal is now."

"How old were you? She's sixteen."

"I was fifteen and Rizelya was only fourteen, youngest in the clan to fight." He puffed out his chest in pride.

Rizelya hung her head. "I had a lot to live up to. Fighting was easier than listening to everyone's expectations of me."

"Hey, sorry," Aistrun apologized. "I was trying to help Laynal, not bring up old stuff for you."

"It's okay."

"You know, when everyone hears about this method of fighting, you'll be as famous as your parents! Their technique uses both their names, Zehis. What are we going to call yours? The Rizelya method?"

"You're that Rizelya!" Laynar exclaimed. "Your parents are Zehala and Histrun?"

Rizelya nodded, heat washing over her face.

"Wait until my grandmother hears about this! She goes on and on about how she worked with them to perfect the Zehis method. I've gotta tell her about this." Laynar ran to the clan house and up the stairs, yelling for her grandmother.

"Now see what you did," Rizelya muttered, hitting Aistrun on the shoulder.

"Sorry, I didn't mean to," he said, rubbing his shoulder.

"Besides, it isn't my method. It's Dehali's and Eiden's and even Leistral's and Naila's. I'm just—"

"Perfecting it and teaching it," Aistrun cut in. "Makes it your method."

"Well, whatever we call it, let's leave my name out of it, huh?"

"Do I have to?" Aistrun sulked. At her nod, he capitulated. "Okay, I'll talk to the others, and we'll come up with something good."

At dinner, the Keep Alphas invited Rizelya to join them at their table. Layhalya spent the evening regaling her with the struggles of the team who'd developed the Zehis method. In one instance, Zehala miscalculated, and instead of forming a fire-ring, she sprayed Histrun with sand, which turned into small globules of glass raining down on him. Rizelya had wondered where he'd received the scattering of scars on his face.

It was late by the time Rizelya ambled to bed. It amazed her how many people had been on the team trying to make fighting the monsters safer for the fighters. Layhalya was as much a part of the discovery and application as her parents, but hadn't received the accolades her parents had. They had been famous Clan Alphas and so all the attention went to them. Rizelya wasn't anything but a squad-alpha, so perhaps for this new fighting technique, the others would get credit, too. Dehali, Eiden, Leistral, and even Naila, had as much—or more—input in discovering their method as she did.

Snuggling under the blankets, she found a new appreciation for her parents. Ever since she was little, they had been larger than life. Layhalya's stories made them people struggling to keep their teams alive in the constant struggle against the Malvers' monsters. She resolved to get to know her father better when she returned home. Maybe he'd tell her the story from his perspective.

Late the next evening, after spending the day with the trainees, Rizelya met with Layhalya.

"You will not leave here until I am satisfied my people can use this new method of yours." Layhalya leaned forward in her chair. "I won't have any more die because we can't kill these monsters." Her gnarled fist struck her desk in emphasis.

"I understand, but I only planned on staying here two days, Alpha," Rizelya argued. "We still have to travel to Strunven Keep, teach them, and reach Strunlair Keep before the clan meeting. We'll never make in time if we stay any longer."

"Yes you will, dear. We know the shortcuts to Strunven Territory." The old matriarch's eyes narrowed. "How is my granddaughter doing, truly?"

"She is quite talented. She's able to create both the cold-air and the fire shields."

"So she says. But that's in training. We'll see how she does in a real battle."

"Well, if the monsters here keep the same schedule as everywhere else we've been, we won't have to wait long for a nest to mature." Rizelya glanced toward the darkened windows. The rain which began in the morning hadn't let up yet. "This rain is keeping them from forming."

"They hate the cold," Layhalya agreed. Her fingers drummed on the desk while she studied Rizelya.

The quiet stretched between them.

The old woman finally stilled her fingers. "You're a fine credit to your parents, Rizelya. A little rough around the edges yet, but you'll make a good leader—that is, when you grow up."

"Maybe I will—" Rizelya smiled "—grow up." The stories Layhalya had told her last night about perfecting the Zehis method floated through her mind. That team had suffered greatly, some of them giving up their lives to ensure the survival of the Posairs. Wasn't it the same thing her squad-pack was doing? She hadn't wanted to be a leader, not even of a small squad. This task force had started out as Histrun and Naila's way of forcing her into a role she'd refused. But now, she couldn't imagine anyone else leading her squad-pack. She'd do everything possible to keep her people safe. It still didn't mean she wanted to lead a platoon or become a Keep Alpha. Being squad-alpha was enough for her.

"You're a leader, whether you acknowledge it or not. Now, off with you. I'm tired." Layhalya's wave shooed her to the door, and Rizelya stood and bowed.

The next morning, Rizelya stretched, luxuriating in not rising with the sunrise. She'd slept deeply, without any dreams. Sitting up, she looked out the window and realized it was almost midday. Her stomach grumbled, reminding her it had been a long time since the evening meal. She washed and dressed quickly and rushed out of the room, braiding her hair as she hurried down the stairs.

Rizelya reached out to open the main door, only to have Leistral jerk it open.

"Oh good, you're awake," Leistral said when she all but ran into Rizelya. "We're to join Laynar." Leistral turned Rizelya toward the stables. "A nest is maturing. We have less than an octar to get there before the monsters emerge."

"But I haven't eaten!" Rizelya protested as they jogged to the stables. Leistral ignored her, rushing to her horse.

Rizelya shrugged and entered Kymaya's stall. Aistrun was already cinching Jezhan's saddle.

"Hey, hurry and tack up Kymaya. We need to leave," he said when he noticed her.

She grumbled along with her stomach as she tossed the saddle on Kymaya's back.

"What are you muttering?" Aistrun asked.

She swiveled around to see him leaning against the doorway. "Why didn't you wake me up earlier so I could get something to eat?" Anger made her voice rough. "I haven't eaten anything yet, and I'm supposed to help fight a control-janack? That's just mean." She turned back to cinch Kymaya's girth strap. Finished, she reached for the headstall and gently tugged Kymaya's head out of her hay. A stray stalk hung from her horse's mouth. "Well, at least someone fed you."

Kymaya whickered softly.

Aistrun joined her in the wide corridor, leading Jezhan. "None of us has had our midday meal."

"You ate breakfast. I didn't!" She heard him chuckling. When she rounded on him, he held out a packet.

"Here, I wouldn't let you starve. I know how snarly you get when you haven't eaten."

She peeled back a corner, revealing a sandwich of roasted billocks and creamy cheese. The fresh bread smelled heavenly. The packet contained two sandwiches, and she devoured both before Laynar called the order to mount. Feeling better, Rizelya rode next to Laynar. She heard a clear laugh and turned in her saddle. Laynal rode at Dehali's side.

"I'm surprised Layhalya allowed Laynal to come with us," Rizelya commented to Laynar.

"She decided she couldn't hold her back any longer. Laynal is quite talented with the new shields you've taught us." Laynar gazed at her sister for a few moments. "Besides, Grandmother realized Laynal would follow us if we didn't let her join us.

She'd rather I keep her close than have her lurking about on her own."

Rizelya laughed. "Smart woman."

"Yes, she is," Laynar agreed with a grin.

They continued to ride at a ground-eating canter. The scouts soon met them on the road and led the platoon to the nest site.

Laynar gave the signal to dismount. They'd leave the horses here and walk the rest of the way. A young woman with golden-yellow hair formed a cold-air shield around the horses. Rizelya approved of the new use for the shield. There weren't any jedash bushes here to protect the horses from any escaping monsters.

Rizelya wondered if the jedash bushes would even grow here. They worked so well in Strunell Territory. She added it to her mental list to talk to Naila about so she could bring it up at the clan meeting.

Aistrun jabbed her ribs to get her attention. "We're here."

Rizelya gasped at the huge nest. So did quite a few of the other fighters.

"Gracious Mother, protect us," Laynar prayed as she caught sight of the nest.

Muttered prayers echoed Laynar's.

"Judging from the size of it," Rizelya said, "we'll be very, very lucky if there's only one control-janack in the swarm." The bottoms of her feet tingled, and an almost subaudible hum skittered over her nerves.

The mass of monsters stirred in the warmth. A heat stalk poked up out of the tangle, and the movement increased.

"They're getting ready!" Laynar yelled. "To your positions."

Men snarled as they changed into their warrior form, while the women surged forward. The fighters sent to the farthest position barely reached it when the nest seethed. Six brechas and three janacks rolled out of the nest. A ring of fire flared around the monsters. The fight was on.

More creatures boiled from the nest. The fighting teams were hard-pressed to keep them contained. The hum increased in volume. Rizelya clapped her hands over her ears, trying to block the sound, but then she saw a break in the seething pile of monsters. Gritting her teeth against the pain, she dropped her hands and gripped her helbraught, unwilling to let the pain distract her from her duty.

"Damn! I hate being right about this," Rizelya swore. "There are two control-janacks." She turned to Laynal. "Looks like you'll get your chance to fight. We'll need both teams at full strength to demolish these monsters."

A control-janack fled the nest with its throng and headed toward the swamp.

"We'll catch that one," Rizelya shouted as she ran. She had to trust the Strunheim pack had learned the shields well enough to keep them safe and to kill their control-janack.

Her people raced behind her, hot on her heels. Relief flooded her when several other Reds and warriors joined them. The group of monsters—two regular janacks and five brechas, along with the control-janack—was too large for her small squad-pack to handle. As she ran, she began to build the fire-ring to stop the control-janack and its minions from escaping into the swamp.

It flared to life.

The control-janack screamed in frustration. It sounded unaccountably like the woman in Rizelya's dreams. She didn't have time to wonder at the oddity. Dehali flung her hand out, sending the cold-air shield to surround them. The control-janack swung its head around, searching for them. Rizelya paused, taking a steadying deep breath. She gestured at Leistral. They would both have to cast the fire shield to contain this mob of monsters.

"Now!" she shouted.

The fire shield burst around them, surrounding them with glowing magic.

The excruciatingly loud humming nearly knocked Rizelya off of her feet, but the fire shield held.

"You'll not stop me like that!" she screamed at the control-janack—and the mind behind it. She raced toward it, with Aistrun keeping pace with her.

Even with the cold-air shield around them, the control-janack seemed to sense where they were. Rizelya finally realized it wasn't tracking Aistrun, only her. She howled in frustration when one of the control-janack's tentacles whipped her off her feet, again and again. She rolled out of the way as a tentacle slammed into the ground. The humming turned into an angry buzz. She had to fight against it drowning her in its fury.

That's it, fury! Rizelya pitted her rage against the anger of the entity behind the control-janack. From all she experienced, she was positive some intelligence rode the janack and controlled it, even as it controlled the other monsters. She built a wall of raging fire in her mind, ringing herself with its ferocity. The buzzing and humming fell silent.

Rizelya feinted to the right. A surge of elation filled her when the control-janack couldn't sense her anymore. She fed fire magic into her helbraught until it glowed orange with intense heat. Using the only technique they'd found to kill the control-janack, she pole-vaulted onto the control-janack and raced up its back to plunge the fiery blade into its head.

"It's going to blow!" she yelled. On impulse, she grabbed the protrusion and sliced it off. Pain burst, streaming from her mind and spreading like lightning through her nerve endings. Screaming, tears flowing down her face, she flung herself from the janack as it exploded. She forced her hand to squeeze the protrusion, not letting it go when she smacked into the ground.

Chapter 8

Rizelya looked up. Aistrun, in his human form, and Leistral stood over her and gazed at her with concern. "I blacked out again, didn't I?"

They nodded.

"Hey, but this time we don't have to go searching for the protrusion." He pointed to Rizelya's still-clenched fist.

The protrusion was a mangled lump of fibers and goo. She grinned. It wasn't buzzing at her anymore.

The thought of the control-janack wiped the grin from her face. The mind behind it had been seeking her. Her heart hitched. She inhaled deeply and blew out her fear. When they reached the Clan Keep, she really needed to visit a White priestess. Hopefully, the priestess could tell her why she could hear and sense the malignant entity that was now stalking her.

The healer in Shaydan's platoon had mixed something for her to combat the headache and fatigue that came from fighting the control-janack. Shaydan had killed the control-janacks during the journey through Strunell, so Rizelya hadn't needed the medication.

Sitting up carefully, she slid a small package out of her jacket. She opened it to find a stack of bite-sized travel bars. Examining one, she discovered it lacked the hated dried fruit, so she popped it into her mouth. Her headache eased within moments of eating it. She'd have to send a gift to the healer and wheedle the recipe out of her so Kaieli could make it. It seemed like the control-janacks were now a permanent part of the monster nests.

"So did the others get their control-janack?" she asked.

Aistrun nodded. "Yes, they did. From what I hear, Laynal not only created the cold-air shield for them but also accounted for one of the brechas." He turned his head toward the other group and tilted his chin at the happy girl. "She's mighty proud of herself."

"With reason." Pride filled Dehali's voice. She took her role as mentor to the teenager seriously.

"Where's Keandran?"

Aistrun inspected the area. He swore a streak, damning Keandran to every possible hell and then some. "The cur isn't here. Neither is Eidstrun."

"Eidstrun must have gone after him," Rizelya said with more calm than she felt. "The idiot probably hied off into the swamp again." She held out a hand for Aistrun to help her up.

"Right you are." Leistral pointed at the edge of the swamp. "Here they come. Eidstrun is furious." She sounded awed. "I've never seen him like this."

Eidstrun, still in warrior form, practically glowed with fury as he drove Keandran forward, cringing in his human form. Swamp crud clung to Eidstrun's legs and chest and covered Keandran. Eidstrun grabbed Keandran by his neck and flung him to his knees in front of Rizelya and Aistrun.

"I will not go after him again," Eidstrun growled as soon as he had shifted back. "The dung-encrusted cur scuttled deep into the swamp. He kept yelling, 'I'm coming, I'm coming.' When I caught up with him, he couldn't tell me what he was doing."

"Where were you going?" Alpha power coated Aistrun's words, demanding an answer.

"I don't know!" Keandran wailed, cowering.

"Tell us what happened." Rizelya added her own power to Aistrun's.

Keandran choked back a sob. Gone was the mouthy, arrogant man. He now cringed before them, sniveling and terrified. "I shifted with everyone else and attacked the control-janack and its beasts along with the rest of you. Then..." Confusion twisted his face. "Then, I..." He stopped again, searching his memory. "There was someone calling my name, I think."

"The next thing I knew, this beast was banging my head against a tree and yelling at me. We were in a slimy pool. Look at me!" Keandran glowered at Eidstrun as he indicated his filthy condition. "I'm covered in slime. How do I know he didn't drag me there to kill me? Huh?" His eyes widened as he lifted a hand to his head, where a trickle of blood dripped. "He was trying to kill me, see!"

"If I had tried to kill you, you'd be dead, cur," Eidstrun sneered, his fists balled up at his sides. He shook with the effort not to use them on Keandran. "I remember what happened, whereas you do not."

At Rizelya's raised eyebrow, he continued. "I had finished killing a janacks and looked around because it wasn't Keandran with me but one of Laynar's warriors. I saw Keandran through a break in the trees. He was already in the swamp. By then, the others had the monsters well in hand, so Leistral opened the fire shield for me. I chased the mangy caitiff. He had shifted back to human and was yelling, 'I'm coming.' I caught him once, and he fought me and escaped. He took me unaware," Eidstrun mumbled the last in embarrassment. Anger filled his voice as he glared at Keandran. "We were deep into the swamp when I caught him again. Bugger moved fast. I had to knock him unconscious to stop him from escaping me a second time. When he came to, he was like this, unable to remember anything but the beginning of the battle."

During Eidstrun's tale, Laynar and several of her warriors joined the group.

"There's something wrong with him," Laynar interjected. "No one willingly goes into the swamps, especially with a nest to destroy. Is this the first time he's done this?"

"No," Rizelya admitted. "He did it in Strunell Territory as well."

"When we return to the Keep, the White Priestess will examine him." She snapped her fingers at the two men, who were still in their warrior form. They descended on Keandran and bound his hands behind his back. When Rizelya opened her mouth to protest, Laynar shook her head sternly. "It's for our safety, and his. This way, he will not be drawn into the swamp again."

Keandran struggled and swore, but the warriors were much stronger than he. They gripped his arms, lifted him off the ground between them, and carried him off the battlefield.

The tightness in Rizelya's chest eased with someone else dealing with Keandran's problem. "Thank you." Rizelya squeezed Laynar's arm.

Laynar patted Rizelya's hand. "Alphas sometimes have to make difficult decisions. Because he isn't one of my pack, it was easier for me. We should get him back to the Keep quickly." She looked around the field where several of the Reds still burned the monster remains. "The rest of my platoon will return when they're finished." Laynar strode toward the horses.

All of Rizelya's pack returned to Strunheim Keep with Laynar, Keandran's guard, and three of Laynar's warriors. They rode quickly. Keandran cursed and screamed at them in a continuous stream until Laynar grew tired of the noise and had him gagged.

When they rode through the gates of Strunheim Keep, Layhalya and the White Priestess waited for them at the top of the steps leading to the Temple. Laynar would have mind-spoken to the Keep Alpha while on their way back.

Rizelya admitted to herself something troubled Keandran's soul. Perhaps a bit cowardly, she'd hoped to have a White Priestess examine him at Strunlair Keep. Then the Clan Alphas could deal with any issues that were found. Layhalya appeared frail, leaning on her cane. Rizelya hadn't wanted to drop any problems in the old woman's lap.

Rizelya twisted in her saddle. Keandran continued to sputter and curse, even with his mouth gagged. The problem had come hunting her down rather than waiting for her timing. She frowned, thinking this was the way of the Goddess. Keandran needed help, and so the Goddess had provided it. Rizelya turned back, settled into her saddle, and guided Kymaya across the courtyard to the Temple.

The White Priestess wore a dazzling white gown of soft silk that grazed the tops of her sandaled feet. The hems of the long, flowing sleeves brushed the priestess's knees. A white gauze veil covered her hair, bound to her head with her coronet of rank, the High Priestess of this Temple. Thin, white side-lock braids woven with tiny crystals descended over her shoulders and reached to her waist. Eight crystal rings encircled her fingers. Each one denoted one of the eight magical Talents. From her neck hung the symbol of the Goddess and Her Consort—an eight-pointed star. The sunlight sparkled on the brilliantly faceted diamond in its center.

The power of the priestesses came from their connection with the Goddess and Her Consort, who ruled the Posairs' world. Their Talent manifested in the color white. All women called to the Goddess had white hair and had a secondary Talent as indicated by their eye color. The Supreme White Priestess, who embodied the Goddess, had unusual eyes: white with black rims. Only the one destined to become the Supreme would be born with such eyes.

The priestesses were the soul workers and spiritual leaders of the community. Rizelya knew if anyone could help Keandran—or her—it would be a White Priestess. They could commune with the Goddess to determine what, if anything, was tainting their souls. Rizelya said a quick prayer to the Mother and Matriarch, praying the evil she had been dreaming about lately hadn't tainted her soul. A wave of dizziness hit her, afraid of what the White Priestess would see within her.

Rizelya dismounted first and approached the steps. The downcast gaze required when approaching a High Priestess helped her grab her fear and strangle it. Clasping her palms together, thumbs crossed, she raised her hands until her fingertips touched the middle of her forehead. She bowed her head with her eyes closed in reverence to the representative of the Goddess. She would wait in this position for hours, if needed, until the priestess acknowledged her.

The creak of leather and soft thuds sounded around her as the others dismounted. She surmised the muffled "oof" was Keandran being pulled from his horse. Movement on either side of her indicated Aistrun and Laynar had joined her in obeisance to the priestess.

A sigh of silk and the perfume of the sacred kehani flower preceded the priestess's gentle words. "Blessings of the Mother, dear children." After a few moments, the priestess touched the top of Rizelya's bowed head. A zing of energy entered her head and a feeling of well-being suffused her.

The blessing gave her permission to open her eyes and raise her head. As she did, she caught the terror on Keandran's face as the priestess blessed the man next to him. *Does he know he's tainted?*

Keandran's shoulders twitched. But the conditioning of years standing like this, waiting for a blessing, kept him still. He squeezed his eyes tight as he awaited the priestess' touch. Rizelya watched in fascination as a beam of white light burst from the priestess' fingertips and passed into Keandran's head. He groaned and then collapsed.

The White Priestess shook her head sharply when Rizelya and Aistrun moved to help Keandran. Rizelya pressed her palm to her heart when Keandran's chest rose and fell.

The priestess quickly blessed the others, and then she strolled to back to Rizelya.

"He is indeed tainted," she said as she regarded Rizelya with eyes the pale blue of a sunlit lake. "Perhaps we can purge it from him. Bring him into the Temple." She motioned to the two men who were still in their warrior form.

When Rizelya and Aistrun tried to follow, the priestess put up a restraining hand. "No. You cannot come. This is a thing for the soul workers to do. We will inform you know when he is well." With a swish of her skirts, she disappeared into the Temple.

Aistrun took Rizelya's arm and turned her back to the courtyard. "Come on, we can't do anything for him except pray to the Mother that he will recover."

She allowed him to conduct her to the horses. As her knees wobbled, Rizelya tightly gripped Kymaya's halter. Hopefully, because she hadn't collapsed at the priestess' touch, it meant she wasn't tainted.

After the evening meal, her squad-pack gathered in her room. They hadn't received any word from the Temple on Keandran's condition.

"Does this mean we can leave him here?" Eidstrun asked, leaning forward and clasping his hands. "Please say we can."

"Hey, it depends on what the priestess determines." Aistrun ran a hand through his hair. Rizelya noticed it was getting shaggy, and a scraggly beard marred his usually clean-shaved face.

"We must depart no later than the day after tomorrow if we're to reach Strunven and Strunlair Keeps on schedule," Rizelya reminded everyone. "If he can travel with us, we'll take him. I don't want to leave him for Layhalya to deal with. She has enough problems with these new control-janacks."

The talk turned to recounting the last battle and the surprise of two control-janacks in the nest. It soon devolved to discussing all the changes in the patterns of the monsters. The tower bells chimed the midnight hour when her people meandered to their beds. For the first time in days, Rizelya drifted easily to sleep.

A dreamless sleep.

In light of Keandran's condition, Layhalya released Rizelya and her squad-pack from training her people. They waited in the pack-house's lounge for word from the White Priestess about Keandran. Rizelya tried reading a book, but couldn't concentrate on the words. The other four set up the keshe board, but soon abandoned the strategy game.

When Rizelya's group wandered into the Keep-house dining hall for the midday meal, everyone stopped talking and stared at them. Hushed whispers followed them as they moved around the buffet tables.

Rizelya listlessly stirred the noodles on her plate, her appetite gone. She glanced at the others. Typically, Aistrun and Eidstrun weren't letting anything get in their way of a good meal. The women didn't eat with quite as much gusto as the men.

"Any word from the White Priestess?" Laynar stood at the end of the table, tray in her hand. Her younger sister, Laynal, beside her.

Rizelya shook her head. She scooted down the bench, nudging Leistral and Dehali to make room for Laynar. The men took the hint and moved to allow Laynal to sit by them.

Rizelya gave up the pretense of eating and pushed her plate away. "I hope we receive news this afternoon. We've already stayed longer than we expected." She could hear the frustration and worry in her voice. "We now have two chedans to reach to Strunven Keep, teach them, and travel on to Strunlair Keep for the clan meeting. If he isn't well enough to rejoin us tomorrow, we'll have to leave him here."

"Grandmother understands," Laynar said. "She's sending me with two platoons to escort you through our territory."

"Hey, expecting trouble?" Aistrun commented, taking a break from his food.

"She thinks there will be more nests like the one yesterday." Laynar put her fork down. "I pray she's wrong."

"Am I going with you?" Laynal asked, hope lighting up her face. "I did really good during the fight. You need me." She nodded knowingly.

"Yes, you create a strong shield," Laynar agreed, smiling.

"So, am I going? Huh? Say that I am!" The young girl wiggled excitedly.

Laynar looked at Laynal for a long moment, and then turned to Rizelya, a gleam of mischief in her eyes. "What do you think? Is she good enough to take with us? Or should we leave her here to deal with Grandmother?"

Rizelya grinned, joining in the teasing and enjoying doing something besides moping. "Oh, I don't know. She is pretty young..."

Laynal made a pleading gesture. "Please say I can go, Rizelya. I'm sure they'll let me if you say it's okay."

"I'm not getting in the way of Layhalya." Rizelya tossed her hands in the air in mock fright and lowered her voice. "She scares me."

"Nothing scares you!" Laynal protested.

Finally, Laynar took pity on the young woman. "Yes, I need you, scamp. You're going."

"Yippee!" Laynal jumped up, banging the table in her haste. Quick hands kept glasses from tipping over, except Laynal's, and juice spread across the table. "I'm going to go pack!" She rushed off, oblivious to the mess she'd made.

"Oh, to be young!" Leistral used the napkins to clean up the spill.

"So, when are we leaving?" Dehali asked.

"In the morning," Laynar replied, "with or without Keandran."

"Good." Dehali stood up. "I'm going to do something constructive. If you need me, I'll be in the practice arena."

"I'll join you," Eidstrun swung his leg over the bench. The two started walking out of the dining room.

Leistral piled a last napkin over the spill and rushed to accompany her pack-mates.

"Doing something constructive sounds good," Rizelya said with a sigh. "I'm tired of just sitting here waiting."

"Well, we do have to plan our journey," Laynar replied. "It will be possible, barely, to get you to Strunven Territory in the allotted time."

"Great idea," Aistrun spoke up. "Let's go."

Rizelya and Laynar stood in the small study they had commandeered, facing each other across the table with maps scattered across it. Rizelya jabbed the map with her finger. "And I say we can travel this distance in two days."

Laynar shook her head, glaring at Rizelya. "We can't with two platoons. I have more experience leading platoons than you do, and I tell you, it will take us three days."

"Hey," Aistrun interrupted them. "We have a visitor." He indicated the door where a novice priestess stood. The young girl of twelve or thirteen hung back, as if afraid of entering.

Laynar beckoned the girl to enter. "You have news?"

"Yes, Lady." Her voice quavered as she wrung her hands together. "The White Priestess wishes to see you and the Strunland alphas."

Rizelya and the others followed the novice to the Temple. She guided them through the main sanctuary, where the priestesses led services and ceremonies to the Goddess. Incense sticks burned on a side altar. The sweet scent of kehani flowers and the tang of frankincense saturated the room.

Rizelya inhaled deeply, letting the sacred fragrances settle her mind and heart. As a Red and a fighter, she attended services infrequently. Her duties took her away from the Keep. The Malvers' monsters didn't observe holy days. Even so, she went to the Temple for private prayers whenever she could. She loved the Goddess, in all her forms, but most often called upon the Mother or the Crone. Rizelya paused as she absorbed the sanctuary's peacefulness. Aistrun had also slowed.

On the far side, Laynar and the novice priestess waited for Rizelya and Aistrun. She hurried toward them. Aistrun quickly caught up with her with his long strides.

"I'm sorry," Rizelya apologized. "It's just been awhile since we've been able to enjoy the peace of a Temple."

"All is well. Perhaps the White Priestess will perform a ceremony for you before you leave."

"Oh, that would be wonderful," Rizelya said with a sigh. Aistrun nodded in agreement. "I'm sure our squad-mates would also appreciate it."

"Then I will arrange it with the White Priestess." Laynar indicated to the girl to continue.

Although Layhalya was the Keep Alpha, Rizelya noticed Laynar did much of the running of the Keep. It surprised Rizelya Layhalya was willing to send her granddaughter with them when she seemed to be needed here. But after their discussion this afternoon, Rizelya was glad Laynar was going to be traveling with them. They would need her leadership and tactical skills.

The novice led them through a door out of the sanctuary. Rizelya hesitated at the threshold. Even when her niece, Wisah, did her priestess training in the Temple at Strunland Keep, Rizelya had never been anywhere in the Temple but the sanctuary. She looked curiously around her, doubting she would have another opportunity like this to see the interior of a Temple.

Closed doors lined the corridor. She wondered if they were rooms for the priestesses who lived within the Temple. Painted murals of the Goddess in her various forms covered the walls.

The first one showed a scene of the Maiden as a young girl, around the same age as their guide, frolicking in a meadow filled with an assortment of animals. Farther down, the mural depicted an older version of the Maiden in her visage of a warrior fighting a nest of monsters.

They turned a corner, and this time the murals were of the Mother, the nurturing aspect of the Goddess. A very pregnant woman nursed an infant in one scene, and in another, the Mother, as healer, tended to her flock of children.

After seeing the paintings, Rizelya supposed she should pray to the Maiden in Her warrior form, but she always felt more comfortable praying to the Mother, the care-giver. She seemed more approachable than the fierce Warrior Maiden.

In the next corridor, the murals depicted the Matriarch, the ruler and leader. A mature woman dispensing wisdom represented this face of the Goddess. Many of the Keep Alphas were in this stage of their life, and they prayed to the Matriarch.

Their guide stopped at a door and knocked before they reached the passageway dedicated to the fourth aspect of the Goddess: the Crone. She ruled death and the world of the beyond. It disappointed Rizelya that they hadn't walked down the Crone's corridor. Rizelya prayed to the Crone frequently because she dealt in death as readily as the Crone did. So did the Maiden Warrior, but the Crone also dispensed justice, and this aspect appealed to Rizelya.

Lost in thought, Rizelya missed the door opening, and before it closed on her, she quickly slid through it. Another priestess waited for them, this one older and closer to Rizelya's age. The young girl bowed to the journeyman and left. "The White Priestess will see you now," the woman said. "Follow me."

Although all priestesses of the Temple were Whites or the rarer Gray, only the leader was called 'The White Priestess.' A Supreme White Priestess ruled the Sanctuary, the White Priestesses, and the Posairs.

Rizelya was glad they were talking to a Keep White Priestess and not the Supreme. Stories circulated about the old woman and her legendary skill of being able to see into the mind and heart of another. Rizelya didn't want her looking inside her anytime soon. Although, the Supreme might be the only one who could tell Rizelya what her strange dreams meant. The thought made her shiver.

"You okay?" Aistrun whispered to her.

Rizelya nodded. "Just cold," she lied.

They followed the second priestess through a short hallway and into a receiving room. Deep blue paint covered the walls, but white fabrics upholstered the carpets and furniture. The White Priestess, who had blessed them the day before, sat in a throne-like chair. Its massiveness only adding to, not diminishing, her presence. Her forearms rested on the chair's arms, and she held herself rigidly straight and alert.

Sitting in a much smaller chair next to her was a Gray. The Gray Priestess's hair was a light silver-gray and her eyes were a pale blue, so pale they were almost white. She wore dove-gray robes cinched with a leather belt dyed a darker gray. Silvery moonstones winked from each index finger and at her ears.

Rizelya, Aistrun, and Laynar made obeisance to the priestesses. When the White Priestess motioned to them, they sat on the empty stools at her feet.

"We have examined your male," the White Priestess said. "There is something, or someone, who is tampering with his mind. I called in my Gray Priestess, who examined him as well. She found tendrils of evil influencing his soul. We do not know what it is or where it is coming from." The White Priestess's face flushed with embarrassed.

The Gray Priestess shifted in her seat. "It has something to do with the Malvers' monsters, perhaps the new one we have heard about, but we're unsure how." She shrugged. "None of us have seen one, so we do not know how it could affect him." She gripped her hands together tightly.

"The control-janack emits a hum," Rizelya admitted. "I don't know why I can hear it and no one else can."

The White Priestess leaned forward slightly. Her eyes blazed with an inner fire as she regarded Rizelya. "Are you not affected and drawn to the evil of the swamps?"

"No, Priestess. I sense some mind control, but I've been able to fight it." She grinned maliciously. "Usually by killing the control-janack and destroying its strange protrusion."

The White Priestess considered this information. Rizelya found it difficult to not squirm under the intense gaze. Inside her boots, she curled and uncurled her toes, needing to move something.

The White Priestess finally sat back and nodded her head once, as if to herself. "This indeed may be the cause. We do not have the skill or resources to fully remove the taint. However, we have blocked it, so it should not lead him astray again." Before they could get their hopes up, she continued. "This is but a temporary measure. The White Priestess at Strunlair Keep should be able to expunge it. And if she cannot, she'll send the male to the Sanctuary for the Supreme to cleanse him."

"We are concerned," the Gray added, "the taint will grow and overtake him completely if it is not removed."

"We're traveling to the Clan-Keep," Aistrun told the priestesses. "When we arrive, we'll take him directly to the White Priestess."

"Is there anything we can do on the way?" Rizelya asked.

The White Priestess gazed down at her rings. When she lifted her head, she wore a grave frown. "The only thing I can suggest is if the control-janack is the cause, keep him away from it."

Aistrun mumbled under his breath about the impossibility of that. Rizelya kicked him surreptitiously. "We will do what we can."

"We will send him to you before the evening meal." The White Priestess gestured to the door, ending their audience with her and dismissing them.

Rizelya and Aistrun stood up and bowed to the priestesses, but Laynar stayed seated. When Rizelya looked at her questioningly, Laynar smiled and mouthed, "Ceremony." Rizelya returned the smile and left.

Anticipating a service, Rizelya happily followed their guide out of the Temple. They were still saddled with Keandran, but he should be better to live with after the priestess blocked the taint.

At least she hoped the evil blight had caused his ill temper.

Chapter 9

The horizon glowed with the rising sun, and in another octar, they would leave. Rizelya took a deep breath, holding it in her lungs before letting it out slowly. She reached high into the air, then bent to touch the ground, her braid swinging. The grassy area had drawn her when she walked by on her way to the stables. Their hectic days hadn't allowed time for stretching.

A short while later, the rest of her squad-pack joined her, even Keandran. Rizelya nodded to them and continued with the familiar routine. The exercises and stretches not only loosened her muscles, but they were also a type of meditation. The ceremony at the Temple last night had done wonders to recenter her spirit. It seemed like ages since she had felt the quiet, loving presence of the Goddess. Bowing at the end of a sequence, she caught sight of Laynar and Layhalya standing off to the side.

"Alphas," she greeted them. "We'll be ready to leave on time." As if on cue, all but Aistrun hurried to the stable. He stepped quietly to stand behind her.

"The boy is well enough to travel?" Layhalya asked.

"So the White Priestess tells us. He does seem to be better," Rizelya replied.

"He's the calmest I've ever seen him," Aistrun assured them. "I hope whatever they did will keep him from running into the swamp when we face a battle, which we'll undoubtedly do."

Laynar nodded. "The increased activity of the monsters ensures we'll run into mature nests."

"I have changed your route slightly," Layhalya told them. She stilled Rizelya and Aistrun's objections with a stern look. "I want you to check several of the nest sites on your way. We must ensure my people can defend us with your new techniques. In addition, I want you to warn the minor keeps along your route. Inform them we'll send them trained Yellows to assist their fighters as soon as possible."

"But we have so little time," Rizelya burst out.

"Ach, you have time." Layhalya waved away her protest. "Strunheim contains fewer hills and valleys than Strunell. You'll move through our territory quickly enough."

Aistrun touched her shoulder, warning her to stop protesting. As the Keep Alpha, Layhalya held a much higher rank. Just as they had obeyed Keshanal's orders, they would obey Layhalya's.

"Yes, Alpha," Rizelya bowed her head in submission.

"Guide them well, Granddaughter." Layhalya patted Laynar's arm, then tottered across the courtyard.

"I guess she's not a fan of farewells," Rizelya commented.

"No, she isn't," Laynar agreed. "Come, we must leave."

Although the exchange with Layhalya hadn't taken much time, Leistral and Eidstrun rode out of the stable, leading Kymaya and Jezhan already saddled. Laynal followed, holding a lead rope to a blue-gray gelding. He had thin white stripes along his sides, white socks, and a white tail. She handed the gelding's reins to Laynar.

The platoon accompanying them stood next to their horses, ready to mount up. Several nibbled on bread rolls filled with meat and cheese. Rizelya's mouth watered, and a loud growl came from Aistrun's stomach. She checked Kymaya's girth strap, shouldering the mare to make her release her held breath, then tightened it again. A young Red ran up to Rizelya, a basket on her arm, and handed her a packet. The girl went around to each of Rizelya's squad-pack and gave them one.

Rizelya held the warm package and lifted a corner of the wrapper, inhaling appreciatively the scent of fresh bread. She had been resigned to eating a trail bar to break her fast, but this was much better. A young boy delivered stoppered ceramic bottles to the waiting riders. When Rizelya opened it, the rising steam carried the smell of spicy taevo.

Once everyone received their food and drink, Laynar called out the order to mount up. Leather creaked as feet stepped into stirrups, and air whooshed lightly as riders settled in saddles. At Laynar's signal, the party urged their horses into a walk. When they were through the gates, Laynar moved her horse into a faster pace.

Rizelya munched on her bread roll and sipped on her taevo as they rode away from the keep. Here, like at home, sheadash stone protected the various sections of fields. Browns with earth Talents already toiled in the fields, along with a few Blues and Greens. Scattered among the women were the men who had chosen not to become fighters. Several adolescent boys and girls, about thirteen or fourteen, drove a flock of sheep down a sheadash and granite gravel lane.

The scene of fieldworkers and herders was so similar to the one she'd witnessed many times at home that Rizelya experienced a moment of homesickness. She blinked at the unfamiliar sight of a young Red fighter, a few years older than the herders, following them sedately on her horse. A young wolf trotted beside her. The two fighters-in-training, guarding the herders and their flock of sheep, provided a meager defense against any marauding monsters. But they could alert their alpha of any trouble, and fighters would quickly be dispatched. Helbraughts replaced the adolescent's shepherd crooks. Although they couldn't use them like the Reds did, the bladed weapons would provide better protection than their usual plain wooden staff.

"I wonder if other Talents could feed their powers into the helbraught blades the way we do with our fire magic," she said to Aistrun, indicating the herders.

"Hey, I don't know why not, other than they haven't needed to. The Reds have always been the fighters."

"Well, we aren't the only ones fighting now."

"Nope, there are also Yellows," Dehali said, entering the conversation. "Their air Talent is now as necessary our fire. I'm sure it would be helpful to include many of the Browns, and perhaps some of the Greens, in this new way of fighting."

"But not Blues." Eidstrun shot a quick glance back at Keandran, who rode several paces behind them. "I don't think it would be a good idea. He has some Blue Talent, and look what's happened to him."

"Are we sure his Talent is the problem?" Leistral spoke up.

"He's the only one who is having problems with the new control-janack," Eidstrun replied.

"Hmm, that's not quite true," Rizelya said quietly. She tried not to let her worry creep into her voice. "I can hear them humming."

"But you don't allow them to manipulate you," Eidstrun grumbled. "You aren't running into the swamp, and I don't have to chase you down."

"Hey, he's right. Rizelya, you're still in control of your mind and fighting the buggers." Aistrun gave her a reassuring smile.

"Helstramiesters create the blades on our helbraughts," Leistral broke in, turning the conversation back to the subject they had been discussing. "The blades hold and direct magic, so why couldn't the other Talents use it like we Reds do?"

Aistrun flicked his reins across his palm. "We need someone who doesn't have any Red Talent to test the theory on."

"Too bad Tami or Kami isn't here with us." Dehali sighed, sadness flitting across her face at their memory. "They were full Yellows."

"But they had some Red Talent too," Leistral reminded her.

"Next time we train the Yellows, let's ask them to try to use a helbraught and make the blade cold," Rizelya said. Her group agreed it was a good idea.

Farther away from the keep, teams of a Red woman and a wolf, able to shift into a warrior if needed, guarded the fields and pastures. These guards were more experienced fighters than the first team with the herder children. Layhalya wasn't taking any chances on the safety of her people. She had been a fighter before she helped develop the Zehis method. She knew how much damage and death a loose nest of monsters caused.

Once the group passed the cultivated fields and the Keep's pasture lands, Laynar picked up their speed. She fell into the trot, canter, trot pace which ate up the measures while keeping their horses healthy.

Their route took them farther north and into the foothills. The contingent rode past the tumbled remains of an old settlement. If there had been a tower, it had long since fallen, and the stone used for building the pack houses. Laynar sent scouts to the nearby nest site.

"Have you ever wondered why," Laynar mused while they waited, "the nest sites are always near where ancient towns once stood?"

Rizelya leaned on her saddle's pommel, examining the ruins. "Yes, quite often. Perhaps all the magic flung around during the Great War created the malignant magic pools? When you encounter an old settlement, you also find a pool somewhere close. The pools and the monster nests go hand-in-hand."

"Maybe someday we can discover a way to drain the malignant magic and end the Malvers' monster's reign of terror."

"Wouldn't that be amazing?" Rizelya sighed happily at the thought. Although she didn't know what she'd do if she wasn't fighting the monsters.

The scouts' returning interrupted their discussion.

"The nest is empty, Alpha," the head scout said, saluting Laynar.

With the good news, Laynar gave the order to ride on.

The group entered a small keep just past noon. The delays made Rizelya unhappy, but she understood the reasoning behind them. Thankfully, there weren't many minor holdings in the district they rode through. A few hearty souls chose to live in the remote garrisons.

"No, I haven't seen any new janacks," the Keep Alpha informed Laynar. "But then again, the local nest isn't active yet. The spring nights are still cold and frost covers the ground most mornings. I expect the monsters to waken with the first planting in another chedan or so."

"Are any of your Yellows powerful enough to learn the new shield method?" Laynar asked.

The alpha tilted her head and pursed her lips. "I have one young woman with Yellow Talent I'll send to the main keep for training. If the nest is as you say, I'd be grateful for any additional help Layhalya and Selestrun can give me."

"I'll let them know to expect your Yellow."

Laynar led the group out of the keep and back onto the road. They rode through rocky, hilly country, the type the monsters avoided because the janacks and brechas couldn't maneuver over rocks. The trail wound up the side of the mountain. Patches of snow covered the path, and in the shadows under the trees, several feet of snow still buried the ground.

Rizelya snuggled into her warm cloak she had put on during their last rest stop. A group of mountain goats climbed the rocky slopes above the path. She gaped with awe as a ram leaped from one outcrop to another.

The sun crept along its downward trajectory as they continued to ride. From Rizelya's understanding, they still had many measures to cover before reaching the pass and the safe house on the other side. If they didn't make it there before nightfall, the rocky landscape ensured they wouldn't face any monsters.

The trail narrowed until only a single horse could traverse it at a time. The mountain's rough rock wall bordered one side, while the other offered a sheer drop. Rizelya rode near the head of the column, and when she reached the switchback, she looked down and saw the tail end of their group coming around the bend below. A few more turns, and they'd arrive at the top. Even with the switchbacks, the steep slope necessitated she stand over Kymaya's shoulders to help her climb. On a curve slightly wider than the path, Rizelya paused and sat back down on her saddle, giving her tired legs a rest.

Pushing on, Rizelya turned the corner of the next hairpin turn and pulled Kymaya to a halt. Laynar stared at the wide stretch of scree blocking the path. Far above them, a scar marred the face of the cliff. The landslide, and resulting field of loose gravel and rock, appeared new. Laynar sent a scout ahead. Rizelya held her breath as the scout dismounted and gingerly walked across the debris. A few rocks skittered down the mountain at his passage. A few more tumbled down on his return.

"Too bad there aren't any Browns with stone affinity with us," Rizelya said. "They could steady the scree and make it safe for us to cross. Do you have any Reds with a strong enough earth Talent?"

Laynar shook her head. "Unfortunately, any we have in the Keep usually join the helstramiesters."

"This is another instance where having a variety of Talents would be beneficial. I'm keeping track to make a strong case to the Clan-Alphas."

"After this, I'll add my support. We can't stop on the path for the night. It's too narrow, and we can't turn around and go back down. We need to cross over the scree and hope for the best."

Guilt squeezed Rizelya's chest. Laynar had chosen this route because it cut days off from their travel to the Strunven territory border. Otherwise, they wouldn't be faced with this danger.

Laynar raised her voice and, Rizelya assumed, mind-spoke to those down the trail. "Walk your horses across. If we take it slow, we shouldn't have any problems." She sent the first riders, her seconds, to traverse the scree while she waited, chewing her lip. Laynar had insisted on interspersing the pack multas throughout the line rather than at the end. Rizelya now appreciated the wisdom of it, as the first group had a multa with them. They would start setting up camp at the top of the pass while the rest made the dangerous crossing.

The shadows grew longer, and Rizelya said a prayer of gratitude that she rode near the front of the line. She'd hate to attempt crossing the loose rock after dark. She wondered if Laynar had misjudged the time it would take to get this many people up the steep slope and over the pass.

Soon Laynar motioned Rizelya forward to go across the rubble. Aistrun would follow, and then the rest of her squad-pack.

Rizelya dismounted Kymaya and gathered the reins in her hand. "Come on, girl, I need your sure-footedness." She urged Kymaya forward, talking gently to her. Taking care of her horse kept her mind off how easy it would be to slip on the loose debris and slide down the slope to her death. She grimaced and held her breath each time rocks slid under her feet. Spots blurred her vision when she stepped off the scree. She draped her arms over Kymaya's neck, breathing deeply while she watched Aistrun.

Rizelya's hands flew to her mouth, stifling her scream.

Half-way across, Aistrun slipped and fell. His big gelding, Jezhan, stood stock-still, then lifted his head, pulling on the reins to keep Aistrun from sliding off the cliff side. Aistrun crawled hand over hand up the reins until he regained his feet. He rubbed Jezhan's nose and then started walking again, taking slower, more careful steps. He held his mouth in a tight line as he fought the terror of his near accident.

She moved Kymaya forward to give him room to move off the scree. As soon as he was off and safe, she threw her arms around him. "I thought I was going to lose you!"

"Hey, never fear, Little Red, you can't get rid of me that easily." His words were light, but he held her just as tightly. Tighter.

"I. Can't. Breathe," she sputtered. He released her.

The narrow path didn't give them enough room to wait for the others. Reluctantly, Rizelya climbed back into Kymaya's saddle. She rode forward slowly, watching behind her to be sure all of her people crossed the loose rock safely. When she turned at the next switchback, Keandran and Tejen stepped off the scree. Kressy, like all the other multas, needed no urging to cross. Her wide, platter-like hooves with their rough pads allowed her to easily grip the slippery surface. Relieved all of her pack had crossed safely, Rizelya returned her attention to the trail.

Twilight cast dark shadows when Rizelya and her squad-pack stopped at the pass. A wide open area greeted them with plenty of boulders and rocks strewn around to ensure no monsters would bother them during the night. Those who had arrived ahead of them had a large community fire burning. Several heavy cooking pots bubbled over it.

One of Laynar's seconds directed them to a spot to set up their tent. As the men worked to put the tent up and secure it, Rizelya and Leistral searched for firewood, and Dehali built a ring of stones. Rizelya didn't worry about the dampness of the wood she picked up. Her fire magic would light most anything, no matter how wet it was. Finished with their tent, the men helped the other tired riders set their tents up, while the women assisted in lighting comforting fires.

Exhausted, Rizelya's crew carried bowls to the community stew pot. She sniffed appreciatively, and her stomach grumbled with hunger. Their fire would be for warmth and taevo. Rizelya kept an eye out for Laynar while she ate.

The platoon leader finally rode slowly into camp after dark. Rizelya hurried over and helped Laynar off her horse.

"Did everyone make it across?" Rizelya asked when Laynar was firmly on her own feet.

Laynar shook her head sadly. "We lost one Red and two warriors. Their horses weren't as well trained as Aistrun's. When the people slipped, they dragged their horses with them."

"I'm sorry."

"It wasn't your fault there was a landslide." Lines of fatigue etched Laynar's face from the exhaustion and worry of getting all her people across the dangerous scree.

"But if it wasn't for my need to hurry, we wouldn't have come this way." Rizelya's guilt flared up anew, knowing there had been casualties.

"We all know how important your task is. We've fought the damned control janacks and have seen the size of the nests. You have nothing to feel guilty about." Laynar abruptly turned away and entered her tent.

Rizelya shuffled to her own tent. Ignoring the others, she crawled into her bedroll and murmured a prayer for the dead.

It surprised Rizelya when she didn't suffer nightmares from falling asleep while praying for the dead. They were lucky only three had died. When she exited the tent to relieve herself and find breakfast, the camp was subdued.

They couldn't retrieve the bodies to burn them properly and release their souls to cross the veil into the Summerland. Nor did a Gray Priestess accompany them to do the full death rites. But they had to abandon their dead fighters for the creatures of the earth and sky often enough that they no longer dreaded ghosts haunting them.

Rizelya wondered if she could convince any Gray priestesses to leave the temple's safety and travel with the fighting-packs. She knew they made rounds to the small keeps in the districts. She pushed aside the wish. So few Grays existed that she doubted the alphas would allow one to serve with the fighters.

"Hey, what are you scheming?" Aistrun asked her as he sat down on a rock next to her. He held out a steaming bowl to her. "I know that look. You were planning something."

"Not planning, just thinking." She took the bowl from him and scooped a spoonful of the hot cereal into her mouth. She hoped he would let it go.

"About..."

She swallowed the porridge. "The people who died and hoping their ghosts would be able to find a Gray to help them cross the veil." At his upraised eyebrow, she continued, "And how it would be helpful to have a Gray travel with the fighting-packs. I hate how often we have to leave a pack-mate who has been killed in the field."

"Me too. But, Rizelya, by the time you're finished rearranging the makeup of the fighting-packs, we'll have all the Talents with us!" He looked scandalized.

"Not all of them," she clarified. "I wouldn't include a White and maybe not even Blues."

"But a Gray? They are almost as rare as the Blacks."

"Now that is what we need! A Black! They're rumored to hold and use all the Talents."

Aistrun laughed. "Good luck. There hasn't been one in ages."

"Well, I can wish, can't I?" Rizelya pouted.

When they returned their bowls to the washing tub, Laynar was there.

"You look better this morning," Rizelya commented.

"Amazing what a night's sleep will do. Kaelyn made me a sleeping potion."

Rizelya's heart sister, Kaieli, had been the first healer to belong to a fighting-pack. The alphas had seen her value, and now there were others. Rizelya had been thankful numerous times on this mad journey across Strunlair Province for the addition of the healers. She still didn't know why she passed out when she killed a control-janack. Not for the first time she wished Kaieli was part of the squad-pack.

Finished cleaning their dishes, they strolled to the picket line.

"The path down on this side is much easier than the one we climbed yesterday," Laynar assured them. "We have two minor keeps to visit today." Laynar must have seen Rizelya clench her jaws. "Going over the mountain saved us three days of travel. These will be short visits, and they're necessary."

Rizelya unclenched her jaw and sighed deeply. "I know they're necessary. I'm just worried about getting to Strunlair Keep in time."

"We'll get you there, don't worry."

"Hey, if we don't get there by the first day of summer, they'll wait." Aistrun sounded positive. "They need the information we have. Besides, we'll most likely be traveling with the Strunven Keep Alphas, so they can't start the meetings without them."

"You're right," Rizelya reluctantly admitted.

"Of course I am!" His reply earned him a slap on the arm. "Hey!"

"Oh, stop grousing."

They reached the picket line, and one of the younger men, barely into manhood, raced to retrieve their horses. Aistrun and Rizelya joined the others of their squad-pack, who busily saddled their horses. While she and Aistrun waited, Rizelya watched Keandran critically. He moved stiffly, and his lips tightened in a grimace.

"Are you all right?" she asked him, coming up behind him.

Keandran gave a sharp nod

"You look like something is wrong," Rizelya insisted, adding a touch of alpha magic to urge him to talk to her.

He stopped adjusting his stirrup and turned around. "It feels like three people are in my head: me, the White Priestess, and someone else." He shuddered, pain burned in his eyes. "They aren't playing nice."

"It must be the block the White Priestess put in place." She reached out to cup his face, letting her hand drop when he flinched away. "Try to fight the taint. Come to Aistrun or me if you need help. We worry about you."

"Yeah, sure," he said with a sneer. "I'll be sure to do just that." He turned back to Tejen.

She threw her hands up in the air, exasperated. Shaking her head and swearing under her breath at Histrun for burdening her and Aistrun with the ungrateful, mangy cur, she stalked to Kymaya.

"Whoa, don't take it out on Kymaya." Aistrun stopped her before she could throw the saddle onto her horse's back. She had already slapped on the saddle blanket. "She didn't do anything to you. What's wrong?"

"Keandran," she spit out. "I don't think the White Priestess helped him much. He's still a nasty piece of work." She took several deep breaths to calm herself down. If what he said was true—and she believed him—then he was struggling. She reminded herself to have compassion. Until Histrun released him, Keandran belonged to her squad-pack.

Aistrun looked at her carefully and then let her arm go. She'd calmed enough to saddle Kymaya and not hurt her. Without a word, he returned to putting on Jezhan's tack.

"Thanks, Wolf," she murmured as she adjusted the saddle on Kymaya's back.

"No problem, Little Red."

A short time later, Laynar gave the signal to mount. Steep switchbacks wound down the mountain path for the first few measures, but afterward the trail gentled into a gradual slope. The farther down they rode, the sun grew warmer, turning into a beautiful spring day. They entered a canyon, and when they exited, a small garrison guarded the entrance.

"Yes, we've seen a... what did you call it?... a control-janack a few days ago," the keep alpha said, running a hand through her cherry-red hair. "We managed to destroy it, but not before it killed five of our fighters, including two Reds."

"We have a new way to distract the control-janack and kill it," Laynar told the alpha. "But it requires a strong Yellow. Do you have any here?"

The alpha nodded vigorously. "We have one." She sent for the woman.

The girl turned out to be in her early teens.

"I can't teach her," Dehali said, crossing her arms over her chest. "She's too young."

"Please," the alpha begged, "you have to teach her. We can't afford any more losses. She's the only strong Yellow in the keep."

Rizelya pulled Dehali aside. "You can't protect her, Dehali. You weren't much older when you joined the fighting-pack."

"Fine," Dehali huffed.

The girl proved to be an excellent pupil and learned quickly. Laynar and Rizelya worked with the alpha to teach her how to create the fire shield. Before they left, Laynar promised the alpha she would tell Layhalya of their losses and send replacement fighters.

Three octars later, Rizelya and her escort remounted and rode off. The small garrison provided them with fresh bread filled with mutton and tangy cheese, which they ate as they traveled. Rizelya tried not to begrudge the time spent teaching them. Her mission included doing what she could to keep the Posairs safe. It wouldn't do any good for her to rush off and leave these people unable to fight the new monsters.

She rubbed her face. The world wasn't as it had been even at the beginning of this lunadar. Neydar, the second lunadar of spring, was usually a time of planting and the birthing of livestock—and dealing with monster nests. But they never had revived as quickly or as profusely as this year. Something had caused the change after centuries of predictability.

Rizelya's thoughts kept her occupied until they stopped at the next minor keep late in the afternoon. They had also recently had trouble with the strange janack. Luckily, this garrison had only lost one warrior.

The woman the alpha brought forward for training was in her forties and a mother with several young children. She didn't want to fight the monsters. But when she found out how horrible this new janack was, she agreed. She would do anything to protect her children.

The alpha was in her seventies. After a couple of tries, she sent a young Red to Rizelya to be taught how to create the fire shield. Dehali worked with the older Yellow, but after the first few attempts, it became obvious it would take longer for her to learn than the young girl had taken.

Since the small keep couldn't feed and lodge their large force, Laynar sent the majority of their people ahead to the next safe house. Dehali, Rizelya, and Laynar stayed behind to continue the training. Aistrun insisted on remaining with them, as did Laynar's partner. A warrior agreed to protect Dehali. Eidstrun had wanted to stay, but Rizelya convinced him to go on to watch Keandran and to accompany Leistral.

Rizelya and the others left the small keep as twilight descended. If they pushed their horses hard, they would be able to reach the safe house before full dark. Rizelya looked forward to a hot meal and bed. Between the riding and teaching, it had been a long day. As their group topped a hillock, the safe house's lights winked at them. The thoughts of dinner occupied Rizelya's mind, and at first, she didn't notice Kymaya's skittishness.

Kymaya jerked on the reins and hopped to the other side of the road. Rizelya blinked and surveyed the area. She had fallen far behind her companions. Now as nervous as her horse, she reached down and unhooked her helbraught.

A deep cough came from the surrounding woods, followed by a dark mass leaping out of the shadows and tearing a gash along Rizelya's right shoulder. She ducked the spiked end of the beast's long, skinny tail. A narhili snarled at Kymaya while another one nipped at her heels. Kymaya bared her teeth at the menace. Rizelya tightened her legs to grip the saddle more securely as she felt Kymaya's hindquarters bunch. She jerked over the pommel at the impact of a hind hoof catching the beast and a soft thud. A yowl split the night.

"Aistrun!" Rizelya yelled as she fed fire into her helbraught, readying for the next attack. The narhili snarled, and red glowing eyes surrounded her and Kymaya. Rizelya swung her weapon, the blade slicing a creature as it snapped at her. It dropped away, only to be replaced by another. She dimly heard the thunder of hoofs as Aistrun and the others raced toward her.

Another swing and another beast yelped in pain. She thrust backward with the heavy staff-end of her helbraught, catching a narhili in the chest as it flew over Kymaya's hindquarters, knocking him to the ground. She dropped the reins, concentrating on fighting—and staying on—while Kymaya twisted, turned, and kicked savagely at their attackers.

Then a howl pierced the night, and an enormous beast entered the fray—Aistrun.

The eight-foot tall warrior shredded a narhili, his reach and claws no match for theirs. Rizelya heard a yip as the other two men, in their wolf form, arrived and tore into the beasts. The red-orange glow of helbraught blades heralded Laynar and Dehali's arrival. With Aistrun in his warrior form, the vicious fight didn't last much longer. An eerie yowl filled the night, and as it died, the surviving narhili fled.

Rizelya grabbed Jezhan's reins. The riders set their heels to their horses flanks, and the horses surged into a gallop. Aistrun ran in the rear, guarding it from any further attacks. The other two men, remaining in their wolf form, loped on either side of the galloping horses. As they raced into the courtyard and the gates banged shut behind them, Rizelya appreciated the safe house as she never had before. Her right shoulder and arm burned from a gash. She wiped the sweat from her forehead. Her hand came away bloodied.

Kymaya skidded to a halt. Eidstrun reached up, pulled her off the saddle, and raced into the building. Leistral grabbed Kymaya's reins and hurried to the stables. Rizelya hoped a narhili hadn't scratched or bitten Kymaya. Narhili wounds on a horse quickly became septic if left untreated. In a person, they could be deadly.

Eidstrun carefully laid Rizelya down on a cot. Kaelyn, the healer, stood nearby. A few moments later, two men carried in Laynar and Dehali. Rizelya knew it was a precaution to prevent further spreading of the poison in case they had been bitten. Someone hung blankets around the cots to provide privacy. As soon as the men left, Kaelyn and her helpers stripped all three women.

When the healer slid Rizelya's pants over her calf, she whimpered, then squeezed her eyes shut when they began removing her tunic. Tears flowed down her face when the leather rubbed against her shoulder. Kaelyn's eyes widened as she examined the wounds, and she crooned a sleeping spell.

I must be bad, Rizelya thought as she drifted off.

Chapter 10

Rizelya woke up with the flickers of the dying fire providing meager light. All three moons had set and sunrise was an octar or so away. She tried sitting up and moaned. Pain radiated from her right shoulder and calf, while the rest of her was clammy.

"Shh... here, I'll help you," Kaelyn's voice murmured. She slipped a gentle arm under Rizelya's back and lifted her, then propped the pillow against the wall. Kaelyn carefully helped her lean back and held out a cup. "Here."

The cool water soothed her dry throat.

"The others," she croaked, and took another sip.

"They fared much better than you did." Kaelyn settled on the chair by Rizelya's cot. "Laynar has a few surface scratches, nothing to worry about. Dehali has a puncture on her forearm, where a narhili tooth cut through her leathers, and a few scrapes. She'll be fine. There's no sign of poison." Kaelyn paused and leaned forward, her elbows on her knees. "Unlike you," she added.

Rizelya figured as much when she woke up sick. "The men?"

"Ach, their fur protected them." The healer smiled and gazed across the room. "That warrior of yours didn't even get a scratch. I understand he accounted for at least three of the beasts himself."

"Yeah, he's amazing." Rizelya moaned as she inadvertently moved her leg.

"I'll give you something for the pain." Kaelyn picked up another mug and held it for a few moments. Dark forest-green healing light pulsed from the healer's hands and into the cup until it, and its contents, glowed. She handed it to Rizelya, who sniffed and screwed up her face in disgust. "Oh, it isn't that bad," Kaelyn admonished. "Just drink it down."

Rizelya gulped the liquid, trying not to taste it. She shuddered and coughed at its awful bitterness. The healer, with a look of disdain, took the empty cup and handed Rizelya another one. After she finished drinking the water, Kaelyn helped her to lie down. In a few moments, sleep reclaimed her.

A commotion in the courtyard roused Rizelya. From the slant of the sunlight shining on the walls, she surmised it was late morning. Someone yelled, "Alpha Laynar! Alpha Laynar, come quick!" When Rizelya tried to sit up to find out what was happening, Kaelyn firmly pushed her back down.

"Oh, no you don't," Kaelyn told her. "If it's something important enough to disturb you, Laynar will tell you."

"At least let me sit up!" This time, Rizelya sat up on her own. Hangings still separated her cot from the others.

Several people ran out of the safe house. After a mumbled exchange, Laynar called out from outside, "Get to your horses! Be ready to leave in ten milcrons." A bench crashed, and the floorboards thundered as the fighters ran from the building.

Leistral threw open the curtains around Rizelya's sick bed. "There's a huge nest maturing by the minor keep we stopped at yesterday afternoon. They need our help. It's triple the size they usually see."

Rizelya tried to throw back her covers, but yelped with the pain the movement caused her shoulder and leg.

"You'll be staying right here," Kaelyn told her. "You're too weak to fight monsters."

"We're going with Laynar," Leistral said. "She's keeping Keandran here. She says it's so he can guard the people remaining here. But I think she doesn't trust him. I thought you should know. Gotta go." She patted Rizelya's uninjured arm and then hurried back out.

In less than the ten milcrons Laynar had given them, horses thundered out of the courtyard. Rizelya banged her head against her pillows in her frustration at being stuck in bed.

Kaelyn brought her a bowl of thin porridge. Rizelya's stomach grumbled, and she realized she hadn't eaten anything since the midday meal yesterday. After she ate, Kaelyn gave her another cup of medicine. Soon, her chin bobbed to her chest, and she jerked awake. The healer had laced the potion with sleeping herbs. It would be several octars before the fighters returned. Resigned to her fate, she laid down and closed her eyes.

Rizelya once again saw the pale, emaciated woman hooked up to the strange device. Rizelya tried to wake up. But the sleeping potion, and the call of the woman, was too strong. All she could do was watch.

The woman and device had become well-known from so many dreams that Rizelya now understood the archaic Posairian language the woman spoke.

"Yes, my sweets, run, kill!" the woman cried. She intently watched a mirror, only it didn't reflect her image.

Rizelya's eyebrows rose. This was new. She hadn't seen this in any of her other visions. The mirror showed the familiar landscape of Lairheim. She recognized the area near the minor keep she'd visited yesterday afternoon. A janack and brecha broke out of the nest before any of the other monsters were mature. Rizelya noted the direction they took. They disappeared over the rise just before Laynar and her fighters arrived.

"No!" yelled the woman. "Not yet, my lovelies aren't ready." Furious writhing came from the nest as the fighters scurried to it. The nest heaved, and a janack with five brechas burst out, racing for an opening. Warriors blocked them while Reds surrounded them with fire. The woman screamed curses at the Posairs. Another heave disgorged the remaining monsters, leaving only the control-janack in the nest.

The woman cackled with glee as a janack whipped a Red off her feet. A brecha leaped on her and raked its claws along her stomach, disemboweling her.

"Yes, yes, my pet, feed!" The woman's eyes closed in ecstasy. Thick, pus-colored smoke filled the tubes and raced down the funnel, where black beads formed and dropped into the bowl.

Rizelya dragged her attention away from the woman to watch the mirror.

The feeding brecha's head flew off and a helbraught thrust into its back. It slumped. The woman cried out in loss. Rizelya jerked back to see the smoke in the device thin.

"No! Damn you to Mordaga's seven hells!" the woman swore. Aistrun and Laynar's partner fought the control-janack. Rizelya assumed someone, maybe Laynar, was on it and making their way to its head. Bright light burst within the mirror as the control-janack exploded. The mirror's perspective shifted to looking up rather than down. Fuzzy waves filled it, and the woman held her head, screaming in pain.

Rizelya clapped her hands over her ears and screamed as the woman's agony echoed in her mind.

"What's wrong? What is it?" Kaelyn rushed to Rizelya's bed, sweeping back the curtains.

Rizelya fought to release the last of the dream's hold on her.

"Get me Keandran, now," she ordered. Rizelya struggled into a sitting position with her right arm in a sling. Grimacing with pain, she covered her face with her hands and rubbed the sleep—and the dream—from her eyes. By the time Keandran and the healer approached her bed, she'd regained her composure.

"You must go find Laynar, and tell her a janack and brecha escaped," she told Keandran. "They were heading east when I saw them."

"How do you know?" he sneered at her.

"I don't know how. Just go!" She pushed some alpha magic into the command. Keandran jerked back as if she'd hit him. *Maybe it was more than a bit.*

"Yes, Alpha," Keandran said stiffly, then turned around and ran out of the safe house.

His horse soon clattered out of the courtyard.

"How did you know?" Kaelyn asked.

"I had a dream," Rizelya whispered, a little embarrassed now her panic was wearing off. "Or was it a vision? Either way, we can't risk it was only a dream."

"What did you see?"

"I saw the nest and a group of monsters leave it before Laynar reached it. I watched the battle. A brecha killed a Red." Rizelya hesitated, then refrained from recounting the rest of the vision. She didn't want to frighten the healer with tales of strange people feeding off of death. It terrified Rizelya enough for the both of them. She hoped it was only a nightmare from the sleeping draft, and no one had been killed during the fight. They would find out when Laynar and the platoon returned.

Rizelya envied Kaelyn's ability to pace while they waited for the fighter's return. The octars dragged by, seemingly twice as long as normal. Finally, the sound of the gate booming open and horse's hooves clomping on the courtyard cobblestones rang through the silent house.

"We need the healer!" someone called.

Kaelyn rushed out to tend the injured. The others who had stayed to guard them hurried out with her. Rizelya, alone and unable to go help, fidgeted, cursing the pain in her leg that made it impossible to get out of bed. The suspense of not knowing what had happened was worse now that an answer was near. At last, Laynar entered the building.

From her downcast gaze and solemn expression, Rizelya guessed her vision had been true. "Did a fighter die?" Rizelya asked.

Laynar looked up, grief on her face. "Yes. How did you know?"

"I had a dream about the battle." She ducked her head, still embarrassed about it.

Laynar came to Rizelya's bedside and plopped down on the abandoned chair, as if her legs wouldn't hold her up any longer. "It was a horrendous battle. It's as if the monsters are learning how to fight us as quickly as we learn how to kill them. We have several fighters injured. The Red who died was from the minor keep." Laynar leaned over, her head in her hands, elbows resting on her knees. "It's a good thing we were there helping them. The woman Dehali taught yesterday, the older Yellow, panicked when the control-janack rose out of the nest."

Rizelya wrung her hands together. Her vision hadn't shown her the incident.

"I don't blame her. The damned things are huge," Laynar continued. "A teacher fighting monsters!" She shook her head. "Did you know that is what the Yellow did before we came along yesterday?"

"No, I didn't."

"Now she is a fighter." Sadness layered Laynar's voice. She swallowed, blinking back tears. "Once Dehali calmed her down, the woman cast a tight, damned-cold air shield. Her fear turned into rage when her friend was killed." Laynar paused, covering her face with her hands, then heaved a sigh. "Is that what we need? More mothers fighting for their children?"

"No, we don't," Rizelya disagreed. "Are any of my pack injured?"

Laynar shook her head. "They fought like the warriors they are, and no one even received a scratch. They are excellent fighters."

"We've had to be. We've fought more Malvers' monsters in the past half-lunadar than we usually fight in a season. Did Keandran reach you with my message?"

"Yes." Laynar gave a curt nod. "After he arrived, we searched and found tracks leading away from the nest in the direction you indicated. Aistrun took your pack and several of my fighters to chase them down. Laynal joined them." She leaned forward, resting her chin on her fists, and her eyes narrowed as she stared hard at Rizelya. "So, have you had many dreams like this one?"

"No, none like this," Rizelya lied with the truth. She hadn't dreamed about a battle before. "I'm unsure if it's linked with being able to hear the hum of the control-janack. I didn't hear it this time. I was too far away." She didn't want Laynar to look at her with less respect. Besides, the White Priestess hadn't detected any taint. If she could stop having these dreams, these visions, she would.

Her corner already created a makeshift infirmary, so when fighters carried in their injured comrades, they placed them on the empty cots around her. She hid her sigh of relief when the commotion made further discussion with Laynar impossible.

Laynar gazed at her for a long time, gauging Rizelya's response. More people came in, and Laynar's second called to her. She stood up, her hands on her hips. "You'll tell me if there is a problem, right?"

"Yes."

"Good." Laynar strode toward her second.

The room grew noisy as the fighters wandered inside, talking about the fight. It always took some time for them to calm down after a battle. Eventually, the common area quieted to the normal levels of conversation, and the soft murmurs lulled Rizelya to sleep.

Kaelyn lightly shook Rizelya awake. "Time for dinner. You should eat."

A commotion at the door drew everyone's attention. Rizelya sat up, without assistance, to see what was happening. Aistrun strode through the doorway with the rest of her pack behind him. Gore covered them, but otherwise, they appeared healthy.

"Thank you, Mother!" Rizelya prayed. She sent another silent prayer of gratitude—her sleep had been dreamless.

"I take it you were successful," Laynar called to Aistrun, as she approached the tired fighters standing just inside the door. She searched them intently, relaxing when Laynal stepped from behind Eidstrun.

"Yes, ma'am we were." Aistrun saluted her and grinned. "A fine merry chase, but we finally cornered them."

"They killed a few animals, but no people," Dehali added.

A collective sigh of relief filled the room at her news. One death today was enough.

"Hey, that smells wonderful!" Aistrun said. "I'm starving."

"You can smell dinner over this stink?" Eidstrun asked incredulously. "I can't. I'm off to wash monster goo off of me."

"You go, I'm eating." Aistrun waved at them and took a step forward.

"Oh, no you don't." Laynar blocked his way and pointed to the door. "You're not eating with us until you've washed."

"But I'm hungry," Aistrun whined.

"Wash, then eat," Laynar commanded.

When he hesitated, Rizelya called out, "Oh, for the love of the Mother, Aistrun, go get cleaned up. You're stinking up the place so no one else wants to eat."

Aistrun's shoulders drooped as he turned around, mumbling, "But I'm hungry." He and the rest of the filthy fighters headed to the bathhouse.

Rizelya tentatively moved her arm and leg. They were stiff and still hurt, but thankfully, they no longer burned.

Kaelyn put a hand on her forehead. "Your fever is down." She unwrapped the bandage on Rizelya's shoulder and calf.

"Hmm, the swelling has gone down and the wounds show no more sign of poison."

She changed the bandages on Rizelya's wounds, then stood up, patting Rizelya's uninjured arm. "You'll live. I'd prefer you to remain in bed another day, but I know you alpha types. You'll be up and moving without my say-so. I'll tell Laynar we can travel tomorrow."

Rizelya threw off her blankets.

"But, I did not say you could get out of bed tonight." Kaelyn pulled the covers back over her. "You stay put. I'll bring your dinner to you."

Rizelya nodded contritely at the healer's orders. As she watched the healer cross the room to Laynar, she chafed at the added delay. They would travel slowly tomorrow. She wasn't the only wounded in the group.

The man next to her moaned in his sleep. A large gash started at his left eyebrow and ended on his right collarbone, and a bandage covered his left eye. Kaelyn was worried he might lose his eye. Kaelyn stitched the cut closed because it was too deep to heal solely with magic. The skin around the injury was gray from the janack's toxins. The warrior hadn't had it cauterized to neutralize the poison. She didn't blame him. Cauterizing a face wound would scar badly and hurt like the Crone's fires. The fur of the men's warrior-form usually protected them from the acidic, toxic ichor of the monsters. But their facial fur wasn't as thick, and it hadn't prevented the poison from entering his system.

She'd overheard Kaelyn and Laynar talking, and they couldn't leave the wounded behind at the small keep. It didn't have a healer talented enough to treat the wounds.

Footsteps approached her cot. Rizelya looked up as her dinner arrived, delivered by Aistrun, now clean.

"Hey, you look much better," he commented as he handed her a bowl. He sat down next to her.

"And you smell much better." She peered at the thin broth in her dish and then at the mashed tubers and roasted rabbit on his plate. "Yours looks tastier than mine. Wanna trade?" A hunting party must have gone out while she napped.

Aistrun laughed. "I don't want to get you in trouble with Kaelyn." At her pout, he relented. "Here, one bite."

He told her about the fight and the chase. Then he regaled her with a funny tale. Soon, first Dehali, then Leistral and Eidstrun, wandered to the side of her bed. Rizelya looked up over their heads, searching for Keandran. He stood alone in the sea of people. She caught his eye and indicated with her head for him to come join them. He turned his back to her.

He's a lone wolf who just hasn't made the break from the pack! Sadness filled her with the realization. Lone wolves didn't survive long, and those that did often became rogues. The alphas immediately killed any rogues to protect the rest of the people from their depravity. Rizelya and her pack constantly held out the hand of friendship to Keandran, and he continued spurning them. Soon they wouldn't try, and he would become what he was: alone.

The healer woke Rizelya up with a light touch and a steaming mug of taevo. A bowl of porridge sat on the small table next to the bed. Other than the wounded, the room was empty.

"Everyone is out getting the horses ready," Kaelyn told her. "Eat." She stood with her hands on her hips. "I don't want you to do any lifting, including using your helbraught, for at least another two days," she said in a stern tone. "Nor are you to put any weight on your leg, or you might lose it. I'm unsure if I caught all the narhili poison."

"Okay," Rizelya said meekly, sufficiently scared. "How am I supposed to get around?"

"Someone will help you."

"Ugh." Rizelya rolled her eyes.

The healer turned away to ready the other patients for travel.

"No sense of dignity," Rizelya mumbled. She flushed with embarrassment when she remembered how yesterday Kaelyn, and then Aistrun, helped her hop to the necessary room. She would have to cope with being an invalid for a few more days. *I wish Kaieli were here. She'd pamper me while I convalesce.*

The noise of the fighting-pack preparing to leave reminded her there would be no lazing about today. She ate the porridge quickly.

When Kaelyn removed the bandage from her calf, a red line surrounded the edges of the bite. She tsked about it, wrapped it with clean bandages, and again warned Rizelya to stay off her leg.

Dehali came in to help Rizelya get dressed. She couldn't lift her arm over her head to slide on a tunic. Aistrun had left his bag, so they rummaged through it and found one of his formal shirts. Wooden toggles held the front closed. Her tight leather pants wouldn't go on over her bandaged leg, so she wore a split skirt with wide legs. By the time she finished dressing, with short boots on her feet and her hair braided, she panted with pain and exhaustion. Dehali hefted Aistrun and Rizelya's bags and carried them to the stables.

Rizelya's injured arm and leg burned fiercely. She wondered how she would survive riding when dressing had her groaning. She almost wished they had a wagon for the wounded to ride in, except it would be bumpy, and even more miserable.

Kaelyn glanced over and saw Rizelya ready to leave. "Here, I have something for you." She strode to Rizelya and handed her several capsules. "Pain killers."

"Hey, Little Red." Aistrun sauntered to where she sat. "Waiting for your handsome warrior?"

"Where? I don't see one?" She looked all around her and then back at him. "I guess I'll have to settle for you, Wolf."

He dramatically put his hand over his heart, swooning. "Oh, have mercy! You're breaking my heart." He picked her up and walked out of the safe house.

"Haven't we decided you don't have a heart to break?" she teased.

"No, we decided you don't. Mine has already been broken many times—" he bumped her forehead with his "—by you."

She expected to see Kymaya saddled and waiting for her. Instead, Eidstrun reached for her.

"Up you come," he said. The long saddle with a high cantle was different from a normal one. It appeared to fit two people on it. The rear rider sat further back, almost on the hindquarters of the horse. Its wide, low saddlebow would allow her to keep her leg raised. As she settled in front of Eidstrun, she noticed the other injured fighters rode double on similar saddles.

Once the healer mounted, Laynar signaled for them to depart.

"These are a good idea," she remarked, after they had ridden for a few milcrons. The strange saddle was more comfortable than she'd expected, at least for now. She'd reserve judgment until after being in it all day.

"It was my aunt's idea," Laynar rode up next to Eidstrun. "She was a healer and had to travel with injured fighters several times. She and our horse master came up with these saddles. They only fit the larger horses."

"Ah, that's why I'm riding with you." She patted Eidstrun's cheek. His gelding, Luchen, was almost as big as Tejen.

He blushed. "Yes, Alpha."

"We will stop at another keep today," Laynar informed her. "It's large enough we can leave our wounded who can't travel. It isn't far, but it will tax our injured to reach it. Even you, I suspect."

Rizelya and Eidstrun talked during the first octar of riding, but by the second octar, her leg throbbed with every step of the horse. The pain killers weren't helping much, and she gritted her teeth against the agony. In the third octar, the man with the gash passed out. Only through sheer willpower, Rizelya stayed conscious.

It took over four octars to reach the keep since they had to move so slowly because of the injured. Rizelya gaped in surprised as they approached the gates. She hadn't expected them to stop at a district keep, which was larger than a minor keep, but not quite as large as the Territory Keep. It housed five, or more, full fighting-packs with hundreds of support people.

At least today they would have more Yellow candidates to choose from. *No more mothers*, she prayed. A shooting pain up her leg made her gasp and grip the edge of the saddlebow. She wouldn't be training them. All she wanted to do for the next octar or two was lie down and sleep.

"I'll be so glad to get off this horse. My butt hurts," Eidstrun complained, fidgeting in the saddle. "Not that I mind riding with you, Alpha."

"Not to worry. My feelings exactly." The saddle made riding for her easier, but had been almost torture for Eidstrun. His legs couldn't hang straight down, but were held at an angle in front of him that didn't allow him to move easily with his horse. Thank goodness they hadn't trotted. Neither of them could have posted to ease the jerkiness of the gait.

Rizelya lifted her injured leg over the saddlebow and wiggled until she sat sideways, waiting for Aistrun to lift her down. While he stretched, returning feeling and movement back into his feet and legs, she watched Laynar rush to greet the keep alpha with joy. Laynal close behind her.

The alpha of this keep was young. Rizelya guessed her to be in her late thirties. As the three women talked, Rizelya could see the resemblance—a sister, she decided. It didn't surprise Rizelya both of Laynar's sisters were Reds. The Talents had a tendency to follow family lines. Since Reds often mated with other fighters, their children were usually fighters as well.

What astonished Rizelya was how the three treated each other like bond-mates. Close family ties, especially between fighters, were unusual. For most Posairs, pack bonds were much stronger than any family bonds, but even more so for fighters. They fostered their children in crèches, and no children lived with the fighting-packs. Raising children wasn't the sole responsibility of the parents, the community packs helped care for them.

"Hey, Little Red, you ready to get down?" Aistrun looked at her more closely. "Maybe I should call you Little White instead. You're so pale. Let's find you a bed to rest in." He gently lowered her off the saddle and let her stand for a moment before lifting her into his arms and carrying her to the Keep House's porch.

"Hey, Laynar, where can I put her?"

"Oh, you have injured, and here I am flapping my jaw with my sisters," the alpha apologized, smiling. Joy lit her face, and laugh lines crinkled around her eyes.

"Rizelya, Aistrun, this is my sister, Laynad," Laynar said, introducing them.

"Welcome to Strunhamde Keep. It isn't much, but we call it home." Laynad swung an arm, encompassing the keep. The other injured being helped off of horses caught her attention.

Her eyes narrowed, and her voice was suddenly serious. "You have had problems, sister. You will tell me."

"It's why we're here," Laynar answered, the smile dropping from her face. "Let's go in where Rizelya can relax, and we'll tell you what there is to tell."

Laynad nodded once, grabbed Laynal's hand, and turned around, leading them into the Keep House. She took the small party to her office. Aistrun settled Rizelya on the couch where she could recline. Laynad moved her chair from behind the large desk, placed it near the couch, and indicated Aistrun and Laynar to situate their chairs the same way. Laynal, obviously comfortable in this Keep, exited and came back with another chair for herself. Since Laynad's alpha partner didn't join them, Rizelya assumed he was busy organizing their fighting force.

A young woman brought in a tray of drinks and snacks. Rizelya gratefully took the glass of chilled juice from her but declined the pastry.

"So what happened? How did you get injured?" Laynad asked as soon as Laynal shut the door behind the server.

"Me?" Rizelya pointed to herself. "I was attacked by narhili. I'll be fine." At least she hoped so. Her leg throbbed, and it felt swollen from the ride.

"Grandmother sent us," Laynar said.

"Hey, Histrun sent us," Aistrun clarified. "Rizelya and I are traveling through our province. At first, it was simply to find out if you were having problems with a strange janack."

Laynad's head rose sharply, like a predator catching the scent of prey. "What do you know of it?"

"We call it a control-janack," Rizelya said, "because it seems to control the other monsters."

"Yes, we have noticed this. And that it is damned hard to kill." Grief pulled her naturally cheerful face into a grimace. "We have lost many trying to kill it."

"It's why we're here, sister." Laynar put a hand on Laynad's knee. "They have taught us how to protect our people while a Red kills the control-janack."

"Then why do you have injured?" Laynad demanded.

"Because the nest was huge!" Laynal threw her arms wide over her head.

"And how would you know?" Laynad scowled at her youngest sister.

"I was there," Laynal said proudly. "Grandmother finally allowed me to fight, Laynad. I'm very good at creating the new shields." Her voice was smug with pride. Then her eyes flashed in annoyance. "If we weren't trying to train the other Yellow, I would have had the shield up faster and no one would have been hurt."

"What other Yellow? What shield?" Laynad looked around the group, confused.

"Let's start at the beginning," Rizelya said and then looked at Aistrun. He had a knack for storytelling. Besides, her pain was getting worse rather than lessening. Her shoulder and arm ached, but nothing like the squirming agony in her leg.

Aistrun caught her cue and wove the tale about their journey. Rizelya's eyelids drooped while she watched him enthrall his audience. Even Laynar had only heard bits and pieces of their story. Fighting to keep her eyes open, Rizelya admired how he knew where to add flourishes and where to edit. She relaxed on the couch, letting Aistrun's voice wash over her. A smile tugged at the corners of her mouth as Aistrun made much of him carrying her off the battlefield.

Rizelya jolted awake when Aistrun put his hand on her head. She'd dozed off while he talked.

"And so, are there any Yellows here who would make good fighters?" Aistrun asked, concluding his story.

Laynad sat a little stunned for a few moments. "Well," she said at last, "I would like to see these shields of yours."

"Oh, they're so beautiful," Laynal breathed, then added, "and effective."

"Let's go see these marvels." Laynad stood up, and the others followed. Except for Rizelya.

"First, Alpha, Rizelya needs to be taken to the healer," Aistrun said, gently stroking her hair. "She really isn't doing well. Where can I take her?"

"Laynal, you know the way. Show him to the infirmary and then bring him to the practice arena." She turned to the door. "Come, Laynar, let us gather the players of this game." Without looking back, they strode out of the office.

Aistrun lifted Rizelya off the couch. She moaned in pain as he jiggled her leg. The infirmary was in the rear of the Keep House. Kaelyn moved around in it, attending to the other injured fighters. She rushed to Rizelya when she saw them enter the room.

"So what hurts?" Kaelyn asked.

"My leg. I swear I haven't been on it at all!"

The healer directed Aistrun to an empty bed, away from the others. Rizelya gasped in pain when he lowered her onto it, but she refused to lie down. She wanted to see what was wrong. Kaelyn lifted Rizelya's skirt to reveal her red and swollen calf. Dark lines ran down to her ankle and up her thigh.

"This is not good," Kaelyn said, calling another healer to her side. Brachen was a Brown, rather than a Green like Kaelyn. They carefully cut away the bandage and pulled it off. The awful smell of putrid flesh made Aistrun gag.

"If you cannot behave, warrior, you must leave." Brachen frowned at him.

"Go," Rizelya told him. "You need to help the others with the demonstration." When he hesitated, she added, "Go on, I'll be fine." He looked at her and the nasty wound and then back at the healers. She knew he didn't want to leave her alone with strangers, but these were healers. They'd take care of her. She made a dismissive gesture at him and laid down, closing her eyes. He patted her uninjured leg before leaving the room.

She sat up and glared at the healers. "Now, what's wrong with my leg? And don't sugarcoat it."

"There is some narhili poison still in the wound, and it's spreading," Brachen told her. "We will need to purge it from you."

Kaelyn handed a cup to Rizelya, tension in her face. "It's a sleeping potion and a painkiller. The cleansing won't be gentle."

Rizelya took the cup and gulped down the contents. Kaelyn put a cool hand on Rizelya's forehead, and her green energy flowed into Rizelya, relaxing her, making her eyes droop and close.

In the fog surrounding her, she felt the first probing of the Brown's power into the wound. In her daze, it didn't seem too bad. And then the energy probed deeper. Even with the painkiller and Kaelyn's energy wrapped around her, Rizelya screamed. And kept screaming, until at last the torture stopped, and she fell into an exhausted sleep.

Rizelya opened her eyes. Sunset streaked across the sky in brilliant purples and oranges. Her mouth was dry and foul tasting from the residue of the healer's potion. The earlier intense pain no longer gripped her. She hoped it meant Brachen had purged the poison from her leg and saved it.

She tentatively moved her injured shoulder and arm. The slight movement didn't hurt too badly, only twinges, so she raised it so she could see the wound better. The healer had removed the bandages, and there wasn't any swelling or redness around the cut. Soon it would be another scar among many. She wore a sick robe rather than her own clothing.

As she lowered her arm, she noticed her toes and relief flooded her as she looked down at her leg propped up on pillows. A tear slid down her cheek. They hadn't had to remove her leg or foot because of the poison, at least not yet. After several milcrons of silent crying, she wiped her eyes and sat up. She took a deep breath to settle the dread in her stomach and lifted the sheet so she could fully see her leg.

The dark lines on her thigh were gone, but the lines on her ankle and foot had only faded to a light gray. She worried it meant some of the narhili poison still lingered. A large bandage on her calf prevented her from examining the wound. Rizelya fingered the bandage, debating on whether she dared take it off herself. She decided she didn't want to chance making it worse. She'd have to wait for the healers to come by to satisfy her curiosity.

Rizelya grimaced at the awful taste in her mouth. She found a glass of water sitting on the bedside table. The cool water soothed her parched throat. Not having anything better to do, she laid back down and soon dozed off. A clatter startled her awake. Glancing at the window, she sat up and realized she hadn't napped long. A young woman, in healer green, pushed a cart in front of her, laden with dishes. Rizelya's stomach rumbled when she smelled the aroma of food.

The girl approached her, smiling. "Oh good, you're awake. Brachen said you could eat if you were awake." She reached under the bed and pulled out a tray, unfolded the legs, and set it over Rizelya's lap. "How hungry are you?"

"I'm starving," Rizelya answered. Her stomach growled loudly. "I haven't eaten since breakfast, that is, if it's still the same day as we arrived."

"It is." The girl laughed and turned to her cart. Humming, she picked up a bowl and added something to it from several small bowls on a lower shelf of the cart. Stirring it, she set it down on Rizelya's tray. She put a slice of bread and a cup of juice on the tray to accompany the soup.

"Are you able to feed yourself, or do you need help?" the girl asked.

"I can do it myself, thanks." She picked up the spoon and dug into her meal. A soft white grain thickened the broth. The girl had added a few cooked vegetables and bits of meat to make it heartier. Rizelya dipped the bread into the soup and savored the rich flavor. She felt better with a full tummy—better able to handle whatever the healers told her.

The same girl came by and took her dirty dishes, replacing them with a bowl of hot water and clean cloths for Rizelya to wash her face and hands. Soon the Brown healer from the day before hurried to her bed. She had the air of authority of a head healer. When Rizelya realized the head healer had worked on her, she swallowed. Her leg must have been bad.

"Let me check you first, and then we'll get you to the necessary room." Brachen pulled back the sheet from Rizelya's leg. Mumbling to herself, she poked and prodded Rizelya's thigh, moving down to her calf, which was tender and sore. And so were her ankle and foot.

"Better, much better. You'll heal," Brachen told her. She handed Rizelya a cane, and when she was standing, propped her up on the side of her injured leg. Rizelya gratefully laid against the pillows after the exhausting hop to the necessary room and back.

"How long before I can travel again?" she asked the healer. "I have to get to Strunven Keep soon."

"It would be better if you stayed in bed for several more days."

"Days! The first of Sandar is in thirteen days."

"But, I know you fighters, unable to sit still for long," Brachen continued, as if Rizelya hadn't interrupted her. "If there aren't any streaks on your ankle and foot in the morning, you'll be out of danger and can leave."

"Oh thank you!"

"I said, *if.* You'll be able to ride *if* you take it easy. You will not—I repeat not—fight for another four days. It would be better if you didn't for at least a chedan." The healer looked around the infirmary and the many patients it contained. "But I've heard of these new control-janacks. I've seen the devastation they, and the increase in the nest's size, have caused. It will be a miracle if you are able to refrain from fighting for four days, let alone a chedan."

"It's why I have to get to Strunven Keep, to teach them how to fight the new control-janacks," Rizelya said. "Otherwise, I would consider staying longer in your care. My heart-sister is a healer. I know how much you worry about your patients, even those who don't listen well."

Brachen laughed. "Especially those. I will help you as much as I can."

She stood over Rizelya. Golden light streamed from the healer's hands and into Rizelya. It tingled where it touched. Soon, the tingling sensation penetrated the inside of her leg, ankle, and foot. Her skin glowed with the same golden-brown light. Brachen continued to work on her for almost half an octar. As Rizelya watched, some of the gray streaks faded away to nothing. A stubborn few remained when Brachen finally took a deep breath and let the light go.

"That is all I can do for now. I hope it is enough."

"So do I," Rizelya replied fervently.

"You can help by going to sleep and letting the healing energy continue to work."

Rizelya obediently laid back down. Brachen covered her with the blankets and touched Rizelya's forehead, murmuring, "Sleep, brave one. Sleep."

Rizelya obeyed the command.

Chapter 11

Aistrun plopped down on Rizelya's bed, making it bounce. "Hey, are you going to go with us?"

Keeping her eyes closed, Rizelya grumbled, "I can think of better ways to wake up." Even with all his jiggling, her leg didn't hurt. She sat up quickly and threw off the covers. A few gray streaks remained on her foot. Hopefully, she had healed enough for Brachen to allow her to leave.

"I believe so," she said happily. Her leg was stiff and a bit sore. It wouldn't hold her weight yet, so Aistrun helped her to the necessary room and back. This time she wasn't panting as badly from the excursion. Brachen arrived soon after she resettled on the bed.

"Let's take a look at it, shall we?" Brachen examined Rizelya's leg. "Hmm, better. These should fade today," Brachen said as she lightly traced the few remaining gray streaks. She carefully cut away the bandage. This time, there wasn't the stink of rotting flesh. Brachen scrutinized the wound and stitches, applied an ointment, and then put a lighter dressing on it.

"Well, can I go?" Rizelya asked impatiently.

The healer gave a reluctant nod. "Remember what I said about fighting. And try to stay off it as much as possible."

"Thank you," Rizelya told her with feeling. "Without you, I might have lost my leg."

Brachen smiled and patted Rizelya's arm. "All in a day's work, my dear." She crossed the infirmary to check on her other patients.

Rizelya sent Aistrun to get her clothes. A few milcrons later, Leistral walked into the room with Rizelya's pack slung over her shoulder.

"The others are still eating breakfast," Leistral said, "and saddling horses. Laynad's going to be riding with us for a while today. She seems to be good people, takes this whole mess with the monsters seriously. She made us stay in the practice arena until everyone she sent to learn the shields could do them with their eyes closed. I'm sure I can do the fire shield in my sleep now. I had to do it so many times yesterday."

Leistral helped Rizelya to a small washroom, where she assisted Rizelya in scrubbing down. Leistral talked all the while, telling Rizelya about the training and the people they trained. Rizelya hadn't realized what a chatterbox Leistral was. With shame, Rizelya admitted she spent more time with Dehali and hadn't gotten to know Leistral very well. That lack was being solved now. Riding with Eidstrun yesterday had allowed her to become better friends with him. The only one in their little troupe she didn't know was Keandran. She wasn't sure she wanted to know him much more than she already did.

Rizelya wore her split skirt again. Her leg was still too sore to pull her tight fighting leathers over her wound. With her hair clean and braided, Rizelya felt better than she had since the narhili attack.

She and Leistral made their way to the dining hall. Most of the keep would have eaten by now, but the kitchen staff usually kept a pot of porridge warm for late diners. "Laynad is going to teach the small keep holders in this area the new technique." Leistral informed her as they walked. "So we don't have to. She changed our route so we won't be stopping at any other keeps until we cross into Strunven Territory. She also knows of a hunter's trail, which will take us to Strunven Keep faster."

"Is it safe?" Some of the trails the hunters used passed precariously close to the swamps.

"She thinks it is." Leistral helped her to a table and then left to go fetch them some food. She came back with a hearty breakfast of eggs, sausage, and toast.

When they finished eating, Leistral assisted Rizelya to hobble outside. When they reached the porch, Rizelya was panting with the exertion. Aistrun saw them and strode up the stairs two at a time. She wasn't sure which would be worse on her self-esteem: hopping down the stairs or having Aistrun carry her.

"Hey, Little Red, time to go." Without asking her, he picked her up, taking the decision away from her. Leistral skipped down the steps behind them and hurried to her own horse. Aistrun put Rizelya down in front of Kymaya.

Rizelya rubbed her horse's nose, murmuring softly to her. Then she noticed the scab on Kymaya's cheek. "She was hurt by the narhili?" she asked in horror. Until then, she hadn't worried that the beasts had injured Kymaya during the attack.

"Only minor scratches," Aistrun assured her. "Leistral took good care of her, and a healer tended to the few wounds that were too deep for general cleaning."

Rizelya looked for Leistral to thank her, but noticed Laynad was on her horse, slapping her thigh with her riding crop impatiently. Rizelya and Aistrun were the only ones still not mounted on their horses.

Kymaya stood next to a mounting block. Rizelya scowled at it, not wanting to admit she needed help to mount her horse. Aistrun snickered as she leaned heavily on him to climb onto the mounting block. He continued smirking at her while he steadied her as she leaned against Kymaya's side, threw her right leg over the saddle, and struggled to a sitting position. It wasn't the most graceful mount she'd ever done, but at least she was on her own horse and not riding double in the awful invalid saddle.

Laynad led them out of the keep at a fast walk. Rizelya had been in so much pain when they arrived the day before, she hadn't paid attention to the area surrounding the keep. They rode through a wide, long valley with the Borleano river winding through it. The road followed the river's path and was spacious enough for two wagons to pass each other.

On their side of the river, large fields, separated and enclosed by the ever-present sheadash stone, were lush with spring growth. On the river's other side, orchards of various fruit and nut trees marched far into the horizon.

"Our valley is fertile and abundant," Laynad said to Rizelya and Aistrun. "We grow enough food to feed most of Strunlair Province. Our prosperity seems to attract the monsters. We have more than our fair share of nests. I suspect we'll be trying your new technique soon."

"I hope it isn't today," Rizelya replied. "Brachen told me I couldn't fight for four days." Fear flashed through her. How would she keep the intelligence behind the control-janack at bay if she didn't have the distraction of fighting? It—she—had certainly been able to enter Rizelya's mind during the last battle when she wasn't even near the control-janack.

"We have enough fighters. You won't need to fight," Laynad assured her. "If we come across a nest, your skill with the fire shield would be welcome in protecting the horses."

"I can do that," Rizelya agreed. It wouldn't tax her strength too much or jar her injured leg. And it would give her something useful to do while the others risked their lives fighting the monsters. Laynad nodded and urged her horse forward.

The exercise soon loosened up Rizelya's tight muscles. It pleased her when her wounded calf stopped aching after the first half octar of riding. An octar after leaving the Keep, they continued riding through the fields. *How much more abundant this lush valley would be if the monsters weren't continually threatening it?*

Wherever people lived—or had once lived—the Malvers' monsters had a nest, but even so, people were still living, still surviving, as the verdant valley attested. Generations had fought the Malvers' monsters, and as fearsome and devastating as they were, the Posairs had prevailed. Rizelya's parents and their team had faced extreme danger and took risks in an effort to control the monsters. Because of them, the fighters had kept the monsters to their nests for the past thirty years. Tears pricked her eyes, and for the first time, she was proud of the accomplishments of her parents. She looked around at the fighters riding with her, at her own squad-pack. They continued the long tradition of keeping the Posairs safe. Because of her visions, she believed someone had created the monsters to destroy her people. They hadn't succeeded. And they wouldn't with this new mode of attack. Her people were fighters and survivors.

Laynad fell back to ride next to Rizelya again. "Can you handle a trot? We need to pick up the pace if we're to cross the river before midday."

Rizelya flexed her leg and then stood up in her stirrups. There was a twinge of aching muscles, nothing more. She nodded to Laynad. "Yes, but not for long, though. We'll take the rear position and follow you."

"I'll send young Laynal to ride with you, then. She knows the way to the river crossing." Laynad rode back up to the front. A few moments later, Laynal rode her horse along the line and joined Rizelya's group. As soon as she did, Laynad signaled to pick up speed, and the troupe kicked their horses into a fast trot.

Rizelya handled posting the trot for several measures, then her leg gave out, and she slowed Kymaya down to a fast walk. Her squad-pack kept pace with her. When she'd rested enough, she picked back up into a trot. They continued this pattern for the next octar. The main force pulled ahead of them and disappeared, but Rizelya wasn't too worried. The road only went one direction. They wouldn't get lost.

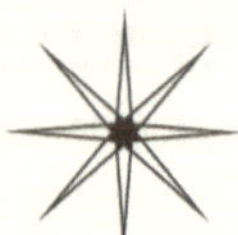

Rizelya slowed her group to a walk. They'd passed the fields, and the road wound through a field of wildflowers. Rizelya kicked out of her stirrups and stretched her legs. She dropped her reins over the pommel and raised her arms. Her right shoulder was stiff, but with slow movements, she lifted it above her head. Breathing deeply, she inhaled the fresh spring air. Then she sat back on Kymaya, bringing her to a halt.

"Do you smell that?" she asked quietly. Although if it was what she thought it was, sound wouldn't lead them to her group, but odor and heat.

Aistrun took a deep breath, his mouth slightly open to get a better flavor of the air. He growled.

Eidstrun swore. "Holy Mother, how did they get here?"

"Monsters?" Rizelya huffed. "So much for me not fighting for several days."

Eidstrun nodded and inhaled again, turning in his saddle, sampling the surrounding air. His sense of smell was one of the sharpest Rizelya knew, even in his human form. He held up two fingers. "Two brechas." He closed his eyes, then held up another finger. "And a janack. That way." He pointed to the left of them, away from the river.

Although the monster nests formed near swamps, they didn't like the fast moving water of rivers. They drowned in them.

Rizelya couldn't hear any humming, so this wasn't a control-janack.

"There's a nest a few measures in that direction," Laynal told them, her eyes wide in fear. It was one thing to battle the monsters with a full fighting-pack, and another to fight them with a group as small as theirs. And Laynal was a new fighter. There were only seven of them, six really, since Rizelya couldn't fight. "Laynad had someone check it yesterday afternoon, and it was empty."

"Well, there's something headed our way now," Rizelya said, a bit sharply to pull Laynal from her fear. "Laynal, you and Leistral will form the fire-rings around the monsters. Don't allow them to get to the road. There are people in the fields. Dehali, you and Aistrun take down the janack. Eidstrun, you fight with Laynal." She put her most fearsome fighter with her least experienced. She glanced at Keandran. If he turned wacky on her again, she wouldn't risk Laynal. Leistral could protect herself.

Laynal moved next to Eidstrun. Dehali and Aistrun looked at each other and grinned.

"That means Keandran, you're with me." Leistral glared at him. "You better stay focused."

Rizelya looked closely at Keandran. He seemed eager to fight. "You aren't going to go crazy on me now, are you?"

"No, Alpha, I'll be good. Let me at those buggers," he answered with a snarl. He was close to shifting.

"Give me your horses." Rizelya held out her hands. "I'll guard them." They dismounted and handed her their horses' reins.

The women pulled out their helbraughts, and the men moved off to shift into their warrior forms. Rizelya crossed the road toward the edge of the river. A crow cawed, and she turned around to face the wooded area. A tentacle reached up and snatched the crow out of the air, its caw breaking off into a squawk.

"Hurry, they're here!" she yelled to her team. She kicked Kymaya into a trot to reach the river's edge. The river was deep and wide, and she wasn't sure if the horses could swim across it if they had to escape the monsters. She had to trust her pack to kill them. She stayed mounted on Kymaya, uncertain if she could get off—or back on—without help.

Leistral and Laynal prepared to form the fire-ring. Rizelya grabbed her helbraught, lowered the tip to the ground, and chanted the spell to create her own fire shield. It flared up around her and the horses as the monsters broke through the overgrowth.

Leistral's fire bloomed, blocking the beasts from the road. Laynal's came to life a few moments later, keeping them from returning the way they had come. A fire shield blazed up into a dome over the fighters and monsters. Laynal, it seemed, had turned her fear into excitement. They didn't need a fire shield with a regular janack. It would, however, keep Keandran from leaving. When Rizelya realized this, she wondered if it hadn't been Leistral who had created the fire shield instead of Laynal.

All the horses Rizelya held were plains-bred, and they stood intently, watching the action. Their eyes were a bit wild with the monsters so close, but they weren't pulling against the reins trying to run away. Rizelya itched to be part of the fight rather than sitting with the horses. She hadn't sat and watched since she was thirteen and had joined a fighting-pack.

Dehali swung her helbraught at one of the janack's tentacles. It flew through the air and Rizelya expected to hear it thud to the ground, but she must be too far away. As she continued to watch, she realized she didn't hear any sounds: no thuds or smacks, no yelps or grunts, no war cries or howls. The eeriness of the quiet fight made her shiver. The shield also distorted her view, but she could see how well her pack fought, even Keandran.

Soon, Eidstrun and Laynal took down their brecha. Laynal jumped on the dead brecha and hacked it to pieces with the blade of her helbraught in her exuberant fury. Ichor flew in every direction, and Rizelya shook her head. Laynal would receive her first acid burns.

Eidstrun raced to help Aistrun and Dehali attack the janack. A tentacle sailed across the glade, sizzling when it hit the fire shield. Another one dropped to the ground, wiggling futilely for a few moments before it stopped. Dehali fought on one side of the janack and Laynal slipped to the opposite side. They timed their strike to coincide with the two warriors slicing through another set of tentacles. The women's glowing helbraught blades slid into its body. The maw snapped once at them before the janack shuddered and died.

Rizelya turned away from the fight at the sound of pounding hoofs. Laynad and Laynar galloped down the road, a fighting force thundering behind them. Rizelya smiled and waved at them and then returned her attention to the skirmish. Leistral and Keandran stood over their dead brecha.

Laynad's horse slid to such a short stop in front of Rizelya that its rump grazed the ground. "What for the love of the Mother happened?" Laynad cried, scrambling off her horse. "Is anyone hurt?"

"We'll find out in a few milcrons, but I doubt it, at least not seriously. Laynal was a bit..." She paused, remembering the fury at which Laynar hacked at the brecha. "Ah... unrestrained and will have some acid burns from brecha ichor. They came from over there." Rizelya pointed to the swath of broken limbs and dying plants.

"But we checked that nest yesterday." Laynad's brow furrowed in confusion. "There weren't even larvae in it."

"Perhaps they came from a different one," Rizelya offered. She didn't know this area or the location of the nests. "Or a new one?" New nests were very infrequent. They only happened where people had committed a malicious or evil act.

"No, no, nothing like that has occurred here," Laynad said, appalled. "We have good people."

Leistral released the fire shield and ring. Laynad and Laynar rushed to their sister, checking for wounds. Laynar, shaking her head, pulled her helstrablade from the sheath at her side and fed fire into it. Rizelya smiled at Laynal's shrieks as the blade cauterized the places where ichor had splashed on her skin. She would be more careful next time. Rizelya fingered a particularly nasty scar under her jaw. She'd learned her own lesson in much the same way.

Leistral and Dehali burned the monster carcasses. Rizelya stared at the path the monsters had carved. *If the nest was empty yesterday, even of larvae, then where did these beasts come from?*

"Do you have any good trackers?" Rizelya asked Laynad. "We need to find out where these came from." She indicated Eidstrun. "He is very good."

"Yes, I have one with me." Laynad called over a young man, not much older than Laynal. He was small for most warriors, with light green eyes and reddish-brown hair. "This is Ledelstrun. He'll go with your tracker."

Eidstrun shifted to his wolf form, and Ledelstrun followed a moment later. They dropped their noses to the ground and took off in the direction of the damaged plants.

"It may be a while before they find anything," Rizelya said. "Should we stay here?"

"Yes. If they discover something, we'll be able to take care of it with the fighters I brought. The others will wait for us at the river crossing."

"Good. I'm tired. I'd like to get out of this saddle."

The men's hearing was extremely sharp, especially in their wolf or warrior forms. Aistrun standing across the road lifted his head and canted it in a listening posture, then loped toward them, still in his warrior form. Putrid green droplets of ichor studded his fur and dripped from his claws. He'd been in the line of fire when Laynal's hacking of her brecha had tossed ichor in every direction. "Need help?" he asked.

"Not until you're clean! You have ichor all over you."

"Huh?" He looked down at himself, grinned, and reached his arms out for her.

"No! I'm not getting burned." She backed Kymaya away from him. "I think I can get down on my own."

"No, wait." Aistrun loped down the slope to the river and waded in. He splashed water over himself, sluicing off the ichor and other monster gore. Soaking wet, he jogged back up the hill and straight toward Rizelya.

He had a gleam in his eye she didn't like. "Oh, no you don't!" she yelled and tried to move Kymaya away from him. He rushed at her and then shook. Cold water sprayed all over her. Wiping water from her eyes, she sputtered and cursed.

"No fun," he said, turning away from her, head bent. He trudged behind a tree to shift back to human.

When he returned, his clothes were soaking wet from his dip in the river. Not looking contrite at all, he strode toward Rizelya. A quick grin was all the warning she received. He reached up and grabbed her, pulling her off Kymaya, then hugged her close, getting her as wet as possible. "There! You're good now. Damn, that's cold."

He released her, and once satisfied she stood on her own, walked to Jezhan and rummaged through his packs. With dry clothes in his hands, he returned to the shelter of the tree to put them on.

Rizelya's clothes were only damp. With a rueful sigh, she limped to her own bags to pull out a jacket. Had she felt better and their situation wasn't quite so dire, she would have indulged Aistrun in a water fight. And pulled in the rest of her squad-pack in the process. She agreed with Aistrun that being an alpha wasn't much fun.

Kressy, their multa, had traveled with their group rather than with the other multas. Rizelya hobbled over to Kressy, using her helbraught as a walking stick to support her. From the packs, Rizelya pulled out a couple of ground cloths and blankets.

"Good idea," Laynar said, as she joined Rizelya. "Here, I'll grab these for you." Laynar took the ground cloths from Rizelya and spread them on the grass under the sweeping canopy of a large tree.

Rizelya limped to the ground cover, carrying a blanket. She folded the blanket into a tight, high square, then sat down and propped her leg on it. During the fight, her injury had started to ache again. She carefully lifted her skirt, relieved to see there weren't any poison lines running up her thigh. Gingerly, she took off her boot to examine her calf, foot, and ankle.

"Your leg looks better," Laynar noted, sitting down next to Rizelya.

"It is. There are even fewer gray lines than there were this morning."

"Hey, I saw you limping," Aistrun said with a grin. "That's better than the hopping you've been doing. You must be healing." He laid down on the blanket and threw an arm over his eyes. "Good idea. I need a rest if we have to fight anymore monsters."

Leistral and Dehali, with the help of Laynal, had burned all the monster bits. They trudged over to where Rizelya, Laynar, and Aistrun waited.

"I'm going to wash this mess off me," Leistral said, throwing a glare at Laynal. Apparently, no one in the circle of the battle had escaped the flying ichor. The leathers the fighting women wore protected them from the acidic ichor in most cases. The green splotches of ichor stood out in contrast to Leistral's bright red leather shirt and pants.

"Any of those serious?" Rizelya could see a few dots where ichor had landed on Leistral's cheek. Dehali had been farther away in the circle and had her back to Laynal, so ichor hadn't splattered her face.

"Naw, Dehali cauterized them for me. None are deep enough to need a healer."

Laynad strode up to Laynal and turned her face from side to side to get a better look at the wounds. Most Reds had small scars on their faces from spattered ichor, one of the minor hazards of fighting the monsters. "You'll learn not to do that again, won't you?"

Laynal nodded and grimaced in pain. A large blotch of ichor had landed on her collarbone. It was big enough to leave a nasty scar. Laynad pulled the neck of Laynal's shirt down to reveal a deep furrow on Laynal's shoulder. It still oozed blood, and the surrounding flesh was turning gray.

"That needs a healer. It's poisoned." Laynad turned around and yelled for someone. An older fighter jogged over to them. He was solidly built, fit and muscular, as most fighters were.

"Take Laynal to the healer, quickly." He nodded and looked at Laynal. She hesitated and opened her mouth to argue, but stopped when she saw Laynad's narrowed eyes. "Move," Laynad commanded. Laynal jerked slightly as the force of the command hit her. She bowed her head in submission and followed the warrior to her horse.

"She's a good kid and will be an excellent fighter," Laynad said, watching Laynal and her escort gallop down the road and out of sight.

Leistral and Dehali, in clean leathers, dropped down next to Aistrun. Using him as a pillow, they stretched out to nap. Rizelya looked around. Someone was missing.

"Where's Keandran?" As she surveyed the area, he loped toward them from upriver. His hair was still damp from his dunking to wash up. "Ah, there you are." She patted the blanket. "Come join us while we wait."

He shook his head and found another tree to rest under. Alone again.

Rizelya awoke from her doze when Eidstrun and Ledelstrun returned. Ledelstrun shifted back to human while Eidstrun hurried to the river and drank deeply before wading in to clean the monster ichor off his fur.

"We followed the monster's trail back to the nest site," Ledelstrun said. "Then we searched all around to make sure the monsters came from it. They did. I don't know how, because I was in the scouting party who checked the nest yesterday. There weren't any larvae in it."

"It's filled with larvae now," Eidstrun said as he joined the group, wiping water from his face. "Beginning stage. The monsters escaped yesterday morning."

"What?" Laynad exclaimed. "Our people didn't see any signs of monsters in it."

"They left before your people arrived and traveled north. A herd of billocks was in that direction. I suspect they destroyed it. They looped around, returned to the nest for the night, then came out when the sun warmed them."

Ledelstrun stared at Eidstrun with his mouth open in shock. "How did you pick up all of that? I didn't sense any of it."

Eidstrun shrugged.

"I told you he was a very good tracker." Rizelya looked smugly at Laynad.

"I have never heard of a nest producing a single janack and two brechas, or for them to hunt and return to their nest. Are you sure?" Laynad asked.

"I'm sure." Eidstrun didn't sound upset at her questioning his abilities. "I haven't either, but that's what my nose told me happened, and I saw the dry slime on the path the janack took. I'm unclear how your people missed it."

Laynad turned to look sharply at Ledelstrun. "How did you?" she demanded.

"We just checked the nest," he said nervously.

"How close to it did you get?"

"They weren't very close," Eidstrun said with a sneer before Ledelstrun could answer. "They stopped at the top of the hill overlooking it. Under most circumstances, it would've been sufficient. Not this time. Had they gone closer to the nest, they would have seen the slime trail."

"In their defense, Alpha," Laynar said, "the monsters aren't adhering to any normal patterns anymore."

"True," Laynad agreed, still glaring in anger at Ledelstrun. "Runner!" she yelled.

A young man hurried over from the group of fighters Laynad had brought with her. She quickly wrote a message and handed it to him.

"Deliver this to my second," she commanded. To the others, she said, "The keep needs to be warned about this. They will have to take care of this nest. We don't have time. Enough lallygagging, let's get moving. We have a long day ahead of us."

After the rouge monster incident, Laynad took no pity on Rizelya and her injuries. An intense urgency drove Laynad as she pushed the horses, and their riders, to the edge of their limits. Rizelya didn't blame her. She gritted her teeth against any discomfort and rode on. Eventually, her leg became so numb, she couldn't feel if there was any pain or not.

Two octars after crossing the river, Laynad led them off the main road onto a smaller one, rutted from passing wagons and thick with spring grass. The riders spread alongside it where the passage was easier. A stone fence marched along a few feet away, protecting it from monsters. The road cut through the orchards Rizelya had admired earlier.

Overhead, blossoms covered the trees, scenting the air with their sweet fragrance. They passed apple, pear, peach, plum, and other fruit trees. The pounding of the horses' hooves caused a white and pink rain of petals. The fruit trees gave way to nut trees, and after fifteen measures, the orchards gave way to a forest of oak, elm, and birch.

Laynad allowed the group to pause in a sheltered glade with a small brook running through it. Throughout the day, Rizelya found it easier to mount and dismount her horse. She still limped, and wouldn't run any races soon, but she was healing from the narhili poison. After getting a drink from the icy stream, Rizelya let Kymaya slake her thirst.

Rizelya's body ached from the fast and brutal ride. She looked longingly at the cold water, wishing she had time to take off her boots and soak her feet. But Laynad only paused long enough for Rizelya to quickly eat a travel bar before Laynad called the order to remount.

The afternoon slipped away as they traveled through the trees, now a forest instead of cultivated orchards. Rizelya's eyes darted from side to side, searching the shadows, praying they wouldn't run into another band of narhili beasts.

The twilight deepened into night by the time they arrived at the safe house. Rizelya stayed mounted, waiting her turn to get into the small stable. So many people in their group would crowd the small safe, but Rizelya didn't mind. She'd much rather be squashed and secure than camp out and risk a narhili attack. They could safely sleep in tents after they crossed into the mountainous Strunheim Territory. The nocturnal narhili beasts preferred warmer, lower climates. Their wrinkled skin didn't provide much protection against the cold.

Rizelya shuddered, thinking about another attack, and suddenly she couldn't breathe. She fought the Malvers' monsters all the time and never had a problem, but one attack from the narhili, and she was panicking at even the thought of them. She slumped on Kymaya's back, gasping for air. Aistrun furrowed his brows at her and opened his mouth to speak, but Rizelya gulped down the panic and rode ahead of him into the stable.

Eidstrun walked over to help her dismount, but she shook him off, trying to calm her pounding heart. She hid her face as she unsaddled and groomed Kymaya. It had been several days since she'd taken care of her horse. The repetitive motions of brushing Kymaya soothed her, and the dread slid from her.

Finished, she stepped out of Kymaya's stall to see all of her pack, except Keandran, hanging out in the center aisle. Tears trickled down her face.

"Shh... shh," Leistral crooned, wrapping her arms around Rizelya. "It's okay."

"We know," Dehali added, stroking Rizelya's hair and back. "We're all tired."

Aistrun and Eidstrun didn't say anything, they just pulled the women into a group hug.

After a few milcrons, Rizelya wiped her eyes and nose. "I'm okay now, thank you." She looked each person in the eye, and felt the bond snap in place, and from the astonished looks of the others, they did too. No matter what happened in the future, they would always be connected. It would be difficult for them to be separated into a different pack.

"Well now, isn't this special?" Keandran sneered.

"It is," she said, and held out her hand to him. "You could join us."

He gazed at her for a long moment. She sensed his ache to belong. But then he shuddered and shook his head. "Not for me." He stalked from the stable.

Rizelya sighed as she watched him. She wondered when he would push everyone away and leave. She couldn't imagine anyone wanting to live alone, separate from the safety and comfort of pack. A few men lived quiet lives as lone wolves. But then there were those who turned rogue and caused problems. Rogues were usually maladjusted, mean-tempered, and angry men, just like Keandran. They preyed on humans, killing them indiscriminately and brutally. The alphas quickly hunted them and put them down. She didn't want anything like that to happen to Keandran. But she'd tried to reach him and let him know there was a place for him within their pack. Whatever the White Priestess had done had only helped him for a few days. He was as sullen and morose as ever.

The next morning, they hadn't ridden far when Laynad led them off the road and into the trees. The path, wide enough for one horse, crawled through the forest. They trailed along single-file behind Laynad. The treacherous path wasn't much more than a game trail. They had to watch carefully to keep their horses from stepping in a hole and becoming lame.

Someone started singing and soon most everyone joined in. Rizelya allowed the song to release her tension from riding in an enclosed area. If a nest of monsters broke free and found them, they wouldn't have space to fight. But birds twittered above them and squirrels scolded them as they passed, assuring her monsters didn't lurk somewhere in the depths of the trees.

Laynad didn't seem troubled or concerned, so Rizelya assumed the path wasn't close to any monster nests. The trail steepened. Rizelya sat forward on Kymaya's saddle to help give the horse more purchase as she dug in her hooves to climb. After almost half an octar of struggling, they made it up the hill and out of the trees. They stood on a grassy meadow looking down into a wide valley. On the far side, Rizelya glimpsed a large keep.

"That's Strunven Keep," Laynad said when Rizelya rode up next to her.

"I didn't think it was this close to the border," Rizelya commented.

"It isn't. We've been in Strunven Territory since the safe house. You can see the trail down." She pulled out a map and pointed the way down to the valley and the road leading to the keep. Laynad handed the map to Rizelya. "We'll leave you here. I'm certain someone from Strunven will notice you sooner rather than later and guide you further. I'm not quite sure it was a pleasure to meet you." She shook Rizelya's hand, then turned her horse around without another word, her people and Laynar's platoon following behind her.

Rizelya gaped in surprise at Laynar, who remained behind.

"What are you doing here? Aren't you going back?"

"No, I'm going with you. I'll rejoin my platoon at the clan meeting. Grandmother says the Strunven Keep Alpha is a bit peculiar, and I needed to introduce you. Otherwise, you might get sent packing without delivering your message."

"But we have letters of introduction from Histrun," Dehali said. "Surely that will let us in."

"Ah, but that is the problem," Laynar said, raising her eyebrows. "It seems this woman doesn't like Histrun. Doesn't trust him." She looked at Rizelya. "Or his offspring."

"Oh, that's just wonderful," Rizelya muttered. "Of course, Histrun wouldn't have warned us. He might even think it was funny."

"Hey, he would at that," Aistrun said, and then grinned. "At least we now have Laynar to save the day. Shall we go?"

Rizelya gazed up at the sun. It was almost midday, and Laynad had set a punishing pace. "No, let's rest here for a while and eat."

The others gave her a grateful look.

"There's a spring over there," Laynar said, pointing across the meadow. She led them to the spring shielded by large boulders.

After they had eaten and rested for nearly an octar, Rizelya wearily woke everyone from their nap. They needed to get down the mountain and to a safe house before dark.

Mindful of Laynar's warning about the Strunven Keep Alpha, she had them pull out their barding gear and put it on their horses. They hadn't bothered with it since Strunell Territory since everyone they had met had been so friendly, and they were, after all, part of the same Clan, Strunlair. Her pack might have had more trouble if they had been traveling in another clan's territory, such as Posanlair.

"I can take the lead," Laynar offered when they remounted. "I have visited Strunven Keep several times before as an emissary for my grandmother."

Rizelya gladly accepted and let the others ride slightly ahead of her. She didn't want to talk. Her leg hurt, her arm ached, and she drooped with exhaustion. It had already been a long trip filled with danger. And they still had another chedan or more until they reached Strunlair Keep. She hoped when they did, they would be able to stay put for more than a day or two. She and her people needed to rest, and she needed to heal.

Chapter 12

The trek down the mountain was uneventful. An octar before dark, Rizelya's group approached the safe house. A Strunven fighting force milled around the courtyard, caring for horses and cleaning off monster gore. They would be testy after a fight. Behind the building, a team readied a funeral pyre, and several bodies laid on the ground next to it.

The barding on their horses proclaimed them as friendlies. Taking the time to put it on could save them trouble with the Strunven fighting-pack.

Rizelya, Aistrun, and Laynar took the lead position, pacing each other. A few paces behind him rode Dehali and Eidstrun, with Leistral and Keandran bringing up the rear. The jingle of the horse's headgear alerted the fighters to their presence. Two Reds rushed to the gate, their helbraughts blazing, flanked by several men. In front of them, a few men, still in their wolf form, wove back and forth, protecting the entrance.

More fighters hurried to stand behind the guards to block the gates. In an undulating wave, they made way for their alphas to approach the riders. The man was tall, even taller than Aistrun, with long golden-red hair he wore loose and that reached to his waist. The willowy woman was almost as tall. She had the same golden-red hair, only a shade darker. They both had the same high cheekbones and slightly slanted green eyes. Alpha partners weren't necessarily lovers and quite a few were, as these two appeared to be, siblings. Antagonism pulled their thin lips into a tight line.

"Greetings," called Laynar, holding out her empty hands. "I am Laynar de Strunheim. We come as friends."

"As they should know," grumbled Aistrun, just loud enough for Rizelya to hear.

Ignoring him, Rizelya held out her hands in the same gesture. "I am Rizelya de Strunland. These are my pack." She indicated those behind her.

The woman turned to Rizelya and sneered. "We have heard of a Rizelya, daughter of Histrun. Are you she?"

"I am."

"You will receive no welcome here."

Rizelya's anger rose. "It is night. All may seek the sanctuary of a safe house," she said coldly. "We will enter." She lowered her hands where she could easily grasp her helbraught from its holder on Kymaya's saddle.

Aistrun urged Jezhan forward a few steps. "Hey, we are all part of the same clan. There's no call for hostilities. We have traveled a long way and need a place to stay for the night. We'll leave in the morning."

The man crossed his arms and growled, "No, you will leave now. We will not let the spawn of Histrun enter our house."

Rizelya looked at Laynar. "You weren't kidding when you said they didn't like Histrun. I can't think why they wouldn't." Sarcasm dripped from her voice. "Sometimes I don't like him. Some help here would be good."

Laynar urged her horse a step forward. "You know me. You know my grandmother," she said. "We can both vouch for the integrity of these people. They have come here at great peril to help you, not harm you."

"You've been having monster problems, haven't you?" Rizelya asked.

The woman's eyebrows raised in alarm. Before she could say anything, Rizelya continued. "Bigger nests, spawning more often than usual, and they have a new strange janack that seems to lead and control them, don't they?" She could tell from both the alpha's faces, they had experienced the same things here. "Well, we know how to fight them and kill the control-janack, without so many people dying. But if you don't want or need our help, we'll leave." She turned Kymaya's head around and retreated down the road. The others in her pack followed her.

They had ridden several horse lengths when the woman called out. "Wait! You know how to kill it?"

Rizelya twisted in her saddle. "We do."

"Then you and yours may enter and find shelter from the night," the man said formally.

The Strunven alphas shooed all their people back to what they were doing. Satisfied, Rizelya returned to the safe house. Quivers ran under her skin from the close call of being attacked by their own clan members. Killing the Malvers' monsters consumed most of the fighters' energy. Once in a while, hostilities would break out between clans, rarely within the same clan. The Supreme White Priestess highly disapproved of this and meted out severe punishment to the perpetrators. The Supreme believed they had enough to do to survive with fighting the monsters. They didn't need to fight each other as well.

As Rizelya's pack entered the gates, the two Strunven alphas joined them and paced to the side of Rizelya and Laynar's horses. Kymaya snorted and tossed her head, not liking strangers near her. Rizelya patted her neck, reassuring her.

When they reached the stable, only a few stragglers remained in the stables. Rizelya ignored them. She grimaced as the ache in her leg flared when she threw it over Kymaya's back to slide off. She still held onto the saddle when her leg buckled to keep from falling in front of these hostile strangers.

"Are you injured?" the female alpha asked.

When Rizelya felt her leg could hold her, she turned around to face the woman. "Yes. I was attacked by narhili beasts a few days ago and am recovering from their poison."

"And still you rode here?" The man sounded incredulous.

"Yes, we help our clan-mates, no matter the cost. It's a long story, and I would tell it better sitting down." Pain glazed Rizelya's voice.

"Our apologies," the woman said. "When you have cared for your horses and refreshed yourselves, we would hear your story." She grabbed the man's arm and dragged him out of the stable and into the safe house.

Rizelya took a step to lead Kymaya to an empty stall, and her leg buckled again. Aistrun caught her before she hit the ground.

"Hey, you okay? You're pale and sweaty."

"I'm fine, just tired and achy."

"If you say so," his voice held disbelief.

"I do say so." She struggled out of his hold. "I need to take care of Kymaya."

"No you don't, you need to sit down and get off your leg," he argued, holding on tighter.

"I'll unsaddle Kymaya, Alpha," Leistral said, grabbing Kymaya's headstall and rubbing her nose. "She and I are good friends. Go take care of yourself. We need you to be strong."

"Eidstrun is taking care of Jezhan for me," Aistrun told her. "Let's go in."

"I'd rather not go into the wolves' den alone," Rizelya said. "We need our people to guard our backs. Let's wait for them."

He considered it for a moment. "Agreed. But you will sit and rest." His tone told her it wouldn't do any good to argue.

She huffed out a breath and settled onto a stool, watching the others unsaddle and curry the horses. When they finished, which didn't take long, together they walked into the safe house. Rizelya refused Aistrun's offer to carry her, but leaned heavily on him as she limped. The room quieted when they entered. The two alphas stepped forward in the silence.

"Greetings," the woman said, holding out her hands, palms up. "I am Saehala."

"And I am her brother, Saehalstrun. Welcome to our territory."

Rizelya introduced her squad-pack. As she did so, she continued to lean on Aistrun. His arm wound around her waist, and his hand gripped her elbow. His support was the only reason she was still standing.

Formalities over, Saehala and Saehalstrun led them to a table situated to the side, away from the others. Rizelya sank onto the bench with a groan. Her people found places around the table. Immediately, two young fighters brought them food and drink. An expectant air permeated the room, as if everyone waited to hear what they had to say. Rizelya ignored it and dug into her dinner.

She smiled in appreciation as Aistrun's friendly, talkative nature saved her from any awkwardness. He kept the conversation to small talk and funny stories. Soon, the Strunven alphas relaxed and laughed at his tales, and so were the Strunven fighters who were close enough to listen in.

Aistrun winked at her, as he launched into another story in which she had a key role. She chuckled as much as anyone else. By the time Aistrun ended his tale, they'd finished eating and cleared away the dishes.

"So, why are you here and how can you help us?" Saehala asked. The room suddenly became quiet again.

"It's a long story, and it's for all to hear, Saehala," Aistrun said. "Let's gather around the fire to find what comfort we may. Our story isn't an easy one, or even a happy tale." Without waiting for an answer, he left the table, grabbed a chair, carrying it to the edge of the large fireplace, and sat down in the traditional storytellers' position. Within moments, the Strunven pack moved the tables. Quite a few of the fighters found pillows or blankets and threw them down on the floor in front of Aistrun. Others carried benches to the center of the room, creating a circle in front of the fire. A kind soul placed a chair next to Aistrun for Rizelya.

When everyone settled into their chosen seats, Aistrun began. "One cold morning, a fighting force left Strunland Keep to destroy a nest of monsters a few measures away. What they found was like nothing they had ever seen. The nest was three times the normal size. Ten janacks at least tumbled out of it.

"In the center towered a huge janack, twice as big as all the rest. A strange appendage protruded from its head. One brave Red—" he glanced meaningfully at Rizelya "—vaulted onto the back of the janack and raced to the head. Daring the wrath of her alpha, she did the only thing possible: she blew up the janack!" He made explosion noises, and the listening crowd gasped in horror. Aistrun paused, surveying the room and catching the eyes of several individuals.

"That was the first control-janack we saw, but not the last."

He proceeded to tell them of receiving Histrun's charge, their discovery of the cold-air and fire shields, and their journey through the territories.

"And so we are here, in Strunven Territory, to teach you how to protect your fighters and kill the control-janack," he concluded.

A log shifted and fell, sending sparks up the chimney. Tension crept through the room as the Strunven fighters turned their attention to their leaders.

Saehala broke the silence. "We have fought such as you describe and have lost many. We'll take you to the keep and vouch for you to our alphas."

Noise erupted as the fighters cheered. More than one fighter voiced their relief with a, "Thank you, Mother!"

A relaxed and friendly Saehala and Saehalstrun led the fighting force from the safe house the next morning. Rizelya and Aistrun rode at their side. After ten measures of riding, they entered a grassy plain. A herd of billocks thundered away from them, then stopped when no one chased them to graze once more on the lush spring grass.

"So why does your alpha hate Histrun so much?" Rizelya asked when the pace slowed to a walk. She wanted to be prepared to refute whatever it was when she met her.

"Ah, she's quite vexed at him," Saehalstrun muttered, rubbing the back of his neck.

"Oh, tell it like it is," Laynar quipped. "Sujeen is a woman scorned and still holds a grudge after all of these years." She huffed. "Grandmother thinks she's a silly fool. She would know. She knew them all."

"Hey, a love triangle, awesome," Aistrun said, grinning.

"Yeah, something like that," Saehala admitted. "Mother thought she and Histrun were bond-mates when Zehala came along and proved her wrong."

"Not only did Zehala have the effrontery to beat out Mother to win the Clan-Alpha competition—when she wasn't old enough to compete," Saehalstrun said. "But she added insult and stole Histrun away, too." He sounded like he had heard the complaint many, many times. He turned to Rizelya. "Sorry about last night, sister."

"Sister!" Rizelya exclaimed, rocking back in her saddle. Histrun never talked to her about his life. She hadn't known he had a family before mating with Zehala, but she should have guessed. He had been an old man of seventy-five when he met her mother. Her much older stepsister, Naila, was Zehala's firstborn from a different partner. When this danger passed, she wanted to sit down with her father and find out more about him. She kept receiving surprising information about him. She thought about his taciturn nature around her and decided she'd ask Layhalya to tell her more. Examining the twins more closely, she wondered if he had spent time with them as children. Had he held them, loved them, as he never had done with her?

"Sister. We are also Histrun's 'get'." He sighed. "Which is why we're sent from the keep as often as possible."

"She says we remind her too much of him," Saehala said with a grimace. "I don't see it. I think we look like her."

Their eyes were the only resemblance to Histrun Rizelya could determine. He had the same slightly slanted, grass-green eyes like theirs.

"Wait," Aistrun interrupted, "if Sujeen was Clan Alpha, why is she a keep alpha now?"

"She wasn't," Laynar answered. "Oh, she tried, many times, but Zehala beat her every time. She lost her keep when she made her bid for the Clan-Alpha position, and it took her years to obtain another one. She hates Zehala more than Histrun."

"Oh, great," Rizelya said, rolling her eyes. "So it isn't just that Histrun is my father, it's also Zehala is my mother. I'm doubly damned. I can't change who my parents were." Panic squeezed her chest. "This isn't going to turn out well. Why don't I ride on to Strunlair Keep, or wait at a safe house while you deal with Sujeen?"

"Coward," Laynar accused her.

"Yep, I'd like to stay in one piece."

"Hey, if she cares about her people, she'll put aside her differences and listen to what we have to say."

"I think she will, especially with us bringing back four riderless horses." Sadness crept into Saehala's voice. "They were good fighters."

Saehalstrun's hands bunched into a fist. "If she doesn't, we aren't the only ones who will challenge her at the Alpha Trials this summer. We aren't quite old enough, but the age requirements aren't written in stone. We have your mother, Rizelya, as precedence. She became the youngest Clan Alpha ever. We only want to be some of the youngest keep alphas."

"It won't help your people now," Rizelya said.

"We are the fighting-pack alphas," Saehala told them. "If she doesn't listen, we'll go to the district keep, Strunvede, learn your techniques, and teach them to the other territory alphas."

"Won't you get in trouble for it?" Laynar asked.

"Of course." Saehalstrun shrugged. "But she can't punish us for long when we're killing the monsters instead of them killing us. She'd have an uprising on her hands and challenged before the summer trials."

Rizelya couldn't believe what she was hearing. Although the leadership of an alpha, any alpha including the Clan Alpha, could be questioned at any time, tradition demanded challengers wait until the Alpha Competitions. The Supreme only allowed unsanctioned challenges when an alpha actively put their people in danger. Those challenges were duels and, for the men, usually to the death; whereas the competitions were tests of strategy, cunning, strength, and leadership. The competitions provided a way to change leaders without the loss of life. The men were more prone to dominance challenges, and the competitions kept these in check. It dawned on Rizelya that Sujeen would endanger her pack if she didn't allow her people to learn the new techniques.

"But what about your male Keep Alpha? Won't he step in and listen to reason?" Rizelya asked.

"No," Saehala answered sadly. "Sujeen has thoroughly cowed him. He doesn't do anything contrary to her wishes."

"That doesn't sound much like an alpha to me," Aistrun snorted.

Saehalstrun shuddered. "Oh, Teraposan is more than dominant enough. He enforces her will with a vengeance. They both rule with an iron fist. Others have challenged him before, but somehow he won the competition." Saehalstrun's eyes narrowed with determination. "He won't win against me. It's time to end their rule."

All is not well in Strunven Territory. Rizelya mused. *Why don't the Clan Alphas do something to end Sujeen and Teraposan's reign of terror?* Although if fear, rather than respect, kept others from challenging Sujeen, then maybe they weren't aware of what was happening here.

The group continued toward the main keep. In the quiet, Rizelya contemplated the upsetting news. Her thoughts ranged back over the past few years, and a pattern emerged. Quite a few people had moved into Strunland Territory from Strunven, more than the usual shifting of fighters. Even stranger—but now she understood why—non-fighters had immigrated, which rarely occurred. She decided to ask Laynar later if Strunheim also experienced the ingress of people since they were riding through the fields surrounding Strunven Keep.

Rizelya approached the gates with trepidation. She braced for the worst, while hoping for the best.

"We'll talk to Sujeen first," Saehala said. "It will be safer for you, Rizelya, if she knows you're here."

Rizelya agreed, and she and her squad-pack waited, along with the twins' fighting force, in the main courtyard. They wouldn't dismount until they knew how Sujeen would react.

Saehala and Saehalstrun approached the Keep House. Laynar paced at their side to add the power of her testimony, and that of her grandmother's, in an effort to convince Sujeen to listen to Rizelya.

They didn't have to wait long to discover Sujeen's reaction.

A few short milcrons after the trio entered the Keep House, a bellow of anger rattled the windows. The twins and Laynar rushed out the door with an old woman, still spry and deadly, chasing them. Sujeen's helbraught glowed and spit globs of fire at their retreating backs.

The fire surged as they ran down the porch steps. Fearing for her half-sibling's life, Rizelya didn't think, she just reacted. She threw a shield between her friends and the enraged woman. "Down!" Rizelya shouted, and the trio flung themselves to the ground.

The flame licked the shield, seeking the edges. Rizelya added more power to her shield. It flared, the red magic deepening to an indigo blue. Her shield sucked the questing fire into itself, absorbing Sujeen's fire.

Furious, Sujeen fed more fire into her helbraught. Rizelya drew this new flame into her shield as well. She sensed it growing stronger as she assimilated Sujeen's magic. Her mouth dropped open. She hadn't known she could do this, and a part of her mind perked up. If others could do this, it would make their shields against the monsters even more effective.

"Who the hell do you think you are?" Sujeen yelled at Rizelya. Fury screwed up her face, making it as red as her hair had once been. "How dare you interfere in my business?"

"I dare because you are wrong," Rizelya said, her voice cold. "You will not harm my friends because you're angry at someone who has been dead for nearly twenty years." Rizelya sat up straighter in her saddle and glared back at the ugly woman. She didn't drop her shield, but instead extended it around herself and the rest of the fighters. She felt Leistral and Dehali add their shields until they protected everyone in the courtyard.

"Why, you impudent, arrogant, little pip-squeak! You're just like your mother, butting in where you don't belong." Sujeen channeled more fire into her helbraught until it glowed with the deep orange that preceded exploding a monster. She lifted her weapon and, leaning over the porch railing, thrust it into Rizelya's shield with all her strength.

Rizelya rocked back in her saddle as the force of the blow connected with her shield. Frantically, she reached out and pulled on the energies from Dehali's and Leistral's shields, blending them into her shield. Cracks slithered up and around the shield, but it held.

With a bright flash, Sujeen's helbraught disintegrated. She toppled over the railing, screaming as the flames ate into her hands. While the fire from a Red's own power wouldn't burn her, the fire of another Red could. A large man rushed to her side, cradling her as she curled around her scorched hands. When he lifted his eyes up to Rizelya's, hatred burned as hot as the flame that had destroyed Sujeen's helbraught.

"You'll pay for this," he snarled, and stood up, his hands in fists. "You saw her hurt the alpha," he yelled at the fighters. "Kill her!"

No one moved to follow his order.

"Kill her, I said!" he screamed.

"It was self-defense, Teraposan," Saehalstrun said, striding to stand nose-to-nose with the larger man, while not touching the still glowing and sparking fire shield. "*We,*" he emphasized the word, "do not murder people. You have just demonstrated you're not fit to be the Keep Alpha. I challenge you!" Saehalstrun's voice rang out with authority. He sounded surprisingly calm for someone whose mother had tried to kill him moments before.

Rizelya surveyed the people in the courtyard. No one seemed angry over the challenge, although they had been plenty upset when Sujeen tried to fry her children. Rizelya dissolved her fire shield now that Saehalstrun had issued his challenge. He would soon fight Teraposan.

Saehala stood next to her brother and stared at her mother. "You're no longer kin and not fit to lead this keep. Your actions in attacking us have proved you're insane. I remove you as alpha."

This pronouncement caused gasps of surprise. Insanity was one of the few instances allowed to remove an alpha rather than challenging them for the position.

Sujeen sputtered with rage, spittle flying from her mouth. Her eyes nearly glowed. She looked quite, quite mad. She leaped up, her helstrablade clutched in her burned hands. With a cry, she lunged at Saehala, blade flashing. Saehala spun out of the way and pushed Sujeen, who landed flat on her stomach.

"Stay down, old woman. I don't want to kill you," Saehala ground out. Sujeen didn't listen and jumped to her feet, surprisingly fast for someone so old and hurt. She swung her helstrablade again. This time Saehala met it with her own, and with her other hand, punched Sujeen. Blood poured from Sujeen's broken nose. She wiped it off, and with a mad cackle, lunged at Saehala. This time, Saehala's knife connected. Sujeen hung for a moment on the blade and then slid off, her eyes glazed in death.

Saehala looked at the body, tears sliding down her face. "I didn't want to kill you, Mother."

A roar of anger broke the tableau. Rizelya tore her gaze away from Saehala. Teraposan shifted to his warrior form as he leaped at Saehalstrun. The crowd shouted in dismay at this outright disregard for the tradition of fighting alpha challenges in human form.

Saehalstrun ducked under Teraposan. A back claw caught him across the chest. He roared in pain, and before Teraposan could land and turn, Saehalstrun shifted to his warrior form.

Everyone scrambled to get out of the way of the battling men. Rizelya had never seen anyone shift so fast, and she urged Kymaya up the stairs and onto the Keep House's wide porch. Aistrun jumped off his horse and stood next to her. The other riders dismounted as well and shooed their horses into the pasture by the stable.

Saehalstrun stood up, opened his jaws wide, and roared again in challenge. His ten-foot-tall warrior form towered over Teraposan. The warriors circled each other, swiping with their claws, snapping at each other. They clashed and parted. Blood streamed off both their pelts from various wounds, although none appeared life threatening. Teraposan howled, ducked his head, and bowled into Saehalstrun, knocking him on his back.

Saehalstrun's longer arms held Teraposan's jaws away from his throat. Teraposan snapped and saliva dripped onto Saehalstrun's muzzle. Tucking his legs to his chest, Saehalstrun wiggled until he maneuvered his feet with their long claws under Teraposan. With a growl, he ripped his opponent open from his neck to his groin. Blood and guts splashed out, covering him in gore. Teraposan collapsed on top of him.

Aistrun and several of the other men raced to pull Teraposan off Saehalstrun before the heavier man crushed him. Saehalstrun struggled free and lay panting. Teraposan's corpse reverted to its natural form. The devastating killing strike was even more evident without all the fur.

"Saehalstrun, talk to me." Saehala ran to him, terrified. "Are you all right?"

He slowly nodded and began to shift. Hurt and exhausted, it took longer than usual. Several of his wounds were deep enough he'd need stitches.

"I didn't want to challenge them like this," he said when he completed his change. "We'll burn them with honor tonight to send their souls back to The Mother and pray they will find peace."

Strunven Keep was subdued the day after the fight, mourning Sujeen's loss. She had been the Strunven Keep Alpha for many years and, until recently, had been a good leader. Teraposan, an interloper from the Posanlair Clan, had used a heavy hand, and Rizelya heard whispers about how glad most people were that Saehalstrun had defeated him.

But the monsters didn't care if grief wrapped the keep. The creatures would continue to form, and grow, and leave their nests to devour whatever was in their path. Saehala and Saehalstrun called a meeting with the fighting-packs right after breakfast.

The new leaders ordered the doors of the great hall opened, informing the residents they were allowed to attend. As Rizelya sat with her team, including Laynar, at a smaller table to the side of the keep alpha's, she glimpsed quite a few non-fighters standing in the back. A few Yellows and other Talents hung around the edges with unconcealed eagerness. She doubted they would have a lack of volunteers here.

Saehala lifted her hands, and the room quieted. "If that was a fire shield you used to protect us last night, I certainly want to learn it."

Rizelya heard several voices muttering agreement.

"It was," Rizelya said. She clutched her hands in her lap under the table. She hadn't spoken to this many strangers. Well, she amended, there might have been as many at Strunell Keep during their first demonstration, but she had been busy teaching and hadn't paid attention to them.

"Hey, it's what we're here to teach," Aistrun spoke up. He enjoyed speaking to audiences. "In case you haven't noticed, we have a strange new janack, and the nests are bigger than ever."

"Yeah, we noticed," a man yelled.

"Why are they bigger?" someone else asked.

"Where did it come from?" another called out.

Aistrun shook his head as he moved from behind the table and to the front of the room. "We don't know. We saw the first control-janack—that's the new beast—just four chedan ago. Our alpha wanted to determine if it was an anomaly in our territory, or if it was happening all over Strunlair Province. We've been traveling all over the province ever since. Seems like we didn't get the only one." He paused and said almost in an aside, "Wish we did, things would be easier." He raised his voice. "They are now in all the nests. Our old methods of fighting the monsters aren't up to the task anymore."

"You can say that again!" a woman yelled.

"But along the way, we've learned new ways to protect ourselves, fight the monsters—" he pointed at the crowd, and then raised his voice and arm in victory "—and kill them."

Everyone in the room stood up, clapping and cheering. Rizelya shook her head in wonder and glanced over at the others at her table. They all held the same bemused look she was sure was on her face. After this, they'd have more volunteers than they needed. Aistrun let them go on for a few milcrons, grinning the entire time.

"Okay, quiet down," he yelled, motioning for them to sit back down. "This new method doesn't only use Red Talent. We also need Yellows."

"Now you're just fooling us," a woman said, scornfully. She stalked to the front, her bright canary-yellow hair indicating her strong air Talent. As she got closer, Rizelya noticed her grass green eyes. "I've been told on many occasions that I can't fight because I'm a Yellow and not a Red. Well, I want to fight! I want to protect my people and pack just as much as any Red ever did." She stood with her feet wide, her hands on her hips, and wore a belligerent scowl, daring them to gainsay her again.

Dehali rose to her feet. "I understand," she told the woman. "I was lucky I have enough Red Talent that they let me fight. But now, I do most of my fighting with my air Talent, forming a cold-air shield so my pack can kill the damned control-janack." She slammed her fist onto the table.

"Show me," the woman said with disbelief.

Dehali gathered up air energy and formed a tight shield around the woman, who shivered. Her face lost the belligerence and softened with delight as she reached out and touched the cold, hard air in front of her.

"Amazing!" she laughed. She gazed at Dehali with something akin to worship. "Just amazing. You'll teach me? And you'll let her?" She addressed the last to her new Keep Alphas.

Saehala nodded, and said solemnly to the woman, "It is our sacred duty as alphas to give you the tools to ensure your safety.

This is another tool. Gehan, I promise you'll get the opportunity to fight, although you may regret it."

Gehan rushed to take Saehala's hands. "Thank you, Alpha! I'm so glad you're now our leader."

Saehalstrun spoke up. "We'll need four powerful Yellow Talent volunteers and four Reds to learn the new shielding techniques." He raised his hands to quiet the clamor. "You must be a *stronf* Yellow in order to hold the shield when facing a nest full of monsters. As we become more proficient, we'll teach others."

"Let's go learn!" Gehan said excitedly. She grabbed Dehali's hand and dragged her through the crowd, which parted with good-natured laughing to let them pass. Gehan and Dehali led the procession out of the meeting hall and across the courtyard to the practice arena.

Amused, Rizelya followed them once the room cleared. Her limp wasn't as pronounced, and she experienced a slight twinge when she rolled her injured shoulder. She didn't need to hurry. Leistral and Dehali were becoming skilled teachers of the new method. She chuckled to herself. Maybe they should name it after them. That would be much better than naming it after her.

With this in mind, she changed direction, returned to the Keep House, and found her way to the infirmary. The healer looked at her wound, which seeped blood from the jostling of the hard ride from Strunheim Keep. Tsking at Rizelya's recklessness, the healer cleaned the injury and used her healing magic on Rizelya's leg. When she allowed Rizelya to stand up, her leg was much stronger and her limp less pronounced.

By the time Rizelya reached the practice arena, it buzzed with activity. Leistral and Dehali had finished the demonstration and divided the trainees into groups. A group of eight Yellows worked on one end. Rizelya inwardly cheered to see so many women had volunteered. Considering the losses this keep had sustained, the double in number of Reds who practiced on the other end didn't surprise her. She climbed to the top of the stands, where she could observe the entire arena.

In the middle, Aistrun and Eidstrun worked with the men. They had developed their own technique for harassing the control-janack. Rizelya watched with interest. She was usually so busy trying to find an opening to leap onto the control-janack that she never paid attention to how the warriors fought. She admired their elegant beauty as they moved in synchronized rhythm, flowing through the forms Aistrun led them in.

The warrior form was magnificent—a beautiful and deadly blend of man and wolf. Men who stood six foot were over eight-foot-tall as warriors. Razor-sharp claws tipped both front and back paws, and their jaws elongated to hold fangs that could rip apart a brecha. The pelt was the same color as the man's hair, except quite a few pelts were striped, spotted, or otherwise marked. The eyes remained the same in either form.

Eidstrun's nine-foot, golden-brown form towered over everyone else, except one. A golden-red warrior with green flecks on his fur stood almost a foot taller—Saehalstrun.

Rizelya pulled her attention away from the powerful men with difficulty. Dehali positioned her group of Yellows several paces apart. The fierce Gehan scowled in concentration. She gave a whoop of jubilation when an air-shield formed correctly. Glowing with pride, Gehan admired it for a few moments, then released it. Immediately she concentrated, made a gesture, and the cold-air shield reappeared. Rizelya's eyebrows rose, and she nodded to herself. It usually took time for people to make the spell work. Another Yellow cried out in victory as she created a cold-air shield. Rizelya smiled at their pleasure. She hoped they could do as well when they faced a real monster.

A flare of light coming from the other end of the arena caused Rizelya to turn toward it. A fire shield burst into being. Saehala grinned triumphantly at it. The other women glanced at it, then returned their attention to their own spells. Soon, all of them had a fire shield blazing around them. They didn't allow them to stay up long before they banished them and formed a new one. Here there were no whoops or excited dancing, only solemn determination to perfect the shields. These women were fighters. They understood what they were up against and were eager to take back control of the fight.

The groups practiced separately for another octar. Then Leistral partnered the Yellows with a Red and two warriors, while Dehali formed the control-janack illusion. The first group to attack consisted of Saehala, Gehan, Saehalstrun, and another warrior. Gehan flung herself with gusto at the janack. It didn't take long for them to it put down.

Seeing the number of groups, Rizelya sighed. Her break was over. They needed her help. She limped down to the arena and joined Dehali in creating the practice illusion. She had done this spell enough over the last few chedan that she could split her attention to yell corrections at the team hitting her janack while controlling the illusion.

When Leistral called a halt three octars later, Rizelya slumped to the ground. Her legs wobbled, and her eyes blurred with fatigue. She wasn't alone. Other fighters sagged to sit where they'd stopped. A few hearty souls wearily made their way to sit in the stands. Rizelya dropped her head to her hands, bracing her elbows on her knees, and sat there for several long milcrons.

She glanced up as a young woman approached her and handed her a small jug. The girl's navy blue hair and clear blue eyes startled her. Blues tended to stay far away from the fighting Reds, especially strong ones like this woman. The violent, passionate emotions of the Reds were usually too much for the gentle Blues.

After Rizelya took the jug, the Blue left to give one to the next fighter. While Rizelya drank the cool water, several other young Blues, Yellows, and Greens wove around the arena, dispensing water.

A cool breeze swept through, drying Rizelya's sweating brow. Someone had flung the large doors open. Four Yellows made gestures, and the fresh air followed the direction of their fingers. A middle-aged woman entered. "We have refreshments ready for you," she announced.

Ragged cheers from the tired and hungry trainees greeted her announcement. Saehala's team sprawled near Rizelya. "That was a good idea," she said to Saehala.

Saehala shook her head, perplexed. "Not mine."

The woman heard them and came over to squat in front of them. A scarf covered her hair. Gold flecked her red eyes. Rizelya wondered why she wasn't a fighter.

"It was our idea, Alpha." The woman indicated all the non-fighters helping the fighters get to their feet. "You're training to protect us and ours from the monsters. The only way we can fight is to help you."

Rizelya considered the woman. She had broad shoulders and muscles rippled under her tunic. She seemed strong. "You would fight?"

The woman nodded. For a large woman, she settled on the floor with grace. "Aye, and many others." She ignored Saehala's sputters and went on. "We train each month in case the monsters break through the protections. Quite a few of us would rather not huddle behind the keep walls while our friends go to battle. We're told we cannot fight because we don't have fire magic. But whose magic gives the blades you use the strength to hold your fire and pierce the hides of the monsters?" Without waiting for an answer, she pointed to herself. "It is us, and our Brown Talent, that allows you to fight."

"You're a metal worker? Do you work the helstrablades?" Rizelya asked excitedly.

"Maendy is one of the finest helstramiesters in the entire Strunlair Province, maybe even all of Lairheim," Saehalstrun said, pride shining in his eyes.

"It's why she can't fight." Saehala glared at Maendy. "We need her too much to allow her to risk herself unnecessarily." It seemed like an old argument.

"I don't need her to fight. I need her knowledge," Rizelya told Saehala. She turned back to Maendy. "You are exactly the person I wanted to talk to. As a helstramiester, you know the properties of the helstrablades and what they can do, right?"

"I do." Maendy sounded wary.

"So can only Red Talent and fire magic be channeled into the blades?"

"No, of course not." Maendy looked indignant. "Although no one has ever used them for more than fire magic."

"I knew it!" Rizelya snapped her fingers, elated. "That means Reds aren't the only women who can fight anymore."

"Why is that important?" Saehala asked.

"We need more fighters. There aren't enough Reds to handle the mass of monsters I suspect are heading our way. I believe we haven't seen the end to the increased size and frequency of the nests, only the beginning."

"You don't think those rogue monsters we fought are one-of-a-kind, do you?" Laynar asked, coming up to stand behind them.

Rizelya's squad-pack and Laynar joined them, carrying plates loaded with fruit, cheese, and crackers with them. They handed plates to those on the floor. Rizelya waited until they sat down before answering Laynar.

"No, I don't. I think the attacks are going to get worse. They already have in the few chedan since we saw the first control-janack."

"Hey, we've been fighting a war with the monsters for a long, long time," Aistrun said. "Our enemy has just changed tactics."

"We've reached a stalemate the past thirty years," Saehala said, "ever since the Zehis method. We can't eliminate the monsters entirely, and they can't annihilate us. Something had to give."

"I wish..." Rizelya began, then sighed wistfully. "I wish we could find some way to rid ourselves of the nests. Then there wouldn't be any more monsters to fight."

"It's been tried," Saehala said, sounding frustrated. "No one has discovered how to drain, destroy, or even neutralize the malignant magic pools where the nests form. The White Priestesses tried when the monsters first appeared, but it didn't do any good."

"They try every hundred years or so," Laynar said. "My grandmother was a child the last time they attempted it. Each time a new Supreme comes into power, she tries to drain the pools. I think it's become some sort of initiation for them."

"Until the White Priestesses are successful," Rizelya said, "it is up to us to fight the monsters. And find better ways to fight them. Using other Talents than simply the Reds is one of those ways." She turned to Maendy. "We need your help. We need to learn what the other Talents can do with the helstrablades and helbraughts. Will you help?"

"Hot damn! A forward-thinking alpha." Maendy slapped her hand on her thigh. "I like you, Rizelya. Of course I'll help. What do you need?"

Rizelya looked at Dehali. "Do you know what your friend Kami did when she killed her brecha?"

"Sure I do. She was so excited." Dehali's face lit up at the mention of the woman she had fallen in love with. "I was so proud of her, a full Yellow killing a brecha! She even did it with a helstrablade instead of a helbraught."

"Impressive," Saehala said, her eyes were alight. "But why didn't she use a helbraught?"

"All she had was a helstrablade," Dehali answered. "Afterward, she tried to use mine and couldn't get it to work."

"That's because it is keyed to you and to Red magic," Maendy said. "What she needed was a blank helbraught that could be attuned to her and her magic. Once anointed with her blood, the blade knows what magic to accept, and that she is its wielder. As you may have discovered, your helbraughts will work for others of the same Talent, but no others. Even another Red's helbraught doesn't work as well as your own."

"Why is that?" Rizelya asked.

Maendy shrugged. "It's the way the helstrim alloy works. It only holds and accepts one type of magic."

"Can you find several women with other Talents who wish to fight?" Rizelya asked Maendy.

Maendy looked at Saehala, who gave a nod of approval. "Yes, there are quite a few. Many are out working today. Not everyone stayed to watch the practice."

"We only need one of each of the other Talents," Rizelya answered. "No sense getting hopes up if this doesn't work."

"Besides," Laynar interjected, "it's one thing to have Yellows fighting because they are creating a shield for the Reds. It's another for the other Talents to fight like a Red. We need Clan-Alpha approval to integrate others into the fighting force."

"Hey, something this revolutionary probably needs the Supreme's blessing," Aistrun added.

"Let's keep this experiment as quiet as possible," Rizelya said. She didn't mind getting herself and her squad-pack in trouble, but these were strangers.

Maendy nodded. "I know just the women to ask. They'll keep it to themselves."

After a quick discussion, they decided only Rizelya's team, and the people Maendy would bring, would meet in the small practice arena an octar after the evening meal.

Chapter 13

Fifteen milcrons before the appointed time to meet at the small practice arena, Laynar knocked on Rizelya's door. Rizelya sat alone on the bed, enjoying the momentary solitude. The rest of her squad-pack had left earlier in pairs. Keandran hadn't returned to the room after dinner.

"Do you really think this will work?" Laynar slumped onto a chair.

"I do. Why are you here?"

"I want to be part of this. What you're proposing goes against all tradition. But the question is, will it hurt or help our people?" Laynar sat forward with her elbows on her knees. Her intense gaze bored into Rizelya. "If it hurts them, I will fight you, but if it helps us win the war against the monsters, I will be your biggest supporter."

Rizelya scooted to the edge of the bed. "We will only train those who volunteer, like we've done so far."

"No, that isn't true. What about the teacher we forced to learn the cold-air shield because she was the only strong Yellow in the keep who wasn't a child?"

"That was a special case and was necessary. You allowed it." Rizelya stood up and paced the room. Remembered malice from the woman in her dreams made her sure more, and worse, was about to hit them. Her voice rose with her passion—and terror. "All of us have to fight, however we can, if we are to survive this next assault."

"How do you know?" Laynar glared at her.

But Laynar wasn't someone she trusted implicitly. She didn't dare tell anyone else, except a White Priestess, of her dreams. She hadn't even told Aistrun the full details. The intelligence driving the control-janacks held a consuming hate and desired the obliteration of the Posairs, every last man, woman, and child.

"Just a gut feeling," Rizelya prevaricated. "Each time I'm near a control-janack and hear its humming, I sense extreme malevolence." That much was true. Why was she the only lucky one to hear the hum and have nasty visions?

Laynar gave her a long look, shrugged, and stood. "Let's go try this experiment of yours and determine if we have new fighters, or if it's still going to be us Reds fighting for our world."

Rizelya and Laynar arrived last at the small practice room. Rizelya's squad pack lounged against the wall. Maendy waited in the middle with a group of five women, each of them holding a helbraught. They seemed familiar with handling them.

"Rizelya, you've met Gehan," Maendy said, touching Gehan on the shoulder. Gehan grinned widely and jumped lightly on the balls of her feet in anticipation.

Rizelya smiled and gripped Gehan's hand as a fighter, hand to wrist. Non-fighters greeted palm to palm. Gehan's eyes widened with the gesture, her smile widening even further. The tension in the other four women eased.

"This is Grazeen." Maendy gestured at a slender and willowy woman with dark forest-green hair. Her eyes were brown and green. She stood a few inches taller than Rizelya.

Maendy nodded to the next woman. "I know I can't fight because we need my skills with the helstrim. But my daughter, Maellyn, can fight." Maellyn smiled. She had the same chocolate-brown hair and red eyes flaked with gold as her mother. She wasn't as broad shouldered from years of work at the forge, but she was strong and muscular.

"I'm Raeleen." The other Brown stepped forward, her hand held out. Rizelya gripped it in the warriors' greeting, feeling the woman's strength. She had dark brown hair with streaks in the same beautiful gold as her eyes. Rizelya felt calluses and scars on Raeleen's hands. The scars continued up her arms, and there was a puckered scar on her forehead, which Raeleen touched self-consciously.

"Stone worker," she said, pulling her hand away.

The last woman wore a hat covering her hair and kept her gaze down. But when Rizelya stepped up to her, the woman looked up in defiance, ripped off the hat, and shook her head. Shimmering sapphire-blue hair streamed down her back, the tips touching her thighs.

Rizelya gasped in surprise.

The woman's blue-green, almost turquoise, eyes narrowed in defiance. She was one of the most beautiful women Rizelya had ever seen. She was curvaceous, but under the softness Rizelya could see the rippling of muscles. Rizelya guessed the woman had an iron will hiding under the velvet veneer.

"Contrary to popular belief," the woman said, her voice was a low contralto, "not all Blues are weak and lack courage. I am Saffren. I wish to fight the monsters that harm our people."

"Welcome, ladies," Rizelya said, "we don't know if our experiment will work—"

"Of course it does," Maendy interrupted. She gave a knowing look to the others. "Show them."

Gehan's helbraught glowed a brilliant yellow. Freezing cold air shot out the end of the blade toward a melon. Ice quickly covered it. Gehan funneled more magic into her helbraught, and the melon shattered, frozen pieces flying in all directions. Gehan grinned. "I can do it with hot air, too."

"My turn," Maellyn said, stepping forward and facing a large leather ball. Her helbraught glowed a dark brown. With a yell, she thrust it into the ball. When it began to smoke and turn red, she withdrew the blade. The ball bubbled and melted, oozing a glowing red substance. "Lava," Maellyn explained, a note of triumph in her voice, "super-heated earth."

"Impressive," Laynar said. "I would never have thought you could do that with earth."

"Watch," Maellyn pointed to the slag that had once been a ball. As it cooled, cracks appeared on the surface, and it darkened to a hard lump of black stone.

"Raeleen, your turn," Maendy said, patting the woman on the back.

Raeleen turned to a hanging leather bag with tentacle shapes sticking out of it. Her lips tightened into a thin, determined line as she clenched her hands on her helbraught. The blade glowed white, with brownish-gray running through it. Raeleen yelled and rushed the bag, slashing at a tentacle. She ducked under the swinging bag and thrust the blade into it. She stabbed again and then stepped back with a satisfied smirk.

Wherever her glowing blade had touched, brownish-gray streaks spread out, growing, until brown and gray mottled the entire surface. The bag quit swinging, dropped to the ground, and with the crack of stone on stone, crumbled into pebbles. Somehow, Raeleen had turned the leather into stone.

"I hope that works on the monsters," Rizelya said as the dust settled.

"It should," Raeleen answered. "It's a type of sheadash stone that they can't stand the touch of it."

"Mine is similar to Raeleen's," Grazeen said, and walked to another hanging bag. She pushed it to get it swinging. Concentrating on the swing of the bag, she fed her power into the helbraught. The blade glowed a deep forest-green, almost the color of her hair. She didn't yell when she attacked, and she moved faster than Rizelya expected. Two large slashes on the bag showed she hadn't missed her target, and the sand flowing out changed from tan to a dark green. The bag also turned green.

It was rather lovely, Rizelya thought, but she doubted turning the monsters green would do much. Suddenly, the bag dripped in clumps, and Rizelya gagged at the smell of rot.

"That smells awful!" Rizelya grabbed her helbraught to burn the rotting bag.

"No, wait." Maendy put her hand on Rizelya's arm. "Watch. Grazeen's magic isn't finished."

Soon, the entire bag turned into a rotten mess, with something long and white squirming in it. Rizelya clenched her jaws against the roiling in her stomach. It took all her determination not to throw up at the sight. The white things grew larger as they became engorged with the rot. When they'd devoured all the rot, they tried to tunnel into the stone floor of the arena.

Grazeen hurried to them, gently picked them up, and put them in a sack she pulled out of her belt. She walked to the door, stepped outside, and stooped down to dump the creatures on the ground. They instantly turned into a churning frenzy and disappeared into the earth.

"What were those things?" Rizelya asked when Grazeen returned.

"Those are snelks. They eat anything rotten," Grazeen said, grinning, rocking on her heels. "I thought about using them while watching them clean up the latrine. They turn our garbage into beautiful, fertile soil."

Rizelya had never paid much attention to what happened to their waste or garbage. It simply disappeared. Now she knew why.

"After that, my little demonstration will be anti-climactic," Saffren said.

"All of what I've seen has been impressive. I'm sure I won't be disappointed," Rizelya said, soothing the nervous Blue.

"Okay, here goes." Saffren turned toward a large melon. Her helbraught glowed a pastel blue. As she channeled more of her magic into the blade, it darkened. Indigo light leaped from her blade to surround the melon, which began to steam as it boiled. The light flickered and changed to a pale blue, almost white. The boiling stopped instantly, and the melon turned to ice.

Saffren put the butt of her helbraught on the ground and swiped a stray strand of hair from her face. "I think I can do this a few feet away and not have to get too close to the monsters. If I can't, I'll stab them like the others do."

"So what do you think of our little squad-pack?" Maendy asked.

"Very nicely done." Rizelya walked around the room, examining the remnants of the targets. She beckoned to Dehali to come forward from where she waited with the others by the door. "It remains to be seen how they react to fighting monsters. Melons and leather bags don't fight back. Dehali will form a brecha illusion that acts like the real thing. Who is first?"

The women exchanged glances. Maellyn raised her hand. "I'll go."

Rizelya motioned for everyone else to stand by the walls and gave the signal to Dehali. A brecha materialized in the center of the room. It stood on its hind legs, head swinging about, scenting for prey. It stopped, dropped to all fours, and rushed toward Maellyn.

Maellyn's eyes widened in fear, but she didn't drop her helbraught or turn and run. She crouched down, her helbraught glowing. As the creature drew closer, she threw herself to the ground, thrusting her helbraught into the brecha's path as it ran over her. The sharp blade slid into its belly. Smoke poured from the opening, and the brecha glowed red. Maellyn rolled out of the way as the guts of the beast, now lava, flowed out. She jumped up and thrust her weapon into the side of the monster. More smoke billowed out of the brecha while lava erupted, covering it. Dehali let the illusion go.

"Dramatic," Rizelya said curtly, "but not the smartest move. The brecha's hind claws could rip you to shreds. You only do something like that as a last resort." She turned to the others, her voice stern. "We do not need heroes or showoffs. We need fighters who are part of the team. If you can't do that, we might as well call this experiment a failure and go to bed."

All of them bowed their head in shame. "Sorry, Alpha," Maellyn muttered. "It won't happen again."

"Good. Time for a change. Put down your helbraughts." She ignored their disappointed muttering as they obeyed and waved the rest of her squad-pack over, including Laynar.

"Form up with the new people in between you so they can see someone wherever they turn." When Maendy hesitated, Rizelya urged her to join them. She examined their positions and rearranged them until they were to her satisfaction.

"These first forms are similar to the ones you've been taught, but then we'll switch to more advanced routines. Learn them well. These will teach your body to move when your mind is busy fighting the monsters." Rizelya took a position in front. They flowed through all the forms once, then again. Sweat drenched her shirt. She had Laynar take the lead for the third set. Rizelya wandered around her new pupils, making small corrections here and there. Overall, they picked up the new forms fast.

"Now get your helbraughts," Rizelya ordered. Aistrun and Eidstrun went to the wall and picked up staffs. They didn't have enough magic to feed into the blades of the helbraughts, but the staffs were good training. She led them through the fighting sequences using the helbraughts. Again, the new fighters caught on well.

After a short break, she gathered them into a group. She looked at her squad-pack. "You know the drills. Pick a partner and work with them."

They quickly scattered throughout the practice arena, leaving Rizelya and Maendy standing to the side. Maendy held a helbraught and looked hopeful.

"I understand why I can't fight, but teach me anyway," she pleaded.

If her premonitions were true, they needed as many fighters as they could get. Maendy seemed to be the leader of this little squad-pack and would likely form another if Rizelya took this one with her. "All right, but you can't teach others," Rizelya warned, following her admonishment with a wink.

"Of course, I won't," Maendy said, nodding her head.

The new fighters made good progress. They moved from forms to partner fighting and then on to attacking the illusion monsters. Rizelya put them to work in teams like they would in a real battle, rather than alone. The techniques the new girls used to destroy the monsters were different enough that it was taking the more experienced fighters time to fall into a rhythm with them. If they added more of these types of fighters into the fighting-packs, they would need some new training drills for them all.

Rizelya sighed, then shrugged. What was another new thing added to all the others she'd been teaching lately?

She finally called a halt to the training after midnight. The next phase of the experiment would be against actual monsters. If the monster nests followed the same pattern, it wouldn't be long before the new fighters were tested.

The sun was just peeking out into the world when the sound of running feet woke Rizelya. Groaning, she wrapped a blanket around her and poked her head out the door. "What's happening?" she asked the first person to run past her.

"All three nests in this valley have somehow formed adult monsters! Hurry, we need everyone." The woman continued down the corridor, pounding on doors, and yelling for people to get a move on.

Rizelya threw on clothes, swiped a cleaning brush at her teeth, and splashed water on her face. Her hair was still braided from the day before, although several strands had worked loose and hung in her eyes. She'd re-braid it later. Her leg didn't hurt when she stamped her feet into her boots. She grabbed her helbraught as she raced out and nearly ran into Aistrun with his hand up to knock on her door.

"Hey, you're ready. Good." He hurried with her down the corridor. "We've sent Red leathers and capes to our new friends. I doubt anyone will notice a few extra fighters with all the commotion. If they keep their hoods up until we get to the nest, no one will know they aren't Reds. We couldn't have timed this better if we'd tried."

"Good thinking. They'll stay close to us. Make sure our people work with them. This will be their first experience with real, live monsters. Damn, I wish we had a chance to work with the illusions again this morning."

Pandemonium reigned outside as three platoons of fighters rushed to get horses saddled. Nervous whinnies and shouts filled the air. Their squad-pack, now doubled, had their mounts out of the stable and in a relatively quiet corner near the pastures. Aistrun was right. No one paid attention to their increased number.

"Saehala wants us to go with the second platoon," Laynar told them when they arrived. "Their nest is the largest, and we have the most experience. She sent Gehan to work with us."

"How awfully nice of her." Rizelya grinned. "Now we don't have to steal her away."

"Our temporary alpha is motioning that she's ready to leave." Laynar pointed toward a group mounting their horses. Rizelya recognized the leader as one of the Reds she'd trained yesterday. "See the teal and purple striped flag? That's ours for the day."

"Mount up and stay together!" Rizelya ordered her squad-pack. She smiled with pride when, in a synchronized movement, they all stepped into their stirrups and swung onto their horses, even Keandran. Rizelya hadn't seen him since yesterday morning. She wasn't sure how he had spent the day, but it hadn't been helping with the training.

They rode to fall into line with the waiting fighters. Within moments, the flag snapped forward. Heels struck flanks, and the horses raced out of the keep gates at a gallop. They had to hurry to reach the nest before the monsters warmed up enough to leave. Rizelya kept an eye on her new pack members. Although everyone learned to ride horses, most didn't ride as often or as far as fighters. Maellyn had a death grip on her reins and a determined and frightened look on her face. But she stayed in her seat. The rest were riding well. Gehan grinned widely and laughed with joy at the fast run.

Less than an octar later, the platoon clattered to a stop. Down below them the nest roiled with monsters, tentacles caressing spikes. It wouldn't be long before they emerged. The platoon stopped far enough away to keep the janacks from sensing their heat. Rizelya directed her squad to wait with the horses while she found out where the alpha wanted them in the battle.

"I want your squad-pack to hang back until we spot the control-janack, if there is one," the alpha told her.

"Oh, there is, I have no doubt." Rizelya winced at the loud hum emitted from the nest. "I haven't seen a nest lately without one. They usually send the rest out first. Are you sure you don't want to go after the control-janack?"

The woman shuddered. "No. I suspect I'll have plenty of practice later. This nest is huge. I'll be busy as it is." She turned away to give orders to her other seconds, but then twisted back to Rizelya. "Keep Gehan safe, okay? She's here to learn, not to get killed."

"I'll treat her like one of my own pack," Rizelya assured her. If this worked, she planned on taking the new fighters with her to the Clan-Keep, with or without Saehala's permission.

She returned to her squad-pack. They'd taken the horses to a small ravine to hide them during the fight. "We get the control-janack." She turned to Keandran. "You'll behave, won't you? No running into the swamp, right?"

"No, Alpha," he said sullenly. "Whatever the White Priestess did, I'm not feeling antsy with the monsters nearby like I did before. I should be good."

She hadn't known he'd been experiencing that. She peered into his pale blue eyes. He was the only one affected by their call. She looked thoughtfully at Saffren, then made a decision. They had a few milcrons yet before the fighting began.

"Saffren, walk with me," she called. The woman's eyebrows rose at being singled out, but hurried over to Rizelya. They strolled far enough away from the others to ensure a private conversation. "Do you hear anything or feel different?"

Saffren started to shake her head, then stopped. "At first I thought I was picking up on all our nervousness, but now you mention it, I think that isn't what it is." She closed her eyes in concentration and then rubbed her forehead. "There's something calling to me, wanting me to join it."

"Can you block the call or resist it? I believe it's the control-janack."

Saffren opened her eyes and frowned. "Of course I can. I don't want to answer the call. It's slimy and nasty. We're taught how to shield from all the emotions bombarding us. I'm a strong Blue, so my shields are also strong. It'll be easy to block, now that I'm aware of it." She quirked her eyebrow up in confusion. "But how did you know about it? You aren't a Blue."

"Keandran is an extremely weak Blue. We've had problems with him suddenly leaving the fight and wandering into the nearby swamp. He just mentioned he felt antsy around the monsters."

"He's so powerless, I doubt anyone taught him to shield because he wouldn't sense very many emotions." Saffren gazed at Keandran, rubbing her upper arms. When she returned her attention to Rizelya, a haunted look filled her eyes. "Keandran picks up more than he shows. He gives me the creeps and reminds me of a man I knew when I was a child. That man had the same pale, watery blue eyes. The only emotion he could pick up and feel was pain, and he enjoyed hurting people. He started on animals and then progressed to people. The alpha had to put him down, like the rabid dog he had become."

"We caught Keandran purposefully mistreating the horses. It's why he rides the brute Tejen. He can't bully him."

"Watch him carefully, Rizelya," Saffren warned. "He hates you... and your entire squad-pack."

Rizelya could hear the sounds of fighting, and the hum grew loud enough she couldn't ignore it any longer. "We need to go. It's time."

They ran back to the squad-pack, and they all hurried to the nest. The control-janack hadn't shown itself yet. The Reds and warriors already surrounded three janacks. Another one boiled out along with six brechas. Rizelya gaped. The humongous nest was the biggest one she'd ever seen. With the nest emptied, the control-janack took center stage of her awareness. Four brechas stalked in front of it, for all the world looking like guards.

They stopped a few feet away from the edge of the fighting. Rizelya looked over at Saffren. "You okay?"

Saffren nodded, her face tight with strain. "It's much stronger the closer we get to that thing. Ah, there, got it." She relaxed. "Ready to fight, Alpha."

Dehali and Gehan worked together, and within moments, they created a cold-air tunnel, leading directly to the nest. Another cold-air shield formed around the nest. Rizelya layered her fire shield over it. She nodded at her team, and they ran through the tunnel. The control-janack screamed in frustration while the brechas widened their perimeter, trying to sense them.

With only three warriors to assist nine women, Rizelya broke her squad-pack up into teams. She put Leistral and Eidstrun with Gehan, Raeleen, and Saffren. Dehali and Keandran joined with Laynar, Maellyn, and Grazeen. Aistrun and Rizelya formed the third team. She prayed Keandran wouldn't run out on them.

Although she wanted to watch how her new squad-pack fought, the screech of the control-janack reminded her she had a job to do. Giving Aistrun the signal to attack, she ran toward it.

She rolled under a flailing tentacle before it crashed down on her. As it began its upward swing, she jumped on it, riding it up until she could leap from the tentacle onto the head. It didn't seem aware of her presence because its focus was on directing its minions. She thanked the Warrior Goddess as she channeled her magic into her helbraught until flames licked the blade. Rizelya severed the protrusion, gritting her teeth against the howl from the controller of the janack, and thrust her helbraught deep into the monster.

"Blowing!" She leaped from her perch toward the protrusion's landing spot. As she hit the ground, she rolled, continuing the momentum to gain her feet and run. Rizelya remembered Gehan and Saffren's technique and tried directing her magic out through her helbraught. A gout of flame erupted from the end of her blade and engulfed the protrusion.

This time, as she destroyed it, she didn't experience the searing pain as the woman screamed in rage. Rizelya sank to the ground, waiting to pass out as monster bits rained down. She looked around in surprise when it stopped, and she was still conscious.

Laughter bubbled up as she took in the state of the monsters left by her new fighters. A brecha boiled on one side while the other side was turning to stone and crumbling. The front half of another one was rotting while molten lava ate the back. The other two brechas had suffered similar fates.

Her experiment worked! Other Talents could—and did—kill the Malvers' monsters just as effectively as the Reds.

The platoon rode back to Strunven Keep, celebrating their victory. They didn't have any casualties and only minor wounds, and they'd destroyed all the monsters from the nest.

Rizelya's experimental group impressed the rest of the fighters. Apparently, when they'd fought the last two brechas, the others had finished their battles and stopped to watch.

Rizelya dropped back to ride next to Saffren. "How are you doing?"

Saffren smiled at her. "Quite well, actually. Better than I expected. The monsters don't have any emotions except all-consuming hunger. It didn't bother me to end their hunger by killing them. After you killed the control-janack, I found it easier because I didn't have to block its call any longer. If it weren't for it, I believe other Blues would do all right fighting the monsters. However, with it around, I suggest only strong ones, who can create extremely good shields, get anywhere close. Its call is powerful. Posairs with weak Blue Talent wouldn't be able to resist it." She gazed pointedly at Keandran, who rode ahead of them. "It's no wonder he cannot. The call appeals to his twisted senses."

"If it's so powerful, why are only Blues affected and not the rest of us?" Rizelya now worried they would be fighting more than the monsters. So far, only she heard the damned hum.

Saffren thought about it for a while. "Because it's an emotional call of yearning. All the fighters I know have a strong sense of pack, of belonging to something greater than themselves. The call is alluring to those who don't have that. It promises someplace where they'll belong, will fit in, and they are wanted."

"What is the control-janack trying to do? Lure them away from the group and kill them individually?"

"Yes, it's a lure. But for what purpose? I don't know." Saffren shrugged, looking as confused as Rizelya felt.

"Then we make sure no one with weak Blue Talent fights the monsters," Rizelya decided.

"More than that," Saffren added, "there can't be any fighters who don't feel like they belong with the pack. It will take those as surely as a weak Blue."

"Well, this battle was informative." She grinned at Saffren. "We learned you and the others can fight, and we discovered more about the control-janack. A good day's work."

A short time later, the platoon rode through the keep gates. The other platoons had arrived ahead of them and worked to unsaddle their horses. Saehala and Saehalstrun waited on the porch of the Keep House for reports. They were still dirty, and a smear of blood ran down Saehala's cheek from a spatter of monster ichor. Her eyes narrowed in anger when she saw the women riding with Rizelya. Saehala angrily gestured to Rizelya to join them.

Rizelya dismounted and gave Kymaya's reins to Leistral. She limped a bit as she walked. Her bad leg ache again after all the running and jumping during the battle. She hoped it was simply muscle strain from the days of inactivity and not a new surge of narhili poison.

"What's the meaning of taking non-fighters with you?" Saehala demanded, her fists on her hips. "They could have been killed. You were very irresponsible."

"No, I wasn't, Saehala," Rizelya ground out as she walked up the steps. "They were there to fight, like we discussed yesterday." She couldn't contain her excitement, even in the face of Saehala's displeasure. She stepped closer, grinning. "You should have seen it. Their magic works wonderfully to kill the monsters. Gehan and Saffren boiled one side of a brecha, while Raeleen turned the other side to stone. Grazeen had the front half of her brecha rotting while lava flowed from the rear half created by Maellyn's magic. Not one of them hesitated. It worked."

"Did my girls do well?" Maendy anxiously asked, stepping out of the shadows. "None hurt?"

"Not a scratch or burn. They did an excellent job," Rizelya assured Maendy. She turned to Saehala and Saehalstrun. "I want to take them with me to Strunlair Keep for the clan meeting. We need to show the territory alphas other Talents can fight, not only the Reds."

"What clan meeting?" Saehalstrun asked, eyebrows furrowed.

"Oh, damn. With everything else happening, I forgot to tell you. Keshanal called a clan meeting for the first day of Sandar to discuss the new control-janacks and the rest of the unusual monster behavior."

"That's eight days away!" Saehala threw her hands up. "We shouldn't leave the keep so soon after the change in leadership."

"But we must," Saehalstrun disagreed. "We must inform the Clan Alphas of our challenge and the reason. We would have to go sooner or later, anyway."

Saehala sighed unhappily. "You're right. I'd prefer it to be later, though." She huffed out another breath. "We'll travel with you, Rizelya, to Strunlair Keep."

"I expected you would. And Maendy's girls?"

The keep alphas looked at each other and then shrugged.

"Of course," Saehala said, still unhappy. "You talked us into how necessary this experiment is. Our approval may help with the others. If we're to reach Strunlair Keep with time to rest before the meeting, we'll need to leave in the morning. There's much to do before then."

Without another word, the keep alphas turned and entered the Keep House, calling for their platoon alphas. Summarily dismissed, Rizelya hurried down the steps to find her squad-pack. She bumped into them where they waited around the house's corner, out of the Keep Alphas' sight. Rizelya shook her head when she noticed Keandran was missing. Her new girls wore shocked expressions about the news they had overheard.

Gehan bounced with excitement. "We get to go to Strunlair Keep with you! I've never been outside of Strunven Keep's environs, not even to Strunvede Keep."

Pleasure lit Raeleen's eyes. "One of my pack-mates is at Strunlair Keep, training with the stonemason there. It will be good to see her again."

"I'm like Gehan," Grazeen murmured, a tremor in her voice. "I haven't ever left Strunven Keep before. But unlike Gehan, I'm more scared than excited."

"There isn't anything to be afraid of," Maellyn assured her friend, putting an arm around her shoulders. "I've traveled with my mother to a number of keeps throughout all of Strunlair Province. We're all part of the same clan. Think of them as distant cousins."

"I'll be going with you," Maendy announced, her stance proclaiming her determination. "I must speak with the head helstramiester about our new needs. She makes her forge at Strunlair Keep."

"Pack lightly and don't forget your leathers and helbraught," Rizelya told them in dismissal.

"We need to restock some of our supplies," Leistral said. "I'll go make arrangements with the quartermaster." Eidstrun trailed after her.

Dehali gazed at the parting women for a moment. "I'll supervise their packing. There's an art to packing what you need." She rushed to catch up to them.

Aistrun and Rizelya looked at each other and shrugged. "Hey, it's just you and me, Little Red." Aistrun raised and lowered his eyebrows in an exaggerated manner. "Wanna join me in a good time?"

"Only if it includes food. I'm starving. I don't know about you, but I didn't eat any breakfast."

"Works for me."

They separated after eating. Rizelya spent the rest of the afternoon getting her clothes cleaned and repacked. When she undressed, she discovered, to her relief, her injured leg was free of any signs of poison. A long soak in the bathing room relaxed her. After jerking awake a few times as she slid under the water, Rizelya climbed out, dressed, and returned to her room to nap.

A commotion outside her door woke her up. She opened the door and hurriedly stepped out of the way as Grazeen's bag bumped the wall. She also carried a saddle bag, a bedroll, and her helbraught. A red cloak slung over her shoulder slipped down, and as she tried shrugging it back in place, her bag banged on the wall again. Saffren and Gehan shambled farther up the hall, while the other two were behind Grazeen, all of them carrying similar loads.

"Oops, sorry," Grazeen apologized. "I guess it takes practice to juggle all this. Since we're now fighters, they're moving us here." She struggled past Rizelya.

"Just for the night," Maellyn clarified.

"Do you think they'll move us permanently?" Raeleen sounded worried.

"I don't know," Rizelya answered truthfully. "It depends on the Clan Alphas." She leaned against the doorjamb. She hadn't thought about what would happen to the girls once they became fighters. They all had other work besides fighting. Maellyn and Raeleen were both accomplished in their fields of metal and stone work. She wasn't sure what work the others did. Since joining a fighting-pack at fourteen, all Rizelya did was fight monsters or hunt.

"For now," she said, "you are part of my squad-pack."

Raeleen nodded and hitched her bag more securely. She solemnly walked into her new room.

Once they'd all entered their new quarters, Rizelya closed her door and leaned against it. She had never considered how much the women's lives would change when they became fighters. The teacher in Strunheim Territory hadn't had any say whether or not she fought, as she had been the only strong Yellow in the area.

Rizelya jammed her rising guilt back down where it belonged. The war with the Malvers' monsters had escalated. She firmly believed if they were to survive, they needed all the capable fighters they could get.

Chapter 14

Late the next morning, Saehala gave the order to leave Strunven Keep. Earlier, a rider from a northern keep rode in, asking for help with a nest too large for the small garrison to handle. The news delayed Rizelya's group's departure since getting the fighters ready to ride took precedence.

Rizelya used the delay to find proper mounts for her new squad members. The ones they had ridden yesterday were fine for pleasure riding. But for the type of traveling her squad-pack did, they needed long-distance runners and horses with steady nerves. The fighting-packs claimed all the plains-bred horses within the Keep. It took a while, but with Eidstrun's help, Rizelya found several mixed-breed horses for her new girls.

Two full platoons rode with them, including a number of yellow- and gold-haired women, and dust clogged the air. Rizelya rejoiced her squad-pack's position was near the front.

The area around Strunven Keep was typical of all the keeps Rizelya had visited. Crushed sheadash stone and walls cordoned off the crop fields and pasturelands. This late in the morning, farmers worked in the fields, and the herders watched their flocks in their pastures.

At dinner last night, Laynar had mentioned the precautions Strunheim Keep had taken. Saehala immediately implemented the practical changes, and now young Reds, accompanied by a teenage warrior, stood guard in the pastures they passed. Some of the smaller fields shared guards. Helbraughts also replaced the shepherd's crooks. Rizelya guessed they would soon learn how to use them with their Talent to better protect themselves and their herds if a monster escaped and attacked them. The way the nests were forming it was a genuine possibility.

They quickly rode through the cultivated land surrounding the keep. The fields soon became a flat grassy plain widely scattered with patches of trees. It would take them several days to cross it. This late in the spring, the verdant green grass brushed the horse's knees. A crushed, compacted stone road cut through the grass. In the distance, a large herd of billocks grazed on the lush vegetation.

The valley reminded her of the great plains in the center of Lairheim. It took over a chedan riding a fast horse to travel from one end to the other. The Haaslair Province, which was even larger than Strunlair, claimed the plains for their territory. She hadn't visited it yet, but if Naila assigned her guard duty at Shandir's Crater, she would ride through it.

Rabbits, squirrels, and chipmunks dashed across the road. Birds wheeled overhead. A herd of long-legged ducorns, their twisty horns almost as long as they were, bounded through the savanna to their right. Rizelya laughed at the way they bounced up and down as they ran, making it harder for predators, such as wolves and cougars, to catch them.

Saehala called a halt at midday beneath a grove of trees. A spring bubbled up in the middle of it, and the water dribbled down a cairn of rocks forming a small pool. A squirrel sat in the tree above the water, scolding them. The paw prints around it indicated animals found it a popular watering hole.

They took turns watering their horses, which took a while, since the pool needed to refill before another set of horses could drink. Rizelya and her squad-pack ate a lunch of cold sandwiches and boiled eggs while they waited their turn. She tossed crumbs of bread to the waiting sparrows. A blue jay swooped out of the trees to snag a large piece before a sparrow nibbled on it.

The area was full of life—just the thing to attract monsters. There most likely was one, if not more, nests in this idyllic setting. Rizelya wandered over to where Saehala and

Saehalstrun rested. "Where are the monster nests in this area? Do we need to check them as we ride through?"

"This road avoids the nests," Saehala answered, her half-eaten apple in one hand. "We shouldn't have any monster problems here."

"There are two minor keeps guarding this valley," Saehalstrun added. "We won't need to fight."

"Good to know." Rizelya wasn't sure they were correct, but didn't want to argue. The monsters had been changing their habits way too much to be complacent because they hadn't attacked this area before. Instead, she returned to her group.

"As we ride," she told them, "be more alert. I have a strange feeling I can't shake or explain." Luckily, her people trusted her and simply nodded they understood. When they remounted, the women loosened the straps on their helbraughts, making it easier to grab them in a hurry.

Saehala picked up the pace after their rest. Several herds of billocks and ducorns scattered as they rode past. Off in the distance, ruins formed a mountain of rubble. Not far from it, the smudge of sedge grasses and thick bushes indicated a swamp.

Rizelya shivered at the menace she felt radiating from it. She cocked her head, listening intently, but didn't hear any humming. She watched Keandran while they passed the ruins and their accompanying swamp. Every few milcrons, his back twitched, and his head snapped toward the swamp. He had to make a real effort to face forward again. She urged Kymaya to ride next to Tejen on the side of the ruins where she could block Keandran if he bolted toward the swamp.

Her shoulders jerked as they rode past. She kept expecting a horde of monsters to attack them, even though it had been many years since an entire nest of monsters had escaped to rove the countryside. Rizelya shuddered at the memory of the nest in Strunheim Territory that had somehow produced just one janack and a pair of brechas out of its regular cycle. Nothing was normal about the monsters anymore.

She didn't relax until they left the ruins far behind them.

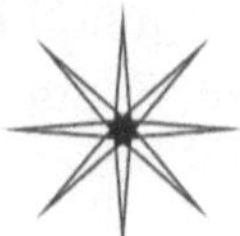

On the third day after leaving Strunven Keep, the plains gradually gave way to scrub oak, then larger trees. Soon they rode through a forest. Birds flitted in the branches overhead, squirrels and chipmunks scurried on the forest floor. Rizelya glimpsed a red fox as it poked its nose out of its den. Their passage didn't seem to frighten the wildlife.

At a crossroads that veered toward a minor keep, a small contingent of fighters turned off the main road. Rizelya noticed a woman with Yellow Talent accompanied the group. Soon, another team sheered off from the platoon to follow a well-worn path.

"Must be a keep in that direction," Laynar commented to Rizelya.

"Saehala was smart to bring additional support for the outlying keeps along our way. But where did she get all the Yellows? We only trained eight, right?" Her squad-pack rode bunched together in the narrower confines of the forest road. Rizelya smiled at the new members trailing behind and their attempts to entice Keandran to join them.

"*We* trained eight," Dehali answered. "Saehala pressed all those we taught, except Gehan, into training others once she saw how effective the cold-air shield is against the control janack. She's sending a Yellow to each major keep, who will then train other Yellows. Those will go to the minor keeps in each of the districts. The ones riding with us are going to the minor keeps beholden to Strunven Keep itself."

Rizelya gaped at Dehali. "How do you know all this? Saehala didn't say anything to me."

"Or to me." Laynar sounded just as confused as Rizelya.

"Ah, but people like me and tell me things," Dehali smirked. After Rizelya glared at her, Dehali relented. "The girls who trained were so excited, they sought out Gehan to tell her, and I was helping her pack, so they told me too."

"Hey, that's a damned fine idea Saehala had," Aistrun interjected. A frown of irritation crossed his handsome face. "It irks me we didn't think of it. We should make sure it gets passed around to the other alphas at the clan meeting."

"I'm positive Saehala will mention it." Laynar slapped at a biting insect that landed on her arm.

"That explains why so many Yellows accompanied us," Rizelya said. "But are they ready?"

"No one is ever ready until they're actually in a fight." Dehali sighed and rubbed her eyes. "I've been giving them additional training in the evening with Leistral and Eidstrun's help."

Pride filled Rizelya's heart. "So that's where you've been disappearing after the evening meal. I wondered where you were going."

"You aren't mad?" Worry creased Leistral's forehead.

Rizelya and Aistrun both shook their heads.

Aistrun snorted. "Of course not. We're proud of you taking the initiative. The more training those women have, the better off they'll be in a fight." He paused, then looked around at their group. "We've been remiss, Rizelya. We should train our new squad-members every night, too. We need to learn to work together with these new methods."

"If we're going to bring them fully into our pack, we need more warriors." Eidstrun scrubbed at the stubble on his chin. "Aistrun and I can't support and protect all you women by ourselves." He glanced back at Keandran and grimaced. "I don't trust him to help us. If that first fight was any indication, it would be wise to have a warrior teamed up with each woman."

"Why?" Rizelya asked, curious. Currently, a typical fighting force consisted of twenty men and eight women with Red Talent. Until recently, the men fought the monsters while the women kept them in the nest and prevented their escape.

Eidstrun chuckled. "Our new girls take the battle to the monsters. It's smart if we have sufficient fighters, because between your magic and our venom, the beasts don't stand a chance. Fighting as a team makes sense."

"We've never had enough Reds to fight as teams." Rizelya chewed on her lower lip. "But with more women joining us, it would be possible."

"I'd bet we'd have fewer injuries," Leistral added. "The men tend to fight individually and no one watches their back. I've seen Reds injured or killed when they tried to help a warrior, because they didn't know how to work together."

"You're right. I've seen the same." Rizelya made eye contact with her core group. "So while we're riding, I want all of you to think about how you would fight together as a team, either in pairs or in groups. Talk to our new members, find out what ideas they have. They don't know how we've always done it, and so they aren't restricted by traditional methods."

"Hey, Eidstrun and I will also scout out the men in this group to determine if any are willing to break tradition." Aistrun grinned and his eyes took on a mischievous glint. "There ought to be a few with open minds here, too."

"We'll exchange ideas and practice tonight after the evening meal," Rizelya said.

Aistrun and Eidstrun nodded in understanding and peeled away. Dehali and Leistral drifted back to join the new pack members. Soon Rizelya and Laynar rode in a pocket of quiet.

Rizelya looked at Laynar out of the corner of her eye. As there was no polite way to ask, she just dove in. "I've been meaning to ask, but didn't want to be rude, but where is your alpha partner?"

"Laenstrun was severely injured in the fight those monsters you caught for us escaped from. If he's recovered enough, Grandmother will bring him with her to the clan meeting."

"Laenstrun? Let me guess, he's related. A sibling, uncle?"

"Twin brother." Laynar smiled. "Grandmother really is trying to set up a dynasty for her offspring. Atypical, I know, for our pack way of living, but then Grandmother isn't a typical Posair woman."

Rizelya had to agree. Layhalya was a feisty, determined, old woman.

"How do you think we can fight these monsters better? Eidstrun's idea of teams is great, but what else is possible?" Both she and Laynar had been battling Malvers' monsters for a long time.

Others soon heard about the discussion and warriors and Reds would ride with them for a while, adding their ideas. Many of the discussions were lively and spirited. Some fought against changing the traditional way of fighting. Those, Rizelya happily noted, were the minority. Most of the fighters welcomed the discussion of new methods to fight their ancient enemy.

By the time they reached the safe house in the evening, the exchange of different, and perhaps better, ideas to kill the monsters had involved everyone open to change. After stabling the horses, a large group gathered in the courtyard. Rizelya,

Dehali, and several others created monster illusions to test the ideas. Some worked, some flopped spectacularly. The group shared cheers and groans with those who succeeded or failed. Rizelya had never seen such bonding, even in their typically close-knit society. Here, there were no alphas, no subordinates. Each person was equal to try their idea.

They put dinner on hold, with only a few people breaking away to eat. Rizelya thought it was a good thing when Keandran stalked into the safe house. The first few ideas had failed, and those were the ones he had witnessed. If whatever entity controlling the monsters lured him into the swamps, then it couldn't discover the new techniques. Keandran also belonged to the minority who believed the old methods were the only right way to do things. She wondered again why he was part of her squad-pack.

Saehala finally called a halt to the testing long after dark. Only when Rizelya stopped to eat did she realize how tired and hungry she was. She wolfed down her food, made almost inedible by the wait, and fell into bed.

A narrow gorge blocked their way, which would allow only a few fighters to slither through the opening at a time. On the other side of the rocky outcropping lay an old nest site, which rarely produced monsters. But with the unusual monster activity, Saehala sent a scout ahead to check.

Rizelya examined her expanded squad-pack as they waited for the scout's return. During the testing last night, each of her new squad members found a warrior, or more, to willingly partner with them. Aistrun and Eidstrun hadn't needed to say much to find volunteers. The girls had made quite an impression during their first fight.

Rizelya would have been happier if the warriors were from her own territory, but then she remembered her new people were all from Strunven. They would be more comfortable with men they were familiar with and had grown up around.

Each woman now had a warrior riding with her. Saffren had three men, and much to Raeleen's surprise, a man rode on either side of her. She believed herself unattractive because of the scars on her arms and face from her stone working. The men smiling and talking to her as they waited didn't seem to even see her scars. Rizelya shrugged, looking down at her hands. Raeleen's scars were similar to the monster ichor scars most Reds carried.

Pounding hooves heralded the return of the scout. "It's active! It's active!" he shouted as he drew up in front of Saehala and Saehalstrun. "Alphas, it's active."

"So we heard." Saehalstrun put a hand on the scouts' horse, calming both horse and rider. When the scout quit gasping, he asked, "What stage and how many?"

"Adult. I'm not sure why they haven't left the nest yet. I saw two janacks, each with six brechas."

While the scout reported, Rizelya rode to the edge of the outcropping. A low hum filtered through the opening. When she moved back, the sound faded. Rizelya leaned out of her saddle, inspecting the rock. The sheadash stone blocked the control-janack's crooning.

"Um, there's more than that," she called out to the others. "I can hear a control-janack's call. More brechas will be in the nest protecting it."

"Damn," Saehala swore. "It's been over a year since that nest was last active. That's why we took this route, and because it cuts a day of travel to Strunlair Keep."

Saehalstrun looked up at the sky, then back at the defile. "Why haven't the monsters left the nest yet? It's almost midday."

"You don't suppose they're waiting for us, do you?" Laynar asked. She seemed appalled at the thought.

"Hey, the way the damned things have been behaving lately, they just might be," Aistrun said.

Rizelya rejoined the group of alphas. "Now would be a good time to test some of our new ideas. How far is the nest from the pass?"

"Not far. We can leave the horses here and walk, or run, to it," Saehala answered.

"Hmm," Rizelya mused aloud, "Saffren's ice curtain should protect us as we move through the opening."

"Put a woman who can work at a distance," Laynar said, "like Gehan or Saffren, on a different team to help take out the janacks."

"Good idea," Saehala agreed. She looked at Rizelya and Aistrun. "Your team will attack the control-janack, as you have more experience. The rest of us will fight the brechas and guard the perimeter as we usually do. We don't want to try too many new ideas at the same time and have them backfire." Everyone nodded in agreement. "Let's go."

The leaders hurried to their respective groups and told them the plan. The fighters took their horses to the makeshift picket lines. A group of warriors and a young Red, barely out of her teens, stayed with the horses to guard them. The rest stalked to the outcropping. The men shifted into their warrior forms.

Saffren stepped to the front, her warriors behind her. She took several deep breaths. Her helbraught glowed an icy blue, and a sheet of ice shot out from it. She walked forward slowly and carefully, creating a thin wall of ice ahead of her. Four warriors and the Red followed. As soon as they neared the nest, the Red would form the traditional circle of fire around it. Saehala waited a few heartbeats, then nodded for the next group to go through.

Rizelya caught Gehan and Raeleen's eye and gave them an encouraging nod and smile. They gripped their helbraughts tight, and then it was their turn to slip through the opening.

On this side of the stone outcropping, none of the battle sounds reached them. Rizelya couldn't gauge if the plan was working or not. Grazeen waved excitedly and Maellyn nodded as they entered the pass. Saehala and her brother crossed with the next group. In just a few milcrons, only Rizelya and her original squad-pack waited to enter the fray. The control-janack was always the last to reveal itself in the nest. She counted to twenty, and then led them through.

The battle was unlike any she'd participated in before. The conflict spread out more than usual, with pockets of concentrated fighting. Each Red enclosed a monster with her fire-ring, while her team of warriors fought the brecha. Seven brecha corpses already littered the ground. Three additional brechas exploded from the nest, and immediately, fire and warriors surrounded them. More than flame and claws attacked the two janacks. A burst of lava melted off a tentacle as Rizelya ran to the center.

Dehali had the cold-air shield already up, and Rizelya's team rushed to the control-janack. It screeched with anger and frustration. Leistral tried a new trick, using her helbraught to create a flaming spear, which she thrust at an oncoming brecha. It pierced the beast and burned it from the inside out. Using the same technique, Leistral drove the remaining three brechas away from the nest and the control-janack.

The resulting scream of fury in Rizelya's head dropped her to her knees. Clapping her hands over her ears did nothing to stop it. She found her own anger and used it to push the shrieking out of her mind to function again. As she did, she regained awareness of the fighting.

Dehali and Leistral lured the control-janack out of the nest and surrounded it with both a ring of blazing fire and one of freezing air. Aistrun attacked the right side of the janack, while Eidstrun struck the left. Their claws slammed into its tentacles over and over, throwing chunks in every direction, and pumping venom into it. The end of Aistrun's tentacle flew off, and he ran to attack another one. Eidstrun roared as he jumped from a thrashing tentacle. It missed him, and he leaped on it with the claws of his right hand extended. His swipe cut through the tentacle.

Dehali saw Rizelya was up and moving again and surrounded Rizelya with a layer of cold air. She didn't have time to be surprised at the amazing developments of Dehali's Talent. Rizelya ran to the control-janack and vaulted onto its head. Instead of cutting off the protrusion, she tried something new. A tongue of flame flowed from her helbraught. She smiled in satisfaction as the protrusion blazed like a candle, cutting off the phantom woman's scream. Rizelya thrust her helbraught deep into the control-janack's head and poured her fire magic through her weapon and into the head until it glowed and pulsed from the heat.

"It's blowing!" she shouted as she jumped, trusting Leistral would throw up a fire shield to catch the debris. She crouched where she landed, twitching as burned monster bits fell around her. Rizelya questioned her bright idea to burn the still attached protrusion. She hadn't passed out, but a colossal headache pounded behind her eyes, and her body felt limp with exhaustion.

After sitting with her head on her knees for several milcrons, she surveyed the area. All the monsters were dead. Her new team had reduced the two regular janacks to misshapen lumps of cooling lava and crumbling stone.

"We did it!" Gehan cried, pumping her fist into the air. "Our ideas worked!"

Numerous fighters joined her in whooping and celebrating their victory.

Rizelya chuckled at their enthusiasm, then noticed Grazeen wandering the battlefield with the Reds. The bits she touched with her helbraught turned bright green, then turned to rot, and finally, the garbage grubs appeared, eating the monster debris. It seemed to take longer than burning them did. Curious, Rizelya counted the milcrons for each. Grazeen's method only took a couple of milcrons more and had the added benefit of leaving the grass a brighter green. Soon, they'd disposed of all the monster's remains.

A man in wolf form loped back through the gorge, and a short time later, the guards returned with their horses. Rizelya crawled onto her feet and swayed.

"Got you, Little Red." Aistrun, back in his natural form, caught her in mid-sway. "You're not going to pass out on me, are you?"

"No, I'm not," she grumbled. "I just have a raging headache, and I'm exhausted. Why am I the only one the stupid things affect like this?"

He shook his head. "Don't know. You're just special." He bent down.

"Oh, no, you don't!" She slapped his arm, stopping him before he picked her up. "I can walk." She took a shuffling step forward. He put an arm around her, and she gratefully leaned into his solid support. "Anyone injured?" she asked as they walked.

"No, no one too bad. There are a few scrapes, cuts, and burns. Nothing serious though. Eidstrun's idea of working in teams made a huge difference. I saw a brecha swipe a warrior's back, but because a Red worked with him, she drove the brecha away from him. It gave the other warrior in his group time to drag him out of the way. If they hadn't worked as a team, he'd be dead."

Leistral and Dehali caught up to them and walked with them. "It was a good fight. What happened to you?" Leistral asked. "You were kneeling on the ground, screaming, and with your hands over your ears. You hadn't formed the fire shield yet, so I did."

"The bad thing about breaking them up like we did is it made the control-janack furious," Rizelya told them. "Its shrieking almost knocked me out. Why am I the only one who can hear the damned things?" she complained, again.

"I don't think you're alone in that anymore," Dehali said after a moment. "I think Saffren can as well. She grimaced with pain when the control-janack started hissing."

Rizelya wondered how Keandran had fared from the intense call. "Where's Keandran?"

"Not again," Eidstrun grumbled, his hands on his hips. "I'm not traipsing around swamp muck searching for him."

"There," Leistral pointed at the far end of the battlefield. Keandran sat near the edge of a small swamp, only a hundred feet in diameter. He had his head on his knees, and Saffren stood over him with her hands on her hips. Rizelya's group hurried over to them.

"What happened?" Rizelya asked.

Saffren pursed her lips in a tight line of anger. "The fool was answering the control-janack's siren call. I had to knock him out to stop him."

"The bitch is lying," Keandran accused.

Rizelya gasped in outrage.

Aistrun slapped Keandran across the face with a loud crack. "Watch your mouth, cur," Aistrun growled. "There will be no insulting the ladies."

"But she's lying," Keandran sputtered. "I came over here to relieve myself."

"In the middle of the fight?" Saffren scoffed. "I don't think so. You heard the call, didn't you?"

"What in the Crone's fires are you talking about?" Keandran squirmed in front of them. He seemed frightened. "Back in

Strunheim Keep, the priestesses did something to me. Maybe their meddling is causing me to black out."

Saffren caught Rizelya's eye and shook her head slightly. Keandran way lying. Rizelya shrugged, uncertain what she could do about it at the moment.

"The others are waiting for us," Rizelya said. "Let's go. We'll deal with this later."

Aistrun helped Keandran up. His fingers tightening in warning around Keandran's arm. Keandran grimaced in pain but didn't fight to get away. Aistrun marched him to the horses and watched with his arms crossed over his chest while Keandran mounted.

We need to watch him carefully from now on, Aistrun mind-spoke to Rizelya as he helped her onto her horse. *I don't trust him.*

Rizelya agreed with him. The binding the White Priestess had put on him seemed to be unraveling. Another day of travel, and they should reach Strunlair Keep. Perhaps the priestesses there could help him more, and if not, the Clan Alphas could deal with him.

That is, if they reached the Clan-Keep before something else happened.

Chapter 15

The pass marked the entry point into Strunlair Territory. Down in the valley a wide road of crushed sheadash stone shone in the sunlight, promising quick and safe travel to the Clan-Keep. Rizelya's team should arrive ahead of schedule, even with all the delays they'd experienced. Exhaustion dragged at her, making her feel sluggish and slow.

"I'm looking forward to going home after the Clan meeting," she told Aistrun as she pulled herself into Kymaya's saddle. "It's been a long, exhausting four chedans."

He lithely jumped onto Jezhan's back, earning a glare from Rizelya. "Even though I still don't like, or want to be, a leader, I've enjoyed traveling and meeting new people. We've made such amazing friends. If Histrun hadn't sent us on this quest, we wouldn't have discovered the innovative ways the other Talents can fight the monsters."

"True," Rizelya huffed a breath, wiggling to get into a more comfortable position. Kymaya flicked back her ears and hopped in irritation. Rizelya leaned forward and patted her mare's neck. "But I miss my bed and cuddling with Kaieli."

She and her pack fell into line as Saehala and Saehalstrun guided the party down the path leading out of the mountains. They'd only ridden a few measures when the horses started snorting and tossing their heads. Aistrun's nostrils flared. He slid off his horse, flinging the reins to Rizelya.

"Shift!" he yelled. "Monsters!" His last word was more of a howl as he began his own change into warrior form.

Rizelya spun Kymaya in a circle, trying to get a sense of where the attack was coming from. A flight of birds, screeching in terror, alerted her to the danger. She whipped Kymaya to the left, already feeding fire magic into her weapon. A janack and three brechas poured out of the forest. The teams fought as if they had been together for years rather than days, and the fight ended shortly.

The various alphas gathered while the younger Reds burned the monster remains. Rizelya loosely hooked her helbraught back onto her saddle. "Where did they come from? The map doesn't show any nest sites around here."

Saehala looked as confused as Rizelya. "I don't have any idea. There aren't any nests. The roads avoid them."

"Remember those rogue monsters in Strunheim?" Aistrun rubbed his chin. "This seems to be like it."

"Crone's Fires! It does," Rizelya swore.

"What happened?" Saehalstrun's eyebrows knitted together.

"We experienced a nest that formed a single janack and a few brechas." Rizelya held up her hands as Saehala sputtered. "I know. It *was* impossible. But the rules regarding the monsters no longer apply. We better find out where they came from."

Rizelya sent Eidstrun to check the creature's back trail, while the rest of the group continued on.

A while later, Eidstrun caught up to them. "I found the nest several measures away." He rubbed his face and ran his hands through his hair. "From what I could determine, the damned things waited to ambush us."

"They don't have the mental capacity for an ambush or the patience." Saehalstrun's mouth pulled down in disgust. "What's going on?"

Rizelya shrugged with the rest of them. They continued forward, sending scouts ahead. A number of men, including Aistrun, stayed in warrior form and ran along the outside of the group. The women carried their helbraughts across their saddles, ready for trouble.

By the time Rizelya and the platoon reached a safe house for the night, they had fought six battles with marauding monsters where there shouldn't have been any. After the first attack, each monster swarm included a control-janack.

The next day was even worse and progressively worsened each passing day. The creatures acted as if they were trying to keep Rizelya's party from reaching Strunlair Keep. They hadn't traveled more than a few measures. A one-day journey had turned into a grueling four-day test of endurance. At this pace, Rizelya doubted they would arrive in time for the clan meeting.

Every night, the gaunt gray woman, urging her pets into mayhem, haunted Rizelya's dreams. She awoke certain the woman had something to do with the strange behavior of the monsters. Rizelya resolved to talk to the White Priestess at Strunlair Keep for help to stop the invasion of her mind.

Kymaya's head drooped, and she walked with a hitch from a splotch of monster ichor burning her right hindquarter. Rizelya rubbed her cheek and winced. She'd forgotten the wound on it. Her leg burned anew from the constant fighting. Aistrun, his red-gold pelt dulled, limped beside her. Blood oozed from a cut on Eidstrun's biceps. Everyone had some sort of injury, and grief hung over the group. During the last battle, the monsters had killed a Red and two warriors. The troop trudged on, knowing safety lay at the end of the road.

Rizelya slumped in her saddle, dreading the cry of warning she knew was coming. When it came, she drew herself up and forced tired muscles to move. When she called on her fire magic, only a flickering of her helbraught answered her. Eyes wide, she pushed away her terror and exhaustion, dove deep into her inner well where her magic resided, and dragged it up her core.

The resulting blaze seared the brecha barreling toward her. Leistral lifted an eyebrow at Rizelya's lack of control. Shrugging, Rizelya kicked Kymaya to avoid a janack's questing tentacle. When she tried again, she directed the fire shooting from her helbraught blade at the janack. The flame sped up its tentacle and covered its head. At the same time, Aistrun swiped his claws, dripping with venom, across its beak. The janack's shriek reverberated in Rizelya's head as it collapsed. It spasmed, jerking a tentacle, and crushed a young warrior as it slammed into the ground.

Tears pricked Rizelya's eyes at the young man's death. She blinked them away. There'd be time to mourn later. Not long after the janack's demise, the fighters killed the rest of the monsters, and the group pushed on.

That night at the safe house, Saehala burned the young man's body. The healers treated wounds, while several people, including Leistral, made a hot meal of beans and rice accompanied by flatbread. Too tired after eating to do more than sit and sip on her spicy taevo, Rizelya surveyed the room. Dehali, Gehan, and Maendy sat at a table, talking quietly. Saffren and Eidstrun leaned over a keshe board, playing with just two players simplified the complicated game. As her eyes roved around the room, she noted all her new friends. She smiled to herself and then sat up straighter. Keandran was missing. Frowning, she pushed herself from the table and strolled through the house, then checked the stables. His horse, Tejen, dozed in a stall, but she still couldn't find Keandran. When she went back inside, Aistrun approached her.

"Hey, Little Red, what's wrong?"

"Have you seen Keandran?"

His eyebrows crinkled. The more he thought, he pursed his lips and narrowed his eyes. "No, I haven't seen him since this morning."

Rizelya asked her squad-pack, and no one remembered seeing him after the day's first battle.

"He's gone," Rizelya admitted.

"He finally succumbed to the siren's call," Saffren added, rubbing her arms. "With all the control-janacks we've encountered, it was only a matter of time before he did."

"Hey, the good news is," Aistrun said, "we don't have to put up with the mangy cur anymore. And, even better, I didn't have to kill him."

"Do you think he can survive in the swamps?" Leistral asked. "I didn't like him any more than the rest of you, but still. The swamps..." she shuddered.

Eidstrun shook his head and crossed his arms over his chest. "I doubt it. I've never heard of anyone surviving alone in the swamps. Good riddance." He made a sweeping away gesture. "He was bad people."

No one argued with him. Rizelya experienced a moment of guilt, quickly squashed. She made the effort to bring Keandran into the pack, but he refused to be drawn in. Without him, her squad would be stronger.

The next morning, the group slowly ate breakfast, stalling the start of another long day of battling monsters, when the safe house gate opened. A large platoon trotted into the courtyard. The dark blue and blood-red barding proclaimed them to be from the Strunlair fighting-packs. Rizelya joined Saehala and Laynar to greet the newcomers.

"You are a sight for sore eyes," Laynar said, lifting her hand in greeting to the alpha leading the detachment.

"Our scouts saw you yesterday, and when you didn't arrive at the keep, we came to help." The alpha threw back her hood and surveyed the exhausted group. She had deep burgundy-red hair and her red eyes were ringed with gold. She was a rare double fire Talent, moderated with a smidgen of Yellow. Seeing her pale skin, Rizelya understood why the woman kept her hood up. She'd sunburn easily. She waited, her hands crossed over the pommel of her saddle, with an air of authority.

Laynar introduced the alphas in the group. When she presented Saehala and Saehalstrun as the Strunven Keep Alphas, the woman jerked back in surprise.

"What happened to Sujeen and Teraposan?"

"We had to challenge them," Saehala said tersely. "We'll explain to the Clan Alphas, not to some platoon leader."

"You will explain it to me." The woman's face reddened, her eyes narrowed, and she sat straighter in the saddle. "I am Beladi."

Saehala blanched, quickly bowing her head and dropping to her knees. She had just insulted the Clan Alpha. "I'm sorry. I didn't know it was you."

The rest followed Saehala's example. Rizelya dropped her head and lowered her eyes, hiding her anger. If Beladi had introduced herself, there wouldn't have been a misstep.

Beladi seemed mollified by the obeisance. "Tell me the story as we ride."

Rizelya's group quickly saddled their horses and readied to leave. With such a large force, Rizelya doubted the monsters would trouble them.

Home. Soon, she'd be able to go home.

The monster's previous bombardment stopped with the arrival of Beladi's large force. The group topped a hill, and Rizelya drank in the sight of the Storanos Lake glittering in the distance. Strunlair Keep squatted several measures from the lake. Histrun told her stories about the keeps enormous keep, but until she saw it, she hadn't understood how large it was compared to other keeps. Strunlair Keep was not only the largest Keep in Lairheim, but the most populous.

They clattered through the gates of Strunlair Keep after a short ride from the safe house. Rizelya sighed in relief. They had made it in time for the clan meeting, and with a day to spare.

Rizelya gazed around the grand keep with interest, as she hadn't been here before. White marble steps led to the Clan-house's sweeping porch, and the building was beautiful gray granite with flecks of mica sparkling in the sun. Columns of black marble held up a balcony, and the double doors leading into the house were dark ironwood polished to a glossy shine. Bands of metal, which looked like helstrim, strengthened the doors. Strunlair had been the first keep built after the Great War and the appearance of the monsters.

The population in most of the territory keeps was between two and three thousand people. Strunlair Keep, as the capital of the province, boasted double that number. Streets led from the central plaza of the Clan-house and Temple. Histrun had told Rizelya tales about the many small plazas scattered throughout the keep and the massive bazaar where one could find goods from all over Lairheim. He wore a belt buckle made from a seashell found on the coast of Keistanlair. Rizelya hoped to travel to the other provinces—once they resolved this mess with the monsters. She'd especially like to visit Haaslair Province in the great plains and see the wild horses galloping across them.

A happy cry spilled from the Clan-house, and the twins, Kami and Tami, rushed out, running toward Dehali. Laughing, they pulled her off her horse and swamped her with kisses. Laynar jumped out of her saddle and hurried into her grandmother Layhalya's arms. Rizelya and her squad-pack rapidly dismounted. Shaydan and Drustrun came down the steps with Keep Alpha Keshanal. Happiness bubbled up in Rizelya to connect with her friends again.

"You made it on time," Keshanal said, giving Rizelya a hug.

"Barely," Rizelya grimaced. "I swear the monsters were trying to prevent us from getting here."

A burst of laughter drifted to them from the courtyard, and Grazeen and Gehan stepped out of the circle of warriors. Their bright green and yellow hair was a striking contrast to all the redheads surrounding them.

"You've picked up a few strays since I saw you last." Keshanal gestured at Rizelya's new pack members. "It's strange to see red fighting leathers on other Talents."

"They are good fighters. Wait until you see what Saffren can do with water."

"A Blue?"

Rizelya nodded, rocking back on her heels. "Yep. An extremely powerful Blue."

As if summoned, Saffren threaded her way out of the crowd. She tossed her long, sapphire hair over her shoulder, laughing at someone's comment.

"I added not only a Yellow and a Blue, but a Green and two Browns to my pack. They have some interesting ways of using their magic to fight the monsters." She leaned closer to Keshanal. "We need every fighter we can get. The monsters aren't following any set pattern now. The nests are bigger, and they're doing strange things like ambushing us. We don't have enough Reds to do the job anymore."

"I can't wait to see your expanded pack's demonstration tomorrow." Keshanal laughed at Rizelya's confusion. "Word of your innovations preceded you. When Beladi heard you were nearby, she rushed out to meet you. You're becoming quite famous."

Rizelya groaned. It explained why Beladi had focused on her during the ride. She didn't want to be famous. She had more than enough notoriety from being her parents' daughter.

Everything she'd done on this trip was to help and protect her people, not draw attention to herself.

She didn't have time for self-pity. A swirl of warmed air warned her as Eiden and Kaieli rushed down the stairs. A moment later, they gathered her in their arms. She nuzzled Kaieli's neck, relishing the touch and smell of her heart sister. The rest of her pack from Strunland Keep clamored for attention. Aistrun's boisterous hugs had everyone laughing.

Behind them on the steps, Naila and Histrun waited for the jubilant greetings to calm down. He grinned at her and gave her a small salute. Rizelya frowned at them and playfully shook a fist at them. Neither she nor Aistrun could go back to being simple fighters now. They had truly become alphas during their quest. Seeing the grin on Naila's face, Rizelya suspected it was their plan, and the monster danger had given them the excuse they needed.

While on this journey, Rizelya had found friends in every keep. The monsters had changed and were doing strange things, but her people rose to the challenge and developed new ways to fight them. Leistral and Dehali were excellent teachers of the cold-air shield and the fire shield. Rizelya gazed fondly at the additions to her pack. They proved women with other Talents besides Red were effective in fighting and killing the monsters.

Now, if she'd quit having those pesky dreams, life could return to normal.

Later that evening, Rizelya dressed for the feast that would begin the clan meeting. Kaieli sat on the bed, her feet curled underneath her. A tight-fitting bodice in bronze silk showed off Kaieli's curves. A long amber necklace caressed the swell of her bosom. She'd piled her deep brown, almost black, hair on the top of her head with a few curls framing her face. Tonight her blue-gray eyes were a slate gray.

Rizelya frowned into the mirror as she attempted to do something as elegant with her own hair. Sighing, she brushed out the mess and pulled the front into a ponytail, leaving the rest long and wavy down her back.

Kaieli had brought Rizelya a dress sewn from the same bronze silk, but with a looser cut to hide her lack of curves. The sleeveless bodice showed off her muscular arms, and the color highlighted the brown tones in her deep auburn hair and made her brown eyes even darker. Other than the red in her hair, her wardrobe didn't include a speck of red tonight. It was a nice change from the red leathers she wore every other day in her life. She smoothed her hands over her gown, luxuriating in the feel of silk rather than leather under her fingers.

"Hey, you gorgeous yet?" Aistrun called as he thumped on the door. Without waiting for an invitation, he strode into the room. He passed a cursory glance over Rizelya and then eyed Kaieli. "Yep, you're gorgeous. Oh, and you too, Little Red."

Aistrun had replaced his red leathers with a crisp white shirt. He wore the laces open to reveal his broad chest. Shiny black leather pants fit his muscular legs like a glove. He fiddled with the antique bronze cuff links at his wrists. A pale gold satin jerkin with burnished gold embroidery finished his outfit. He had shaved and cut his red-gold hair, which had grown past his shoulders in the several chedan they'd been traveling.

"May I escort you beautiful ladies?" Aistrun bowed slightly and held out his hands in invitation. "Please. The food smells amazing. I'm about to shrivel up and die of starvation."

Kaieli giggled, then allowed him to help her off the bed. Rizelya rolled her eyes and shook her head, but took his elbow. The three friends headed down to the feast. At the doors leading into the huge dining hall, they met the rest of their squad-pack. The ladies looked lovely in their brightly colored gowns and the men were handsome in formal jerkins or jackets. Grief gripped her heart when she searched for and didn't spot Keandran.

The group swept into the dining hall. Rizelya gasped. The china and crystal place settings on the long tables must be ancient. There hadn't been such craftsmanship since the Great War. The tablecloths were in the colors of the different keeps. Rizelya approached the table with the rose and turquoise tablecloth. Next to it was the sapphire blue and carmine red of the Strunell Keep. Shaydan was already sitting and gave Rizelya a little wave. On the other side was the sky blue and pink of Strundale Keep. Rizelya hadn't gone there and didn't know anyone at the table. Further down the room, Strunven Keep's teal blue and purple covered a table. She glanced at Grazeen, Maellyn, and the others from Strunven.

"Do you wish to go sit with your friends?"

Maellyn gave her a wry smile and shook her head. "No, we're part of your pack now. Besides, we spent all afternoon with them."

"Unless you don't want us anymore," Raeleen said, her eyes wide.

Rizelya reached out and patted Raeleen on her arm. "Of course I want you. You're my pack."

The group settled around the table with the Strunland contingent. Eidstrun sat next to his twin sister, Eiden, their yellow heads tipped toward each other, shoulders touching. Her table, beside those living in Strunlair, was the only one with representatives from other Talents. Otherwise, only a few Yellows and Brown healers dotted the sea of Red.

A dais at the front of the hall held a table for the various keep alphas. Naila caught her eye and raised her cup. Rizelya couldn't hide from Naila and Histrun much longer. She'd spent the afternoon relaxing. First, she basked in the hot waters of the bathing room and then Kaieli treated Rizelya to a marvelous massage, during which she fell asleep. She'd slept until Kaieli woke her to get ready for dinner.

Clan-Alpha Nestrun stood and tapped his glass. As people noticed Nestrun's imposing presence, chatter ceased and everyone turned respectfully to listen to their alpha. Nestrun was tall, almost seven feet, and was a big man. The crystal goblet appeared tiny in his giant hand. Green streaked his close cut red hair. Laugh lines surrounded his pale green eyes.

"My people," Nestrun began, his voice a deep baritone, "we are gathered for the direst of circumstances. After a thousand years, our ancient enemy, the Malvers' monsters, has changed and threaten our survival more than ever before. We must fight differently than even our parents did in order to win. Luckily, we have some innovative young people who are showing us the way. Tomorrow, they'll begin teaching us their new techniques, including old wolves like me. Tonight, we celebrate and honor their accomplishments." Nestrun held up his glass. "To Rizelya, Aistrun, and their squad-pack."

Everyone turned to face Rizelya's table and toasted them. Rizelya's ears burned with embarrassment.

Nestrun sat back down, and young people streamed into the room, carrying heaping platters of food. The amount and variety astounded Rizelya. After five chedan of living mostly on soups and stews, she missed eating mashed tubers, crusty hot bread, and tender lamb chops. Flaky berry pies finished the meal. By the time Rizelya pushed away from the table, her stomach hurt. Aistrun's eyes were heavy lidded after the massive amounts of food he'd consumed.

A group of Yellows and Browns brought out instruments, and soon, lively music flowed through the dining hall. People carried the tables to the side, nestling them against the walls, to create space for dancing. Aistrun pulled Rizelya onto the floor for a spirited dance. She whirled away from him. Eidstrun caught her, and they danced for a set. When he twirled her around, she landed in Histrun's arms.

"You've done well, girl," he said with pride. "I knew a leader was in you, waiting to come out."

"You and Naila have ruined me and Aistrun. There's no way we can return to being simple fighters."

"It was about time. This situation, as bad as it is, was too good to pass up. You two were the only choice for the mission."

"Why didn't you just call a clan meeting like Keshanal did and save us the trouble?" Rizelya frowned at him.

Histrun laughed. "We could have, but you needed to stop hiding from your abilities. Besides, it gave you the opportunity to find new methods to fight the monsters. We wouldn't have discovered what the other Talents were capable of without you."

She dropped her head and blinked back tears. He rarely expressed his pride for her. After a few more turns, she looked over his shoulder. Naila danced with Aistrun. Histrun spun and whirled Rizelya, taking her off the dance floor. Aistrun and Naila were right behind him.

"Now, talk. No more hiding." Naila pointed at the hall's door.

Rizelya sighed and gave her alphas a wry smile. They crossed an inner courtyard and entered a small office.

After they were all settled in chairs, Histrun leaned back with his arms crossed over his chest. "Report," Histrun snapped. "We'll hear everything that happened on your journey."

Rizelya motioned for Aistrun to take the lead. He didn't leave anything out, including her propensity to faint after killing the control-janack. Histrun and Naila listened without interrupting. They'd drill them with questions once Aistrun finished.

"And—" Aistrun glanced at Rizelya "—she's been having strange dreams."

She should have known he would tattle on her. She wanted to punch him but couldn't with the alpha's gaze boring into her.

"Dreams? Of what?" Naila said, leaning forward.

"When the control-janack is present, I hear humming. I don't *faint* from touching the protrusion." Rizelya glared at Aistrun. "When I touch it, I see a strange woman, and her angry screaming is so loud it makes me pass out. The same woman appears in my dreams, or perhaps they're visions. She is gaunt and has very pale gray skin, so pale it's almost translucent. Her hair is charcoal-gray hair, and her eyes are black. She wears a strange device on her head which harvests some sort of food for the others."

Rizelya paused and gazed at her fingers as they twisted and untwisted. She replayed all her dreams of the woman and the sense of a mind behind the control-janack. "I'm sure the woman controls the monsters," Rizelya said, her voice bleak. "I think she even created them. She calls them 'her pets.' The monsters aren't our ancient enemies. She and her people are."

Naila's elbows rested on the arms of the chair, and she dropped her head into her hands, shaking it. Histrun groaned, then stood up and went to the window. When he turned back, all the color had drained from his face.

"If there's someone controlling the monsters, we don't have a chance," Histrun said.

"The Sanctuary. The Supreme Priestess," Naila said quietly. "She needs to know. She'll know what to do."

Histrun leaned against the windowsill. "Yes, she will. I'm sending you to the Sanctuary to tell the Supreme White Priestess about this and your theories. Rizelya, don't hold back. Tell her everything."

Rizelya rubbed her face. She had known this was a possibility and why she had avoided Naila and Histrun all day. This delayed her going home for some unknown time.

As soon as breakfast was over the next morning, Rizelya and her squad-pack led a procession to the practice arena. Keshanal gave her an encouraging nod. Shaydan and Laynar walked behind the keep alphas and would lend a hand in the demonstrations and training.

Eiden beamed with pride when Dehali exhibited the cold-air shield and how to use it.

Beladi gazed at Eiden with new respect. "Nicely done."

"That will be extremely helpful in the field," Nestrun said, nodding with approval.

"It's even more effective in conjunction with the fire-shield. I learned it from Naila." Rizelya and Dehali showed how the two shields worked separately and together.

Nestrun stood up, applauding. "I heartily approved of these new shields." He glared at Naila. "Although I'm disappointed in you for not sharing this with us earlier."

"Mother developed it," Naila croaked. "Same time as Zehis method. Assumed everyone knew it."

"In that case, we forgive the oversight." Nestrun rubbed his hands together. "Now, what other wonders do you have to show us, Rizelya?"

"Next up is the demonstration from my new pack members, showing how the other Talents battle the monsters."

While she'd talked with the Clan-Alphas, her team set up melons and leather targets. As a group, the mixed Talents stepped into the arena.

"What is she doing out there?" A man at the front sneered and pointed at Saffren.

Her braided sapphire blue hair, hanging down her back, contrasted vividly with the red fighting leathers she wore.

"Blues can't fight! Get out of here," someone else yelled.

Rizelya glared at the audience.

Beladi stood up, her hands on her hips, facing the crowd. "Those comments are uncalled for. We treat each other with respect! If I hear another outburst like that, I'll send you all out of here. And I'll punish the culprit." She turned back to the women waiting on the arena sands. "Ladies, please continue with your demonstration."

The group had planned on demonstrating in the same order as before, with Saffren showing her ability last. Instead, Saffren glowered at the crowd and strode onto the sand, standing several feet away from the first leather target. She gripped her helbraught so tight her knuckles turned white. Rizelya smiled at her and gave her a nod of assurance. Saffren visibly relaxed.

Her helbraught glowed with pale blue light, and a stream of icy water flowed from the blade, freezing a melon. Then the color of the blade changed to deep indigo. A flash of light, and the melon boiled. An astonished yelp came from the crowd.

"That should be almost as good as fire," Beladi said.

"It is. And her ice curtain allowed us to get past monsters that blocked the pass into Strunlair." Rizelya lowered her voice so only Beladi could hear her. "But because of the control-janack, we can only allow very strong, dark Blues to fight. Otherwise, we could have another Keandran."

Beladi nodded in understanding. Before breakfast, Rizelya had briefed the Clan Alphas on what happened during their journey.

Grazeen went next, exhibiting the rot and the resulting snelks.

"It works on the monsters," Rizelya told Beladi and Nestrun. "These methods are battle tested. We had enough battles the last few days to test a multitude of techniques." She shuddered at the memory of the monster's unending onslaught.

When Raeleen showed turning monsters into stone, and Maellyn burned hers with lava, the Clan Alphas nodded, pleased smiles on their faces.

Gehan's freezing air was a bit anti-climactic, given the previous spectacular lava destruction.

"Yes!" Eiden yelled, jumping up from her seat. "I can actually fight now!"

"We must train as many people as possible while Rizelya and her team are here. We can't afford to hope the Malvers' monsters will return to normal, and we won't need this."

"I agree," Nestrun said with a curt nod. He stood up and faced the crowd. "Anyone who wants to learn these new techniques is free to do so. However, I will require you to travel with the various keep alphas and pass them along to their people. I want every keep, no matter their size, within Strunlair Province to contain at least one squad with varied Talents to fight the monsters as soon as possible."

"Thank you!" Layhalya cried. "Even with the cold-air and fire-shields Rizelya taught us, we're having problems with the growing number and size of the nests. We simply don't have enough Reds."

"Same in Strunland," Naila agreed.

Keshanal nodded. "As in Strunell. We're also experiencing the odd janack and accompanying brechas the nests are throwing out now. They've killed several people. More would be dead if I hadn't instituted the old policy of having our warriors-in-training guarding the fields and pastures."

"These methods are too valuable, and needed, to keep to ourselves," Beladi said. "We can't wait until the next Alpha Council to share them. As soon as we have enough experienced teams, we'll send representatives to the other seven provinces to teach them the new techniques. We'll need volunteers for those squads."

"Sign up forms will be posted in my office within the octar," Nestrun announced.

Rizelya gaped at the number of people rushing from the arena, talking excitedly about signing up for training.

Over the next three days, Rizelya and her team taught the new methods to so many people, Rizelya lost count. At the end of the third day, Histrun and Naila called Rizelya and Aistrun into a meeting.

"You're leaving tomorrow for the Sanctuary," Histrun told them.

Rizelya nodded. She'd expected it. "Who is going with us?"

"Your squad-pack." Naila's eyebrows scrunched in confusion.

"Does that include my recent additions?"

"Oh," Naila said as understanding washed across her face. "No."

"But they're my pack!" Rizelya crossed her arms, ready to fight for her people.

"Yes, they are," Histrun agreed. "But they'll wait here for you to return."

"But why can't they come with us?" Seeing Naila's tight lips, Rizelya changed tactics. "Surely the Supreme needs to know about our new fighting methods, doesn't she? My team could show her."

Naila frowned at her. "Not the Supreme's concern."

"The Supreme doesn't care how we fight the monsters." Histrun folded his arms across his chest and leaned back in his chair. "We need your people here to help us complete the training of all these new squads. You don't need them to accompany you through an area that hasn't ever seen a monster attack."

Rizelya's shoulders slumped, and she huffed in defeat. "Oh, all right. Just as long as when I return, they rejoin me."

Aistrun cleared his throat. "Alpha, we'd like a change in our squad-pack."

Rizelya smacked her forehead. How could she have forgotten? Since arriving at the Clan-Keep, Dehali and the Strunell twins, Kami and Tami, were inseparable. They were quickly becoming bond-mates. It would be unkind to make them wait for her return from the Sanctuary to be together.

"Dehali would like to be transferred to Strunell Keep. Keshanal says she'd be delighted to take her," Rizelya said.

"Already done," Naila said with a smile. "Not too old to see love."

Rizelya leaped up, rushed to her sister, and hugged her. "Oh, thank you, Naila. They will be so happy."

Her squad-pack had begun as six, then swelled to twenty, including the warriors attached to her new girls, and now it was down to four. On her way to her room, Rizelya stopped to tell Dehali of her transfer. Dehali swamped her with deliriously joyful tears. Rizelya was still smiling when she entered her room.

"What's happened?" Kaieli asked, putting down the scroll she was reading. Strunlair Keep was home to the healing college of the country. Healers from all over Lairheim traveled to the college to study with the masters, and Kaieli was taking advantage of the opportunity to consult with them.

"Naila transferred Dehali to Strunell Keep."

"That's marvelous news! Finding bond-mates is always special."

"Are you sorry we never became more?" Rizelya knelt in front of Kaieli, holding her hands.

"No, we're what we are meant to be: heart sisters." Kaieli cocked her head to the side. "What's wrong?"

"I'm leaving for the Sanctuary tomorrow."

"I'm confused. That's good news. The Supreme needs to hear about your dreams."

"But we've seen each other so little. I'd rather be going home with you."

"Oh, I'm not going home."

Rizelya pulled back in surprise.

"I'm going to Posanlair Province. There's been an outbreak of a strange plague, and they need help. I came here to consult with the master healers before leaving."

"Oh. You're an excellent healer, and they're lucky to have you." Rizelya threw her arms around Kaieli's waist and buried her face in Kaieli's lap. "I'll miss you. Who knows when we'll see each other again?"

Kaieli kissed the top of Rizelya's head. "It will go fast. You've monsters to kill, and I have a disease to destroy. It's what we do."

That night, with Kaieli's soft breath on her shoulder, Rizelya allowed herself to wonder what life would be like without the monsters. What if they could destroy them forever? Kaieli would still have diseases to fight. All Rizelya had ever known was fighting monsters. What else would she do?

Chapter 16

Rizelya's small pack saddled their horses in the early morning light. Dehali solemnly boosted a large bundle onto Kressy's back. Over the several chedan since they'd acquired her, the multa had shed her winter pelt. The pale cream and warm gray had turned to light green. Glancing around to see that everyone was ready, Rizelya called the order to mount up and led her group out of the keep.

Not far from the gate, a commotion caused Rizelya to turn in her saddle. A familiar, stubborn stallion galloped toward them, trailing his broken lead rope. She reached out and grabbed Tejen's bridle. He tossed his head at his cleverness in catching up to them, and Kymaya whickered at him. The horse trotted happily along with them. Rizelya knew it was hopeless to take him back. Obviously determined to accompany them, he'd just escape again and follow them.

They rode north toward Strunhelos Territory, and the early summer sun warmed their backs. The first two days, they experienced pleasant riding through the fields and orchards. It was becoming common for teenage Red girls and their wolf counterparts to guard the non-fighters as they worked. Rizelya reflected that soon every keep in Lairheim, large or small, would institute the practice until the monsters returned to normal.

But Rizelya doubted they would.

Her visions convinced her that the only way to end the monster's reign of terror was to defeat whoever controlled them. In her dreams, Rizelya had glimpsed others besides the strange woman, and all of them held malice for the Posairs.

The second night from Strunlair Keep, the visions began again, more horrible than before. Rizelya saw a young boy herding a small flock of sheep. During their grazing, they had wandered away from the rest of the herders. A brecha burst out of the tall sedge grass with another one close behind it. They ripped the sheep apart. Pus-colored smoked roiled in the woman's tubes, forming beads as the brecha devoured the animals. The boy ran screaming with a janack rolling after him, thick slime coating the ground. Its long tentacle stretched out and snatched the child, lifting him high in the air and dropping him in its open maw. The strange woman laughed gleefully when the pus-colored smoke turned black. The black pearls dripping into her bowl were larger than the others. She popped a pearl into her mouth and sucked greedily on it. Other hands reached for the pearls.

Rizelya woke up screaming. Aistrun gathered her in his arms and held her for the rest of the night. Whenever she closed her eyes, the boy's death replayed, and the woman's exultant laugh rang in her ears. The monsters killed two more people in her dreams.

The dying people's terror sizzled through Rizelya's veins. Even in the bright light of day, the images haunted her. A heavy lethargy settled around her, and she slid from Kymaya's saddle, coming to when she hit the hard ground. After the second time, Aistrun insisted she ride in front of him.

They reached Strunhelos Keep as twilight ignited the snow-covered peaks of the White Mountains. After dinner, their host led the group to a room high in a tower. The meal and the safe confines of the keep revived Rizelya. Dreading more dreams, she forced herself to stay awake while the others slept. In the dark, Rizelya stood staring out the window. The Sanctuary hid in the mountain's depths, and it would take them three days to reach it. Rizelya leaned against the cold glass. Would the mountains offer her sanctuary from the attacks on her mind and sanity?

Unwilling to see any more people dying in her dreams, Rizelya spent the night drinking copious amounts of taevo in an effort to stay awake. By the time the others woke up, her eyes were bleary, and she shook from the caffeine. While trying to saddle Kymaya, she fumbled the buckles and straps so badly that Leistral pushed Rizelya's hands away and finished the job.

The steady sway, and the warmth of the sun, lulled her, and Rizelya drifted to sleep. Dream after dream of monsters killing people assaulted her. The woman's gleeful cackle as she and her compatriots fed on the death essence echoed in her head.

Aistrun pulled her from her saddle, and she stumbled against him while he guided her to sit on a log. She blinked her eyes, trying to stay awake. Rizelya covered her ears with her hands, attempting to stop the ongoing cackle, and she curled into a ball until her face rested on her knees. Her jaw ached from clenching it tight to keep the scream inside. She was vaguely aware when someone threw a sleeping fur over her. Another dream assailed her, and the next time she floated into consciousness, Aistrun carried her into a tent and laid her down. He wasn't grinning.

The woman's attack on Rizelya's sanity didn't stop. By morning, the dreams became all Rizelya knew. In rare moments of clarity, she heard the clopping of horse's hooves, and felt Aistrun's strong arm around her. She'd lean back against him, soaking in his strength, until the next dream stole away her awareness. She awoke once when Leistral spooned warm broth into her mouth. Leistral's eyes were red rimmed, and worry etched lines on her face. Then another vision swooped into her consciousness, and terror engulfed her.

The clatter of hooves on cobblestones intruded into Rizelya's dreams. The steady clip-clop rhythm penetrated through the mists of horror, and the dream began to slip away, ceasing entirely a few moments later. Rizelya tensed while she waited for the next dream to hit her. When it didn't, she let out a breath and relaxed against Aistrun's shoulder.

Jezhan came to a shuddering halt. "We're here." Rizelya heard Aistrun tell her.

"You're safe." Gentle hands, matching the voice, caressed her arm. At their touch, Rizelya jerked awake, truly awake for the first time in days.

"Where are we?" Rizelya's voice cracked.

"The Sanctuary."

A woman stood next to Jezhan. The familiarity of her voice teased at Rizelya. She blinked, then narrowed her eyes. A blue band pulled the woman's creamy white hair with thin streaks of gray back from her face, and she had kind, pale blue eyes. She was about the same age as Rizelya. Recognition finally dawned.

"Wisah!" Rizelya slid off the horse and into the waiting arms of her niece. Wisah was Naila's only daughter. Zehala had been in her mid-fifties and Histrun in his seventies when Zehala's pregnancy with Rizelya surprised them. At the time, Naila was thirty and pregnant herself. Wisah and Rizelya had been raised together in the pack nursery until Wisah turned five and had gone to the Sanctuary to train her White Talent. When she was thirteen, she had returned to Strunland Keep as an apprentice priestess, and the two had renewed their friendship. But they hadn't seen each other since the Supreme recalled Wisah to the Sanctuary six years ago.

"You've looked better." Wisah kept an arm around Rizelya's waist to support her while smoothing her hair. "Why are you here?"

"Can't I just come to see my niece?"

"No. What's wrong?"

Rizelya wrinkled her nose. "I need to talk to the Supreme about my strange dreams. They could be visions."

"Sounds important."

"It is."

"I'll make arrangements for you to meet with the Supreme. Let's get you settled first." Wisah turned to Aistrun, who pulled her into a hug. "You, however, can't come any further. No males are allowed into the Sanctuary cloister."

"Hey, Wisah, can't you make an exception for your favorite wolf?" Aistrun made a sad face.

She laughed at him. "No, not even for you. There's only one man, except the Consort, who has ever seen the cloisters, and that was Blazel. He was only a boy then."

"I remember Histrun talking about him. Where's Blazel now? I'd like to meet him."

"Gone. Chariel sent him south."

A young girl about ten years old with white hair approached them and bowed. "I'll take you to the men's ward, warriors." Her voice and body trembled.

"Be gentle, Aistrun," Wisah warned. "She rarely sees any warriors here."

Aistrun nodded, and he and Eidstrun pulled their packs from their horses and followed the girl to a door across the courtyard. Another girl took the horses' reins and led them away.

"Come," Wisah said, "let's get you and Leistral settled. Tell me about home."

Leistral and Wisah each put an arm around Rizelya's waist, supporting her as they walked to the cloister.

Rizelya stretched, and her leg hit a solid presence where none should be. She opened her eyes and scrambled out of bed.

"What... where... who...?" She couldn't form thoughts, much less words, in her terror. The woman assaulting her mind was here, on her bed.

"I'm Chariel," she said, in the soft tones used for calming spooked horses. She lifted a hand to swipe a strand of hair away from her face.

Her long, tapered fingers caught Rizelya's gaze. Fingers, not claws. Her thumping heart slowed to a normal pace. At first glance, the woman from her dreams and this one could be twins. Rizelya forced herself to study the woman's face. It was fuller, healthier, and her eyes were different, too. They weren't brimming with hate, but with concern. And they were dark gray, not black. Chariel's pale skin glowed rosy in the morning light rather than being a pale gray. However, they both had the same charcoal-gray hair. All the Grays Rizelya had seen had much lighter gray hair and eyes.

"What..." Rizelya swallowed the last of her fear. "What are you?"

Chariel looked at her quizzically. "I'm a Gray..." she said hesitantly, as if it wasn't obvious.

"You look like the woman in my dreams." Rizelya grimaced, then began pacing the room. "An evil, malicious person who hates all Posairs."

"Ah," Chariel said, understanding in her voice. "I'm sorry I frightened you. I just wanted a better look at the woman in my visions."

"Visions?"

"I have visions." Chariel shrugged. "You are quite prominent in many of them recently. You are important to our survival."

"Me?" Rizelya frowned. She was a simple squad-pack alpha. "How?"

Before Chariel answered, Wisah breezed into the room. "There you are, Chariel. Oh, good. You two have met."

"You could say that," Rizelya said with a snort.

Wisah whirled to face Chariel. "You didn't scare her with one of your prophecies, did you?"

Chariel shook her head, but suddenly stopped in mid-motion, a silver film covering her eyes.

"Newfound friends," Chariel said in a deep, monotone voice.

Rizelya glanced at Wisah, who shushed her and grabbed a pen and parchment. Her quill scratched to keep up with the words flowing from Chariel.

"New Talents appear. Unlikely travel companions, danger they find. A rogue for a guide into the Deep Mountains. Long-lost allies to fight once more. Ancient enemies coming into the light. A menace comes. No allies, the enemy wins and all die. All must go or none will return. Horse and hawk, fire and warrior, white and gray." Chariel turned her blind eyes to Rizelya. *"You must lead. He will follow. We will follow."*

Chariel's eyes rolled to the back of her head, and she slumped to the ground. Rizelya caught her before she banged her head on the floor. Rizelya looked up at Wisah, who was still scribbling furiously.

"What was that?"

"A prophecy." Wisah finished writing. She knelt next to Chariel, gently stroking her hair. "She's an oracle."

Chariel's eyes flickered, and she groaned. "I had a prophecy again, didn't I?"

Wisah nodded. "Yes. It sounds like a group is going on a quest to find old allies to fight our ancient enemy. But who are our enemies except the damned monsters?"

"I have a feeling I know." Rizelya helped Chariel sit up. "I think my dreams are a clue. Maybe the Supreme knows who this woman is who plagues me."

"The one I remind you of?" Chariel said. "I told you, you are important." She closed her eyes and held her head in her hands. "Hmmm, this is unusual. I rarely remember my visions, but this one remains fairly clear. Rizelya, you were in it, which makes sense since you triggered it. Blazel was there." She looked up at Rizelya and grinned. "He's going to love you. There was a Haaslair horse man, and—" she tilted her head "—what, who else... Oh, Crone's fires!"

"What?" Rizelya and Wisah asked at the same time.

Chariel moaned again, then turned bleak eyes to Wisah. "We're the White and Gray who go with them."

"But you've never left the confines of the Sanctuary." Concern filled Wisah's voice.

"I know." Chariel's eyes widened.

"Any idea who the lost allies are?" Wisah prompted.

"Ah, yes. The Gryphons. You remember Blazel telling us about them? We need their flying abilities. Something is in the air that we can't fight, but they can."

"Gryphons?" Rizelya asked. "Aren't they only mythical creatures? Who are they supposed to fight?"

"I don't know," Chariel snapped. "I'm shown bits and pieces, just enough to get things moving. Or scare myself. The Goddess never shows me all of it because we have a choice to do as we will. Our actions and choices change the future."

"But there isn't anything that we need the flying capabilities of the Gryphons to fight."

"Not yet. My vision says there will be. Soon. It warns none of us will survive the coming danger if the Gryphons don't help us."

"And Blazel is the only one who can negotiate with them," Wisah said. "Now we know why you sent him to the Deep Mountains. But why, for the love of the Mother, did you send him to the southern swamps?"

Chariel shrugged. "My vision told me he had to go there. Again, our survival depends on it."

"Do you think he'll get back in time to help us?" Wisah looked skeptical.

Chariel walked to the window and gazed down. When she turned around, she wore a smug smile. "Yes, I do. He's coming up the road now."

A bell chimed. "Oh, damn," Wisah swore. "Rizelya, I came up here to get you for your appointment with the Supreme. Hurry and dress. We have just a few milcrons. The Supreme hates tardiness."

Rizelya threw on fresh clothes, splashed water on her face, and quickly cleaned her teeth. She grabbed a brush and tugged it through her hair. As they hurried down the stairs and through the halls, she wove her hair into a braid. She wasn't paying much attention to where they were going until she heard the clatter of horses on the cobblestones. Wisah had taken them to the entrance courtyard.

"Isn't the Temple and the Supreme back there?" Rizelya asked, pointing toward the door.

"Blazel is here," Wisah said with a grin, continuing to walk along the courtyard's rear wall. "I wanted to see him first. The Supreme will forgive us for being late, if we tell her about Blazel's arrival."

Across the courtyard, a wild-looking man dressed in startling red leathers laughed with one of the stable women. He wore his dark auburn hair in long tangled ropes. When he turned his head, Rizelya gasped at the scar running from his right cheekbone, across his chin and neck, and disappearing into his shirt. Other than the scar, he was quite handsome. Their eyes met, and Rizelya felt a shock go through her. She remembered Chariel's words: "Blazel's going to love you." She had thought it was a sarcastic comment, but now she wondered.

Blazel waved at Wisah as they crossed the courtyard. The horses moved to reveal he wasn't alone. Rizelya and Wisah gaped at the strange sight of Blazel's companion. Most Posair men only shifted into wolves, but the men of the plains were as comfortable as a horse as they were a wolf. Rizelya had heard the stories of the few Haaslair men who shifted into half man, half horse. Once they did, they could never shift back to man or horse. They lived the rest of their lives in the half-shape. Blazel's comrade was one of these centaurs.

Chariel's prophecy rang in Rizelya's mind. "Horse and hawk" must mean the centaur and a Gryphon. She assumed the 'fire' was her and the warrior was Aistrun. The rogue had to be the wild Blazel. She tipped her head back to peer at the mountain's tall peaks. She shivered. No one, except apparently Blazel, had ever gone into the Deep Mountains and returned.

The centaur noticed them gaping and gave them an open, friendly smile.

"We don't have time to go greet them," Wisah sighed. "But I can't wait to meet Blazel's friend. I've never met a centaur before, have you?"

"No." It wasn't the centaur Rizelya wanted to meet, but the man with him.

Wisah guided Rizelya through another door in the back wall of the courtyard, and they hurried through the well groomed gardens. The garden pathways led to the largest Temple Rizelya had ever seen.

The Sanctuary was home of the Goddess and Her Consort, and the Temple reflected this. Inside the public chamber, familiar murals and statues depicting the Goddess's four faces filled three of the walls. Rizelya turned curiously to gaze at the fourth wall. Images of the Consort covered it, showing him flowing through life. He started as a small boy, experiencing the joy of shifting to his wolf for the first time. Then it continued until he became a venerable sage with a long beard, wrinkled face, and kind, wise eyes. She gaped at the Consort's warrior form. This painting showed the Consort as a Black Talent, rare even for women, and unheard of in men.

Rizelya wanted to linger and ponder its meaning, but Wisah walked past it as if it weren't unusual and went through a door in the back. Richly painted murals of The Goddess and Her Consort decorated the corridor. Wisah hurried through the hallway, not giving Rizelya a chance to get more than an impression of the stunning paintings.

They stopped at an enormous ironwood double door with an image of the eight Talents etched in the center. The top of the circle started with the symbol for the Whites, then the Grays,

Reds, Yellows, Greens, Blues, and ending with the Browns. The black background symbolized the eighth Talent, Black: one who could work all the other seven magics. Carved above the circle was the cycle of the three moons—Kelar, Zelar, and Chelar. A woman stood guard on either side of the door. They wore red leather and clutched a helbraught. Red veils covered their faces. At Rizelya and Wisah's approach, the one on the right opened the door.

A tingle ran along Rizelya's skin as she passed through the threshold. A spell guarded the entrance just as surely as the two women outside the door did. White sheadash and marble formed the floors and walls of the audience chamber, which could fit several hundred people. White curtains hung on the windows, and white pillar candles provided additional illumination. The only color in the room was Rizelya's auburn hair, red leathers, and boots. Her heels striking the floor sounded loud in the quiet.

Across the room rose a dais where a woman sat on a throne carved from a single massive piece of clear crystal. She wore a long, dazzling white silk gown and a white veil covered her hair. She had white hair and white eyes. Only a single girl child on the continent possessed white eyes: the one destined to become the Supreme White Priestess. And she was born when the current Supreme neared the end of her life.

Ten paces in front of the throne, Wisah gestured Rizelya to stop. Together, they made the gesture of obeisance and honor to the representative of the Goddess and dropped to their knees. Rizelya trembled from the power she sensed emanating from the Supreme.

"You may rise," the Supreme said after several long microns.

Rizelya stood up and raised her head slowly. Around the Supreme's neck hung the symbol of her office, an eight-pointed star. The large diamond in the center of it caught the light in the room and tossed it at Rizelya. She blinked away the dazzle and found the courage to look at the Supreme's face. She was an old, old woman.

"Supreme," Wisah said, again bowing her head, "this is my Aunt Rizelya. Ever since coming into contact with the first strange janack, she has had weird, frightening dreams. We believe they are important, and she is here for you to interpret them."

The Supreme drummed her fingertips on the arm of her throne. Her nails clicked on the crystal, creating a soft chime. Instead of eight rings circling her fingers like the High Priestesses, she wore ten. The rings on her thumbs represented the Goddess and Her Consort.

"So I have heard. Come closer, child." She stopped drumming her fingers and beckoned to Rizelya.

All her life she had been taught to respect and follow the White Priestess's guidance. This was an order she could not disobey. She moved forward, stopping at the steps leading to the dais.

"Closer," the Supreme urged.

Rizelya hesitantly climbed the stairs. The Supreme motioned her forward, halting Rizelya when she stood directly in front of her.

"Kneel." The Supreme placed cool fingers on Rizelya's face, her fingertips lightly touching Rizelya's temples. "Relax. I'm not going to hurt you."

Rizelya closed her eyes and performed the mental exercise to relax her muscles.

"Good. Now start with the first occasion you sensed the woman and recall in detail what you saw or experienced. Then move forward, remembering every instance, every dream."

The Supreme's calm and soothing voice eased Rizelya into a trance. The images and malevolent feelings rushed through her awareness. It seemed like it took days, and yet no time at all, for all the dreams to be wrung from her mind. The Supreme removed her fingers, and Rizelya slid to the cold stone floor, shaking. The shadows on the walls indicated it had taken several octars for Rizelya to recount her dreams.

Wisah's gentle strokes and voice stopped the Rizelya's trembling. She placed a cup next to Rizelya's lips, and the cool water revived her enough she could sit up. Wisah helped Rizelya to her feet and together they moved to the edge of the dais.

The Supreme leaned back in her throne with her eyes closed and appearing haggard.

Rizelya took a deep breath. "I can't shake the feeling there is someone, some intelligence, behind the monsters, especially the control-janack. Whoever it is hates the Posairs, and is very angry, blaming us for some horrible wrong against them." She stopped as a sudden insight hit her. "They want to obliterate our entire race. Supreme, who are these people, and why do they would hate us so much?"

After a long time, the Supreme opened her eyes. Fear and anger swam in their depths.

"So, our old enemies are not dead."

Rizelya's brow furrowed, uncertain how that would help her end the assaults on her mind. "Supreme, do you know who the woman is?"

The Supreme scrunched her nose, as if smelling something repugnant. "I do. She is a Malvers."

Rizelya looked at Wisah and saw the same confusion she felt reflected on Wisah's face.

"Malvers are the people we fought in the Great War," the Supreme continued, her voice low. "We won, just barely. Shandir's amazing magical achievement defeated the Malvers, creating the crater in the process. We exiled all the survivors, hoping they would die and leave us in peace. My predecessors thought it would be better for our people if they forgot about the Malvers and their nasty blood magic. They stripped the memory of them from the records. The janacks and brechas you fight, Rizelya, are their creation. We believed they had lost their magic when no new monsters attacked us. Some of the past Supremes even proclaimed them dead. Wishful thinking, it turns out."

Her fingers started drumming again on the throne. This time, it sounded like a battle call. "Now we have proof they still live and are gaining in strength. Goddess help us if they return to the continent."

Rizelya's stomach gripped in fear. If these Malvers made the Supreme afraid, what hope did the rest of them have?

"Chariel experienced a vision just before we came here," Wisah said. "She saw flying creatures, and the Gryphons fighting them." Wisah dug the parchment with Chariel's prophecy written on it from her pocket, read it aloud, and then handed it to the Supreme.

She gazed at it, then allowed it to fall into her lap. Her hands tightened around the arms of her throne, and she leaned forward. "This doesn't bode well for us, especially after hearing Rizelya's dreams." She sat back and picked up the parchment. The fingers of her left hand tapped a staccato as she re-read Chariel's prophecy. "Gryphons? Blazel? Isn't he at the southern peninsula?"

Wisah shook her head. "No, your grace. He arrived at the Sanctuary this morning."

"The Goddess provides in strange ways." The Supreme covered her amulet with both hands and raised her eyes to the heavens. "We shall soon discover how this new prophecy of Chariel's plays out."

Epilogue

The Supreme White Priestess watched the young Red, Rizelya, leave the audience chamber. She wasn't having dreams. Somehow she and the Malvers woman were linked. Extraordinarily, it seemed like the girl was developing Gray Talents. The fiery, passionate, warrior personality of a Red opposed the gentle mind-healing of the Grays.

"Malvers!" she whispered to the empty room. "We should have killed them then, not exiled them."

The Supreme walked slowly back to her quarters, waving away her assistants. In the rooms that had housed the Supremes for ages, she entered a hidden alcove. Inset into the wall was a panel with ancient symbols carved into its surface. Lifting her heavy necklace over her head, she flipped it around so that the diamond faced the panel, and pressed her token of office into the corresponding eight-pointed star. The jewel flared with bright white light, and the Supreme turned the key in a set sequence, unlocking the secret safe.

She reached inside and pulled out a gold and silver coffer, then carefully carried it to her desk and sat down. She stared at it for several milcrons, not wanting to open it, not wanting to reopen old secrets. The chest's lock also required the key of her necklace. Taking a steadying breath, the Supreme lifted the lid with trembling fingers.

The coffer had been handed down from Supreme to Supreme since the end of the Great War. It contained the Malvers' histories. They had erased everything relating to the Malvers from history and the minds of the populace. However, the Supremes' job was to remember—remember all the atrocities committed by their enemy, all of their secrets, and who they once were.

The Supreme shuddered, recalling the reason for the war. The Malvers practiced a malignant form of magic, creating only things that devoured and destroyed. This was anathema to the Posairs, who used their magic to improve life. The Posairs had hated what the Malvers were doing and stopped the creatures, but that hadn't caused the Great War. The Posairs discovered the Malvers went even further against the ways of the Goddess.

They used forbidden blood magic.

She fisted her hands. *We can't allow them to return to the continent to practice their evil once more!* Her eyes narrowed in anger. One was trying to do just that through young Rizelya. The Supreme recalled the image of the Malvers woman haunting Rizelya—she seemed familiar. She said a quick prayer of gratitude to the Goddess that Rizelya was strong willed and resisted the Malvers' call.

During her training to become the leader of the Posairs, the Supreme had studied the contents of the coffer in depth. She delved into it now, retrieving ancient portraits preserved with magic over the ages. She flipped through the pictures of all the exiled Malvers and stopped when she saw a familiar face. *How could it be the same one? How has she managed to survive all these centuries?*

The Supreme gripped the edge of the coffer so tight her rings dug into fingers. She reached out with her mind, as her predecessor had taught her so many years ago, and touched the magical barrier. She gasped. It was failing. The last time she checked it, at the turn of the year, it had still been strong. *How did it weaken so fast?*

She struggled to repair the damage until her strength ran out, but she knew her repairs weren't enough. It would give her people a few lunadar, at most a year, to prepare for the invasion surely to come.

As she came back to herself, she recalled Chariel's prophecy. She'd send the young people on their quest to find the Gryphons. Perhaps there was yet hope for her people's survival.

And this time, the Supreme vowed, the Malvers would be destroyed.

WHAT TO READ NEXT

The story of Rizelya and her team continues in *Ancient Allies,* the next exciting episode in the completed Legends of Lairheim series!

You can purchase this, and all my books, directly from me at *Shop.ToraMoon.com* or at your favorite retailer.

A prophecy revealed...
A reluctant leader's quest...
An alliance to save the world...

Prophecy thrusts Rizelya, a Red with fire Talent, into a perilous journey north to the Deep Mountains to seek the mythical Gryphons. Struggling with newfound leadership, she strives to unite her diverse group into a cohesive force. Blazel, a lone wolf in every sense, returns to Posair society after years of isolation, facing the daunting task of reintegrating with his people and forging pack bonds.

Joined by an eclectic team—a centaur, a warrior, a White Priestess, and the Gray Oracle—Rizelya and Blazel venture into uncharted territories. Their mission: to rekindle the ancient alliance between the Posairs and the Gryphons, whose help is essential to combat an emerging threat. As the questers struggle to survive, deep bonds of friendship and unexpected love blossom.

Old wounds and mistrust surface, threatening to derail their quest. A new threat emerges from the sky, bringing a powerful enemy that could destroy them all. Can Rizelya and Blazel convince the mythical Gryphons to unite with the Posairs to save Lairheim from annihilation?

Ancient Allies is the second book in the epic science-fantasy series, Legends of Lairheim, where epic battles and mythical creatures intertwine with the enduring power of unity.

Discover the thrilling world of Lairheim today!

APPENDIX

THE CAST

(IN ALPHABETICAL ORDER)

Aistrun - (Aye-strun) Co-squad-pack Alpha with Rizelya; Strunlaind Keep; Rizelya's squad-pack

Beladi - (Bell-ah-de) Double Red with Yellow; Strunlair Clan Alpha

Bestrun - (Bae-strun) Strunell Keep Alpha

Brachen - (Bray-chen) Brown - healer; Strunhemde Keep

Bren - (Bre-en) Red and Green, with some yellow; Strunell Keep

Chariel - (Char-ee-el) Gray, also known as the Gray Oracle; The Sanctuary

Dehali - (Dee-haa-lee) Red and Yellow; Strunland Keep; Rizelya's squad-pack

Drustrun - (Drew-strun) Strunell Keep, squad-pack Alpha

Eiden - (Eye-den) Yellow, twin to Eidstrun; Strunland Keep

Eidstrun - (Eyed-strun) Strunland Keep; twin to Eiden; Rizelya's squad-pack

Gehan - (Gay-han) Yellow and Green; Strunven Keep

Grazeen - (Gray-zeen) Green and Brown; Strunven Keep

Histrun - (His-strun) Former Strunlair Clan-pack Alpha; Strunland Keep, Rizelya's father

Kaieli - (Kai-ee-le) Brown and Blue; Strunland Kee

Kami - (Cam-ee) Yellow and Green, identical twin to Tami; Strunell Keep

Keandran - (Kae-an-dran) Originally from Andranlair, transferred to Strunlair Keep; Rizelya's squad-pack

Kelstrun - (Kel-strun) Strunland Keep Alpha

Keshanal - (Khe-shan-al) Red and Brown; Strunell Keep Alpha

Laenstrun - (Lay-en-strun) Strunheim Keep Alpha; Laynar's twin brother

Layhalya - (Lay-hall-yah) Red and Green; Strunheim Keep Alpha

Laynad - (Lay-nad) Red and Green; Strunhamde Alpha; older sister to Laynar and Laynal

Laynal - (Lay-nal) Red and Yellow; Strunheim Keep, younger sister of Laynar

Laynar - (Lay-nar) Red; Strunheim Keep, granddaughter of Layhalya

Ledelstrun - (Lay-del-strun) Strunhemde Keep

Lehaas - (Lay-haas) Strunell Keep; horse master

Leistral - (Lay-ee-straal) Red with Green; Strunland Keep; Rizelya's squad-pack

Leistrun - (Lay-is-strun) Strunland Keep

Maellyn - (May-lyn) Brown with Red; Strunven Keep

Maendy - (May-en-dee) Brown and Red, with some Yellow, Helstramiester; Strunven Keep

Naila - (Neigh-la) Red and Yellow; Strunland Keep Alpha; Rizelya's sister

Nestrun - (Nay-strun) Strunlair Clan Alpha

Raeleen - (Ray-leen) Brown with Yellow; Strunven Keep

Rizelya - (Rha-zeel-yha) Red with Brown; Strunland Keep - main character

Saehala - (Say-hall-la) Red and Green; Strunven Keep Alpha

Saehalstrun - (Say-hal-strun) Strunven Keep Alpha

Saffren - (Saff-fren) Blue with some Green; Strunven Keep

Selestrun - (Say-les-strun) Strunheim Keep Alpha

Shandir - (Shan-deer) Legendary hero from the Great War, a White Priestess; the huge crater in the south is named after her, Shandir's Crater, also called Shandir's Misery.

Shaydan - (Shay-dan) Red and Brown; Strunell Keep

Sujeen - (Sue-jean) Red and Green; Strunven Keep Alpha

Tami - (Tam-ee) Yellow and Green, identical twin to Kami; Strunell Keep

Teraposan - (Ter-ah-po-san) Strunven Keep Alpha

The Supreme - White; the Posairs' spiritual leader; The Sanctuary

Wisah - (Wee-sah) White and Grey with some Blue; The Sanctuary; Naila's daughter, Rizelya's niece

Zehala - (Zay-hal-ah) Red and Brown; Naila and Rizelya's mother (Deceased)

THE HORSES

Caela - (Say-la) Leistral's mare

Jezhan - (Jay-zhen) Aistrun's gelding

Julay - (Ju-lay) Dehali's mare

Kressy - (Kress-ee) Rizelya's multa

Kymaya - (Kai-may-ah) Rizelya's mare

Luchen - (Lou-chen) Eidstrun's gelding

Tejen - (Tee-jen) Stallion rode by Keandran

THE WORLD

The main continent is called Lairheim. The Barrens is an area of desolation, with only petrified wood and sand-glass in it. It covers a hundred-mile radius from Shandir's Crater, which is in the center of the isthmus between the main continent and the sub-continent. After the Great War, travel south of the Barrens became taboo, and so no one knows what the area is like. The sub-continent is believed to be covered by one huge swamp and is located south of the Barrens.

No one sails the oceans anymore because of the sea monsters created during the Great War. There is limited travel along the coasts.

The Provinces

There are eight provinces, each divided into eight territories. Each clan takes the name of the Province.

Strunlair

Ledonlair

Andranlair

Posanlair

Haaslair

Dehanlair

Ronanlair

Keistanlair

Days and Time

Milcron - equivalent to a minute.

Octar - roughly equals an hour. There are 16 octars in a day.

Chedan - roughly a week, consisting of eight days.

Lunadar - a month consists of eight chedans, or 64 days.

A year is eight chedans, or 512 days.

Measure - term for distance, a little less than a mile (5,000 feet)

The Months

Ahdar - Month one; Spring

Neydar - Month two; Spring

Sandar - Month three; Summer

Drudar - Month four; Summer

Godar - Month five; Autumn

Rokdar - Month six; Autumn

Eyedar - Month seven; Winter

Hondar - Month eight; Winter

The Moons

Kelar - the largest moon takes 64 days for a full cycle, measurement of a month.

Zelar - the middle-sized moon takes 32 days for a full cycle.

Chelar - the smallest moon's cycle takes 8 days, measurement for chedan, or eight-days.

Magical Abilities of the Women

There are eight types of magic, called Talents, worked by the women. Men exchanged the ability to do magic (except very basic skills) for the gift of shapeshifting into their warrior form when the Malvers' monsters appeared after the Great War. Hair and eye color indicate of the type of magic the person uses. Hair color indicates the person's major Talent and the eye color their secondary Talent. The darker the hair or eye color, the more powerful in that Talent the person is. A woman with fire magic is called a Red, one with water is called a Blue, and so on. Hair color pales with age.

The Powers

Whites - have shades of white hair. Priestesses — mind and soul workers, spiritual leaders. (Unseen in men.)

Grays - have shades of gray hair. Priestesses — also mind and soul workers but they work more with the transitions of the soul. This is a rare Talent. (Unseen in men.)

Reds - have shades of red hair — the fire workers and warriors.

Yellows - have shades of blond hair — the air workers.

Blues - have shades of blue hair — the water workers.

Greens - have shades of green hair — earth workers, plants, and are healers.

Browns - shades of brown hair — earth workers, animals and minerals/metals, and are healers.

Blacks - shades of black hair (extinct) — can work all types of magic.

GLOSSARY

billocks - a wild, large herd beast and resists domestication

brecha - (bray-cha) one of the symbiotic pair of monsters collectively called the Malvers' monsters

ducorn - (dew-corn) a type of antelope with two twisty horns

helbraught - (hell-brac-kt) the magical halberd type blades the women use to fight the monsters; the wooden staff is the height of the woman with a 16"-24" inch blade made from helstrim attached to the end

helstrablade - (hell-stra-blade) knives made from helstrim but not keyed to any type of magic

helstramiester - (hell-sta-my-ster) masters of the helstrim alloy

helstrim - (hell-strim) a special alloy that accepts and holds magic used to make helstrablades and helbraught blades

janack - (jan-ack) one of the symbiotic pair of monsters collectively called the Malvers' monsters

jedash - (jay-dash) a bushy plant resistant to monster toxins and cools the area around them

jelehan - (jay-lay-han) a throwing game using sticks of varying lengths with colored bands

kehani - (kay-han-ee) the flowers of the kehani tree are sacred to The Goddess and are used by the priestesses in the temples as perfume and incense

keshe - (kay-she) a strategy board game. It can be played with as few as two players or up to ten players; the more players added, the more complicated the game becomes

mookti - (mook-tee) an early ripening spring berry that is sweet, dark purple, and grows in small clusters

multa - (mul-ta) a pack animal with cloven, platter-like feet able to carry heavy loads

narhili - (nar-hee-lee) also called narhili beasts, predators that live in the swamps during the day and hunt the surrounding area at night

oyt - a nonsensical term used to activate the fire arrows.

paether - (pae-ther) a canid-like predator found in the northern part of Lairheim

sabertiger - a large white and black striped feline that lives in the Deep Mountains

sheadash - (shea-dash) a type of white stone that repels and negates any malignant magic. The Malvers' monsters can't cross it and so it is used for buildings and roads

snelks - (snell-ks) a grub which eats rotten matter

taevo - (tay-vo) a stimulating drink made from the leaves and berries of the taeve bush

Stay In Touch!

Sign up for Tora's newsletter to keep in touch with what's happening in the world of Tora. Receive exclusive extras, news, and discounts on my books, products, and art. I have lots of ideas and always have a project—or three—in progress.

ToraMoon.com/subscribe

Also By Tora Moon

Legends of Lairheim (Epic Science-Fantasy)

Ancient Enemies (Book 1)
Ancient Allies (Book 2)
The Scourge Incursion (Book 3)
Exile's Vengeance (Book 4)
Redemption - A Novel

The Sentinel Witches (Urban Fantasy)

Crossroads to Destiny (Book 1)
Descent Into Darkness (Book 2)
Well of Sorrows (Book 3)

Indie Author Guides

Business & Accounting for Authors
Business Plans for Authors

To get an up-to-date listing of all my books or to purchase visit
ToraMoon.com

Thank You!

I hope you're enjoying discovering the world of Legends of Lairheim world and Rizelya and her team's story.

If you have a moment, please help others enjoy these books too by leaving a review on my shop or the retail site where you purchased this book, review it on a blog, share it on your social media, or even just tell your friends about it.

Reviews help other readers choose what to read and authors depend on reviews to get the word out on good books. Honest reviews and genuine word-of-mouth recommendations make all the difference.

I'm not asking for one of those awful book reports we did at school. Leaving a review will only take a minute: it doesn't have to be long or involved, just a sentence or two that tells people what you liked about the book. This will help other readers know why they might like it, too, and help me write more of what you love. But please, no spoilers!

The truth is, VERY few readers leave reviews. Please help me by being the exception.

ABOUT THE AUTHOR

Tora Moon writes Goddess fantasy and science fiction, skillfully melding different sub-genres to create unique, memorable stories. Her completed series, The Legends of Lairheim, combines elements of epic, paranormal, and science fiction into a breathtaking tale of magic, courage, and the enduring power of unity.

Her series, The Sentinel Witches, blends her love of urban/magical realism, mythology, and portal fantasy—and skates close to the edge of thriller and horror. Throughout all her works, you will find Tora's love of Goddess mythology as she weaves aspects of these into her stories.

As Tora-Iresh'nai Moon, she writes about Goddess Spirituality and shares her nearly fifty years of experience of connecting with the Goddess and the Feminine Divine.

Tora is also an artist who explores drawing and watercolor painting. Her current passion is creating and coloring mandalas inspired by the Goddess. Tora also expresses her creativity through various handcrafts.

You can find out more about Tora, her books, and her art at: ToraMoon.com